JJ BLACKLOCKE

REFUGE

THE TRADEPOINT SAGA BOOK ONE

D1784956

www.aethonbooks.com

ALSO IN THE SERIES

DAY ONE

TRADEPOINT

Gredin te Balamont arrived on Tradepoint, shivering with wonder.

She had little memory of her journey on the River, beyond a dazzling sense of light and a strange inner calm that blurred the passage of time. But now she stood on the arrival dais beneath a protective dome, just as the Traders had described it, and her nose, her ears, her very skin prickled with excitement and an awareness of *other*.

To her left, Beda squeezed her hand reassuringly. On her right, Ingarra fussed with her shawl, like a bird resettling its feathers after a rain shower. And Gredin recognized Tetralanna, First Speaker for House Balamont and official Voice for the Vennan delegation, standing a few steps in front of them, silhouetted by the harsh lights of the room beyond.

It was a room unlike any Gredin had ever seen. Broad and deep and high, it was windowless, and devoid of color variation or ornamentation. The silver floor beneath her feet simply continued out and up, as if some Craftsman had poured molten metal to form the huge chamber.

A vibration shook the soles of her boots. Overhead, the dome parted.

"Wait a few moments more," said Burlon, the Traveler who had conveyed their group.

Slowly, the halves of the dome sank down to vanish into the platform's edge, and the floor became still.

"Down the steps, now," Burlon instructed. "Clear the dais for the next group."

Gredin reached up to clasp the smoothness of her flamestone pendant — Dreff's present to her on the night of their Choosing. Around her, other members of House Balamont gathered their small items, while Travelers managed the larger bundles brought for the four-day stay.

Ahead, Tetralanna descended the steps of the dais.

"Our turn," Beda prompted.

Gredin picked up her bag and hopped nimbly down the broad steps.

"Where is the sun?" Ingarra asked indignantly, arriving more sedately at Gredin's side.

"Our sun is too far off to be seen," Burlon told her. "The Prett world has one of its own."

Ingarra gave him a disgruntled look. "Then where is it? Why can't we see the sky? We might as well be in a cave."

Gazing upwards, Gredin had to agree; it was strange to see nothing overhead but an expanse of silver, interrupted by blue-white lights so intense they made her eyes sting.

Beda grabbed her elbow, dragging her to an abrupt halt, and Gredin realized that she had almost blundered into Tetralanna, who had stopped.

Gredin flashed Beda a grateful smile. He knew she was hoping to talk Tetralanna into lessons in their shared gyfte. Tetralanna had given her original refusal to act as her Mentor long ago. Surely, she would see that Gredin had changed and was worthy of a second chance.

But not if Gredin began the trip by knocking her over.

Ingarra looked around. "Where do you suppose we'll be staying?"

At that, Tetralanna turned to face them. "Follow Burlon. He's escorting those from House Balamont. Gredin and I are lodging separately. I explained to the organizers that I needed privacy to prepare for the Trisectoriana, and it made sense to keep my translator close at hand. Come along, girl."

Gredin hesitated, taken aback. Preparing for this trip, she'd felt confident and optimistic. Now, she had to quell a flare of panic at being singled out, like a rista kidlet separated from the herd. Still, if serving as Tetralanna's translator required her to lodge separately from the other House members, that was how it must be. There was no cause for alarm. She was an adult, if only barely. Adults handled unexpected changes without protest, and they did not need to sleep near their Guides.

As if reading her misgivings, Tetralanna said, "Of course it makes sense. Don't make a fuss, Gredin. It's a privilege to have a private space set aside for us."

Gredin's face grew hot.

Well, it was only for three nights. She could manage anything for three nights. And it was flattering that she and Tetralanna had been paired as working partners. "Of course, First Speaker. But before we part, I would like to introduce my Guides—"

"Later, perhaps. It's a long walk. We need to get settled," Tetralanna said, sparing only a quick nod for Ingarra and Beda. "There will be time later for introductions and conversation."

Gredin grimaced in apology. "I'll try to find you at evening meal," she told Ingarra and Beda, and hurried to take her place at Tetralanna's side.

The group from House Balamont veered off to the right, the long line of them following Burlon. But Gredin and Tetralanna moved straight ahead, walking toward a distant dais identical to the one upon which they had arrived.

Tetralanna seemed to know where she was going. Gredin wondered if that information had been part of the information session she had missed during her golden days with Dreff. They walked on, and then farther still, seeming to get little closer to their goal at the far end of the room despite their efforts. "Tetralanna?" Gredin said at last, shifting her bag to the other shoulder.

"Yes?"

"Why don't we simply Send to where we're going?"

Tetralanna swung about to face her, wearing a look of such alarmed disapproval that Gredin took a hasty step back. "Didn't you pay attention at the meeting?"

"I wasn't there."

"Four days ago?" Tetralanna persisted.

Gredin shook her head. "Four days ago, Dreff and I were still in our dydanin." She blushed at the remembered glory of discovering her life-mate, and of the twenty days and nights they had spent in seclusion, aware of nothing but each other. She offered a rueful smile. "I suppose I felt as if everyone's life simply held still while I was away. I was just happy."

"Happy," Tetralanna echoed, her expression softening slightly. "Well. Hardly surprising, I suppose. I didn't realize you were so recently emerged." She sighed. "Still, that meeting was important, for it dealt with our safety. While we are here, we have been told not to Send."

"At all?" Gredin asked, dumbfounded.

"Walking is slower, but safer." Tetralanna made a sweeping gesture that encompassed the gleaming metal wall far ahead of them and the metal plates beneath their feet. "This place is like a cloud, hanging in the sky far above the surface of the Prett home world. Burlon says there is no air to breathe, on the other side of these walls." She shuddered. "If you made an error while Sending, you could end up outside of Tradepoint, and it would end your life."

The thought was alarming, but also rather silly. "Make an error while Sending? I have Sent without incident since I was a youngling. Why would that skill desert me now?"

Impatience marred Tetralanna's expression. "Because you are easily distracted. Because your mind is preoccupied with thoughts of your Chosen. Because you have just Traveled the River for the first time and may be feeling the effects of that experience. Besides, we were told that Travelers and Traders never Send in front of other races on Tradepoint. It isn't a talent those other races appear to possess. It might unsettle them to see us do such a thing. And so we walk."

"Yes, Tetralanna," Gredin agreed.

But it was a long and pointless trudge.

When they finally reached their destination, which proved to be a row of five featureless metal doors within a shallow alcove, Tetralanna pointed. "That door, on the far left, will be the historian's chamber. The middle three are storage rooms for the craft demonstrations' equipment. And this, on the right, is ours."

As they approached the door, its panels parted down the center and slid sideways, startling Gredin as the panels vanished into the walls.

A room of modest proportions stood revealed, furnished with a table and two benches, all fashioned from metal. The table held a carafe and two cups. The ceiling was lower than in the area they had just traversed, but the same harsh light flared down from overhead.

It was a graceless place, colorless and unwelcoming, a room of abrupt angles and stark shadows. Three doorways punctuated the far wall, and Tetralanna gestured at them in turn. "Your sleeping chamber, the cleansing chamber, and my sleeping chamber."

Gredin wondered if she would find a metal slab awaiting her in her sleep chamber. But when she looked, she was relieved to find a thickly quilted sleeping mat and a pile of folded blankets. Better still, someone had set a small luminth in the corner. Prettily carved in the image of a glowmoth, the luminth was roughly the size of her fist. Beside it sat her pillow from home, the one that Ingarra had long ago decorated with clusters of embroidered ildarian blossoms.

Gredin transferred energy into the luminth until it shed a warm, friendly glow. Carrying it into the outer room, she squinted up at the blue-white glare. "Is there a way to douse that light?"

Tetralanna emerged from her own sleeping chamber and walked to a vertical panel of buttons set into the wall near the main door. When she pressed her finger to the bottom button, the overhead light winked off, leaving the room bathed in the golden glow of Gredin's luminth.

"Well, that is an improvement," Tetralanna conceded. "Unpack your belongings. It will be time for our meeting with the Tradepoint Director soon."

"Oh!" Gredin's spirits lifted. "What should I wear?"

Tetralanna surveyed the pants and jacket Gredin had donned for their Travels. "What you have on will do well enough. You are here to facilitate conversation between the Director and myself. He and I will be talking to each other, *through* you, not *to* you. Drawing attention to yourself would defeat the purpose of your presence."

Chastened, Gredin nodded, wishing Dreff had come. She missed his good-natured advice. Would he have agreed with Tetralanna or suggested a change of outfit?

"Today's meeting is a formality," Tetralanna continued. "I will meet the Director and thank him for organizing the presentation. And you, I suppose, can discover whether you actually understand this language that he speaks. If not, Cirin says that the Director can manage somewhat in Vennan. Or Burlon can translate, if it proves to be beyond you."

Gredin was confident of her skills in both Prettian and Tradetalk, but she made no response to Tetralanna's jibe. Long ago, at the onset of her language lessons with the Traders, she had asked about the homeworld of people who spoke Tradetalk. The Traders had laughed, though not unkindly. Tradetalk, they'd explained, was an artificial language created by the Prett, a crude tongue that most anyone could master.

There was nothing lyrical about Tradetalk. Unlike Vennan or Prettian, it had no finesse. But it enabled individuals from different races to broker deals while maintaining a level of basic civility, despite their widely differing customs and expectations. At home, a Trader negotiating an exchange between two Vennan Houses might say, *How many skeins of your yarn will you offer in exchange for three wheels of my rista cheese?* That same proposition in Tradetalk might become *My three cheese you want. Your yarn how many give?* It was utilitarian, with an emphasis on numbers and terms of possession. Nouns were numerous and simple, while adjectives were few, since samples of the products in question were usually displayed as part of the negotiation.

Gredin had taught some Tradetalk to Dreff during the luxurious days and nights of their dydanin, substituting Vennan nouns. It had become a source of amorous amusement. *My three caresses you want*, Dreff would say. *Your kisses how many give?*

The memory made her smile, and she felt a thrill of longing. Twenty days and nights of intimacy had primed her body to crave the gratification of Dreff's attentions. The three nights she would spend here, alone on her solitary mat, would be tedious compared with the intoxicating tangle of limbs and lips and sleep-warm bodies...

"Gredin?"

Tetralanna's voice startled her from her reverie. "Your pardon. My wits wandered."

"No doubt they wandered to your new-found Chosen,"

Tetralanna said, and her look of irritation softened. "It is ever so, for those freshly emerged from dydanin — and, indeed, beyond. My own Chosen, Elander, is a Traveler, so we are often parted. When he returns home, our reunions are sweeter than even a Speaker can express." She gestured toward the table. "For now, though, you need to pay attention. I have a word of guidance to offer before your official duties begin."

Gredin pulled out a bench and sat down.

Tetralanna remained standing. "I am aware that Frake te Santelle became your Mentor when I declined to undertake that role. Your subsequent work with Frake is not unknown to me."

Gredin tried not to wince; the subject was a sore one.

"To be forthright," Tetralanna continued, "though Burlon and Cirin wished to bring you to Tradepoint as translator, I counseled against your inclusion."

"Against?" Gredin stared, stung. "Why?"

"This delegation needs to reflect well on House Balamont and our world." Tetralanna smoothed a hand over the sleek fabric of her trousers. "When Unter invited me to act as Voice here, I nearly turned him down. But I reconsidered." A look of longing flitted over her face. "Elander delights in Traveling the River, and he wishes me to accompany him to other worlds. Thus far, I have declined. If I find this trip as distasteful as I fear I shall, I would rather my Chosen not witness my reaction. He is on a Tradeteam mission to Anderlith, due to return shortly. In the meantime, my participation here will bring honor and profit to our House, and give me a private opportunity to see whether I can bear such a trip, and so I agreed."

"But you didn't think I should come?"

"Burlon and Cirin asked my opinion. It would have been dishonest for me not to share what I know about you." She sat down across from Gredin. "You have matured somewhat, during your studies with Frake te Santelle, but you are still very young. Your gyfte is considerable and yet, despite your training, Frake says it still often masters you, rather than you mastering it. Your enthusiasm appeals to people, but your excitable nature distances you from Control of your gyfte. I had hoped for someone steadier. Someone less... erratic."

"I've worked hard at my lessons in Focus and Control," Gredin asserted.

"Yes, and you have made progress in those disciplines, according to Frake. But I suspect that Focus and Control do not lie at the root of your problem."

"What, then?" Gredin asked anxiously. "Tell me, and I will work harder still. I wish to do proper honor to Frake's instruction. I wish to serve my gyfte proudly. I wish—"

Tetralanna lifted a hand. "Hush. It is not a question of working harder. Frake says you apply yourself sincerely to your lessons. He finds no fault with your devotion to your gyfte."

"But you perceive some other fault?"

Tetralanna shrugged. "Do you not perceive one, yourself? Is your mastery of your gyfte all that you would have it be? Does it answer fully to your will, when you call upon it?"

Gredin's spirits plummeted. This was not at all the discussion she'd hoped to have with Tetralanna, but she had to speak the truth. "Not always," she admitted. "Why is that? What is wrong with me? What holds me separate from my gyfte?"

Tetralanna waved a hand. "The gyfte of Speech requires us to master ourselves. How can you calm others, if you are not calm? How can you resolve their fears, if you give way to your own?"

Gredin's cheeks heated with mortification. "So then, what are you saying? That I talk too much? That I do too much? What new instruction should I undertake?"

"In Frake's opinion, it is not additional lessons you require."

"Then in what area am I still lacking?"

"Frake believes that you feel too much."

Gredin stared at her, bewildered.

"When you are happy, no one is more filled with joy. When you are sad, the sun may never shine again. Rarely can you quiet yourself and simply... be. Rarely is your spirit at rest for two consecutive breaths. Emotions color your perception of the world, making it difficult for you to understand anyone else's position. And if you do not understand their position, how can you represent them fairly?"

"Then what am I to do?" Gredin asked, fighting to hold her voice steady. Why had Frake discussed these things with Tetralanna, rather than talking to her directly?

"Do? Well, you are barely an adult. Time may eventually grace you with enough maturity to access your gyfte fully. Or, if not, you may simply have reached the limits of your ability to exercise your gyfte." She shrugged, as if distancing herself from Gredin's growing distress.

"And in the meantime?"

"While we're here, you need only translate for me. That shouldn't overstress your gyfte."

Gredin bit hard on her lip to keep the tears from falling.

"Self-pity is pointless," Tetralanna said, and stood up. "I suggest that you unpack. Perhaps take a short nap."

"And what are you going to do?"

Tetralanna looked startled by the question. "Change my outfit for the meeting, of course. I am the delegation's Voice. My appearance will matter," she said, and retired to her chamber.

Nine hundred and thirty-seven Vennans.

It was such an astonishing, ludicrous, potentially problematic number that Wyve, Director of Tradepoint, could only marvel at it.

Over the past three hundred sectora, Tradepoint had hosted many Vennan travelers and traders, but always in small numbers — often as few as four, and never more than a dozen at a time. Now, instead of four or eight or twelve individuals, nearly a thousand Vennans had come.

Wyve hadn't even been sure the Vennans would warm to the notion of a Trisectoriana ceremony. Instead, to his shock, they had announced plans to attend in such numbers that he'd had to assure his own government that the usual time limitation on the Vennans' stay would be observed. No trade delegations remained on Tradepoint longer than it took the station to orbit the Prett planet two thousand times. That worked out to forty sects — one for arrival and unloading, thirty-eight for active trading, and one for pack-up and departure.

For clarity's sake, every enclave on the station was equipped with a countback monitor. Upon a group's arrival, the figure *2000/2000* lit up, and thereafter showed the number of orbits remaining. When it reached *0/2000*, departure was mandatory.

Thirty-eight sects of active trading was long enough for a delegation to justify the length of its journey and accomplish its business on Tradepoint, although races like the Beng consistently flirted with the deadline, postponing their departure until the final few orbits, ever hopeful that some new arrival would afford them one last, lucrative trade before they left.

But Vennan trade teams never lingered. They came, traded, and left, often within a sect or two of their arrival. Even now, despite the huge number of Vennans here for the Trisectoriana, they only planned to stay for four sects. The station could accommodate that short-term influx.

The members of the Vokastra had professed themselves mollified. That was no surprise; the value of the Prett trading partnership with Venna could be counted on to outweigh most other concerns.

It hadn't always been that way. In their earliest dealings, Venna had traded only in luxury goods. Their trade items had been elegant and appealing, but no one lost any sleep over when the next consignment of goods from Venna might arrive. But that all changed, due to the Hesch.

The Hesch, a tall, bird-like race, were intimidating traders. They commonly offered edible items for barter, from fruit preserves and nutmeats to unusual liqueurs, many of which appealed to the Vennans. But striking a counter-deal with the Hesch had proven challenging. Then some observant Vennan trader noted that the Hesch liked things that glittered. As a result, the Vennans submitted a new trade item for Prett approval, hoping it would interest the Hesch.

The item was a packet of geddel crystals, which the Vennans used in jewelry and to embellish clothing. The Tradepoint Director of that era, Wyve's predecessor by more than two hundred and fifty sectora, had nearly swooned when the Vennan Trader emptied out a pouch of geddel crystals of unparalleled clarity and quality — crystals for which the Prett had a pressing and far more practical need than mere ornamentation.

That canny Director, with the support of the Vokastra, awarded the Vennans 'Favored Trader' status, on the condition that the Prett thereafter have the right of first refusal for all geddel crystals the Vennans brought to Tradepoint. Crystals that were flawed or too small for industrial use were then made available for the Vennans to sell to the Hesch and any other races showing an interest.

The Prett were a scientific race. The Vennans, it quickly became apparent, were not. They had no understanding of the technological uses to which the Prett put geddel crystals. But the quantity and quality of the crystals they'd provided to the Prett over the past three hundred sectora had gradually transformed Prettian industry in general, and power production in particular. If the Vennan supply of geddel crystals were ever to be interrupted...

Well, suffice it to say that the Prett had no intention of offending the Vennans, even if it meant smiling politely while an inconveniently large delegation of Vennans descended on Tradepoint, turning the carefully planned Trisectoriana into a logistical nightmare.

Wyve found Vennans both perplexing and enticing. They eschewed science, responding with a shrug to any question that began with "Yes, but *how* do you...?" Even Burlon, normally quite a talkative Vennan trader, looked blank when scientific topics were raised.

Take the matter of transport. From Cirin te K'lar's first shocking appearance on Prettig to the present time, Vennans had come and gone without the use of a starship. When asked about it, Cirin stated, to the consternation of the Prett, that he "traveled the river."

It had quickly become clear that he was not talking about some physically impossible body of water flowing through the universe, but rather (the Prett were forced to conjecture) some path of energy, undetectable to their instruments but undeniably existent since Cirin was, demonstrably, *there*. Unfortunately, all attempts to further clarify or quantify "the river" in scientific terms had met an exasperating dead end. Indeed, tech of any kind seemed to make the Vennans uneasy. "We don't use *griimoni* on our world," Cirin told Wyve, pronouncing the Prettian word for "machines" as if it tasted unpleasant on his tongue. "We don't need them. We have our gyftes."

The subject of Vennan gyftes was a mystery to Prett scientists and to Wyve himself. Asked to elaborate, Cirin simply said that Vennan children were born with a standard array of lesser gyftes and one or two major gyftes, and that all gyftes were respected. When the Vennans announced they were coming for the Trisectoriana in such large numbers, Wyve had asked if they would all be travelers and traders. Burlon, clearly amused, had replied that Vennans with many different gyftes would attend, along with someone to act as their delegation's Voice.

"A government official, like one of our Vokastra?" Wyve had inquired.

But Burlon had said, "No. She has the gyfte of Speech, but she speaks on behalf of others. She is an official emissary, but not politically powerful."

Upon further discussion, Wyve had been charmed to learn that all of the Vennans attending planned to take an active role at the reception, giving demonstrations of craftsmanship, performing music, and offering other cultural displays. As Tradepoint Director, he would only need to deal with any small difficulties that might arise in the process.

It helped that the interior structure of Tradepoint was designed for easy reconfiguration. The abrupt influx of nearly a thousand individuals put their ingenuity to the test, but his workmen had relocated cargo, turned warehouse space into living quarters, and increased the number of refreshers per module, to handle the increased volume of solid and liquid waste.

In four sects, when the Trisectoriana was over and the Vennans had departed, those alterations would all need to be reversed, but Wyve considered it effort well spent. The Vennans' presence on the station — unlike that of several other races he could name — had always been peaceful and businesslike, and he expected their stay to be a smooth and productive one.

The mat beneath Wyve's feet vibrated; someone was approaching his office. A glance at the monitor showed it to be Figg, his assistant director. As a rule, he and Figg divided their work cycles, each on duty for half a sect apiece, with a small overlap at either end for consultation.

Many races did business at Tradepoint, each with an inborn biorhythm, making it impractical to proclaim a single wake/sleep cycle for the entire station. Instead, Tradepoint never slept. Station-wide displays indicated which races' maartzas were open for business in the Traders' Market at any given time. Either Wyve or Figg was always available, along with a constant Prett security presence in the corridors and areas of public interchange.

Personally, Wyve was grateful that Vennan biorhythms so closely mimicked those of his own race. It gave him many opportunities to interact with them. But not all races' biorhythms matched so well. The F'lala and the Wilra both needed a rest cycle much sooner than any Prett. And it was counterproductive to prevent either race from leaving a meeting prematurely. The last time he had tried to extend a meeting between himself and a F'lala until an agreement could be reached, the white-haired creature had simply put its head back and begun to snore.

For today's official welcome, Figg was interrupting her off-shift sleep cycle to greet the Vennan representatives. As she entered, Wyve nodded a greeting to her and consulted the monitor again. "Before the Vennans present themselves at our door, perhaps you and I should discuss last shift's difficulty between the Polpethtira and the Thalken. What, precisely, was the Thalken's complaint, *this* time?"

"Remember, all of you, that you're on Tradepoint. It isn't like being at home, where everyone's a kinsman," Burlon te Bentain cautioned.

Gredin reflected that he and Cirin looked quite impressive in their close-fitting Trader's jackets of forest green. She looked around at her group — three men and three women, including herself. She knew Tetralanna, and she had been introduced to Burlon and Cirin, but the other two members of their party were strangers to her.

"Some of you are from different Houses and may not have met, so I'll make introductions before we begin our walk to the Director's office. As you must know by now," Burlon said, "we are your delegation co-leaders. I'm Burlon te Bentain, Traveler and Trader. And this—" He clapped a hand briefly on his companion's shoulder. "—is Cirin, First Traveler for House K'lar."

It struck Gredin that Cirin's relaxed demeanor as a First was quite a contrast to Tetralanna's straight-backed stance.

Burlon tilted his hand and said, with a polite smile, "Here we have Tetralanna te Balamont, First of Speech for her House and official Voice for this delegation."

Tetralanna, elegant in a sleeveless, full-skirted gown, nodded graciously to the others. On her bare upper arm, First Speaker's hlette glittered in the harsh lights. It was beautiful, twining like a pair of vines, and the grace of its curves seemed to speak to something deep within Gredin.

"And," Burlon continued, "this is Gredin, also a Speaker from House Balamont, who will translate for the delegation. She is proficient in both Prettian and Tradetalk."

"I'm curious to hear how that came about," the unknown man said.

Burlon laughed and nodded toward the speaker. "This is Keegan te Fliss. He is a historian, which means he hungers to discover the reasons behind everything for himself or, failing that, to talk with someone who knows."

"And I am Sill," the final woman said softly, before Burlon could introduce her. "I am First of Memory for House Torr."

A thrill of wonder passed through Gredin at the realization that she was in the presence of three individuals who wore a hlette as First of their gyfte.

"It pleases me to meet you all," Keegan said. "My written account of this delegation should include sketches and descriptions of each of you and, for those who possess them, of your hlettes, if you will allow."

Tetralanna turned to stare at him. "Written account? What need is there for a written account when we have a First of Memory with us?"

Before Keegan could reply, Burlon said, "That debate is best left for another time. Let's be on our way to the Director's office. But first…" He cast a stern eye over Tetralanna's elegant gown. "Doors on Tradepoint open and close on their own, sometimes quite quickly," he warned her. "Be mindful, or you may get your skirt caught in one." His gaze swung to include the others. "And none of you should wear your hlao with the ends trailing, except when we're here in the enclave. Wear it as a circlet instead. That's safer. It attracts too much attention, the other way."

Gredin hurried to comply, and saw her companions reach up to do the same.

"Good," Burlon said, and gestured for the group to move ahead.

Tetralanna took the lead and entered the huge, vaulted antechamber that lay before them, gathering her skirts closely about her as she went. Gredin followed, with the rest of their little party.

"Well, Burlon?" Tetralanna said, her tone sharp as she reached the far side. "Open the outer door so that we can be on our— Oh! Oh my!"

The recessed door panels had slid into place behind them, closing them off from the enclave. Gredin heard a hissing sound, and a cool mist permeated the air, smelling faintly of fresh-sliced tongue-peppers.

With an agitated squawk, Tetralanna cupped her hands over her nose and mouth.

"Don't do that," Burlon said. "It's just bio-mist. Breathe it in. It's for your own protection, and everyone else's."

Tetralanna made a sound of protest, her eyes wide above the frail barrier of her hands.

Burlon extended a finger and poked Tetralanna in the ribs.

At the touch, Tetralanna drew in an affronted gasp and whirled to face him.

His answering smile was full of mischief. "There. Now you're breathing properly. The bio-mist keeps us all safe. The air on Tradepoint gets recirculated, so what you inhale now was likely exhaled by a trader of some other race, earlier today."

Tetralanna made a strangled sound, looking horrified.

"It's why you — and they — get treated with bio-mist, every

time you leave or return to your enclave after venturing into the public areas. Be grateful for it."

Tetralanna didn't look grateful, but the outer door opened soon thereafter, allowing them all to spill out into the broad corridor, where Burlon took the lead.

Gredin walked behind Tetralanna, whose gown shimmered in shades of cobalt, sapphire, and ildarian blue. The older woman's hair was elaborately braided, and she wore an array of rings on her delicate hands.

By comparison, Gredin felt drab. She had simply traded her jacket for a short-sleeved tunic of light green, which she wore over her dark green travel pants. To comfort herself, she raised her hand to the flamestone pendant Dreff had given to her on the night of their Choosing, a teardrop of intense colors against her pale tunic. The pendant wasn't a hlette, of course, but its presence made her feel special. She wondered what Dreff was doing, at home. Was he thinking of her, missing her as she was missing him...?

A pair of white-haired individuals passed by, walking in the other direction. Startled out of her reverie by the sight of them, Gredin realized that she had been wit-wandering. Again. That wouldn't do, especially as they were sharing the public corridors with unfamiliar races.

In the next moment, a new individual came into view. The dark creature was tall and gaunt, with bare, claw-like feet. The shape of its body was indeterminate beneath loose layers of black and green gauze wound around and around it, gathered tightly at neck, wrist, and ankle. It cocked its dark, hairless head as they passed it by, then opened and closed what appeared to be a long, gleaming bill.

Gredin felt unsettled, convinced that the glittering gaze was trained expressly on her, tracking her every movement.

It was a relief to round the next corner and leave it behind.

The next folk they encountered seemed less threatening,

though no less strange. Short and stocky, they had high-pitched voices that teased at the upper range of her hearing. Brown haired and light skinned, dressed in identical green coveralls, they stood in a group, milling about in such a way that it was impossible for her to count them accurately. They were clustered around a single figure of some other race, immensely tall and sturdy, an individual whose grey-brown skin looked as rough as tree bark. The tall figure looked down at the green-clad people and spoke to them briefly in a deep, rumbling voice that Gredin felt as much as heard.

And she recognized the words! Excitement flashed through her as she realized that the tall figure had spoken in Tradetalk. *No*, it had just said. *You go back to...* Its final word was one she didn't know, but she repeated it silently to herself, trying to memorize it. Later, she would ask Burlon for its meaning.

One of the short ones turned, then, and caught sight of Gredin looking at them. An instant later, the entire group spun around to look at her, chattering loudly amongst themselves.

=Don't stare.= The silent reminder that blossomed in her mind came from Cirin, behind her. =Move up and walk beside Tetralanna.= Then he called aloud to the green-clad strangers, in Tradetalk, "Meeting. Talk later."

Gredin was embarrassed to have drawn a reprimand from Cirin. Still, it was exhilarating to hear Tradetalk in its actual environment. She quickened her pace to walk beside Tetralanna and behind Sill, fixing her gaze conscientiously between Sill's elegant shoulder blades. The woman's gyfte was Memory, but Gredin had only a hazy notion of what skills that gyfte entailed.

Ahead of Tetralanna, Keegan te Fliss began to cough, and Sill came to a sudden halt. Gredin drew a breath and found herself gagging as a horrible stench filled her nostrils. The smell was appalling, somewhere between wood smoke and rotting vegetables, so visceral that it clawed at her senses, stinging her eyes and making her stomach roil.

=Cover your nose and mouth, if you need to, but get Control of yourselves.= Burlon's words burst into her private mind, harsh and commanding. =Now!=

A trio of tall creatures in bright yellow shirts and black trousers moved past them in the corridor. They walked swiftly, their steps precisely matched, their reddish-brown heads bobbing in unison as they strode along.

Burlon called out to them, in Tradetalk, "My people new. Not Traders. Sorry. You, me, we talk soon."

Gredin realized that the creatures were the source of the hideous smell, and that Burlon was apologizing for the Vennan group's reaction. Beside her, Tetralanna swayed. Gredin reached to steady her, but Cirin got there faster, slipping his arm around her and holding her upright.

"Keep moving," Burlon said, and they began to walk again, with Keegan still coughing convulsively.

Each step took them farther from the creatures, but there was no immediate relief, as the smell seemed to linger in the air. Gredin raised her arm and pressed her nose into the crook of her elbow. Tetralanna continued to lean heavily on Cirin. Ahead, Sill seemed to have steadied, and she reached over to pat Keegan's back from time to time, as spasms of coughing shook him.

Gredin noticed that Burlon and Cirin seemed largely unaffected.

"Unlucky timing," Burlon said as they proceeded. "Those were Mamoran traders. Nice enough folk. Their scent is natural, and Tradepoint has yet to find an effective way to counteract it. It's a touchy topic, since the Mamora are as clean as any of us, and entirely oblivious to their own aroma. Just know that, while it's unpleasant, it isn't harmful."

By the time they stopped again, the miasma from the Mamora no longer hung in the air, and Keegan's breathing had steadied. Tetralanna, however, still looked shaken. A nervous wariness had supplanted her customary aura of calm, and her fingers gripped convulsively at the sleeve of Cirin's jacket.

"The Director's office suite is through this next set of doors," Cirin informed her. "Can you deal with the meeting, or should we take you back to the enclave?"

Tetralanna straightened, looking affronted. "Proceed," she said, and released his sleeve.

"As you like," Cirin said.

Burlon pressed the palm of his hand to a screen set into the wall of the corridor. A quick trill of notes came from the panel, making Gredin think of birdsong. Then the two halves of the door slid apart.

"Stay close," Burlon advised, and led them inside.

The transition from the corridor to the Tradepoint Director's office was short, but the contrast was extreme. Where the corridor had been bright and bare, this area was softly lit, its walls covered in tall panels that housed ever-changing arrays of color.

"Welcome," a deep voice said. "I am pleased you have arrived."

Gredin turned and saw that, while the words were Vennan, the individual speaking them definitely was not. It was tall and thick-built, with rough, grey-brown skin, like the person she had seen speaking to the short creatures in the corridor.

Was this a Prett?

Burlon and Cirin stepped forward, each smiling and crossing their palms. "Wyve!"

So, this *was* a Prett. In fact, it was *the* Prett. Wyve, the Director of Tradepoint.

Burlon added, in Prettian, "Thank you for receiving us."

Tetralanna bridled and stared at him as if Burlon had suddenly sprouted a second head.

Keeping her voice to a murmur, Gredin translated. "Burlon is greeting the Tradepoint Director and thanking him for arranging this meeting," she said, and waited for Tetralanna to step forward and add her own expressions of greeting and gratitude.

Instead, Tetralanna said, in a strangled whisper, "Inform the Director that we were accosted in the corridor."

Gredin felt her face grow hot, but she knew that silence was not an option. Turning to the Prett, who was gesturing for them to enter, she selected words from her store of Prettian vocabulary. "A moment, Director, if you will. We passed Mamoran traders in the corridor. Our Voice, Tetralanna, was troubled by the encounter. She wishes you to be aware of the event and asks whether it is likely to recur."

Cirin looked annoyed.

Burlon's expression was harder to gauge. Before the Director could reply, Burlon said, still in Prettian, "My fault, Wyve. No ill intent, and no harm done. I knew the Mamora were in port, but I didn't expect our group to encounter them in the hallway."

The Director of Tradepoint gave a slow nod. "Unfortunate. I am sorry the Voice was distressed on her first walk through the station." A change of expression came over the rough-hewn face, an expression that Gredin thought might be a smile. "As it happens, however, the Mamora are in port *because* of you."

"What do you mean?" Burlon asked, clearly startled.

"They remained because of your upcoming reception. They are determined to attend, as a gesture of support and goodwill." A tip of the head. "With all due apologies to the Voice, there is no graceful way to avoid it — or them."

"I would never wish to avoid the Mamora. It will be fine. Have no worry."

Tetralanna hissed, "What are they saying?"

Gredin turned to her, balancing between tact and truth. "The Director is aware. Burlon is certain that future encounters will have a more satisfactory outcome."

Tetralanna's mouth tightened. "The most satisfactory

outcome would be not to *have* future encounters," she muttered, but she inclined her head to the Director and, at Wyve's second gesture of invitation, moved forward with the rest of the group.

The inner office was spacious and gently illuminated. A large, sleek table of metal and glass stood near the back wall, with two tall chairs positioned behind it.

In front of the table, seating was provided in a broad curve — wide, padded benches, some with upholstered backs. Behind the Director's desk, one of the tall chairs was already occupied by a second Prett, who rose as they approached.

"This is Figg, Assistant Director of Tradepoint," Wyve said. "While your delegation is here, address any questions or concerns to Figg or myself. She or I will be on duty at all times. Now, would you present your group, informing us of their names and functions?"

Gredin nodded. She supposed that Tetralanna would take umbrage at not being addressed directly, but it was clear that she had not yet fully recovered from the shock of the Mamora. And what could she expect, when she shared no language with the Director? Gredin was simply relieved that her own grasp of Prettian was proving sufficient.

"The Director presents Figg, whose title is Assistant Director of Tradepoint. Figg is identified as female," she added for the group's benefit. "Wyve and Figg stand willing to assist us, at need, and Wyve invites us to sit, and asks Tetralanna to identify everyone."

Wyve settled into the other chair behind the table. Tetralanna claimed the bench at the midpoint of the half-circle, facing him. Burlon and Cirin settled to her left, leaving a gap between themselves and her, while Keegan and Sill sat to Tetralanna's right.

When Gredin moved to take the seat on Tetralanna's left, Tetralanna said, "Stand behind me, Gredin. You are not here as an individual. You are here to translate my words."

Gredin obeyed, stung at being singled out to stand, but she

recognized a certain logic to Tetralanna's direction when she saw that Wyve's direct line of sight could now easily encompass them both.

At a nod from Wyve, Tetralanna said, in Vennan, "Greetings to the people of Prett from the people of Venna. We come in recognition of the relationship between our two worlds, as trading partners and as friends."

Gredin translated, retaining Tetralanna's phrasing and content. Her lessons with the Traders had only involved translation of isolated words and phrases, or times when they all practiced speaking solely in Prettian or Tradetalk. Never before had she tried to do justice to a conversation between two people, each speaking their own language. And yet she found, as she conveyed Tetralanna's greeting, that her gyfte rose to uphold her.

As soon as Gredin paused, Tetralanna said, "You already know Cirin te K'lar and Burlon te Bentain. We are also joined by Sill te Torr, First of Memory for House Torr."

Gredin rendered that into Prettian, finding her footing in the alternating flow of words.

Tetralanna continued, "Sill will observe the proceedings and make a Memory of our visit available, if anyone should express an interest in it when we return home."

If.

The inclusion of that one small word made it difficult to translate Tetralanna's statement in a properly complimentary way. Taking a deep breath, Gredin said instead, "Sill will closely observe everything that transpires here, so that all Vennans may have the pleasure of sharing in this experience when we return home."

Burlon smiled wryly; he'd noticed her amendment. She wished she could have spared Sill the insult, but First of Memory had understood Tetralanna's words all too well.

A slight gesture of acknowledgment from Wyve was

followed by a question. "What does it mean, this title of First? Is it ceremonial or functional?"

He was asking her directly, so she offered no translation to Tetralanna. "Both," she replied. "It identifies Sill as the most accomplished in her gyfte within her House."

"Venna has sent us their best," Wyve observed. "We thank you for that."

In front of her, Tetralanna stirred, likely impatient with the incomprehensible exchange. "Your pardon," Gredin murmured to her. "He requested a clarification regarding Sill's rank."

That seemed to mollify Tetralanna, who continued. "Also with us is Keegan te Fliss, who functions as a historian. He will keep a written account of our stay here."

Gredin saw that Keegan had opened his bundle and was already doing so, using a reed pen and a small vial of ink to make marks on the topmost page in his notebook.

After Gredin provided the introduction, Wyve replied, "Tell your historian I am doing the same, here where I sit, although we Prett do not employ paper or inks. When our meeting concludes, I would be happy to show him our method."

Gredin nodded and said to Keegan, "The Director says that he, too, is making notes, although in a different manner. He extends an invitation, at the conclusion of the meeting, for you to observe how he does so." She was curious, herself; there was nothing in front of the Director but the table's shining surface, over which his hands moved, blunt fingers tapping.

Tetralanna said, in Vennan, "Director, I am Tetralanna te Balamont, First Speaker of House Balamont and appointed Voice for this Vennan delegation. Shall we begin?"

Gredin hesitated. Begin? Clearly, that was Tetralanna's intent. And, just as clearly, Tetralanna saw no need to introduce Gredin, apparently viewing a translator as a mere tool of convenience, like the Director's table or Keegan's reed pens. For a moment, mortification stirred to life again within Gredin, but she quelled it and plunged into speech, doing what a Speaker was trained to do — defuse awkward situations.

"Seated in front of me is Tetralanna te Balamont, First Speaker of House Balamont, the appointed Voice for this Vennan delegation," Gredin said, the Prettian words rising easily to her lips. She added, "Please do not ask my name at this time. It would not be appropriate while I am translating. First Speaker invites you to begin the important business of this meeting, if you will be so kind."

Out of that flow of Prettian, Tetralanna would only have been able to discern her own name and that of the House. The other words would be nonsense to her ears. But Gredin hoped she had forestalled Wyve from asking a question that could only be adequately answered by speaking her own name, in defiance of Tetralanna's wishes.

"Very well," Wyve said, although Gredin fancied that there was a bright directness in the look he gave her. Then his gaze shifted to Tetralanna. "Are you finding the accommodations adequate to your needs and comfort? Have any problems arisen?"

"We're all fine," Cirin interjected before Gredin could translate.

"Good. In that case, I would like to clarify the agenda for the Trisectoriana. The ceremony will be held in the Communications Center, just down the corridor from here. I will make a few opening remarks, after which there will be several speeches from members of the Vokastra — one from the Prett President, one from the senior Trade Commissioner, and possibly one from the senior Economics Commissioner, although we are trying to gently discourage that, in the interest of brevity. It is also possible that the Vokastra will order the Melding Mediator to take part in the proceedings, although that is less likely, as he is technically a member of our Tradepoint staff, not the Vokastra." He paused and looked to Gredin.

Taking her cue, she rendered his statements into Vennan, wishing she could ask for further clarifications. *Vokastra? Melding Mediator?* The Director's words were unknown to her. She could only repeat the sounds as she had heard them. But Tetralanna uttered no questions.

Wyve continued, "Because of the importance of these individuals, their crowded schedules, and the transit time that shuttle transport would require, the President and the others will not be physically present. Rather, they will attend by communication link, able to see and hear all that transpires, and they will make their speeches by..." He looked to Cirin and Burlon, speaking another word that Gredin didn't recognize.

Burlon nodded and turned toward Gredin. "We'll see their images as they speak. It will look as though they're in the room with us, but they won't actually be there."

She translated Wyve's words and Burlon's explanation to the rest of the group.

"After that," Wyve said, "a token of appreciation will be presented to Cirin, in recognition of his status as the first Vennan ever to visit Tradepoint, three hundred sectora ago. Cirin will be given an opportunity to express his thanks. Then a present will be offered from the Prett government to the Vennan government. At that time, the Voice will be welcome to offer her thanks on your government's behalf. When she has finished doing so, I will make a brief closing remark, and the ceremony will conclude."

Gredin realized an odd misconception in the Prett Director's phrasing. Wyve seemed unaware that there was no single 'government' on Venna to whom such a present could be given. Each Vennan House was entirely independent. And yet there was to be only one present from the Prett Vokastra.

Gredin began slowly, choosing her words with care. "The Director informs us that two presents will be given to us at the ceremony. The first is intended solely for Cirin. The other..."

Inspiration rescued her. "…the exact nature of which has not yet been made clear to me, will be a token of esteem from the Prett government. It is intended to circulate among the Houses of Venna so that each House, in turn, might enjoy the honor of possessing it for a time. Upon its presentation to us at the ceremony, Tetralanna is invited to speak on behalf of all of the Houses of Venna, expressing their thanks to the Prett government."

Tetralanna nodded approvingly, while Burlon and Cirin looked amused.

Wyve added, "The Trisectoriana will be widely broadcast on the planet. This ceremony is a Tradepoint tradition. We acknowledge each of our trading partners on their three-hundred-sectora anniversary as a Tradepoint participant. I will take particular pleasure in this ceremony since it is the first such Trisectoriana to be reached during my tenure as Tradepoint Director."

Gredin translated, hoping it would bring the meeting to a close.

Instead, Wyve leaned back in his chair. "I have now spoken at length about our plans for the Trisectoriana. Thank you for your patience. If you have questions, I will entertain them. And I have questions about the reception you plan for that evening."

Gredin said to Tetralanna, "The Director says his comments have covered the necessary facts about the Prett government's presentation. If you have questions, he will address them. If not, he has questions about our plans for the reception at the enclave."

Tetralanna waved her hand airily. "The Director may ask."

Gredin offered Wyve a smile. "Your presentation has been most thorough. We will gladly respond to your questions regarding the reception now."

"Excellent." Wyve leaned forward, with every appearance of lively curiosity. "May I hear the agenda for the Vennan reception? The order of events?"

Gredin translated for Tetralanna. "The Director thanks you for listening to his agenda for the Trisectoriana. Now he asks you to inform him of the order of events for the reception we will hold afterwards, in the Vennan enclave."

For an unsettling minute, Tetralanna said nothing. Then, shifting her gaze, she said, "Burlon, explain to the Director."

Confused, Gredin looked to Burlon.

He shrugged and smiled before replying directly in Prettian to Wyve. "Your Trisectoriana honoring Cirin is a government event. Very proper. Very structured. A Vennan reception is quite different. There is no agenda."

Wyve looked perplexed. "I am sorry. Have I misunderstood? You wish the Trisectoriana to be the end of the matter?"

"No, no, no," Burlon said. "I say only that there will be no formality at the reception."

"Then what *will* there be?"

"Music," Burlon told the Director.

"And food," Cirin added.

"Dancing."

"Drink."

"Artists and artisans."

"Singers."

"Laughter," Burlon elaborated. "Definitely laughter. I doubt whether there will be any laughter at the Trisectoriana, so we will be in great need of laughter, by evening."

"But…" Wyve seemed to be searching for words. "Which of those will happen first?"

"All of them," Burlon said, and he and Cirin grinned at each other. "Do the Prett never have parties, Wyve? Is everything always according to an agenda?"

Figg, the Assistant Director of Tradepoint, cleared her throat and said, "There is a reason for the Director's question, good travelers."

Burlon and Cirin quickly quieted themselves and gave her their attention.

"There have been inquiries," Figg told them, "about attendance at the reception."

"Inquiries from…?"

"From the Shodekekeen. From the Thalken. And several more who are in port."

"I'm not having the Hesch there," Burlon said, scowling.

"Or the Beng," Cirin groaned, rolling his eyes.

"Or the—"

Figg held up a hand, as if pleading for them to stop.

They fell silent, eyeing her warily.

"To admit some and exclude others would invite hard feelings," Figg cautioned.

"Well, to admit the Beng is to risk losing everything we own," Cirin groused.

Tetralanna turned her head slightly. "Why are they arguing with the Prett woman?" she demanded under her breath, looking perturbed.

The exchange had all been conducted in Prettian. Gredin said hastily, while the debate continued, "A question about reception guests. A moment, please."

" —listen to the Thalken whine all night, you're sadly mistaken," Cirin protested.

"The Shodekekeen are welcome," Burlon stated. "And the F'lala, since they're in port. If the Wilra or the Nairn or the

Yaylay arrive before then, they can come. The same for the Kikaradd or the Anamadansit, though not both. But not the Chibi. They would only cause trouble. And despite today's incident in the corridor, we're happy to include the Mamora."

"Mamora?" Tetralanna echoed sharply, apparently catching that one name out of the rapid exchange of Prettian. "Gredin, what are they saying?"

"More talk of who should guest and who should not," she answered, most of her attention pinned on the rapid exchange between the two Travelers and Figg.

"Your attention, all," Wyve said loudly in a voice that rumbled like thunder.

Gredin turned to him, noting that everyone else did, too, eyes wide, mouths shut.

"Whatever your concerns," he said, "I am certain you have no wish to cause lasting harm to your trading relationships. Therefore, I propose a compromise."

Cirin looked suspicious.

Burlon continued to scowl.

"Three guests from each race's enclave, if they so desire," Wyve said, and held up three fingers, each half as broad as the palm of Gredin's hand. "Each delegation will sign a written agreement, if they wish to send representatives. And Prett security will be assigned to remain with the guests throughout the evening."

"Security with each group or with each individual?" Cirin asked. "Beng can scatter quicker than grain lice. One security officer can't keep track of three Beng."

Wyve sighed. "One security officer per individual, then. Each set of guests will arrive in a group. They will depart as a group. No one is compelled to attend, but any who wish to must agree to our conditions and precautions."

"There's more than three Shodekekeen I want to invite,"

Burlon objected, "and if the Rodorno reach port by then, their whole enclave is welcome."

Wyve tilted his head to the side, and Gredin wondered if it was the Prett equivalent of a shrug. "Be that as it may, the limits must be the same for all," he said. "Surely, with the proper precautions, you can tolerate three Beng."

"Why three?"

"Fewer seems restrictive. And more... Well, my security forces are not inexhaustible. Think strongly about three. It is a number that seems manageable. Discuss it with your people."

"Why bother?" Cirin scoffed. "They can't tell a Shodekekeen from a Thalken."

Gredin pitched her voice to reach them. "We can tell a Mamora from a Prett, and that is a start," she dared to say, and saw Burlon smile. "Surely the Director knows a great deal about those who frequent his station. Can we not depend on his advice?"

"What *is* this disagreement?" Tetralanna demanded.

Gredin looked beseechingly at Burlon and Cirin.

To her surprise, they both relaxed, the tension draining visibly from the set of their shoulders. "Our apologies, Wyve," Burlon said.

"Certainly," Cirin concurred. "At this rate, you'll regret offering to honor me at all."

"Truly, we ask your pardon, old friend," Burlon added. "Three of each race it shall be." He shrugged. "And if any stray Shodekekeen should venture to our door, we'll be certain it's before or after the official groups attend. Will that keep the peace?"

"Indeed," Wyve said, and the set of his broad shoulders relaxed, as well.

"Gredin?" Tetralanna prompted again, her voice very nearly a growl.

"The point of contention has been resolved as the Director

advised. Prett security will oversee all members of other races who attend our reception, and the number of such attendees will be limited to three from each race," Gredin told her.

Before Tetralanna could respond, Wyve looked to Gredin. "This lack of ordered events that Burlon describes — it is common on your world?"

"Yes," Gredin replied. "A time of relaxation and pleasure. The reception will be our chance to show others what it is to be Vennan. Sample our foods. Observe us as we create our Craftwork. Enjoy performances by our dancers and musicians." She smiled shyly at Wyve. "We hope you will find it enjoyable, as well."

"Will it not be chaotic?" he asked, the twinkle in his eyes softening his question.

"Perhaps a little," she conceded. "But that can be pleasant, as well."

"And this is what Vennans enjoy?"

"We are a happy people. To share that happiness pleases us deeply."

"Ah, I see. For one with no name, you are most enlightening."

He was teasing her. Flattered and a little embarrassed, she said, "I have a name. At another time, I will share it with you gladly. Just not right now, please."

"As you wish." He made a show of looking directly at Tetralanna. "Is there anything else that might enrich your stay?" he asked, with a sudden air of gravitas.

"The Director inquires whether he can make your time here more enjoyable," Gredin told Tetralanna in Vennan, with what she hoped was equal solemnity.

Tetralanna appeared mollified. "My thanks to the Director, but I need nothing."

"The Voice thanks you, but her needs are met," Gredin assured Wyve.

"Tomorrow, your people might enjoy a tour of our Traders' Market. Cirin, can arrangements be made for them to explore our facilities during their brief stay here?"

Looking less than thrilled, Cirin replied, "Most will be busy preparing, tomorrow, but I suppose we can find a Trader willing to take a group to the Market."

"Hey!" Burlon exclaimed. "Don't be promising away my Traders' time. Take people to the market yourself, if you're so eager to oblige their curiosity."

Wyve said, "My apologies, but we will need Cirin to attend a rehearsal in the communications center tomorrow, after your midsect meal."

"There, you see?" Cirin said, grinning at Burlon. "I'm important. You're not. If you're so concerned about your Traders, you could offer to take a group yourself."

"I have two trade negotiations scheduled. But I'll find someone else to take the groups."

"Gredin?" Tetralanna prompted.

She wanted to say, *It's nothing — just Burlon and Cirin teasing one another*. Instead, she clung to the literal truth of the exchange, and said, "They are discussing a possible tour of the Traders' Market, tomorrow, and the need for Cirin to attend a rehearsal in the communications center in preparation for the Trisectoriana."

"Ask the Director whether I am required at the rehearsal. If so, I will need you there with me, to translate."

Gredin dismissed a stab of disappointment. She was here to fulfill a specific function, not to explore Tradepoint. Catching Wyve's eye, she said, "Director? The Voice asks whether she should plan to attend tomorrow's rehearsal?"

Again, his eyes twinkled. "Oh, I think she would feel quite insulted otherwise, don't you? By all means, inform her that we wish her to attend." He spread his hands. "And now, if there are no further matters to explore, I expect you would all benefit from an opportunity to relax in the Vennan enclave. I look forward to seeing you tomorrow."

"Thank you for your time, Director."

"Do you desire a security pod to transport you back to your enclave?"

"No!" Burlon and Cirin said firmly, nearly in unison.

"We'll all be fine," Cirin temporized more moderately. "We need the exercise, and Burlon and I will stay alert for any…complications."

Burlon stood up. "So, shall we be on our way?" he asked in Vennan.

"Pardon," said Keegan. "Is there time for what the Director wanted me to see?"

Gredin had entirely forgotten Wyve's offer to the quiet historian.

Cirin said, "I imagine the Voice would rather return to the enclave without delay. But I can walk there with her and Sill, while the rest of you talk with Wyve."

Tetralanna rose from her bench with a nod to the Director. "Gredin, translate for the historian. Don't pester the Director with questions. And don't linger. It must be nearly time for evening meal. I will see you in our chambers afterwards. The two of us have matters to discuss."

With that, she left, and Gredin finally dared to relax.

By the time Gredin returned to the Vennan enclave, evening meal had begun.

She and Burlon and Keegan had shared an enjoyable span of private time together in the Director's office with Wyve and Figg after the others left, observing the Prettian manner of notation and demonstrating that of Venna. But the interval was now at an end, and the two men offered her a cheerful word of farewell and headed off, doubtless to join the members of their own Houses for the evening meal.

When they had gone, Gredin looked around in confusion. At home, groups of kinsmen often ate together in one of the many dining chambers instead of their private quarters. But this room was immense, filled with unfamiliar faces. She scarcely knew six people here, despite sharing a House-bond with over a hundred of them.

That seemed daunting... until she recalled the alien races in the corridor. At least the strangers in this vast room were Vennan. Compared to the strange individuals she'd seen in the corridor, any Vennan was a familiar sight and potential friend, regardless of which House might be theirs.

Still, that attitude wouldn't survive their homecoming, where House defined everyone. You grew up there. You found your Chosen there. You bore your children there. You exercised your gyfte there, unless you were a Traveler or a Trader. Some lived entirely within their House and its Holdings, never encountering folks from another House. She herself was a bit of an exception, since Unter had looked beyond the bounds of the House to find her Mentor, Frake te Santelle...

Frake. Her spirits fell as she remembered his criticisms of her, as Tetralanna had relayed them. It stung Gredin's feelings, as well as her pride, that her Mentor had made such comments to Tetralanna, even if the two of them *were* First Speakers of their respective Houses.

Stop, she admonished herself. *You're hungry and tired. Don't dwell on unhappy thoughts tonight.* So resolved, she approached an unknown group, to seek a place at their table.

=Nifflin!= The touch of Ingarra's pet name for her blossomed within her private mind.

Gredin scanned the crowd. = Ingarra! Where are you?=

=Not far. Stay put. Beda is coming for you.=

When she spotted Beda threading through the clustered tables, Gredin hurried forward, murmuring apologies as she brushed past people. Reaching him, she threw her arms around him.

"Such a day of new experiences," he said with calm cheerfulness. "And more of them for you than for most, I imagine. Come and eat."

At the long table where Ingarra waited, someone had already joined her, a woman with broad cheekbones, a cheerful smile, and sandy hair tidied into neat little braids. "Miri, this is our Gredin," Ingarra said. "And this is Miri te Kendar. Her Chosen, Zanther, is a Trader. Miri Tends in the kitchens. You'll know why we befriended her, once you taste what she's prepared."

As Gredin sat down, a glass, a plate, and two small bowls

appeared in front of her. The first bowl held a bounty of berries, from deep-red galens to dusky blue choff, purple vokes and, her favorite, pale green lentz. The second bowl held steaming vegetable broth. The plate bore miniature pastries, their aromas so savory that her stomach growled.

The top crust of each pastry bore the symbol of one of the Houses of Venna, golden brown and beautifully detailed. "They're too pretty to eat!" Gredin protested.

"Nonsense. Eating is what they're made for," Miri said, looking pleased. "Each one has a different filling. We're experimenting, to help us decide which ones to make for the reception."

"Did you really make a different flavor for each House?"

"Of course. Thirty-three Houses, thirty-three fillings."

"So much work!" Gredin marveled.

"So much pleasure," came Miri's prompt reply.

"My favorites," Beda confided, "are Deldora, Joth, Santelle and, of course, Balamont."

"Fliss was best," Ingarra volunteered, "although Torr and Avilar were nearly as good."

Gredin considered her own plate. Six tiny pastries bore the emblems of Bentain, Kendar, Hetamar, Balamont, Olifan, and Portamara. Choosing her own House's symbol first, she lifted a pastry, popped it into her mouth, and bit down on what proved to be flaky pastry with a warm center of melted cheese, redolent of herbs. She chewed slowly, savoring the tastes whispering across her tongue. "Bayette," she murmured, "and nepp... and is that astinelle?"

"It *is* astinelle," Miri affirmed, "though only a tiny pinch. Most folk don't notice it. Do you have a gyfte for Tending in the kitchens?"

"No, only for appreciating what others prepare," Gredin said, and her Guides laughed.

"It's true," Ingarra said. "She has a clever tongue, for flavors *and* for words. Gredin's Chosen has a minor gyfte for food Tending, although his primary gyfte is for Making. He is quite skilled at working with metals and gems. Indeed, he fashioned Gredin's flamestone necklace."

"Oh!" Miri's face lit with interest. "Will he be demonstrating his Craft at the reception?"

"No," Gredin said. "We just completed our dydanin, and he is moving our belongings into our new chambers. But what of you? Is your Chosen here?"

"No, he is on a Tradeteam mission to Sprygale." Miri looked wistful, then brightened. "Here. Try another pastry."

Gredin did as she was bidden, choosing the one for Miri's own House of Kendar. Again, crisp pastry, but this filling was a spicy minced mixture that sent little shivers of sensation over her tongue. "Sunmint," she said. "And tongue-peppers! But what have you minced for the base?"

"Benroot. Baked, it has a pleasant texture."

Gredin was astonished. Benroot was simple to grow and quick to sprout. Beda had given her seeds when she was just tiny, so she could plant them in the garden and watch them grow. The small vegetable was often included in stews, or cut into long slivers and eaten raw, mostly for its crunch, but she had never been fond of it — until now. "You've made it taste glorious."

Miri beamed. "I wanted to bake something unusual. I'm so glad you like it!"

Gredin felt an unexpected rapport with this woman and her bright chatter.

"I worried," Ingarra said, "that nothing could make this cavern look festive. But Miri showed me items she brought to decorate the tables. It made my luggage packs seem paltry."

"Well, what's the use of producing good-tasting foods, if the setting doesn't please the eye?" Miri asked. "Things will look festive on the night of the reception, I assure you."

The other pastries were flavorful, but the one bearing House

Kendar's emblem remained Gredin's favorite. By the time she'd finished the pastries and most of her broth, her eyelids were growing heavy. The day had begun at home with Dreff and was ending here in the skies above another world. A yawn escaped her. "Your pardon. I'll take my berries and seek my bed."

"A fine idea," Ingarra agreed. "Tomorrow will be busy. Rest while you can."

"Perhaps we'll see you at morning meal," Beda said. "Shall I walk you to your room?"

"No, I'm fine. Miri, it pleases me greatly to have met you. My thanks for this wonderful meal." Rising, Gredin crossed her palms to the three of them, then picked up the little bowl of berries. "A fine night's rest to you all," she said in farewell, and started toward the far wall, munching berries as she walked.

By the time she reached the entry to the rooms that she and Tetralanna shared, the bowl was empty. She set it on the final table she passed, knowing the Tenders would gather it up.

Empty-handed, she approached her door and waited while its two halves slid apart.

Inside, Tetralanna sat at the little table with an empty plate and glass in front of her. "Ah. Gredin. I began to think you had lost your way."

"No, I was dining with my Guides. You said we'd speak after evening meal, and so—"

Tetralanna waved her to silence. "What is that on your hand?"

Gredin looked down and saw that, while her left hand was clean, the fingertips of her right hand bore bright stains of berry juice, blue and red, green and purple. Hastily, she Tended them clean. "Berry stains," she said. "Didn't you have berries with your evening meal?"

"No. I had little appetite."

Concerned, Gredin asked, "Are you unwell? Shall I request an Assessor?"

"No, it has simply been a troubling day. A night's sleep is what I need. But I wanted to speak with you first. What did you think of today's meeting?"

"The Director was unexpectedly genial. I worried that he might be stern and reserved. It must be no small responsibility to manage Tradepoint. But I found him quite kind."

"And what of your translations? Are you confident that you understood him well?"

"Mostly, yes. I believe I was able to provide him with an accurate sense of all that you said."

"And a great deal else," Tetralanna said dryly.

Gredin stilled, startled. "Your pardon?"

"At times, your conversations with the Director seemed to carry on far beyond a simple rendering of my words into Prettian. Or am I mistaken?"

There was no overt anger in Tetralanna's tone, but her expression held no approval. Gredin framed her reply carefully. "I sometimes lacked the precise Prettian words to do justice to your message. At those times, I elaborated so that your finer points wouldn't be lost."

Tetralanna pressed her fingertips briefly to her temples. "I imagine you're doing the best that you can. But remember your role. When you become drawn into side conversations with the Director, it slows the meeting and distracts from our purpose here. Simply convey my words to him and translate his replies, as accurately as you can." She took a breath and released it slowly, then drew another. "Tomorrow, after the rehearsal, I'll be spending my time in the reception hall, making sure everything goes smoothly."

"Why would it not?"

Tetralanna's smile was wry. "Because of the nature of people, I suppose. This is a strange place to them. Preparations for the reception may not go smoothly. The facilities provided may bewilder them. Or they may simply long for their House members or their Chosen. For all those reasons, tempers may be short and people's moods uncertain. I will walk among them, admiring their handiwork, encouraging those whose spirits seem low, and mediating any frictions or disagreements." She gave Gredin a measuring look. "You may come along, if you wish."

"I would like that very much."

"Well then, I bid you a peaceful night," Tetralanna said, and went to her room.

Pushing back her own bench, Gredin sought out the cleansing chamber. There had still been no time for Burlon to provide instructions or explanations, and her need was now pressing. She would just have to puzzle it out for herself.

The room, harshly lit from above, was fashioned all of metal. There was a tall inner chamber with a perforated floor and ceiling, separated from the rest of the room by a translucent barrier that slid on a track. Near it, at waist height, two slanted openings were set into the wall, roughly a hand-span apart, but their purpose eluded her understanding.

Lastly, the room contained a broad bench with a cutout whose shape made its purpose clear. Unfastening the pants of her travel outfit, Gredin sat, allowed her body to empty, Converted her waste, and Freshened herself. When she rose from the seat, something made a clicking sound, and a sharp, unnatural scent tainted the air briefly and then subsided.

The unexpected sound and smell made her uneasy. Refastening her pants, she resolved to ask Burlon or Tetralanna to explain, in the morning.

Leaving the cleansing room, Gredin reclaimed her luminth and retreated to her sleeping chamber, exhausted by all that had happened since dawn. She was bewildered that her successful interactions with the Director had drawn more criticism than praise from Tetralanna. And though she was pleased by the thought of the day's new acquaintances, both Vennan and Prett, she felt a faint niggle of concern that, elsewhere within Tradepoint's walls, so many other races resided. The names she had heard Burlon use for them rang in her mind: the Beng, the Hesch, the unpleasantly fragrant Mamora...

Right now, however, she should close her eyes and sleep. But she would have to do so without Dreff beside her. He had teased her, last night, nestled together in their bed on the eve of her departure. "Gredin, my joy, what will you do tomorrow night when you have no one to warm your cold feet?"

"How sad. My Chosen has already begun a list of my faults," Gredin teased. "Because you find my feet too chill, you are unmoved by my approaching absence."

"Unmoved? By you?" Dreff took her in his arms. "Never." Then he had wooed her with kisses and caresses and the presence of his own beloved body within hers, continuing his attentions until a completion overtook her, and her very wits fled, leaving her limp and satisfied, with pleasure ripples lapping deliciously through her body, from core to fingertips.

But that was last night. Now she was on Tradepoint, floating above the Prett home world, sharing quarters with Tetralanna. Her mind wanted to race, determined to examine everything she'd experienced on this astonishing day. But she knew how to prevent that. She spread blankets on her sleep mat, added her pillow, and stepped out of her clothes. Then she withdrew the pouch that was always with her from her trouser pocket and settled cross-legged on the bed. Untying the cord, she teased the pouch open and tipped out her stones.

They tumbled free, clicking and clacking, and landed in a cluster on the coverlet, as if clinging together upon finding themselves so very far from home. "Be bold," Gredin whispered to them. "We are having an adventure." She stirred the pile gently with her fingertip. Twelve stones. Twelve little pieces of Venna... Well, thirteen, if she counted her flamestone pendant. She lifted each in turn, remembering where she found them and what each looked like before it Became. Then, calmed, she returned them to their pouch and tucked it beneath her pillow, knowing sleep would now be possible. Tetralanna would have no reason to find fault with her, tomorrow.

So decided, Gredin climbed beneath the covers, drained the luminth down to darkness, closed her eyes, and drifted smoothly into sleep.

Gredin?

She was warm, and her need for sleep wasn't nearly satisfied. Closing her eyes more tightly, she nestled into the pillow. But there was a glow against her eyelids. What was it?

Beloved?

Oh, unfair. She couldn't resist the sweet murmur of Dreff's voice in her ear.

Lie still, he soothed. *You need do nothing but listen.*

She made a drowsy sound of assent, for there was nothing she would deny him. He had only to ask. And it was sweet to lie in boneless repose while he whispered to her.

Something has happened. Hear me, Gredin, and be brave.

Brave? She tried to rouse, but her eyelids were sealed. She could only listen. And worry.

I am gone, beloved. House Balamont, the Ocean Holding, our entire world is gone.

Worry turned to terror as the relentless words continued.

In an instant, everything ended. Everything! But I rejoice that all who accompanied you to Tradepoint are safe, despite the loss of so much else. Is it not wondrous?

She was trapped in a terrible night-thought from which she could not awaken.

Keep the others from falling into despair. Their lives must be lived, not wasted. There are Chosens to be found, babies to be born, gyftes to be celebrated, losses to be faced — losses that can only be survived if people stay strong. Every individual has been ravaged by this disaster. Let that pain unite you in common concern. Act as one House, watching over one another.

You are a Speaker. Step into the fullness of your gyfte. It will take time to recover from this blow, but time is the one advantage our race possesses in abundance. All must rebuild their lives. It can be done, decision by decision, action by action, child by child by child...

The voice that had seemed to be Dreff's was changing, growing deeper, taking on a resonant echo.

You are stranded in a place that is not your own. Recovering from these losses will take tears and remembrance. Entrust your memories to Sill te Torr. Her gyfte will bring comfort and enlightenment when the path grows uncertain.

Watch over Salderon te Indirin and the minor Healers, for your community must avoid any more losses. Urge every individual to look vigilantly to their Balance and hlinga and safety, so that the Healers will not be taxed beyond their limit.

Most importantly, protect your own strength and spirit. Forge new paths. Do not be swayed by those who resist your counsel. Speak with authority. You have a glorious gyfte waiting to blossom forth.

Find the value in every survivor.

Keep them safe... keep them safe... keep them safe...

Then he was gone. The torpor left her limbs. In panic, she opened her eyes — and gasped.

Her body was glowing in the dark.

Sitting up, Gredin reached for the luminth. The hand she extended toward it glowed brighter than a full moon. Sobbing with fear, she snatched up the luminth and poured energy into it, but it shone like a raging hearth fire. On the edge of panic, she drained it completely, then fed tiny trickles of energy into it until its illumination looked more normal.

She was starting to look more normal, too. Only her hands still glowed, their silver aura at odds with the golden light from the luminth. Her breathing slowed.

Then she recalled Dreff's words: *I am gone, beloved. Our entire world is gone.*

Wailing in despair, she kicked free of the coverlet, snatched up her stones, and ran to tell Tetralanna.

[9]

It seemed an impossibly long way to Tetralanna's sleeping chamber. As soon as the two halves of the closed door parted, Gredin darted inside and flung herself to her knees beside the sleeping mat. "Tetralanna! Tetralanna!"

The older woman woke with a start, eyes slitted against the glow from the luminth, her normally serene expression contorting into a mask of alarm. "What?" she demanded hoarsely. "What is happening?"

Fresh tears sprang to Gredin's eyes, and her throat seemed to swell shut. She gasped for air, struggling to frame a reply, yet dreading the moment when she would have to turn the terrible knowledge into words. Letting the luminth drop, she buried her face in her shaking hands.

"Answer me, girl!" Tetralanna ordered. "What's wrong? Has someone come to the door? Is there trouble on Tradepoint?"

She shook her head in negation, feeling as if her insides were trying to rise up through her throat.

"Gredin!" Tetralanna's voice, pitched low, cut through her panic, forcing her to listen. "Take a breath."

With difficulty, Gredin dragged air into her aching body.

"Good. Push it out and take another."

It felt odd to do so, an unfamiliar chore that required her concentration, but she managed, and the room seemed to steady.

"Now look at me."

Reluctantly, she lowered her hands and met Tetralanna's troubled gaze.

"Are we safe?" Tetralanna demanded.

The question was so wrong as to be almost funny. Gredin nodded.

"Then why did you wake me? What is the matter with you?"

Gredin swallowed, fumbling for words. "I... I had a...." She had no adequate name for what she had experienced. "It... it was a kind of night-thought. But more...real."

"A night-thought?" Tetralanna demanded, repeating the phrase. "Is *that* all?"

"No. I mean, it wasn't really a night-thought."

"Then what?"

Gredin began to shiver. "It was Dreff. He spoke to me. He said—"

"Dreff did not speak to you," Tetralanna interrupted testily. "You had a night-thought about him. Not surprising, I suppose, so soon after your dydanin. But truly, Gredin, how inconsiderate of you to wake me and frighten me over nothing. Go back to bed."

"No, you don't understand!"

"Then explain yourself."

Again, the words drained away from her, like water seeping into parched soil.

Tetralanna made a visible attempt to Control her irritation. "Tell me where we are, Gredin."

"On Tradepoint."

"And where is Dreff?"

But the answer to that was too horrible to contemplate.

Gredin rocked with distress, unable to subdue the sobs that rose within her.

Tetralanna released a long-suffering sigh, pushed her blankets away, and stood up. Reaching down to grasp Gredin's upper arm, she said, "Come with me." She tugged firmly, drawing Gredin to her feet, then stooped to sweep up the discarded luminth from where Gredin had dropped it. Guiding her, Tetralanna took Gredin to the table in their common room. "Sit," she said.

Dizzy with distress, Gredin dropped onto a bench, flinching as her bare skin came in contact with the chill metal. "It was Dreff," she insisted raggedly. "He woke me, and he said—"

"Hush. You can tell me later." Tetralanna poured water from the carafe into a cup and handed it to Gredin. "Here. Drink."

Gredin shook her head. "You need to listen. I have to tell you!"

"After you take a sip."

Conflicted, Gredin sat immobile, cup in hand, wrestling with the memory of Dreff's words. She felt as if she should be running through the enclave, shouting to wake the sleepers, alerting them to the terrible news... and yet, if Dreff was to be believed, the worst had already happened. *I am gone, beloved.* That's what he had said. *Our House is gone. Our world is gone.* If that were so, what did she suppose could be done about it? What could be accomplished by rousing everyone from a peaceful slumber, only to shatter their spirits as hers were shattered? Why not take pity and let them sleep, while they still could?

"Drink," Tetralanna prompted again.

Numbly, Gredin obeyed, but it was hard to swallow. Sobs kept welling up from some unplumbed depth within her, wracking her body, and it was a challenge just to retain her hold on the cup.

At last, Tetralanna took it from her and, sitting down across the little table, grasped both of Gredin's hands in her own. "Listen to me," she said, and Gredin could feel the pull of Power with which Tetralanna laced the words. "Think back to this afternoon. Do you remember when I spoke of how your emotions separate you from the fullness of your gyfte? This is precisely such a time."

Gredin opened her mouth to protest, but Tetralanna swept on, overriding her, weaving a web of calming persuasion.

"You are young. You are newly Chosen. You have passed beyond the confines of your House for the first time and ventured upon the River. You have been exposed to many strange and unusual sights, and you have been subjected to the presence of beings that belong to races other than our own. You have called upon your gyfte as you translated our interactions with the Director. This day has been long and taxing, and it is no great surprise that your sleep was troubled. But we have important tasks ahead of us, these next two days, tasks that will require strength and Focus. I am going to return you to your bed, now, and I want you to put these night fancies aside, and get the rest you need. In the morning, you will feel much improved, and the disturbance you're experiencing now will be only a shadow." She released Gredin's hands. "Take a last sip and go back to your bed. You need your sleep, and so do I."

Gredin sat silent for a moment, feeling as if she were swimming after being cast into the sea, struggling to keep her chin above the chop of the waves. "Tetralanna, our world is gone," she whispered, the words stinging her tongue as she spoke them.

Tetralanna sighed. "No, we are merely gone from our world," she countered, "soon to return to it. I warned the organizers that you would be unable to deal with this journey. I foresaw that trouble would result if they brought you, and you are proving me right. Nevertheless, I should hope that the need for your services at the Trisectoriana is not lost on you."

"Tetralanna—"

"Hear me, girl. I expect you to sleep, and allow your body and mind to restore themselves. You will feel very foolish tomorrow, when you think back on this night. For now, I ask that you quiet your mind and go back to your bed."

"But Dreff said—"

Tetralanna's face tightened in anger. "Dreff said nothing. Look around, Gredin. This is Tradepoint. Your Chosen is not here. You imagined him in a night-thought, nothing more." Abruptly, she stood. "Enough. Consider me, if you refuse to consider yourself. Morning will arrive all too soon, bringing a number of necessary tasks with it. We owe it to our House and to this delegation to be alert and capable, not dragging about because we sat up half the night, spinning troubles from thin air."

Tears stung Gredin's eyes. "But none of that matters now," she said, in as much voice as she could muster.

"It matters to me," Tetralanna snapped, "and to every other Vennan in the delegation. I should think you'd be embarrassed to admit that it doesn't matter to you. I cannot even imagine what Unter will say, when he learns of how you've carried on. Thank the Power that I'm the only one hearing you. Are you determined to bring shame to Balamont?"

But there was no Unter any more, and no House, except for the hundred and fifty-six other kinsmen from Balamont who had come to Tradepoint. Dreff was gone. Her sister was gone. Her mother and father were gone...

"You are going to do yourself a harm if you keep crying like that," Tetralanna said, and came around the table to draw Gredin to her feet. "This is nonsense. You are upsetting yourself over nothing. The sooner you go back to sleep, the sooner you'll be able to put this all behind you. Remember, you are the one who was so eager to visit Tradepoint. Where is the cheerful girl who thought today's ordeals were so intriguing, and who found those impossible creatures we encountered fascinating rather than disgusting? You dealt quite smoothly with the Director at our introductory meeting, and you seemed to take his massive size and odd appearance in stride. Can you not think on those accomplishments, instead of recalling this night phantom?"

Gredin tried to resist the persuasive flood of words. "No, Tetralanna. Please. We should be making plans for the morning, for telling the others. This is no time for sleep." Sobs rose to choke her. "I mustn't go to sleep! I'm supposed to—"

"Stop!" Tetralanna's exasperated voice was a lash, cutting across her words.

"But—"

Tetralanna gathered herself up and spoke, this time infusing her words with the Power of her gyfte. "Go to your bed. Now. And stay there until I come for you in the morning."

Gredin shivered. Step by reluctant step, aware that she was fighting a losing battle against Tetralanna's Voiced orders, she let herself be herded back to her sleeping chamber. What point was there in trying to speak the truth? Tetralanna refused to listen to her, convinced that the morning would bring a fresh view of matters.

She wished desperately that it could be so, but she couldn't escape the knot of dread at her center, nor could she disown the impact of Dreff's words. She could only take the remainder of the night to mourn privately for all that had been lost: the loved ones, the kinsmen, the House itself, the flowers, the hlaolings, the ocean, the very future that should have been hers.

All too soon, this night would end. And when it did, she would need to find the strength to explain to everyone that they, too, should be mourning.

For now, however, she let Tetralanna chivvy her back to bed, then watched as the older woman turned away and left, taking the light with her. Alone in the darkness, Gredin stared sightlessly up toward the ceiling, feeling the hot tracks of the tears that fell unceasingly as she waited for the new day and its intolerable burden to arrive.

DAY TWO

THE TRADERS' MARKET

1962 OF 2000 ORBITS REMAINING

As a rule, Burlon was quite fond of mornings on Tradepoint, since they normally consisted of a leisurely meeting with his Tradeteam over the first meal of the day, discussing who was in port and laying their plans.

Today was not normal.

His main complaint was the crowd. You couldn't cram nearly a thousand hungry Vennans, along with the tables and benches to accommodate them, into an enclave's warehouse area without causing a bit of a crush. And the noise level was wildly at odds with the usual echoing quiet. On a regular trade run, the enclave's high-lofted space would be filled with tradegoods. This mass of people, by contrast, was a shock.

But there were compensations. In fact, two of those compensations were seated with him: Sill te Torr and Keegan te Fliss. Sill hadn't spoken a word during yesterday's meeting in the Tradepoint Director's office, but Burlon had encountered her twice before, and liked what he knew of the self-possessed woman. And Keegan had spoken up for himself yesterday when the group had almost swept him out of there before he'd had a chance to accept Wyve's offer to observe Prettian annotation.

Both Sill and Keegan were unusual people, in their quiet way. Since Burlon had a bottomless appetite for the unusual, he had invited them to join him today for morning meal. "Do either of you wish to attend the Trisectoriana rehearsal?" he asked. "There won't be much to see, but I'm sure Wyve would welcome you if you're interested. If not, we could—"

Sill raised her hand suddenly, forestalling his words. "Your pardon, Burlon, but I have just been contacted by Tetralanna. Something has happened to the girl who translated for us. Tetralanna asks that I hurry, if you two will excuse me."

"I know where they're lodged," Burlon asserted, not pleased to think that something had befallen Gredin te Balamont. "We'll come with you. At least, I will. Keegan? Do you prefer to stay and finish your meal?"

But Keegan was already rising from his bench. "I'll come."

While they walked, Burlon considered contacting Cirin. After all, he and Cirin were the official Vennan organizers for the Trisectoriana. If something was going wrong, Cirin would have strong opinions about how matters should be handled. Cirin *always* had strong opinions about how matters should be handled.

Still, this matter might prove to be a fuss over nothing. The day had scarcely begun. Whatever was worrying Tetralanna te Balamont, they had an entire morning in which to set it right before the afternoon rehearsal. And Cirin, after all, was the honoree. Let him have a peaceful morning meal with his Chosen and his kinsmen. Time enough to summon him later, at need.

When their little group reached the access to the rooms where the two Speakers were being housed, Burlon stepped to one side. "Sill, you're the one Tetralanna asked for. I suspect she'll be better pleased if it's you she first sees when she comes to the door."

Sill reached out to touch his arm. "You aren't leaving, are you?"

Burlon grinned. "Never fear. Keegan is kind, and I'm curious, so neither of us will be going anywhere until we find out what has Tetralanna so concerned. Just let her know you're here. We'll stay close at hand," he promised, and composed himself while Sill contacted Tetralanna's private mind to announce her arrival.

The room doors slid open almost immediately, and Burlon was shocked to hear a high, keening wail rising from within.

Clearly, the sound wasn't emanating from Tetralanna, whose lips tightened into a thin, hard line when she saw the trio at her threshold. "Sill?" she said, her tone reproachful.

"We were at morning meal together…" Sill began, on a note of apology.

But Burlon was having none of that. Something was clearly wrong, and they were here to help, not to beg Tetralanna's pardon. He slid past them both, looking for the girl.

"Then you had best all come in," Tetralanna said, "so that I can shut this door before the entire enclave hears her."

Burlon went deeper into the room, following the eerie sound to the open doorway of a small storage room that had been made over into a sleeping chamber. Gredin was there, sitting on the floor on a quilted mat, rocking in distress, her face hidden behind hands that trembled visibly.

"Gredin?" he said, alarmed.

At the sound of her name, the girl fell silent, but when she dropped her hands and met his gaze, Burlon was taken aback: she looked terrible, her face blotched, her eyes red and swollen, her shoulders hunched. She stared up at him blindly for a moment, then buried her face in her hands, and the keening began again.

Burlon whirled to confront Tetralanna. "What ails her?" he demanded, concerned beyond all expectation. "Is she hurt? Ill?"

"Nothing of the sort. She's been crying, that's all."

"But why? Is she in pain?"

Tetralanna's glance was withering. "She frightened herself with a night-thought."

"Your pardon?" Burlon said, certain he had misunderstood.

"A night-thought," Tetralanna said with unblinkable clarity. "She woke me from a sound sleep, carrying on about something she claimed her Chosen had just told her."

Burlon looked around the small chamber. "Well, then, where is *he* in all of this?"

"Oh, he isn't here. He never was. Dreff is at home — which is precisely where I told you this unsteady, unreliable girl should be left, no matter how many languages she speaks. If you had listened to my counsel, we wouldn't *have* this difficulty."

A squabble with Tetralanna te Balamont was no part of his plan for the morning. "Gredin's here now, regardless, and we'll need her, later today. Can't you just—?"

Tetralanna raised her hands as if warding off his words. "I am not equipped to deal with this situation, and neither are you." She looked past him. "Sill, you are a First of Memory. Harvest this night-thought of Gredin's and get rid of it."

"Harvest... a night-thought?"

"Yes. Take it out of her mind so she can calm herself and get on with the day."

Burlon turned to Sill, startled. "Can you do that?" he asked. "Pluck a night-thought out of someone's mind?"

"I don't think so," Sill said. "We aren't speaking of a bag of diller beans that can be picked up and moved from one storage shelf to another."

Tetralanna's face grew red. "Your pardon," she snapped. "Memory is not my gyfte, so my wording may be imprecise. But folk do speak of harvesting a memory, don't they?"

"Yes," Sill conceded.

"Then do whatever it is that you do when you harvest a memory. Anything is better than this," she said, and cast a dire look toward the room where the girl still huddled, weeping, while Keegan te Fliss knelt beside her, murmuring soothing words.

Sill sighed. "But night-thoughts aren't real, Tetralanna."

"Of course not. That's exactly what I told Gredin."

"No, what I mean is that my gyfte may have no effect at all on a night-thought. When I harvest a memory from someone, it is clarified through my gyfte. I replicate their perception of the incident itself, down to the scent of the air and the precise words that were spoken. A night-thought is different, an imaginary thing fashioned out of emotion and impression, knit up into a wispy scarf of fancies."

"I don't care," Tetralanna insisted. "Whatever it is, it's obviously still upsetting her. See what your gyfte can do. Perhaps the touch of the Power when you attempt to harvest this thing will steady her. Something certainly needs to." She turned to Burlon, her expression darkening. "And if Sill cannot help her, summon an Assessor."

"To what purpose? There's no injury for a Healer to mend."

"The Assessment itself should calm her, at least temporarily. And if none of that helps, then you must find someplace else for her to stay — perhaps with her Guides, since it is clear she hasn't yet outgrown her need of them. I cannot properly carry out my duties at this Trisectoriana if I am kept awake half the night by a weeping child who should never have been brought here in the first place."

"That's a bit harsh," Burlon objected.

"No harsher than my being deprived of a night's sleep because Gredin cannot Control herself. And if she remains useless, you must step in and act as my translator instead."

That notion was certainly unappealing. "Don't be hasty," Burlon said. "You summoned Sill, so let's see if there is something she can do for the girl. If it turns out that she cannot, that's time enough to discuss alternatives."

Sill nodded. "I will try. Of course I will try. But it will take a bit of time. Tetralanna, why don't you go out and share morning meal with the delegation? It would do them good to see you, and I imagine you could benefit from a meal eaten in peace."

Tetralanna closed her eyes for a moment, then nodded. "Very well. I suppose that is the wisest course. I'll be back before long."

"No need to hurry. One of us will stay with Gredin until you return."

Burlon hid a smile. "On your way, First Speaker," he encouraged. "The food Tenders have outdone themselves, this morning. Be sure to sample the tipcakes."

Still tutting and dithering, Tetralanna stepped out into the reception hall, the noise of the crowd swelling and then resolving to silence as the doors slid open and closed to permit her exit.

To Burlon, the relief of her absence was palpable.

"Sill te Torr," he said, "you are a wise and clever woman. My fervent thanks."

Sill smiled. "It isn't an easy thing, being a Speaker. Tetralanna seems well-respected within her House, given what idle gossip I heard at table. She just isn't a cozy sort of woman." She smoothed her teslan. "Well, it sounds as if Keegan has calmed the girl a bit. I'll go see if I can help the poor thing."

Burlon shook his head. "What could there be in a night-thought to make her so upset?"

"Perhaps I'll be able to find out."

Sill entered the sleep chamber, and Keegan came out, cueing the inner door to close, shutting Gredin and Sill in together.

"Join me," Burlon invited from where he sat at the little table, but Keegan chose to pace the room instead, moving back and forth until Burlon finally pushed the other bench out with his foot and said, "Sit down, Historian. You'll wear a path in the floor."

Keegan sat.

"So," Burlon continued, "the girl quit making that awful

noise, once you'd been in there for a while. Thank you for that. Did she say what's troubling her?"

Keegan nodded.

"Has Tetralanna been short with her?"

"No. Well, probably. But that's not why she was crying."

"Why, then? Is she missing her Chosen?"

Keegan gave him an odd look. "She says her Chosen spoke to her in the night-thought." He rubbed the back of his neck. "She said he told her... that he is dead. That everyone we left behind on Venna is dead."

Burlon stared at him, shocked. "What sort of nonsense is that?"

Keegan shrugged. "The sort that keeps a girl up all night, crying, it would seem."

"Sounds as if a Healer may be what she needs, after all." It was Burlon's turn to rise from his bench and pace. "Scabs, what a terrible thing to claim. Truly terrible. What could be going on in her head, to conjure a night-thought like that?" He scowled. "She has to know it's pure foolishness."

"Then why is she still crying?"

More pacing. "How long do you suppose Sill will need?"

"I have no idea. Are you suddenly in a hurry?"

"In a hurry to resolve this." He pointed at the outer door. "We have almost a thousand people out there, eating their morning meal, about to prepare for tomorrow's Trisectoriana and reception. And the day after that, we'll all head home again. My grand ambition is to get through these next two days without an incident. But *that*—" He swung to point at the door to Gredin's chamber. "—has all the makings of an incident."

Keegan nodded in unhappy agreement.

More troubled by the moment, Burlon reached out to his First Friend's private mind. =Cirin, it seems we have a difficulty.=

=One that's beyond the talents of the brilliant Burlon te Bentain to resolve?=

=One that I thought you might bestir yourself to help me with, unless you're too busy shoveling food into your mouth.=

=I've nearly finished shoveling. Where is this mysterious difficulty located?=

=In the rooms the Speakers are sharing.=

=That sounds ominous.=

=You have no idea,= Burlon lamented.

=In that case, open the door and let me in.=

Burlon crossed to the outer door and opened it, revealing Cirin, who looked smug.

"You Sent," Burlon accused.

Cirin grinned. "You begged for my help. It seemed best to come quickly." He looked around the room. "I must say, nothing here looks amiss. I could have stayed and finished my last tipcake."

"Have patience," Burlon said grimly, and stepped back to usher Cirin inside. As soon as the outer doors were closed, he said, "It's Gredin. She had a night-thought, according to Tetralanna, and the girl's been caught up in a weeping fit, ever since."

"How festive."

"Yes, well, not what the Prett have in mind, either, for a translator. And we certainly don't want her upsetting the entire delegation. If she's in no fit condition to translate, perhaps she should just take to her bed for the day and—" He broke off as the inner door opened.

Gredin and Sill walked out, silent and subdued. Sill's color was high, but she looked weary, as if it were day's end instead of morning. Her arm was wrapped protectively around the girl's shoulders, and she seemed oblivious to Cirin's arrival.

"Good morning, ladies," he said. "Or not so very good, I see.

Gredin, I'm sorry to hear that you had a difficult night. Are you feeling better now?"

The girl stared at him, her blue eyes red-rimmed and puffy. "How can I feel better? Tell them, Sill. *Tell* them!"

Sill fiddled with her braid, then said, "Gredin believes that Venna is gone."

Cirin drew back. "What do you mean, gone?"

"Destroyed," Sill clarified.

He began to laugh. Approaching Gredin, he said, "Such dark night-thoughts from such a sunny girl! Well, don't upset yourself. I assure you that Venna is right where it has always been. Shall I prove it to you?"

The girl retreated a pace, and then another. "You have to believe me. This is no matter for laughter. Everyone we love, everything we had…" Her face contorted, and she sank to the floor, her shoulders shaking with silent sobs.

Cirin heaved a gusty sigh. Then, more gently than Burlon was accustomed to seeing him move, he hunkered down by the weeping girl and crooked a finger under her chin. Tilting her face up so that he could meet her gaze, he said, "Stop. You'll make yourself ill. Be at peace, Gredin. Go back to your bed. The morning can manage without you, while you get some decent sleep."

"But Tetralanna—"

"Has no need of a translator until this afternoon. I tell you what — I'll go pick a flower from your garden and bring it here to you. Would you like that?" he asked, then jerked in surprise as she clutched his arm, her fingertips pressing hard against his skin.

"Don't jest about it!"

"I'm not jesting. I'll pop back to House Balamont and—"

"No! You can't!" Her gaze was frantic. "Weren't you listening? There are no flowers. There is no garden. No House. There is nothing there now. Nothing!"

Cirin pulled his arm free and stood up. "Burlon, I suggest you call for an Assessor. This girl needs a Healing."

"Promise me," Gredin said, her voice wobbling and wavering. "Swear to me by the Power, Cirin te K'lar, that you won't try to Travel the River to Venna."

"I promise no such thing," Cirin said, looking affronted. "No Traveler would."

"It isn't *safe*!"

He didn't laugh, this time, but he couldn't quite hide his smile. "Ah, Gredin, how little you understand about the River. I am in no danger. Even if this fantastical night-thought of yours were true, which it certainly isn't, I would be safe. The Power would never permit a Traveler to leave the River and step onto a world where he couldn't survive. There would simply be no inlet there, no way to exit the River's flow. I would Travel on to Palomar, refresh myself there, and then return here. You are frightening yourself over nothing. You need to Focus on serving your own gyfte, instead of attempting to tutor me in mine."

She flinched at the rebuke, but still persisted. "Don't go. I don't *want* you to go."

"You don't want a flower? Or perhaps a word from your Chosen?"

Her face went so pale that her golden skin looked sallow. "I have had all the words from my Chosen that I can bear to hear," she whispered, and something in the way she said it made the hairs on Burlon's arms stand on end.

But Cirin was dismissive. "Fine, then. I'll go for my own sake, not for yours."

"Don't!"

"You don't get to decide that, youngling."

Unsettled, Burlon bestirred himself to say, "Keep in mind, Cirin, that Wyve won't be pleased if you miss the rehearsal."

"Such worriers you both are! Very well. I won't leave until after Wyve's precious rehearsal. Seriously, Gredin, you need to put the night behind you and get on with today." He looked around at the others. "Someone should take her to morning meal."

"Not with her eyes all swollen like that," Burlon objected. "Anyone who sees her will want to know what's wrong."

"Then call for an Assessor and a minor Healer," Cirin suggested, with an air of long-suffering patience.

"And tell them what?"

"That's she's homesick, I suppose."

At his words, Gredin began to wail.

Cirin eyed her balefully and shook his head. "Good fortune to you, Burlon," he said, and headed for the door. "I'm off, since it's clear I'm doing no good here. Or are you coming, too?"

It was tempting, but it seemed unfair to leave Sill and Keegan to handle the matter. "No," Burlon said, "go on. I'll catch up with you later."

"If you're quick enough," his friend teased, and left.

With Cirin gone, it felt as if half the light and energy had been drained from the room. Burlon gathered his wits, trying to decide what should be done next. Keegan had hunkered down by Gredin, watching with concern as she struggled to contain her tears.

Sill stood a bit apart from them, a frown on her face. Burlon crossed the room to join her. "So," he said quietly, "did you harvest this strange night-thought of Gredin's?"

Sill's mouth tightened. "No. There was nothing there for my gyfte to grasp."

"So this is all just empty talk? Did she make the whole thing up?"

"I have no way of knowing. In the case of someone's memory, I observe it. I retain it. But I found nothing here but a cloud of emotion."

He wasn't about to argue with Sill over the strictures of her gyfte. Instead, as was his habit, he tried to discern what the next practical step might be. The Trisectoriana was still a day distant. The midday after that, they'd be homeward bound. From now until then...

"I definitely don't want this girl frightening everyone with wild talk of death and destruction," he told Sill. "In fact, until Cirin returns with proof that this is nothing but a troubled girl's nonsense, I don't want her talking at all. It's fine for her to translate other folks' words, if we can calm her enough to do that, but I refuse to have a pointless panic spread through the enclave because of someone's outlandish night-thought. For the moment, you, Tetralanna, Keegan, Cirin, and I are the only ones aware that anything is amiss with Gredin, and I'd like to keep it that way. Can we agree that we will say nothing of this?"

Sill considered, then nodded. "Very well."

"Not even to your Chosen," he challenged.

The look Sill gave him was cool. "I am not in the habit of troubling Marin with other people's memories, and I see no reason for that to change now."

"My thanks, Sill. I'll caution Cirin to keep the matter close, and Tetralanna seems anxious to forget that this night-thought ever occurred, so there should be no difficulty there. As for me, I have no Chosen yet, and Cirin is the only one I might have been tempted to tell." He looked over his shoulder. "Keegan?"

"I have no Chosen, either," Keegan said. "I'll not discuss it with anyone."

That assurance eased Burlon's mind. "Good. This way, we won't have people fretting over nothing, and no one will tease Gredin about it, once we're all home."

Without warning, the outer door opened again. He thought it might be Cirin returning, but it was Tetralanna. Her expression grew grim at the sight of Gredin still weeping, and she cast a reproachful look at Burlon.

He was in no mood to take any share of the blame. "We've just been discussing the need for all of us to keep this matter to ourselves, speaking of it to no one," he said. "May we assume you agree with that strategy? Not that it will do us much good, if you mentioned it to anyone at morning meal, or if Gredin herself begins to speak about it, but..."

"I did no such thing. And Gredin won't be a concern," Tetralanna said.

"Oh? How so?"

Her chin lifted. "You appear to know little of what a Speaker's gyfte can do." She waved her hand. "Historian. Move aside."

Keegan rose and backed away from Gredin.

Tetralanna walked closer and closer, until she towered over the girl. "Gredin," she said, her voice vibrant.

The girl looked up at her immediately, blinking away tears.

"Give your hands to me," Tetralanna ordered.

Gredin reached up to do so, extending her arms to bridge the distance between where she sat on the floor and where Tetralanna stood.

Burlon saw Tetralanna's many-ringed fingers tighten, gripping the girl's hands firmly in her own. "Hear me, Gredin te Balamont. You will not speak to anyone about your night-thought." The words seemed to tremble on the air, laced with Power. "You will not speak of Venna. You will not speak of your Chosen. You will not refer in any way to what you claim has transpired there in our absence. If questioned about the reason for your apparent distress, you will make no reply."

A visible shiver ran through Gredin, as if she were attempting to pull her hands free, but Tetralanna's grip tightened further, and the girl subsided.

"You may converse freely in other regards, on other topics, but you are now Silenced where anything at all to do with your night-thought is concerned." She released Gredin's hands, as if tossing away something for which she had no further use, and Burlon saw that Tetralanna's color was high. Her eyes glittered brightly, and her breathing had quickened — the look of someone who had just exercised their gyfte to a significant degree.

On the floor at her feet, Gredin looked drained, as if she barely possessed the strength to hold her head up.

"What is your name?" Tetralanna demanded.

"Gredin," came the faint reply.

"What color is my teslan?"

"Purple."

"What is your Chosen's name?"

Gredin's mouth opened, but no sound came out. The girl swallowed convulsively and tried again, to no avail.

Tetralanna turned away from her. "There," she said to Burlon, then looked at him sharply. "Why do you stare at me like that? I agreed with you that she needed to be kept silent about her night-thought, and I have seen to it. Now we needn't worry."

In truth, he felt both impressed and horrified. "It seems..."

"Effective?"

"Unkind."

"No. Allowing Gredin to upset the entire delegation the way she has upset me would be unkind. I haven't harmed her. The Silencing will dissolve by tomorrow morning. I'll renew it then, and the next morning. After that, we'll be home again, and it won't be an issue any longer, because she will see for herself just how foolish she has been."

That drew a whimper from Gredin.

"Can you handle matters from here?" Tetralanna asked Burlon. "You *are* supposed to be in charge, aren't you? And I'm needed, out in the reception hall."

He realized that he was eager to have her gone. The exchange between First Speaker and the young translator wasn't sitting well with him. There was too great an aura of personal triumph in Tetralanna's manner to suit him. "Yes," he said, his own voice gone slightly unsteady. "By all means. Go."

"Don't look so apprehensive," she said to him. "Trust me, I

know this girl. She is excitable, but she is also easily distracted. Put a meal in her and she'll be fine." Tetralanna turned her gaze to Gredin. "And you. Focus on conducting yourself as a Speaker should. I will see you at the rehearsal, after midday meal," she said, and swept out of the room.

When the doors had closed firmly behind her, Keegan said softly, "What now?"

Shaken, Burlon tried to turn his thoughts to the next necessity. "Well, she's right that Gredin should eat... although, for that, the girl will need to be calmer. I suppose Cirin and Tetralanna both had the right plan, after all. We'll call for an Assessor and a minor Healer. That should help." He considered the people he had recruited for the journey to Tradepoint, and recalled two names that might serve. "I'll ask Norian te Kendar and Dint te Darius to come to us here." Moving slowly so as not to startle Gredin, he knelt by her and said, "Norian will Assess you, and Dint will take away the swelling from your eyes and the stuffiness from your nose. You'll feel better afterward, so long as you don't start crying again."

But that seemed a distant hope, unless he could find something to distract her from her present misery...

Inspiration struck. "Gredin," he said with fresh energy. "Do you remember yesterday, at Wyve's office, when I spoke about the Traders' Market?"

She nodded, and although he saw her gulp back a sob, she looked up at him with something like a spark of interest.

"After Norian and Dint have done what they can for you, and after you've eaten something for morning meal, you and Keegan could go along to see the Traders' Market. Would you enjoy that?"

She didn't answer, but she didn't look away.

"Then that's what we'll do," Burlon told her. "I'll alert a Trader or two, and some folk from the enclave who've already voiced an interest. You can go down with them and take a look, and still be ready in plenty of time to translate for Tetralanna at this afternoon's rehearsal."

A flicker of interest woke in her gaze, blunting a little of the misery he saw there.

Burlon relaxed a bit, confident that he had come up with a successful diversion. There was no place quite like the Traders' Market to catch a person's interest and hold it. The goods there changed constantly, depending on who was in port and what they had brought to trade. Entering the Market was as energizing to him as launching himself upon the River, a joy that never failed to thrill. It was just what Gredin needed to distract her from her imaginary woes.

So decided, he reached out to Norian's private mind and made Gredin's need for an Assessment known.

1959 OF 2000 ORBITS REMAINING

A short time later, feeling somewhat benumbed, Gredin drifted through morning meal, finding each bite an effort.

Norian te Kendar's Assessment, coupled with the Healing efforts of Dint te Darius's Healing, had removed the physical discomforts of aching head, congested breathing, and unsettled stomach that had plagued her. The Assessment had even granted her a fragile shell of calm, although she knew it would soon fade. For now, it was like standing on the shore, looking out over the waves. The water might sparkle in the sunlight, but appearance did nothing to change the reality beneath the surface. That was where the ocean truly existed, in the depths that couldn't be seen from the beach.

In that same manner, she now had a surface available to the casual view of anyone who passed by, but her appearance told them nothing about the horrible secret locked within her by Tetralanna's Silencing.

"Have you eaten all you wish to?" Keegan te Fliss asked.

She looked down at the plate in front of her, which still held a quarter of a tipcake and a plump little slice of spangin.

Her first impulse was to Send her dishes back to the Tenders

in the kitchen so that they could dispose of the uneaten food…
but a new realization stopped her: *This may be the last slice of
spangin you will ever be offered. The orchards are gone now, the
crop destroyed.*

The realization sent such a pain searing through her that she
almost cried out.

Trembling, Gredin slid her hand into her pocket and slipped
a single finger into the little pouch she had tucked there. To calm
herself, she stroked the topmost stone, Focusing on the coolness
of its smooth surface. Then, with conscious care, she used her
right hand to scoop up the slice of spangin and slip it into her
mouth.

When she bit down on it, the fruit's delicate flesh gave way
between her teeth, releasing a flood of sweet juice.

The taste of Venna.

Incipient tears stung her eyes.

Not now, she told herself. *Not here. Not when you can't
explain.*

Desperate for distraction, she said, "I'm sorry, Keegan."

"Sorry? For what?"

"For taking up your morning. For making you venture to the
Traders' Market with me."

"That will be no hardship. I need to go there, anyway. I don't
have enough paper."

That surprised her. At Wyve's office, Keegan's notebook had
appeared to contain a substantial number of blank pages. "To
write your account of the Trisectoriana?"

"To make a list of all who are here."

It seemed like a most peculiar answer. "Why should you
need such a thing?"

It was his turn to look surprised. Dropping his voice until it
was barely audible above the hum of conversation in the huge
room, he said, "Because we are all who are left."

The meaning behind his words ran through Gredin like an icy stream. "You believe me?"

Keegan nodded.

"Why?"

"I listened carefully to your story, earlier in your chambers. Do you recall what you said?"

Gredin thought back to when Keegan and the others had arrived. It was largely a blur of despair, but she did remember the comfort of his presence and the kindness of his voice.

"Mostly..." She lifted a hand to her throat, helpless to continue. "But I can't talk about it. The words..."

Keegan nodded calmly. "I know what Tetralanna did to you. Before she returned from her meal, though, I sat with you in your chambers, and you spoke of the night-thought that had come to you while you slept."

"It wasn't just a ...," Gredin choked with bitter indignation. "It was more than that! So much more."

He gave her a gentle smile. "I agree."

"Why should you believe me, when Tetralanna doesn't?" she challenged.

"Because you said that, when you first awoke, you were glowing."

Gredin stared at him. Lost in the turmoil of Dreff's message, she had almost forgotten the strange illumination of her skin.

Keegan's smile faded to a look of solemnity. "I have lived long and long, and my gyfte has afforded me many opportunities to gather knowledge. I know only one explanation for why a Vennan's skin would glow as yours did. It occurs when they are in the presence of the Power."

Her hands began to tremble. Carefully, she lowered them to her lap, out of sight. "Don't."

"Don't believe you? Why not? Have you told an untruth?"

"No... but if you believe me, I will have to believe it, myself."

"You already do," he said, with such kindness and pity in his gaze that she had to look away.

"No one else believes me," she said, her voice as soft as his. "Not Tetralanna. Not Cirin. Not Burlon. Not even Sill, although I think she was troubled by what I related to her." She darted a glance at him. "Cirin plans to return to Venna soon after the rehearsal, despite my warning." She shuddered at the thought. "Wouldn't you rather withhold your belief until he has proven or disproven my claim?"

"No. I would rather prepare." He inclined his head in a slight nod, indicating the expanse of people seated behind her. "You and I know. They do not, yet. Once they do, everything will become more difficult. People will seek guidance and comfort, lost in their grief. How can we help them if we aren't even certain who they are?"

"Help them?" she echoed bleakly. "There is no help to be had, for us or for them."

"Not so. A short while ago, Burlon brought Norian and Dint to ease your headache and reduce the swelling around your eyes. That was a help, was it not? But if Burlon hadn't been there, I wouldn't have known whether there was a Healer to summon, or who that Healer might be. How can we steady ourselves and meet our people's needs if we don't know what gyftes are available, and who wields them? We need lists."

"Lists?"

His smile was apologetic. "It's what I do. I write things down. I collect personal tales. I make inventories of belongings. But I can't do any of that without paper, and reed pens, and ink. I packed what I thought would be more than enough for a four-day stay, and now… now, it frightens me to think how quickly all of what I brought will be used up. So you see, it is no hardship for me to venture to the Traders' Market with you. Rather, it is a necessity."

"You frighten me," she admitted. "You speak as if the responsibility for what is to come will fall upon you alone."

"Upon me, and upon you, and upon others like us," Keegan said.

"Me?" Gredin stared at him. "No. Others, older and more experienced, will take charge." But even as she protested, she remembered Dreff's voice, the Power's voice, telling her otherwise: *Our people's hopes and ambitions rely upon you now... Lead them, beloved... Do not doubt yourself, or allow others to doubt you.*

"Are you so certain?" Keegan asked. "We have no Heads of House here with us at Tradepoint. Not a one. And I am only aware of a small scattering of Firsts, like Sill and Tetralanna and Cirin. We have the delegation itself, but it is headed by Travelers and Traders, and they are used to thinking only about their next trading trip. Do you seriously envision any of them stepping forward to manage matters for longer than a four-day journey? It is neither their nature nor their gyfte."

"Then what will become of us?"

"The Power spoke to you, Gredin. It chose you, out of all of us. Yours will be the hand that directs us through this time of sorrow and grief, although I and others will help you, at need," Keegan said. "For now, we should explore who and what we are. There will be time enough, after that, to explore what we need to become."

"You sound so certain."

That drew a grimace from him. "Do I? In truth, I am certain of nothing... except that I believe that what your night-thought said is true. And, because I believe it, I know we need to begin by visiting the Traders' Market." He reached across the table and gave her plate a little push. "So finish your tipcake. Then we will retrieve the notebook from my room and go."

Was it only yesterday that Tetralanna had explained that Keegan's room was at the opposite end of the small alcove where the chambers that she shared with Tetralanna stood? The details of her arrival, although clear in her mind, seemed to have taken place long ago, back when the world and her place within it were calm and established facts. Back when Dreff still awaited her return. Back when...

Fighting back tears, Gredin followed Keegan meekly as he went inside to pick up the little leather-bound notebook and the cloth roll that held his pens and ink. "Do you need anything from your rooms?" he asked as they came back out, but she shook her head and kept her gaze averted from the place where the Power had revealed such calamitous truths to her.

By the time they had made their way across the enclave again, nineteen other Vennans were gathered at the doors, ready to join them in the walk to the Traders' Market. The group was in the charge of a female Trader unknown to Gredin. *A new face to learn*, she reflected, mindful of Keegan's words. *A new kinswoman of mine, regardless of her House.*

"I am Ellis te Vell," the woman announced, "here to take you all to the Traders' Market and back. If that is not your intent, you should leave us now."

There were murmurs between those who waited, and people exchanged excited glances, but nobody retreated.

"Right, then," Ellis said briskly. "This is the first of several groups who wish to see the Market today, so our visit won't be a long one. It's important that you all stay together, and that you follow a few simple rules. Touch nothing. Remember that the foreign traders don't speak or understand Vennan. If you see an item at the Market that interests you, address my private mind. I will advise you of the item's worth, and whether the race offering it is one with which we commonly trade. And," she added, with a sudden grin, "I suggest that you show no obvious interest in the item. If you do, its price might well double."

There were a few answering smiles.

"The only way to leave the enclave is to pass through the antechamber on the other side of these doors," Ellis continued, gesturing. "While we're in the antechamber, a mist will fill the air. Breathe it in deeply. It's a measure employed by the Prett to protect the health of all who come to Tradepoint, regardless of which world they claim as home."

Another little murmur of comment flowed through the group, but no one seemed unduly concerned. Gredin wondered why Burlon had not given them such an explanation before their walk to the Director's office, the previous day. Perhaps he was so used to the procedure that it hadn't occurred to him, until Tetralanna reacted.

Or perhaps Tetralanna's reaction had been exactly what Burlon wanted. Her demeanor had certainly been less brash, after the warning about getting her skirts caught in the door, and her panic over the bio-mist. It had made their walk through the strangeness of the corridor quieter... and perhaps safer, when they encountered the stench of the Mamora. Had that been Burlon's conscious intent?

Gredin didn't know... but it was something to think about.

Ellis opened the inner doors, and the group moved forward in an orderly fashion, entering the antechamber. There was a ripple of reaction when the doors to the enclave closed behind them, but people remained calm, taking their lead from Ellis's nonchalant manner.

Then the mist began to descend.

"It smells like tongue-peppers," Gredin murmured to Keegan.

She had only intended her comment for his ears, but others must have heard it, as well, because she heard the phrase repeated, and a few people chuckled.

Then the mist was gone, and the outer doors opened.

"Stay close behind me," Ellis instructed as they began their journey down the corridors of Tradepoint.

Not wanting to be overheard again, Gredin hung back, letting others pass her, until at last she had enough privacy to murmur to Keegan, "How are we to pay for the paper that you need?"

"However we must," he replied, stubbornness asserting itself on his genial features. "I will speak to the Director of Trade-point, at need, and make him understand our necessity."

"No! You cannot talk to the Director about..." Her voice choked off as the Silencing halted her words. "...about that," she finished lamely. "Not yet. Not until Cirin returns. Did you not give Burlon your word that you would not?"

Keegan sighed. "Just so. Well then, for now, we may have to settle for discovering which traders offer the items I need. But immediately after Cirin returns, we must find a way to obtain what I require."

"After Cirin returns, everyone will understand the need," Gredin said, and felt dread rise within her. Despite Cirin's assur-ances regarding the safety of the River, it terrified her to think of him leaving Tradepoint and attempting a return to Venna. She had no idea what had actually happened there. Perhaps their world still existed but something had ended the lives of all who had dwelt there. Or perhaps the world itself was utterly gone, as inconceivable as that seemed.

Either reality was a tragedy that could threaten Cirin's well-being. He seemed far too confident to take proper care, speaking blithely of the protection the Power afforded him. Where had the Power's protection been when Dreff's life ended?

Something touched her hand, and she stiffened.

Keegan gave her fingers a squeeze. "Don't cry," he cautioned softly. "Shall I take you back to the enclave?"

Grief and panic scrabbled inside her chest like some sharp-clawed little forest creature seeking to escape, thwarted only by the thin, calming veneer of the Assessment that Norian had performed on her. She longed to retreat to the sanctuary of her bed... but what purpose would that serve? With nothing to distract her, the cycle would simply begin again: memories of the night-thought, her longing for Dreff, and the horrible, para-lyzing grief of imagining all of the loved ones who were now gone beyond recall...

No. The last thing she wanted was to be alone. But the price of companionship was equilibrium.

"Help me be calm," she whispered to Keegan. "Talk to me."

"What about?"

"Anything. Anything but... that."

She saw him hesitate, and realized that for him, as for her, the night-thought and its ramifications dominated his awareness. But he rallied and said, "Despite Burlon's blustering complaints, I was surprised to see that he'd passed this group into someone else's care. I thought he might take us, himself. I wonder where he is."

I hope he is off talking sense into his friend Cirin, she thought. But she said, instead, "Perhaps he has gone ahead to the Traders' Market, to be certain no Mamora are there."

"Indeed." Keegan's face took on a thoughtful look. "There is some trick to that," he said. "When we encountered them, yesterday, neither Burlon nor Cirin seemed particularly troubled by the smell."

"Then it would be a trick worth learning." Gredin looked ahead through the group, then glanced behind. "Today, we have encountered no one at all in the corridors. Do you suppose that is by coincidence or plan?"

Keegan considered. "Tradepoint is a large place, and I have no notion whether our 'morning' is morning for the other races, too. This empty corridor might well be coincidence. Certainly we are going to encounter others at the Market itself, so it can't be that they hope to isolate us entirely from the other races here."

Remembering the dark, bird-like creature who had peered at her so intently, Gredin repressed a shudder. "I suppose not." She looked over her shoulder again, remembering that sense of being observed. "I'm surprised that our Traders take pleasure in these encounters. I understand that Trading is their gyfte, but would they not have been happier simply Trading between one House and another?"

When she heard her own words, it was as if a stranger had spoken them, and she realized that she and Keegan and the other Vennans on Tradepoint would all be dead, if that had been the Traders' attitude. Her life would have ended last night, along with Dreff's. She would not be walking this strange corridor, bearing this terrible knowledge. She would be nothing but a glimmer of Power, without memory or sorrow.

"Happier?" Keegan said. "Likely not, since Traders are a friendly and curious lot." His cheerful tone made it clear that his thoughts had not followed the same dark path as her own. "New tradegoods, new faces, new customs — I imagine it all intrigues them. In truth, it intrigues me, too. I am going to the Market in search of things I need in service to my gyfte, but I will gladly look at everything else displayed there, as well. The Traders have brought many beautiful and interesting things back with them from Tradepoint and the other worlds, in the course of my lifetime, and it will be wonderful to finally see some of the races that create those objects."

In Gredin's mind, a swirl of lavender took form — the fabric that had become Trethen's first-dance gown, and which she herself had so recently worn for her own first dance, the night she found Dreff.

Her breathing faltered at the realization that the dress was in her luggage bundle now, brought along to be worn at tomorrow night's reception. In her haste, she had packed it without giving a thought to its origin, but she reflected now that this was Tradepoint fabric returning to Tradepoint. Which race had woven it? Would they recognize the provenance of the fabric, if they attended the reception and saw her dress?

Could she even bear to wear it, knowing that both Dreff and Trethen were lost to her?

"Gredin?"

She pulled herself back to the present moment and fought to regain her calm.

"Your pardon," she murmured.

He gestured forward. "I think we are nearly there."

Looking ahead, she saw that Ellis te Vell had taken up a position in the center of the corridor, just short of a set of tall, metal panels, and was gesturing for everyone in the group to gather close.

When they had done so, Ellis said, "The Traders' Market lies within. Enjoy yourselves, but I remind you again of the necessary precautions, and a few additional matters. Stay together. Touch nothing. Remember that there is no point in speaking to anyone outside of our group, since they won't understand you. Alert me if an item seriously interests you but pay no obvious attention to it. Look at the objects displayed for trade as much as you like, but do not look too directly at individuals. You will encounter a great many odd people in the Market, and customs vary. To some, staring is considered quite rude, while others find it completely natural. For today, unaccustomed as you are, better to keep your gaze lowered and your manner calm and quiet, to avoid giving unintentional offense. On the other hand, some of them may stare at *you*. Vennans have never visited the Market in such numbers. Any stares you attract will be born of curiosity, not malice.

"Each race of traders occupies a separate structure, called a maartza, with display space at the front and private storage at the rear, usually behind a curtain. Be aware that only one race of customers is allowed within a maartza at a time. You can tell at a glance by looking at the entry. If someone else is already trading there, the edges of the entire entrance will be framed with a bright strip of light, all the way around. If no light shows, no one but the owners of that maartza are within. Therefore, if I take us into a maartza, rather than simply having you look at the shopfront display, you can be sure that no one else will join us while we are inside. We may pass a number of empty maartzas, since they are only open when representatives from that race are present here on Tradepoint. The interior of an active maartza will be lit and accessible. Inactive maartzas will be dim, with a transparent barrier across their entrance, but there may still be items on display behind the barrier."

Ellis shifted from one foot to the other. "Enough talk, unless one of you has a question or concern. No? Then stay close by me, and we'll go in," she said, and pressed her palm to a lighted disk set into the wall.

The door panels opened, and sounds rolled out to greet Gredin: high voices mingling with lower ones in energetic discourse; some sort of rhythmic clanking sound; a thin, querulous call that put her in mind of seabirds; and a dozen other noises she couldn't begin to identify.

With Keegan at her side, Gredin stepped into the Traders' Market, the last of their group to do so, and the doors slid shut behind them.

It didn't look at all as she'd imagined, which she supposed simply meant that it didn't look the least bit Vennan. To begin with, it was immense and, as was the case in the enclave, the Traders' Market ceiling was so far above their heads that she could barely make it out against the bright glare of the lights. The Market itself consisted of an orderly pattern of metal buildings, each shaped exactly like the others, all lined up in orderly precision, with broad avenues separating each one from its nearest neighbors.

But although the outlines of each building were identical, that was where the resemblance stopped. Some of the structures sported colorful awnings that arched over their entrance, while others bore no embellishment at all. And, of the few into which she could see from where she stood, the amount of lighting varied, as well. The interiors of some maartzas looked warm and inviting, while others were as harshly lit as the Market itself, employing those blue-white lights that made her eyes sting.

Everywhere Gredin looked, colors dazzled her eye, and each breath she drew was freighted with unknown scents, from the subtle to the bold — although none, to her relief, were anything like the acrid pungency of the Mamora. Based on her experiences of the first day, she had begun to think of Tradepoint as a bare and sterile place. The Traders' Market banished that impression with vigor. And the people—

Keegan tugged at her hand. "Ellis and the group," he prompted, and drew her forward.

She followed where he led, but her attention was largely consumed by the individuals they passed. Before venturing to Tradepoint, she hadn't given much thought to how other races might look, assuming that they would be shaped more or less as Vennans were, differing mostly in the manner of their dress, and perhaps to some degree in the coloring of their skin and hair.

Now she realized how naïve and uninformed that expectation had been. Yesterday, she had seen the massive Prett, the tall and unpleasantly fragrant Mamora, the little green-clad people with brown hair and pale skin who had gathered around the Prett security guard, and the dark, thin birdman who had unsettled her so. Now, within her first few steps, she was passed by a trio of waist-high, blue-furred creatures, each lumbering along on six appendages.

Keegan tugged at her hand again.

Pay attention, she admonished herself, and turned her gaze to the first set of display tables they were approaching.

Keegan was scrutinizing what appeared to be stacks of shiny, openwork metal boxes in varying sizes and colors. Some were square, some oblong. The smallest would have fit easily on the palm of her hand, while the largest was nearly the size of her head. There were even a few huge ones resting on pedestals behind the display table. Were the boxes intended for storage, or decoration, or some other purpose she could not yet imagine? If she picked one up, would it be heavy or light? What world had created them? Perhaps she could afford one of the tiny ones. With its delicate, lace-like grillwork, it would make a wonderful present, perfect for hanging a sweet-smelling sachet of flower petals at the head of Trethen's bed…

Trethen, who was no more.

Gredin stood motionless, stricken afresh by grief.

Oblivious to her distress, Keegan took a slow, sweeping look at the table's contents, then said, "Come. We should stay close to the group." And he took her hand, drawing her along as he followed Ellis and the others to the next building's display of wares.

This time, the objects offered for trade were presented in a series of woven baskets suspended at different heights from the ceiling of their maartza, the entire display overseen by a pair of smooth-skinned beings who squatted, side by side, on a beautiful carpet of black, white, and green. The pair were hairless and wore no clothing, but their deep-purple bodies were covered in meticulously painted white designs not unike the patterns woven into the carpet.

Gredin stood back carefully at the front edge of their area, still trying to regather her composure. The objects in the nearest baskets were roughly egg-shaped, and their proper purpose was as unknown to her as that of the open-work boxes at the previous maartza.

Ignoring the objects, she noticed that the baskets themselves were beautiful, tightly woven in patterns that soothed the eye. She would like to have known whether the baskets themselves were available for purchase. Still, she had no specific need for the baskets, beyond her appreciation of their craftsmanship, and she had nothing of worth to trade for them. There was no point in alerting Ellis to her interest.

Since the maartza entrance showed no frame of bright light, Gredin was sufficiently emboldened to glance down at the purple-skinned proprietors of the display and say to them softly, in Tradetalk, "Your baskets good. Much, much good." Then she crossed her palms to them, nodded, and moved on with the group toward the next display front, while the purple-skinned people stared after her, open-mouthed in apparent surprise.

Keegan was staring at her, too. "What did you say to them?" he demanded in a shocked whisper.

"Nothing."

"Something."

She shrugged. "I just told them how beautiful I thought their baskets were."

"Baskets?"

"The display baskets. Never mind. It doesn't matter. Have you seen anything useful yet?"

"No," he said bleakly. "Nothing."

"Well, don't lose hope. We've hardly begun to look," she reasoned.

"I know…but it isn't just a question of what's being offered for sale. I haven't yet seen anyone using a pen or paper. They're all holding little machines like the one the Director's assistant had, yesterday. Or like the top of the Director's desk, but tiny. Gredin, what if no one here has what I need?"

With a pang, she remembered the sobering reason why they had come to the Market. Mere moments after feeling the pain of Trethen's loss, she had allowed herself to become distracted again, like the silly girl Tetralanna accused her of being. Her world and her loved ones had been destroyed… and she was admiring baskets.

Ashamed of herself, she said to Keegan, "Wait and see. Don't frighten yourself with problems that may not arise. We have most of the Market yet to explore. And if nothing you need is here today, speak to Burlon. He may know of traders who aren't currently here at— What?" she demanded, for Keegan was suddenly looking past her.

"There," he whispered. "Walking toward the door. That person with the white hair. Look at what they're carrying."

Gredin turned around, scanning the throng of moving individuals until she spotted a plump figure whose head was covered in fuzzy white hair, with a package tucked under its arm — a package wrapped in what appeared to be a speckled sheet of yellow paper.

Keegan took a rapid step into the aisle, as if to follow, but Gredin grabbed his arm. When he resisted, she cautioned, "No. At best, it is only one sheet, and I doubt whether my Tradetalk is sufficient to explain that you want the paper, not the item wrapped within it. The paper must have come from somewhere here in the Market. Better to find the source than assail some creature in the corridor."

The sense of her words must have penetrated Keegan's determination, because the tension drained out of him, and he turned back to her. "You are right, of course," he conceded, looking forlorn.

"Be happy," Gredin said. "At least, now, we know that what we seek is here somewhere."

When they turned to look ahead again, it took a moment for Gredin to spot the blond braids of the Vennan group, the last few of whom were rounding the corner of a building that sported a striped awning, a considerable distance ahead. With a pang of conscience, she hurried to catch up.

As they came abreast of the striped awning, however, the sound of high-pitched voices made her hesitate. Glancing inside the maartza itself, she saw that it was filled with mounded stacks of bulging sacks, piled head-high. And in the midst of the sacks she spotted a bustling group of the same thick-set little creatures in green coveralls that she had seen in yesterday's corridor, their sameness and milling motion making them appear even more numerous than they were.

"Pretty lady," one called out to her in Tradetalk, and they all swiveled their heads to stare at her.

It had been a mistake to look. Unsettled by the abrupt mass scrutiny and the crowd of identical faces, Gredin groped for some Tradetalk phrase that would allow her a graceful escape. "Good day, you," she managed to say, and hurried onward.

"Wait!" she heard them cry, peeping like hungry nestlings. "Wait! Wait!"

But she didn't wait. She wanted no dealings with them. If they were the source of the yellow paper, Keegan would have to pursue it later, when she wasn't with him.

She rounded the corner of their building, intent on rejoining Ellis and the group, but there wasn't a Vennan in sight.

"Pretty lady!" came the cry from behind her. "Pretty lady!"

She refused to look back. Taking Keegan's hand, she plunged along the aisle. It felt safer, somehow, to have individuals from other races around her. She hoped that the presence of others would discourage the little creatures in the green coveralls from pursuing her.

At the next juncture, she turned to her right and had to step aside quickly to avoid a pair of the tall birdpeople. They clacked their bills at her in obvious disapproval, and light reflected off the black skin that covered their hairless skulls.

One of them cocked its head, eyeing her, and raised a scrawny arm to point a skeletal appendage in her direction, the black and green gauze of its tight-cuffed sleeve swaying in graceful loops as it made some comment to its companion.

The other birdperson leaned forward, its thin neck contorting, and she realized that it was staring directly at her flamestone pendant.

Shuddering, Gredin dodged around them.

"Wait," she heard Keegan call from behind her as she rounded the next corner. When he finally caught up with her, he asked anxiously, "What happened? Is someone chasing us?"

"I don't know." Daring to glance behind, she saw no sign of the birdpeople, and she heard no more calls of *Pretty lady*. Gasping for air, Gredin slowed, then halted, and turned to Keegan in apology. "Not now," she admitted. "At least, I don't think so." She tried to calm herself and catch her breath.

"We need to find Ellis and the others," Keegan counseled. "She won't be best pleased with us for straying off."

"I know. I'm sorry. I didn't realize there would be so many aisles, so many maartzas. We..." A flicker of yellow caught her eye. A tiny being, wearing a towering headpiece, was leaving a nearby maartza. As it made its mincing way into the aisle, ducking slightly to make certain that its headgear cleared the awning under which it had been standing, the bright light around the maartza entrance behind it went out. The little trader held a bundle in its thin arms — a bundle wrapped in speckled yellow paper. "There," Gredin said softly to Keegan, and nodded in that direction.

He looked and stiffened.

Of one accord, they waited in silence, watching. As soon as the being moved off, Keegan darted across the aisle, with Gredin at his heels.

When they entered the maartza, its air was heavy with some unknown scent that managed to seem both sweet and sharp. The size of the interior was difficult to judge because lengths of fabric hung everywhere, festooned from poles, draped over the rungs of slender ladders, folded on shelves and counters, even filling large baskets scattered about on the floor. The material ranged from rich, heavy satins to dense woolens, and included a rainbow of ethereally thin gauzes that eddied in the slight breeze created by their arrival.

"Beautiful," Gredin breathed, astonished by the wealth of colors.

"But there's no one here," Keegan said, disappointment etching his features.

"What seek?" someone asked in heavily accented Tradetalk.

Gredin looked around wildly.

"Here," the voice prompted, and Gredin saw that its source was one of the six-legged, blue-furred creatures she had seen earlier. This one had been resting on the floor in a tight curl, nose on rump, but it roused itself and raised its head to regard her.

Unsure how to proceed, Gredin crossed her palms and offered the creature a slight bow.

"What seek?" it repeated. Extending a delicately curved claw, it tapped at a broad metal cuff that encircled one of its topmost limbs. Gredin jumped as the bright light around the entryway flared to life again. The trader sat up by straightening its central pair of legs completely and lifting the front-most pair off the floor. "What cloth? What weight? What color?"

Gredin knew her color words in Tradetalk, but she didn't know how to explain Keegan's particular needs. "Yellow," she said. "But no cloth."

The creature thrust its head forward. "Yellow," it repeated.

"Yes. Yellow. But no cloth."

A little ripple ran over its body, disarranging and then reset-tling the fur. "No cloth?" It waved a forelimb, indicating their surroundings. "I trade cloth."

"Yes," Gredin acknowledged, and added apologetically in Vennan, "Your pardon."

"Seek... yellow?" With a grunt, it shifted onto all six feet, and Gredin took a hasty step back and stifled a squeak of alarm, startled by how much room the waist-high creature suddenly filled within the confines of the maartza aisle.

It appeared to take no offense from her retreat. Making low, melodic noises under its breath, it fished a small basket out from beneath one of the ladders. The basket brimmed with transparent orbs the size of Gredin's fist, each filled with sandy grains of a different brilliant color — powdered dye, perhaps. "Yellow," the creature said on a note of triumph, unearthing an orb of that hue.

"Yes," Gredin conceded, "but... no."

The confusion of their attempted conversation was compounding, and Gredin worried that her awkward attempts to clarify would exhaust the merchant's patience. Looking over her shoulder at Keegan, she said, "A piece of your paper. Quickly."

He fumbled with his notebook and, with a wince, tore out a blank page, which he offered to her with an anxious air. She took it carefully and held it out to the creature.

"What call this?" she asked. Indeed, *'What call this?'* had been one of the first Tradetalk phrases she had ever been taught, and its utility was now apparent to her.

The creature came closer and peered at the paper, then lifted both forelimbs and pressed its palms to the single sheet, one above, one below. Slowly, its palms moved in opposition, examining the paper caught between them. Then, withdrawing the top palm, it partially extended a curved claw and flicked the edge of the page delicately, once and then again. Leaning in, it sniffed at the paper, then eased back. "Bahnt," it said, the single syllable coming out in a guttural grunt.

"*Bahnt*," Gredin repeated, trying to replicate the sound. She indicated Keegan, handing the notebook page back to him. "Seek yellow *bahnt*," she said, then felt a stab of uncertainty over what to do next. Even if the furry trader produced an entire stack of the yellow paper, Gredin had nothing to offer in exchange for it. Belatedly, she recalled Ellis's caution: *I advise you to show no obvious interest in the item. If you do, its price will likely double.* If that happened now, she would have no one but herself to blame.

Dropping down again, the creature moved past her, then past Keegan, making its plodding way to the farthest recesses of the maartza. "Bahnt," it said, and beckoned.

Keegan cast a wary glance at Gredin.

"You may as well go and look," she said. "If he does have paper, I wouldn't be able to tell whether it suits your needs or not."

With a look of grim determination, Keegan stepped deeper into the maartza to examine what the blue-furred creature was displaying. "Oh!" Gredin heard him say a moment later, and saw him kneel down quite willingly at the creature's side. "*Bahnt!*" he said with sudden animation, and Gredin smiled, pleased for him. Whatever difficulty might ensue, she and Ellis would find some way to make a trade work.

As she waited, a piece of fabric that rested on the bottom rung of a ladder near the entrance snagged her attention. The bright lighting seemed to ignite the scarlet material, making the color appear so vibrant that Gredin half expected to feel it give off heat as she knelt to examine it more closely.

The weave was tight and sleek, as smooth as liquid when she stroked it with a single fingertip. Slipping her hand beneath the top layer, she saw the color alter, shading from the lively red of galen berries down to a scarlet so deep-hued that it almost appeared black. The effect was beguiling, and she tilted her hand, watching the play of light.

A shadow fell, dulling the color.

A second shadow followed. Then a third and fourth and fifth, in rapid succession.

"Pretty lady," a voice whispered in her ear, and the phrase repeated like an echo —*pretty lady pretty lady pretty lady pretty lady* — as tiny fingers touched her sleeve, her braids, her cheek, her hlao.

Gredin, recoiling violently from their touch, overbalanced and tumbled sideways, knocking one of the cloth-laden ladders over onto herself. It bumped against her head and shoulder, burying her beneath its fragile burden of material, and all the while she felt the little fingers continuing to pluck at her. Deeper in the maartza, she heard the blue-furred creature roar in surprise and anger, then shout in hoarse Tradetalk, "You! Out! Out! You go out!" Keegan was calling her name, his voice sharp with alarm, and she opened her mouth to answer, but then she felt a small finger snag on the cord that secured Dreff's flamestone pendant around her neck.

"No!" She tried to lunge to her feet, but she was tangled in the ladder and the lengths of fabric, her vision obscured, her body weighed down by grasping hands that pulled her one way while another set of hands tugged the cord in the opposite direction, straining it close to the snapping point.

In panicked desperation, Gredin Sent.

Her destination was the nearest vacant space she could clearly envision: the area just outside the huge doors of the Traders' Market—

—which, she realized in horror, wasn't an empty space anymore. Flailing as she fought to get her feet under herself, she collided with someone and stepped down with unintended force onto something so brittle that it made a noise like kindling sticks being broken to length.

A piercing shriek split the air, making her ears ring. Strong claws dug into her arm, piercing her skin through the fabric of her jacket, jerking her sideways as a hot wave of vertigo flashed through her. Knees buckling, she hung in the painful grasp, blinking against a flood of tears. Then she heard the resonant rumble of a Prett voice as it commanded, "You, Hesch. Let go that one."

"No," came the thin, nasal reply. "I, Nitikikani, say this one you take. Take and hold. I claim—" And it spoke a further word of Tradetalk that she didn't recognize.

"What name you?" the Prett demanded.

Claws bit more deeply into Gredin's arm, and the thin, nasal voice of Nitikikani of the Hesch demanded, "Speak! Tell Prett. What name you?"

She hadn't realized that the Prett's question was aimed at her. On a gasp of air, she said, "Gredin. Gredin te Balamont. Vennan. Please, I talk Director, I talk Wyve."

The Hesch made a cackling sound. "Oh yes, Vennan. I talk Director, also. I claim—" The unfamiliar word slid past again, something guttural that sounded like *gegitt* or *kekitt*. "You talk Director? He talk *you*. He talk you much and much." Another spasm of pain jolted through her as the Hesch's claws bit deeper into her flesh. "Prett, you take this Vennan," the Hesch demanded. "You hold this Vennan good. We go talk Director. Now!"

"Bloody blisters, can't you hurry?" Burlon snapped at Tetralanna as they dodged around two Thalken who were strolling languidly down the middle of the station corridor.

Tetralanna gave him a sour, affronted look. "Your legs are longer than mine."

"I've got no time to coddle you," he told her, and it was the truth. Ellis's words still echoed in his private mind. =*Come quickly. Gredin has injured a Hesch. Wyve is going to pronounce Judgment on her.*=

Burlon's mouth tightened at the memory, and he quickened his pace. "You're here because I need someone to take charge of Gredin after the hearing, and you agreed to come. I need to reach Wyve's office as quickly as I can. With the Hesch involved, this could turn into a complete disaster."

He turned the corner, his increased pace causing Tetralanna to break momentarily into a trot to remain at his side.

"Ellis says the hearing has already started," Burlon told her, "so keep up or, if you can't, I'll leave you here and ask Prett security to return you to the enclave."

"Don't you dare leave me! None of this is *my* fault."

Burlon struggled with his temper. "I seem to remember you bragging that Gredin would settle down and be quiet, once she'd eaten."

"Don't attempt to blame me, Burlon te Bentain."

Burlon bit back another curse. "We could have avoided this mess if you'd kept a closer eye on her. Why didn't you accompany her to the Traders' Market?"

"I had no idea she was going. If I'd known, I'd have forbidden it. I have far more sense than to go out amongst these creatures voluntarily," Tetralanna said coldly. "I warned you that the girl was flighty and unpredictable. The last I knew, she was going off to morning meal with Keegan te Fliss. If you wanted her watched beyond that, you should have taken charge of her yourself."

"Oh, right. Certainly. Why not? We all know that *I* have no other responsibilities with regard to this Trisectoriana. I'm only the organizer. By all means, I should have found the leisure to watch over *your* House member."

Tetralanna's eyes narrowed. "I have duties, too, you know. And although she and I inhabit the same House, I am not her Mentor. In fact, I told you clearly that I didn't want her here in the first place."

"Well, she's here now, and we need to deal with her."

Tetralanna snatched a few breaths and said, "Or... perhaps we don't."

"What's that supposed to mean?"

"There's a simple solution. Tell Cirin te K'lar to take her home with him, after the rehearsal."

It was an appealing notion, but hardly practical. "Gredin is your translator."

"*You* could translate for me, tomorrow at the Trisectoriana. That would be more appropriate anyway. You *are* one of the organizers." She smiled tightly, her gaze calculating. "Cirin doesn't plan to leave until after today's rehearsal, so we may as well use the girl's skills for that. Keeping her busy will also keep her in our sight and out of any more trouble. But if Cirin takes her home, afterwards, your — our — problem will be solved, don't you think?"

He had to admit it was a tidy solution. And it was probably best for Gredin, as well. Once she was home again, she would see that her fears were nothing but an errant night-thought.

Before he could reply, however, Ellis contacted his private mind again. =*Burlon? Where are you? The Beng are here now, too. I don't like the looks of this.*=

The Beng were involved? Small wonder Ellis's contact held an undercurrent of panic.

Breaking Tradepoint protocol, Burlon grabbed Tetralanna's arm and ran.

[18]

Wyve, Tradepoint Director, stood behind his desk, doing his best to exude an aura of calm, all the while wondering why this debacle couldn't have developed during Figg's shift.

But no. If it had, he would no doubt have been roused from his bed to help adjudicate the matter. On reflection, it was better that he be wide awake, with all his wits about him.

The unraveling of his well-planned morning had begun with the arrival of a Prett security guard from the Traders' Market, accompanied by a limping Hesch and a weeping Vennan. Not an auspicious start. Since then, it had devolved to include a clutch of yammering Beng, a conscience-stricken Vennan Trader, an indignant Shodekekeen vendor, and Keegan te Fliss, who was pale with distress.

Feeling distinctly outnumbered, Wyve had sent for Figg.

To give her credit, she arrived with gratifying speed. But when she reached his office door, she hesitated on the threshold, clearly shocked by the array of individuals gathered there, many of whom were holding forth simultaneously, their assorted voices creating a cacophony that bordered on the physically painful.

Being Figg, she recovered her composure, stepping carefully between the various contingents to join him behind the bulwark of his desk. "A routine morning, I see," she murmured, deadpan. She took her place at his side.

"Quite. We are, of course, recording. I would appreciate your personal notes, as well."

"Of course."

Figg settled but Wyve remained standing, and the room fell obediently silent except for the crying girl and a few Beng who continued to chitter until a direct look from him quelled them, at least for the moment. "Assistant Director Figg now here," he said in Tradetalk, acknowledging Figg with a nod of his head. "We make official account. No talk until I ask. When speak, be concise."

One of the Beng stood up, waving its arm in a frantic bid for attention.

Wyve acknowledged it with a reluctant nod.

"Too much big word!" it protested.

This was the plague of any meeting that involved the Beng. Whether honestly or as a manipulative tactic, the Beng claimed to have only the most rudimentary grasp of Tradetalk. Privately, he and Figg suspected that it suited the Beng quite well to maintain a thicket of confusion between themselves and any matter not directly related to trade.

Squaring his jaw, Wyve said, "Simple. No talk until I say Beng talk. Yes?"

Mutters and murmurs within the group, then a sullen nod from the one who had lodged the complaint.

"Good," Wyve said. "Beng sit." When it had done so, he lowered himself into his own chair and said, "We begin. Vennan turn talk first." Before they could object, he turned his gaze to Ellis te Vell. "Stand. Speak," he instructed.

She stood up, shifting uneasily. Wyve had, by intent, isolated the three Vennans from one another, although doing so tugged at his conscience when he saw the abject misery into which Gredin te Balamont had sunk. But the Hesch were involved. It was important to proceed with irreproachable propriety.

Ellis te Vell cleared her throat and said, "Burlon say take twenty Vennan to Traders' Market. They want see. I take." She shot a look at Gredin. "Later, in Market, I count eighteen."

"You know then who gone?"

"No, Director. Know number, not names. Told all 'Stay close.'"

"So. Two gone. What you do?"

"Talk Prett security. Say two Vennan lost in Market. He check com, tell me one lost. Say other Vennan here your office." Her hands fluttered in a gesture of frustration. "I call two Vennan Trader. Tell them come Market. Tell one look for lost Vennan. Tell other, take group back to Vennan enclave. I come here your office, seek other Vennan. You tell me trouble, detention that Vennan. I call Burlon. He come soon. Detention maybe mistake we hope, Director."

"No mistake," the Hesch countered darkly.

Wyve gave it a stern look, then said to Ellis, "You say more?"

"No. I wait Burlon."

Wyve nodded and turned his attention to the Shodekekeen. "I hear you now, yes?"

The Shodekekeen reared up onto its hindmost legs, which made it slightly taller than the Vennans and nearly the equal of the Hesch. "Yes," it said, in the thickened accent its blunt muzzle created. "Quiet day. One Thalken place order. Then two Vennan come. Seek bahnt. While I show bahnt, Beng come," it said, its lip curling back from prominent teeth. "Make trouble. Cause damage."

The Beng chittered in protest, but Wyve was having none of that. "Beng no talk!"

They subsided.

"Trouble," the Shodekekeen repeated, glaring at the Beng. "Bother customer."

The accusation carried the potential for serious consequences since, by common agreement, no race was permitted to enter a vendor's maartza if another was already present there. Wyve made a notation. "Then?"

The Shodekekeen grunted. "That one—" It gestured at Gredin. "—gone. This one—" A nod toward Keegan. "—left behind. *They*—" A swipe of one long-clawed paw in the direction of the Beng. "—run away."

That triggered another round of protests from the Beng. Wyve stood up. "Beng stop!" he rumbled, drowning them out.

They cowered and covered their ears, although he knew he had not actually scared them. Unfortunately, Gredin te Balamont *did* look frightened. Wyve had conducted many Judgments as Director but he could not recall an accused as openly emotional as Gredin.

It was at this sorry juncture that Figg keyed the office door. It opened, admitting Burlon and Tetralanna te Balamont.

Displeased, Wyve sat down.

"What the piercing point is all this about?" Burlon growled in Vennan as he stalked in.

The phrase meant nothing to Wyve, but Ellis blinked, and Keegan gaped, while Tetralanna drew back, stiffening with affront.

Gredin wept on, oblivious.

Burlon's glare grew darker as it swept from the Shodekekeen to the Beng to the Hesch. Then he surveyed the Vennans, ending with the weeping girl. "Stab it," Burlon muttered, and belatedly crossed his palms to Wyve and Figg. "Your pardon," he said in Tradetalk "I was—"

Tetralanna interrupted sharply, in Vennan, "Gredin, come here and translate."

Gredin cast a desperate look of appeal at Wyve.

It was Figg, however, who said in crisp Prettian, "No, Gredin te Balamont is not at liberty to do so. You have arrived in the midst of a Judgment. Either be silent or leave. Burlon, translate that for your Voice."

As Burlon did so, the Vennan woman's face reddened, and she cast a blazing look at him.

Burlon added, "Their station, their rules."

The lone Hesch and the group of Beng turned to stare at Tetralanna, perhaps annoyed by the flow of Vennan, which was incomprehensible to them. Under the force of their joint regard, Tetralanna retreated a pace.

Wyve looked to the Shodekekeen again. "You say more?" he asked the merchant, returning to Tradetalk.

"Damage," asserted the Shodekekeen, its neck fur beginning to rise. "Damage cloth. Damage equipment. Beng make damage and run."

"No! Not so! Not so!" the Beng shrilled in chorus.

The Shodekekeen snarled at them, and Tetralanna gasped audibly.

Wyve slapped his palms onto the desk. "Quiet! Beng no talk. Vennan no talk. Stop noise or go out." Then he added in Vennan, for Tetralanna's explicit benefit, "Stand silent or leave."

"But I—"

"Silent or leave. Choose!"

Her mouth snapped shut. It was clear she had taken offense, but Wyve simply cast a hard look at Burlon, who had brought the woman into this fraught situation, and said to him in Tradetalk, "Your citizen. Make behave or take her out."

Burlon nodded.

"Apologies," Wyve said to the Shodekekeen, whose entire ruff was now bristling. "I hear your words. Affront. Loss of customer. Damage. You say more?"

Looking slightly mollified, the Shodekekeen shook itself, resettling the fur on the back of its neck. "No complaint on

Vennan. Customer. Polite. No trouble. All trouble Beng. Formal complaint Beng."

Burlon's face betrayed some relief at that, but Wyve suspected it was premature. The Shodekekeen complaint was one thing. The Hesch's would likely be quite another.

Predictably, the Beng again protested their innocence. Wyve strove for patience, only to find that Figg had reached her flashpoint. Rising from her chair, she bustled around to confront the Beng contingent, looming over them. "One Beng speak for group," she insisted. "One! Which Beng speak?"

After a hurried consultation, a Beng raised its hand.

"All other Beng leave," Figg said, "Go Beng enclave. No go Market. No stay corridor. Go enclave. Now."

"We quiet. We stay."

"No. Talk, talk, talk. No chance left. This Beng stay. Other Beng go now. Go!" And she stamped her foot for emphasis.

They scattered and scurried, heading for the door. One of them blundered into Tetralanna and grasped at her skirts to regain its balance.

She shrieked and darted sideways, jostling Burlon.

That won audible laughter from the four retreating Beng, who tumbled out through the doorway as it slid open.

And then they were gone.

Tetralanna bristled and pointed at the lone remaining Beng. "Go!" she demanded in Vennan. "Leave with the rest!"

The Beng wrung its hands, darting anxious glances from Figg to Tetralanna.

"Out!" Tetralanna cried, her hand shaking visibly as she pointed at the door.

Figg said, "Security, remove this Vennan. Return her to her quarters."

When two uniformed Prett approached Tetralanna, she recoiled. "Burlon, who are these men?" she appealed, her eyes widening in fear.

"They're Prett security. You've disrupted the Judgment. Go with them. They'll take you back to the enclave."

"But—"

Wyve nodded to the waiting guards, who herded Tetralanna out of the office, her flow of protests still audible until the door closed behind them.

The tension in the room eased immediately.

Figg strode back to her bench and sat.

Reorganizing his thoughts, Wyve braced himself to tackle

the unavoidable. "Now Beng talk. What happen Market?" he asked the solitary remaining Beng. "You tell. I listen."

The Beng gave him a surly look. "Beng go Market for trade. Beng make no trouble. Beng make no damage."

"Shodekekeen say damage cloth, damage equipment. Who make damage?"

The Beng crossed its arms. "Pretty lady."

"Pretty lady?" Wyve repeated uncertainly.

The Beng pointed at Gredin. "She."

That drew a snarl of dissent from the Shodekekeen.

The Beng rose on tiptoe, its gaze a challenge. "Beng no touch e-quip-ment. Beng no touch cloth. Beng no make damage. Pretty lady touch cloth, touch e-quip-ment, make damage. Truth I tell. You ask. She say no, she lie!"

The Beng were sly. The Beng were slippery. The Beng were evasive. But the Beng, in Wyve's experience, had never been particularly artful liars. Their nervousness tended to betray them, through a ragged laugh, a facial tic, or an unwillingness to make eye contact.

No such signs were in evidence now, and Wyve's heart sank.

At the back of the room, Burlon looked no happier.

Figg said, "I have question for Beng."

Wyve nodded for her to proceed.

"Beng go Shodekekeen maartza?"

A wary nod.

"Light at entrance to maartza on or off?"

The Beng shuffled its feet. "Not sure."

Figg snorted. "You trader, yes?"

"Yes."

"Every trader know to check light at maartza entrance, every time."

The Beng shrugged.

Figg persisted. "Vennan in Shodekekeen maartza when Beng arrive?"

"Not understand," the Beng claimed.

Wyve suspected that the Beng understood far too well for its own comfort. Extruding a fingertip, he called up a desktop hologram of the Shodekekeen maartza and beckoned the Beng closer. "You look. Shodekekeen maartza." Another flick of the controls placed a small blue marker near the back of the structure. "Shodekekeen. Yes?"

Reluctantly, the Beng nodded.

A third flick created five green markers, just outside of the structure. "Beng those."

"Yes."

A fourth flick created two yellow markers, also outside. "Vennan, yes?"

A nod.

Now they were down to it. Wyve placed the yellow markers within the maartza outline. "Shodekekeen inside. Vennan inside. Beng *not* inside. Yes?"

The Beng maintained an obdurate silence.

Figg chimed in. "Shodekekeen and Vennan in maartza. Why Beng come inside?"

The Beng pointed across to where Keegan te Fliss stood. "One Vennan trade, talk Shodekekeen here." He pointed at the very back of the maartza. "Beng no talk Shodekekeen and trader Vennan."

Wyve moved one yellow marker to the rear, along with the blue marker. "So?"

The Beng nodded.

Wyve pointed to the yellow marker that represented Gredin "Show where this Vennan."

The Beng pointed a stubby finger at the front margin of the hologram.

Wyve edged the marker close to the entrance, but still inside. "Here?"

The Beng offered a token shrug and said, "This Vennan no trade. No talk Shodekekeen."

"Other Vennan trade. Why Beng go in?"

Making no reply, the Beng turned away, walked back to its place, and sat down.

Wyve slid a glance at Figg. The Beng position appeared to be that, although they had contravened Market rules by entering the Shodekekeen maartza while another race was present, they didn't feel it was a serious offense, since they had only interacted with Gredin, who was not actively trading with the Shodekekeen at the time.

The Beng position was weak because the rule was unequivocal: only one race of customers at a time was permitted in a maartza. Still, it was less serious than if they had interrupted Keegan and the Shodekekeen in the midst of trade negotiations.

"You say more?" Wyve asked.

"Beng make no damage!" the Beng replied, and crossed its arms with finality.

Why is nothing ever simple? Wyve wondered. He organized his thoughts for the next step in the process: interviewing the Vennan historian. "Burlon, translate for Keegan te Fliss, yes?"

Burlon nodded.

"Ask him speak what happen."

In Vennan, Burlon conferred with Keegan, who replied. After a minute, Burlon said to Wyve, in Tradetalk, "Keegan Gredin go Trader Market seek bahnt."

In Wyve's view, it meant that their trip had been a fool's errand. Vendors at the Traders' Market offered a wide array of goods, but the scientific sophistication required to navigate a starship to Tradepoint meant that these races relied on electronics or gel-tech for communication, not bahnt and reed pens.

The Vennans, of course, were the exception. The cultural mismatch put them at odds with every other civilization at Tradepoint. "Seek bahnt," he echoed dryly, and he and Burlon shared a look.

But then Burlon shrugged. "*Found* bahnt," he pointed out.

And that was true, though Wyve could not imagine why

there had been bahnt in the Shodekekeen cloth merchant's maartza, or how the Vennans had discovered its presence there.

Still, that wasn't the issue at hand. "Go on," he directed Burlon, who turned back to Keegan te Fliss and prompted him, in Vennan, to continue.

The account was brief: the two Vennans entered the Shodekekeen maartza, Gredin explained what they sought, and the merchant took Keegan to the back to view the bahnt. At that point, there had been a commotion, display racks had tumbled over, and Gredin had vanished.

"Ask about Beng," Wyve prompted.

The answer was inconclusive: Keegan te Fliss had been facing the Shodekekeen and, while he had glimpsed figures fleeing and could confirm that they were Beng, he had seen nothing to identify *which* individual Beng had been present. His concern had been for Gredin, afraid at first that she'd been crushed beneath the fallen racks of fabric, and then concerned because she was *not* under the racks and fabric, but had disappeared entirely.

The Beng looked smug.

Refusing to be ruffled, Wyve expressed his thanks for Keegan's testimony and considered the two individuals who had not yet been interviewed: the Vennan girl and the Hesch.

After a moment's reflection, Wyve decided to address the Hesch first. Its involvement in the day's events had been relatively brief, occurring only at the end. Gredin, by contrast, had been present from start to finish. And perhaps the delay would give the girl time to compose herself. He certainly wasn't looking forward to questioning her in her present state of distress.

"Nitikikani of Hesch," Wyve intoned, inclining his head, "I thank for wait. Speak now. I listen."

The Hesch twisted its neck slowly, raking the room with a cold stare. Only Burlon and Ellis met its gaze, wearing the impassive expression common to Vennan traders. Everyone else — even the Beng — found somewhere else to fix their attention.

As if content that it commanded the room, the Hesch said, in a thin, scratchy voice, "Vennan assault me. I charge kegitt against this one." And it pointed a long forefinger at Gredin.

At the back of the room, Burlon swung an alarmed glance from the Hesch to Ellis to Gredin, then back to the Hesch again.

"What happen?" Wyve asked, keeping his own voice level. "Tell place. Tell action."

"Corridor. Trader Market door. I approach. Door open. *This* one collide. Assault."

Wyve considered that account. "You approach Market door," he summarized carefully. "This Vennan come through door, collide you, yes?"

"No."

Startled, Wyve deconstructed it further. "You approach Market door."

"Yes."

"Door opens."

"Yes."

Then where are we failing to agree? "This Vennan come through door," he said, indicating Gredin.

"No," said the Hesch.

Confusion and hope warred with each other in Wyve's mind. Perhaps, despite the Hesch's gesture, Gredin was not the intended target of the accusation. "Some other Vennan?"

"This Vennan," the Hesch said firmly. "Not through door."

Wyve suppressed a sigh. "Not through door? Then from where?"

"No from." The Hesch made a jerky gesture. "Was."

"Not understand," Wyve said flatly.

The Hesch fixed him with a beady look that clearly meant, *Stupid Prett.* "Not there," it stated. "Then there. Collide. Assault."

Although the words were said with haughty dignity, they sounded like nonsense to Wyve... until his gaze strayed to Burlon, a Vennan whom Wyve knew and liked.

Burlon looked aghast.

Stop trying to clarify, Wyve counseled himself sharply. *There is more involved here than you realized. Take the Hesch at his word and move on.* "What Judgment you ask?"

The Hesch blinked three times. "Formal apology. Leave Tradepoint, this one." He fell silent, but Wyve wasn't fooled. There had been three blinks. There would be three demands. The Hesch clacked its bill and added, "Thirty point nine five seven credit, for six sectora."

The Beng's eyes widened dramatically. Burlon's face reddened with temper. Even Figg sat up a little straighter on her bench.

But Wyve swallowed all reaction. What the Hesch requested and what the Hesch eventually received might very well be two different matters. Still, it deserved the chance to make its demand without interruption or comment from Wyve or anyone else.

"You say more?" he invited, completing the ritual.

But the Hesch simply clacked its bill again, the noise resounding in the quiet office.

And that left only Gredin te Balamont to be questioned, however distasteful Wyve found the remainder of his task to be. He couldn't even legitimately ask Burlon to translate, as he had for Keegan te Fliss, since Wyve knew that the girl was quite fluent in both Prett and Tradetalk.

"Gredin te Balamont," he said, because speaking her name aloud committed him to begin. "We hear Ellis te Vell. We hear Keegan te Fliss. We hear Shodekekeen. We hear Beng. We hear Hesch. Now need Gredin's words. Tell from start, please."

She nodded and took a visibly shaky breath. "Keegan seek bahnt," she began. "Keegan speak no Tradetalk. I go, speak for him. We… I…" Her face crumpled. "Your pardon," she gasped, and ran the flats of her fingers across her cheeks, pressing hard as she wiped tears away.

The Hesch looked unmoved, while the Beng seemed entirely too interested. The Shodekekeen dropped down onto all six feet, swaying slightly from side to side, as Shodekekeen were prone to do when they were unhappy. Ellis looked uncomfortable, and Burlon frowned.

Wyve tried a new approach. "Gredin," he said, "if I ask questions, you answer, yes?"

She nodded.

"Good. You go Traders' Market with group?"

"Yes. Twenty Vennan."

"Twenty Vennan go Market. Only two Vennan go Shodekekeen maartza. You, Keegan leave Ellis and group. Why?"

"We seek bahnt," she replied. "Busy look. Walk too slow. Hurry then, seek group, seek Ellis. No see Ellis. See maartza."

"Shodekekeen maartza?"

"No. Beng maartza." Her voice took on a note of urgency, and the pace of her words quickened. "Beng see. Beng say 'pretty lady.' Beng come follow, say 'pretty lady, pretty lady.' Not good. We hurry more. Turn corner, no see Ellis. Walk more, hurry more. Turn again, more new maartza but no see Ellis. No see group."

The Beng squirmed as if words were trying to burst from its mouth, but Figg pointed a cautionary finger, and the Beng subsided, glowering.

"We see person come out from new maartza. Person carry bahnt."

Wyve made a note. "What you do?"

"We go that maartza. Go in. Shodekekeen there. I ask. He say yes bahnt. I tell Keegan go look. I wait."

Now they were coming to the crux of the matter. "Keegan, Shodekekeen go look bahnt. You say you wait. Wait where? Outside Shodekekeen maartza?"

"No. Inside maartza. No want go out. Afraid see Beng. Stay in maartza, look cloth. Down low, see beautiful cloth," she said, her voice softening at the memory.

"What color this cloth?" Wyve asked, hoping the detail might later prove useful in pinpointing her exact location within the Shodekekeen's structure.

"Red," she replied, then waved her hand in apparent frustration over the simple word. "Much, much red. Deep. Where light touch it, make red much beautiful." A grimace distorted her face. "Then many Beng come, stand close. No light touch cloth."

"Beng come where?"

"Inside Shodekekeen maartza."

Ah. That was clear-cut. "Beng do what in maartza?"

"Touch me — touch hair, touch sleeve, touch hlao, touch face. Say 'pretty lady.' Many Beng, too close, too much touch. I —" Her face was now a portrait of distress. "I try stand up—" She half turned and called out a string of words to Burlon in Vennan.

He replied in Tradetalk. "She try stand, bump cloth rack. Rack and cloth fall on her."

Gredin's attention swung back to Wyve. "Beng too much close, too much touch," she asserted. She reached up to her throat and pulled a cord and its pendant from beneath her clothing. "Beng try touch... this."

It was a flamestone, its deep colors startling against the pale blue of her outfit. Flamestones were rare, even on Venna, according to Burlon. As a result, they were extremely valuable and were rarely offered for trade by the Vennans. Wyve had never seen this stone's equal in size or brilliance, in all his sectora as Tradepoint Director.

The Hesch took a hobbling step toward Gredin, its eyes narrowing with interest.

"Beng try touch stone," Wyve said, nodding his comprehension. "What you do?"

"I..." She swallowed hard. "I go out. Go out from Shodekekeen maartza. Leave Beng." She grimaced. "Leave Keegan. Leave Shodekekeen. Leave all. I... go out," she said, ashen.

The Beng could hold its silence no longer. "How?" it demanded, its curiosity so intense that it was nearly bouncing in place. "How go out, pretty lady? How you leave Beng? How?"

"Beng no talk!" Wyve thundered, in part to quell it, in part to buy another moment in which to organize his own thoughts. This was where the two parts of the tale joined, somehow. Gredin left the Shodekekeen maartza… and ended up at the Traders' Market entrance, where she injured the Hesch. He suspected Burlon understood both matters, and yet the Vennan appeared anxious for Wyve not to attempt to clarify the matter.

But clarifying the matter was precisely what Wyve's position as Director compelled him to do. "Gredin te Balamont," he said quietly, when silence had once again fallen, "you leave Shodeke-keen maartza and go Market door, yes? So I ask — how you go Market door?"

"I… make… be there."

"Gredin make Gredin be at Market door. How? Walk?" He made two of his fingers move across the desktop slowly, as if pacing.

Gredin shook her head. "No."

"Run?" he asked, quickening his fingers' pace.

"No."

"Then how you go?"

"No Tradetalk words," she said again.

"Then say Vennan words. You *speaker*, yes? So say."

"Great gaping wounds, Wyve, stop it!" The angry flood of Vennan words came not from Gredin but from Burlon, at the back of the room. "Leave the girl be," he continued heatedly. "Leave her be and I'll tell you what you want to know."

The Hesch, the Beng, and the Shodekekeen all glanced briefly at Burlon in confusion, unable to understand his language but alarmed by his harsh tone. Then they turned their attention back to Wyve, clearly expecting him to take control of the situation.

Wyve said firmly, in Vennan, "Then tell me. I will listen."

"Watch," Burlon said, his eyes narrowed in exasperation. "And pay attention. I only intend to do this once."

Do what? Wyve drew breath to ask. But before he could do so, Burlon was suddenly standing on the other side of the room, a good ten paces from where he had begun. And then, an instant later, he was back to where he'd started.

The Vennan said, in his own language, "*That* is how Gredin passed from the Shodekekeen maartza to the Market door. She should not have done so. She and the others were all instructed not to do so, during their stay here on Tradepoint. But she is young, and she was frightened, and so she did it, to get away from the festering Beng. Now, in the name of the Power, can you finish with this so we can take her out of here?"

Unable to understand Burlon's remarks, those not in the

Vennan group were still looking at Wyve at the front of the room, seeming unaware of what had just transpired behind them.

That was just as well, in Wyve's opinion. He did not try to tell himself that his senses had deceived him. He knew precisely what he had just seen. The ability Burlon had demonstrated was astonishing. How had Vennans managed to frequent Tradepoint for three hundred sectora without anyone else being aware that they had such an ability?

Of course it *had* been known, since Cirin's first arrival, that Vennans used no ship to traverse space. By their own explanation, they 'traveled the river.' Because of that, they had henceforth conformed by arriving and departing Tradepoint from within the bio-safety — and privacy — of the Vennan enclave. Once arrived within Tradepoint's hull, however, Vennan Tradeteams had moved through the corridors like any other race, walking from place to place.

It had never occurred to Wyve to wonder whether that was from necessity or choice.

"What wait?" the Beng made bold enough to say. "What Vennan say? Why we sit wait? You done? We go?"

Wyve refocused with a jolt. "No," he said sharply. "You wait. Done soon." He forced his attention back to Gredin, who was clinging to the edge of his desk as if it were all that kept her upright. "Done soon," he repeated, this time saying the words directly to her. "You go Market door," he said to her in slow, clear Tradetalk. "Hesch there, yes?"

She replied in a torrent of Vennan. "Yes, he was there, and I injured him. It was all my fault, not his. Please, help me make him understand how sorry I am!"

Wyve lifted a hand to silence her. He had intended to guide her, question by measured question, through an account of her interaction with the Hesch. Instead, she had just blurted out a confession. The Hesch's demand for reparations was already steep, but it was apparent to Wyve that there had been no malicious intent behind Gredin's actions. The resulting accident had been minor, mostly an affront to the Hesch's prickly pride. The settlement should reflect that.

But that wouldn't happen if Gredin openly claimed full responsibility for the incident.

Pointing at her, he said sternly, also in Vennan, "This is more serious than you realize. Answer only my direct questions, no more. You comprehend?"

She nodded, large-eyed, and Wyve hoped his words would at least make her reflect before speaking again. In Tradetalk, he started over. "You go Market door. Hesch there, yes?"

"Yes."

"You bump Hesch?"

"Fall into Hesch. Try not fall down." She grimaced. "Step Hesch foot."

Stop, Wyve willed. *Stop right there.* But he already knew, from the look on her face, that more words were coming. He could only hope they would be innocuous, perhaps an apology.

Instead, with regrettable clarity, Gredin te Balamont said, "Hesch foot break."

Wyve stared at her, shocked. Surely she was mistaken. The Hesch was here, standing before them. Yes, he had limped when he came in, but there was nothing in his bearing or demeanor to indicate a serious injury. Or so Wyve hoped.

Then again, what had he ever been able to tell by looking at a Hesch's face? Their anatomy was so radically different that expression conveyed very little. And this wasn't about what he *wanted* the facts to be. Gredin had just made a potentially damning admission, one that had been heard and comprehended by everyone in the room. Additionally, it prompted serious concern about the welfare of the Hesch itself, if Gredin's assertion proved accurate.

"Why you think break?" he asked.

"I hear," she said and, raising her hand, snapped her fingers several times in quick succession. "Hesch cry out." With that, she pivoted away from Wyve to face the Hesch directly, crossing her palms to him. "Much sad," she told it. "Much, much sad I make break."

The Hesch leaned toward her, cocking its head in that disconcerting way that Hesch had. The overhead lights made its dark eyes glitter, and it opened and closed its bill several times, with the softest of clacking sounds. But it offered no spoken reply, just that intent stare, as if it were memorizing Gredin te Balamont's appearance from head to foot.

On Tradepoint, no race was permitted to touch another without express permission. That was no small part of the offense that the Beng had committed against Gredin — and theirs had been only superficial contacts, with no physical harm inflicted. If Gredin was correct in her description of the Hesch's injuries, the situation could result in a financial setback that might take multiple sectora of skilled trading to offset.

"Nitikikani of Hesch, this Vennan say break bone. What say you? Is so? Is not so?"

The Hesch continued to train its gaze on Gredin as it replied. "Vennan step foot. Insult."

"You ask big penalty on Vennan. I listen, think now maybe yes. Ask again, break bone?"

The Hesch hunched its shoulders, still peering at Gredin.

"What mean that?" Wyve demanded. "Mean yes? Mean no? Mean not certain?"

The Hesch made no reply.

Figg shifted slightly on her bench, and Wyve took it as a signal: *Wrap this matter up.*

He agreed. The hearing had already been lengthy. Prolonging it would serve no good purpose. He didn't have all of the facts, but when did he ever have all of the facts? There was only one essential piece of information missing. He would simply have to work around it.

"Judgment," he announced firmly, and stood up.

A ripple of shock raced through the room.

"Two races bring charges — Shodekekeen and Hesch," he continued. "Two races charged — Beng and Vennan. Charges connect. Judgments connect."

All eyes were on him now, even the Hesch's.

"Shodekekeen Judgment first. Beng break rule, enter maartza with Shodekekeen and Vennan. Judgment — Beng pay fine of two point two five for one sectora. Beng hear?"

The Beng's face was set in a sour look of protest, but the fine was a long-established consequence. "Beng hear," it muttered.

"Next, Shodekekeen say damage cloth, damage equipment. I say Shodekekeen make tally, submit damage amount my office. Judgment — I take damage amount from Beng account, add to Shodekekeen account. Beng hear?"

"No!" the Beng cried, the picture of disbelieving outrage. "Wrong! Beng no touch Shodekekeen e-quip-ment. Beng no touch Shodekekeen cloth. You no take amount from Beng! Wrong Judgment, Prett Director. Much wrong! Why you do? Why?"

Wyve lifted his hand, demanding silence. When the Beng finally managed to stifle its protests, Wyve said, "Say I lift bench, throw bench. Bench damage desk, injure Assistant Director. Where fault? Blame bench? No. Blame me." He pointed at the Beng. "Vennan inside Shodekekeen maartza, all good. All calm. You go in Shodekekeen maartza. Wrong. You touch Vennan. Wrong. Bad things happen. If Beng follow rule, no wrong, no damage. Beng choose break rule, Beng pay damage. Beng hear?"

"Beng hear," the Beng grumbled, but it cast a resentful look at Gredin.

"Judgment," Wyve intoned for a third time. "No Beng speak this Vennan, no Beng touch this Vennan, no Beng come same place this Vennan, next three sect." By that time, happily, the trouble-prone Vennan girl would no longer be on Tradepoint, and would therefore no longer be Wyve's concern. "Beng hear?"

The Beng balked. "This Vennan be tomorrow reception? Beng want go reception."

Wyve felt a flare of temper, and took a calming breath. Slowly, with precision, he said, "Three Beng only register this office tomorrow. Three Beng only go reception. Beng come, short stay, Beng go." He raised a cautioning finger. "All other time next three sect, no Beng speak this Vennan, no Beng touch this Vennan, no Beng come same place this Vennan. Beng hear?"

"Beng no *want* speak, touch, go same place *that* Vennan," the Beng said spitefully.

"Beng hear?" Wyve repeated, relentless in his pursuit of the formalities.

"Beng hear," the Beng said. Its mouth worked, puckering as if it might spit on the floor at Gredin's feet, but a sharp sound from Figg made it reconsider and subside.

"Hesch Judgment," Wyve announced, determined to bring the matter to a conclusion with as much dispatch as he could muster.

Tense silence.

"Gredin te Balamont touch Nitikikani of Hesch. No dispute. I need know big touch, small touch. Need proof. Prett ask Hesch come Prett Clinic, have foot scanned. If no damage, I fine Vennan two point two five for one sectora. If touch big and bone break, Hesch ask I fine Vennan thirty point nine five seven, for six sectora."

Every eye in the room was fixed on him now.

Wyve put on his most sober demeanor. "Judgment — If Hesch refuse come Clinic to scan foot, I award small fine to Hesch. If Hesch come Clinic and scan show bone not break, I award small fine to Hesch. If Hesch come Clinic and scan show bone break, I award thirty point nine five seven for six sectora to Hesch."

It was an unprecedented amount, for an unprecedented duration. It meant that for every sale negotiated by a Vennan trader for the next six sectora, nearly a third of the purchase price would be diverted directly into the Hesch's account.

A murmur of comment ruffled the silence, then died away.

"Judgment," Wyve said again. "Whether small fine, whether big fine, I take one-third of fine from Vennan account, I take two-third of fine from Beng account. Vennans hear?"

"Vennans hear," Burlon affirmed from the back of the room.

"Beng hear?"

"Unfair, Director, unfair! Beng protest!"

"Protest?" Wyve folded his arms. "No ground for Beng protest. Same like Shodekekeen damage. Beng no enter Shodekekeen maartza, no bad thing occur Hesch. Beng make choice. Beng pay price." He pointed at the angry Beng. "Beng listen me now. If no bone break, small fine, I advise Beng pay. If Hesch bone break, big fine, I give Beng two choice. First choice, pay. If no want pay, second choice is leave Tradepoint for six sectora, then come back, all settled."

The Beng sputtered.

Wyve turned his attention to the Hesch. "What say, Hesch? Come Clinic, scan foot? Or add small fine to Hesch account, say matter done?"

If the Hesch had possessed an upper lip, it would have curled it. "Scan," it said, as if the word tasted bitter.

"You stay here," Wyve instructed, relieved. "I call transport pod."

"Wait," said Nitikikani.

Wyve eyed the Hesch warily. "Wait why?"

"Judgment not complete," came the accusation.

Wyve spread his hands. "What more you want me say?"

Nitikikani pointed a long, thin finger at the girl.

Of course. Wyve realized that he had, indeed, forgotten something. Trust a Hesch not to forget a single detail that was in its own self-interest.

"Yes," Wyve conceded. "Judgment. This Vennan, Gredin te Balamont, leave Tradepoint two sect from now."

Nitikikani stiffened. "No 'two sect.' Leave now."

"No. Vennan reception in one sect. Next sect after reception, she go."

Silently, the beak parted, then eased closed in grudging acquiescence.

Relieved, Wyve looked out over the rest of the room. "Thank all who come. Thank all who speak. Thank all who listen. Beng, remember terms of Judgment — no talk, no touch, no go same place this Vennan. After scan, I send word to Beng, word to Vennan. Beng leave now. Then Shodekekeen. Then Vennan." He clapped his hands together twice. "Judgment done. Go."

The Beng glared at him, and Wyve felt a brief flicker of sympathy for it, knowing that it would now have to return to its enclave and relate the details of the Judgments to the rest of the Beng contingent — not a pleasant fate. Still, they had brought the matter upon themselves, even if they hadn't foreseen how far-reaching and expensive the result would be.

Selecting a carefully neutral expression, he nodded to the Beng in dismissal.

Again, the little mouth worked and puckered.

Again, Figg made the merest noise.

With a muttered curse, its shoulders slumping in defeat, the Beng turned and left.

"Transport pod for the Hesch is on its way," Figg murmured, and Wyve reflected — not for the first time that day — how fortunate he was to have her as his Assistant Director. When the time came for him to step aside from his role as Director and resume life on the world below, Tradepoint would fare well under Figg's steadfast guiding hand.

With the Beng gone, the scenario in the room shifted, but only slightly. The Shodekekeen merchant had extricated Burlon from the rest of the Vennan delegation and was having a private word with him, but everyone else stood in isolation: the Hesch, who had lowered himself onto a bench; Ellis te Vell, whose gaze moved from Vennan to Vennan as if she were belatedly determined to keep an eye on all of them, after her failure to do so at the Market; Keegan te Fliss, who looked worried and exhausted.

And Gredin.

Gredin te Balamont still stood near Wyve's desk, making no attempt to join her group. Her hand had come up to clutch the flamestone pendant that she wore, as if it were her only anchor in a world gone mad.

"Gredin te Balamont," Wyve said mildly.

She flinched, but her gaze came back into focus, fixing on him.

"You are free to return to your enclave now," he told her in Vennan.

Wyve was surprised to find, despite the morning's missteps and trespasses, all of which had Gredin as their point of origin, that he was sorry to see her go.

But he supposed it must be his most foolish thought of the

morning, because it was increasingly clear to him that matters on Tradepoint were unlikely to regain any semblance of normalcy until the Vennan delegation, and this young woman in particular, had bidden him farewell and headed home.

Gredin found the walk from the Director's office back to the enclave long and bleak.

Burlon had stayed behind, still conversing with the blue-furred Shodekekeen merchant, but Ellis was there to lead the way, with Keegan at her side. Gredin trailed along behind them, winded and weary, her head congested from the endless tears she had cried, her legs unsteady beneath her.

At the outer doors to the Vennan enclave, Ellis and Keegan stepped into the antechamber. Gredin crossed the threshold after them, relieved that the long walk was at an end. The bio-mist felt soothing on her face, a cool touch in a world that had grown too warm for comfort. But when the cycle was complete and the inner doors opened, she took a single step into the enclave and found Tetralanna waiting for her there.

Flinching, Gredin said, "Excuse me, but I am going to retire to my room now."

"To what purpose?" Tetralanna demanded, looking affronted. "It is time for midday meal. Come to table and eat. Rest afterwards, if you must."

Gredin longed for a span of private time, a chance to sit in silence and finger the stones from her pouch. She needed an opportunity to reassemble her fractured sense of who she was, in the face of so many losses. Instead, Tetralanna expected her to sit on display in the reception hall, surrounded by strangers, some uncaring, some too curious. "My eyes are red and swollen," Gredin murmured, mortified.

"And whose fault is that? I'm told that Burlon arranged a Healing for you, just this morning, and you have already undone all of the benefit that intercession won for you. You have been nothing but a disruption. At least *try* to fit yourself back into the pattern of the day. A meal is what you need. You and I will require strength and clarity, this afternoon, for the rehearsal."

The rehearsal? Gredin's spirits plummeted further. She had forgotten entirely about the rehearsal. But she supposed she did need to eat. And this meal, however little she wanted it, might at least be an opportunity to mitigate the terrible impression of her that the morning's events had made on Tetralanna. She would try.

Gredin let herself be directed to the first table with available seating. The room around them throbbed with motion and noise, quickly robbing her of her resolve. Gredin huddled into herself, trying to block it all out, wishing with bitter, despairing fervor that she could simply evanesce and return to the Source.

It was a shameful thing to think. A terrible, cowardly thing to think. But it was truly the only coherent ambition her belea-guered mind could muster. Dreff was forever gone, and she lacked the will to go on without him, weighed down by the enormity of all that she had lost.

"Stop that," Tetralanna hissed, and Gredin realized that she had begun to weep. "I should think your appetite for attention would be quite sated, after that incomprehensible affair in the Director's office. Compose yourself."

But the memory of the Judgment redoubled the threat of tears. The mean-spirited contempt of the Beng. The piercing stare of Nitikikani of the Hesch. The disarming kindness of the Shodekekeen merchant, when it had insisted upon her innocence. The cool manner of the Assistant Director, and the unexpected pity she had glimpsed in the eyes of Wyve. Of her fellow Vennans present at the Judgment, everyone but Ellis had known that their loved ones and their home world were lost to them forever. How could Tetralanna and Burlon and Keegan maintain their calm demeanor, in the face of a truth that was crushing the very life out of her?

But she knew how. It was because they didn't believe her.

Well, Keegan claimed to believe. But Burlon was no more convinced of the truth of her night-thought than Cirin te K'lar, while Tetralanna—

"Eat your meal," Tetralanna prompted.

Gredin picked up a glass and raised it to her lips, then set it down without drinking. Her insides were too roiled from the morning's misadventures to tolerate even a sip.

Tetralanna noticed. "How can you expect patience from others when you make no effort to mend your ways?" she demanded. "Last evening, I was exhausted from the demands of the day. Do you suppose *I* had my normal appetite? No. But I made myself eat a small meal, in spite of that. Even now, having just been subjected to that hideous mist, I am consuming the food and drink that my body requires. Self-discipline, Gredin. If you have no self-discipline, you cannot serve your gyfte. The time for the rehearsal will be upon us before you know it. There is no time to dawdle. Eat your food."

The thought of the upcoming rehearsal made Gredin shudder. How could she face the Director again, so soon after her public disgrace? And Cirin would be there, as well. What new, more compelling words could she find to dissuade him from attempting a return to Venna? This morning, he had spoken confidently of Traveling the River on to Palomar if her warning about Venna proved true, but that seemed a flimsy safeguard. Far better for him not to go at all.

Still, he was a stubborn man, prideful in his gyfte. She wished she had any confidence in her ability to make him listen. Most of all, she wished she could just be wrong, no matter how foolish it might make her appear.

There were a great many things she wished, none of which would be coming true.

"At least make an effort," Tetralanna said. "How do you expect to retain your Balance if you neglect your body? Besides, you'll hurt the kitchen Tenders' feelings if you leave all that food uneaten. And be quick about it. We need to leave soon."

"Gredin!" someone called out from behind her, the voice nearly lost in the general hum of conversation.

Grateful for the reprieve, she twisted on the bench, hoping for the sight of Ingarra, or Beda, or even Miri te Kendar. But her relief turned to alarm when she saw Burlon striding toward her, carrying a bundle under his arm — a bundle wrapped in a length of speckled yellow paper that looked all too familiar. "I'm seeking Ingarra te Balamont," he announced as he reached their table. "Have you seen her?"

"Not since yesterday's evening meal. Is something wrong?" Gredin asked. Anxiety tightened her throat. So much else was already lost — she didn't know how she would bear it if something had befallen Ingarra, as well.

But Burlon brushed her concern aside. "Nothing's wrong. I just need a moment of her time." He looked down at Gredin's loaded plate, next to Tetralanna's near-empty one. "Are you planning to eat that?" he asked, indicating a neat little egg-and-cheese pastry that sat untouched there.

"No. Take it, if you like," she offered, glad to be rid of it.

He lifted it from the plate and popped it into his mouth, then hurried off, at speed.

"That man's manners are a disgrace," Tetralanna said. "I

should think House Bentain would be ashamed to have him represent them."

But Gredin disagreed. Burlon had come to her defense in the Director's office, however reluctantly. And he would have been justified, just now, if he had added his own reprimand to those she had already received. Still, she lacked the fortitude to directly contradict Tetralanna.

Ashamed of herself for not defending Burlon, and curious as to why he was seeking Ingarra, she watched as he dodged between tables. Several people stopped him along the way, and she saw him shake his head in sharp negation as he spoke a few words to each before moving on.

It appeared that Burlon was having a difficult day, too.

Difficult. What a hopelessly inadequate word.

"Are you listening to me?" Tetralanna demanded.

"No," Gredin replied without thinking.

It was the simple truth, but it launched Tetralanna on a reprise of her complaints, ranging from "those horrible little men in the Director's office" to Tetralanna's indignation over having been summarily ejected from the hearing. And, of course, no recitation of her woes could be complete unless she expressed her bitter disapproval of Gredin. "If I had realized how little use you were going to be, I would have insisted that they leave you home. But you're here, and I expect you to pay attention during the rehearsal so that matters can go smoothly tomorrow at the Trisectoriana. Do you suppose you can manage that, at least?"

Beleaguered, Gredin peered at her. "I will do the best I can," she said. "But do you truly not understand what has happened?"

"How can I? I was forced to leave! And even before that, you wouldn't translate!"

"No," Gredin said wearily, "I'm not talking about the Judgment. I'm talking about..." The Silencing closed her throat. Frustrated, Gredin said instead, "...what happened in the night. I'm talking about..." Again, the ability to speak abandoned her, forcing her to find other, vaguer words. "...what I *told* you when I woke you."

"Stop." Tetralanna raised her forefinger and pointed it, bringing it to a halt less than an inch from the end of Gredin's nose. "Not one more word of that nonsense. Do you hear me?" Her voice dropped to a growl, and she lowered her hand. "You will *not* ruin this event for everyone, like some spoiled child intent on having her own way. You are a Speaker, and your gyfte carries with it a deep responsibility to those around you. I will not have you distressing them and embarrassing us both in this way. You have made a bad beginning here, Gredin te Balamont, a very bad beginning. But there is time yet to redeem yourself, and I expect you to do so. For the remainder of your stay, you will comport yourself with the dignity that our gyfte requires and deserves. You will keep your emotional outbursts to yourself. You will translate for me when I call upon you to do so, and you will most certainly not involve yourself in any more behaviors that force the rest of us to apologize for your actions to the Director of Tradepoint. Do you hear me clearly?"

It was the ritual phrase. Gredin gave the required reply. "Your words reach me, First Speaker."

But hearing them was one thing. Finding sufficient Control to comply, Gredin feared, would be quite another.

Cirin decided that preparing to be honored was a rather tedious undertaking.

Waiting while a communications difficulty was worked out between Tradepoint and the Prett homeworld below, he did his best not to fidget, unwilling to give offense. The Prett were good trading partners, and he approved of how smoothly Tradepoint ran under Wyve's calm direction. That hadn't always been true of Wyve's predecessors, although they had done their best. The Prett were an odd people, so dependent on their machines, but they were generally well organized.

They were also deeply invested in protocol and procedures, which didn't always make for an easy fit when dealing with independent-minded traders from a wide range of worlds. The Mamora were a perfect example. On the face of things, dealing with a Mamoran presence on Tradepoint presented certain... challenges. Bluntly put, they stank. A more judgmental and less tolerant race than the Prett might never have granted the Mamora permission to offer their wares on Tradepoint. But the Mamora had turned out to be honest, good-natured people who always gave good value when they traded.

Moreover, if the Prett had not been open-minded enough to give them a chance to participate as traders, everyone would have been the worse for that decision, because the Mamora were the sole source of one of the most universally popular items available on Tradepoint — kithris.

Kithris was the rarest spice on Tradepoint. A single sack of kithris nuts could pay for a hundredweight of many common goods. The spice was usually sold in smaller quantities, packaged in transparent orbs that allowed the number of separate nuts to be counted and dispensed. Legend had it that, upon the occasion of Tradepoint's Octasectoriana, the shavings from a single kithris nut, dissolved in the Great Bowl, had been enough to enhance the celebratory punch consumed by attendees from over a dozen worlds.

Cirin didn't doubt it. Sweet or savory, no dish or drink he had ever encountered failed to be enhanced by the addition of a dusting of kithris. The very thought made his mouth moisten in happy anticipation. Every Vennan who had ever tasted kithris adored it, so far as he knew, and the same apparently held true for races ranging from the pleasure-loving Rodorno to the ascetic Hesch. Last sectora, the Beng had exchanged an entire cargo of grain for five hundred kithris nuts, and the general consensus on the station was that the trade had been a good one.

And that pleasure might never have been available to any of them if the Prett had been too fastidious to admit the Mamora to Tradepoint.

On the other hand, Cirin had to wonder which long-ago Director had decided to admit the Beng. It was true that they were a steady source of a variety of grains, a universal foodstuff that was stable in transport and tolerant of a wide range of storage conditions. But the Beng themselves were untrustworthy little pests. Burlon was convinced that their identical coveralls and haircuts were intentionally adopted to make it all but impossible to tell one Beng from another, the better to prevent any single Beng from being held to account for their mischief.

Cirin and Burlon sometimes made a game of it, with points awarded for any difference that could be spotted, but they often ended a stay on Tradepoint with a score of zero to zero. On rare occasions, they might see a Beng with an oddly shaped earlobe, or a scar on its chin, and once there had been a Beng with a right eye that was a darker shade of brown than its left eye. But they'd never yet spotted the same aberration on two separate trips. The same height, the same build, the same features, the same clothing: a Beng was a Beng was a—

The doors of the audience hall opened, and Tetralanna te Balamont swept in, looking for all the world as if she believed that *she* was the guest of honor. And behind her came young Gredin, chin tucked, eyes swollen and red, as if she didn't dare to claim her own shadow.

When no one made an effort to greet them, Tetralanna took up a position at Cirin's side. "The rehearsal hasn't yet begun?"

"No," he said and, feeling contrary, didn't elaborate.

"Well, that's a relief. I was afraid we would keep everyone waiting. I fear Gredin is feeling the ill effects of this morning's upheaval."

"Still not over her night-thought?" Cirin asked, with a touch of asperity.

"That as well," Tetralanna said, her expression darkening. "But I was referring to the unfortunate encounter at the Traders' Market."

Connections began to click into place in Cirin's mind: his banter with Burlon yesterday about the planned outing to the Market, then a recent, harried mind-touch he'd received a short while ago from Burlon, stating that he'd be holding an urgent meeting with the Traders concerning some incident that had transpired... and now Tetralanna's oblique comment. "Encounter?

What happened?" he asked as casually as he could manage, and saw Gredin te Balamont shrink even further into herself, tears welling anew in her eyes.

Tetralanna shook her head, looking annoyed. "I don't understand all the details. Burlon can explain it, when next you speak with him. Some disagreement involving a blue creature, an oversized bird, and an entire horde of those little, rude ones."

A Shodekekeen, a Hesch, and a clutch of Beng? That wasn't a trio of races that would normally intersect... "And Gredin witnessed whatever went on?"

"I gather," Tetralanna said in a tone of frosty disapproval, "that, whatever happened, she was at fault. Some sort of *debt* has been incurred, according to Ellis te Vell. As Voice for this delegation, I should have been consulted." Her jaw tightened. "And your friend Burlon involved himself, there in the Director's office, in language that became quite inappropriately profane. I intend to have a word with his Head of House about it, when we get home. It certainly is not the way I wish our trading partners to think of Venna."

Cirin scarcely knew which part of that alarming statement to tackle first. They'd ended up in Wyve's office? Debt had been incurred? Burlon had blasphemed — perhaps in front of Wyve, perhaps *at* Wyve? Even if he had, Tetralanna was presuming she had the right to run to House Bentain about it, telling tales? And Gredin was somehow entangled in the matter? "But what—?" he began, floundering.

At that moment, however, Wyve turned from his conference with the technicians and said, "There. That seems to have done it. Shall we begin?"

Beyond him, a column of light took form and, within it, three Prett appeared.

Cirin had seen such a thing once before, on the occasion of his first journey to the Prett homeworld. His appearance there had caused quite an uproar, complicated by his inability to communicate with the Prett. But he had dealt with initial encounters before, on other worlds, and it hadn't taken him long to establish the essentials: that he meant no harm, that he would tolerate no harm from them, and that he wanted to strike up a friendly trading interaction.

It was when he'd tried to communicate the concept of an exchange of small presents as a token of good intention that the Prett had shown quite an interest, first by expressing their enthusiasm for the idea, and then by using just such a column of light as this one to put him in contact with the individual — Wyve's several-times predecessor — who turned out to be the Director of Tradepoint. That Director had presented a flood of information: images of other races who frequented Tradepoint, a drawing that made it clear that Tradepoint hung in the sky above the Prett world where he stood, and, best of all, the first basic lessons in Tradetalk.

From there, matters had progressed quickly. As much as Cirin enjoyed the challenge of new contact and new worlds, it was a relief to stumble upon a multicultural site that was already established. And the Traders, of course, had been enthralled.

Now, in an odd sense, things had reversed themselves; this time, he was on Tradepoint, gazing at that same column of light, and it contained images of individuals standing on the Prett homeworld.

But that, too, soon grew tedious. Initially, Cirin had been patient, aware that Wyve was trying to establish the contact. Now, it became apparent that the rehearsal was more like teaching a very young child how to play pletkin. *This piece will move here. Then that piece will move there.*

He indulged them, hiding his impatience, wishing they would bring things to a close so that he could seek out Burlon, listening as Wyve outlined the order of events that would take place tomorrow, then stepping forward when he was directed to do so, and stepping back.

Matters quickly grew more interesting when it was Tetralanna's turn.

To begin with, Wyve seemed uncertain whom to address. From yesterday's welcome meeting, he knew that Tetralanna had absolutely no grasp of the Prettian language, and yet Wyve seemed strangely reluctant to address the girl who was assigned to translate. After clearing his throat — which always sounded more like an ominous rumble, coming from a Prett — Wyve said, "Cirin, will you show the Speaker where to stand for her remarks?"

"Certainly," Cirin replied, also in Prettian, "if you will first explain to me why you are ignoring the capable translator who stands at her elbow."

In three hundred sectora, Cirin had never seen a Prett blush. Given the roughness and coloration of their hide, he doubted they were capable of doing so. But Wyve managed to look abashed as he said, "I intend no disrespect. The young one has had a difficult morning. I thought perhaps it would be kind to—"

"It would be kind to let her serve her gyfte, as she has come here to do, and kinder yet to do so now, before the Voice starts demanding to know what you and I are discussing."

"As you think best," Wyve said. He shifted his focus to Gredin. "Please convey these instructions to the Voice. After Cirin has accepted the token we present to him, and has offered his thanks, the officials from my government will offer a token for the Vennan government. When they do, Tetralanna te Balamont should advance to this point on the floor and speak whatever words of acceptance she deems appropriate. Once she has done so, I will make a closing remark, the ceremony will conclude, and the hologramatic image of the Prett governmental officials will stop transmitting. Would you please ask her to come and stand here for a few moments, while we adjust our equipment?"

Gredin turned to Tetralanna and said quietly, in Vennan, "Once Cirin has expressed his gratitude, the Director's people will make a presentation to the Vennan people. At that time, you are invited to step forward to the spot the Director just indicated, and offer your words of acceptance. When you conclude your remarks, he will bring matters to a close, and the ceremony will end. He would like you to stand there briefly now, while they make a few adjustments."

Wyve gestured an invitation, and Tetralanna stepped forward onto the designated spot.

As she did, Gredin swung to face Cirin. "Please don't go," she murmured, her voice fraught with tension.

"Go? I'm right here," he said lightly.

"No. I mean, don't leave Tradepoint," she elaborated, her voice cracking.

Cirin sighed. "Calmly," he cautioned.

"Then promise."

"No. I will not disrespect you by telling you an untruth. Your fears are baseless, Gredin. I'm leaving once we're done here. And I'll be back by morning."

"Cirin, you can't. You *mustn't*!"

The words escaped loudly enough to make Tetralanna glance over her shoulder at them.

On the instant, Gredin desisted. "Your pardon, Tetralanna. Is there anything you would have me ask the Director on your behalf?"

"No." Tetralanna eyed her warily, despite the girl's humble tone and subservient manner.

Cirin caught Wyve's gaze. "Is this rehearsal concluded?" he asked in Prettian.

"Yes," Wyve replied. "We have all of the readings we'll need for a smooth broadcast tomorrow. My thanks for your patient attendance."

"Well, then, I'll walk this pair back to their rooms, and we'll see you tomorrow." He offered Tetralanna a polite crossing of his palms. "Shall we return to the enclave?" he invited in Vennan, and escorted her out, with Gredin trailing along behind.

He had assumed that walking beside Tetralanna would shield him from any more importunate requests from Gredin, and that proved to be true.

What he hadn't expected was for Tetralanna herself to stop their progress and initiate a conversation in the middle of the corridor. "I will allow Burlon to give you the details of this morning's fiasco," she stated. "But you should know that Gredin has disgraced not only House Balamont but all of Venna."

Gredin's face crumpled, and fresh tears began to track down her cheeks.

Cirin raised an eyebrow. Clearly, the girl was young and inexperienced. Tetralanna, who had no such excuse, was being insufferable and mean-spirited. He had no trouble deciding which woman he preferred.

"An entire world? I had no idea the girl was so formidable."

Tetralanna bridled. "Are you mocking me, Cirin te K'Lar?"

"Now, why would I do that, First Speaker? I can scarcely wait to hear more about Gredin's dark accomplishments."

"You and Burlon are too much alike," she groused, "going about as if you know all."

"I am more than happy to deliver you back to the enclave so that you can be free of me." *And I of you.*

"And I will be happy to be back among our people. But I need to speak to you of something else, first."

"By all means," he said, waving a hand. "Speak, since that is your gyfte."

"Burlon and I wish you to return Gredin to House Balamont when you Travel to Venna today."

Gredin gasped and took a step back. "No! I told you that... that..." Her mouth worked frantically but no more sound emerged.

Watching her struggle, Cirin found the effect eerie and off-putting.

"You see?" Tetralanna said with satisfaction. "My Silencing holds. It was not *my* failure that resulted in Gredin being banished from Tradepoint."

Astonishment nearly stole his breath. "Banished?"

Gredin began to sob.

"It was part of the Director's judgment against her. That horrible bird person demanded that Gredin leave the station, and the Director agreed. Now that the rehearsal is over, I have no more need of her, so Burlon and I have agreed that you should take her along when you go, rather than risk more trouble by allowing her to remain until the delegation's general departure."

Before Cirin could respond, Gredin darted forward and grasped his arm, clearly panicked. "Please don't make me go, Cirin. I'll stay in my chambers here. I won't come out, even for meals. I promise to do and say nothing. Just don't make me go with you, I beg you."

The girl was white-faced and frantic. Cirin felt pity for her, but he realized that Tetralanna was right, as much as he disliked admitting it. Gredin belonged at home with her Chosen, who would be able to deal with her odd notions and bring her some comfort.

Tetralanna smiled, seeming to sense that she had won.

"The schedule will be tight, but I want to be entirely in Balance for the trip," Cirin said, and gently removed the girl's hand from his sleeve. "Pack your belongings, Gredin. We'll leave as soon as I've found my Chosen and mated with her. I'll contact your private mind when I'm ready. You can meet me at the departure dais." He smiled at her. "Rest your fears, youngling. This interlude with my Chosen will ensure that our journey on the River is an easy one."

Gredin began to keen.

Tetralanna gave her a critical look. "Control yourself, Gredin. You've wasted enough of everyone's time. Some creature could pass by and hear you. Do you want Cirin to have to explain why you are carrying on like this?"

Cirin gestured at the hallway. "Tetralanna's right. We aren't the only ones around, Gredin. Some of the delegations aren't particularly nice, and even the friendly ones have their own plans and schemes. The Prett keep a decent lid on the pot, but we'd all do well to be quiet and watchful when we walk these corridors."

Tetralanna looked alarmed. "Are you saying we're in danger?"

"I'm saying no one but the Prett really cares whether we're happy here, and there's danger to be had if we act foolishly enough to invite it. Tradepoint is a big place. You can never be sure who's staying in the next enclave or walking down the next cross-corridor. For all our sakes, I suggest we finish this walk in silence, so that I can pay proper attention to our surroundings."

On the instant, Tetralanna closed her mouth as if her lips had been sewn shut. Gredin gave the outward appearance of doing the same, but Cirin suddenly became aware of her tapping at his private mind, soliciting his silent attention.

He could sense her urgency, steeped in concern and distress, but it was an urgency born of ignorance. Lacking a gyfte for

Traveling the River, she had no idea what it was like for him, and his attempts to explain had clearly failed to persuade her. The only way to put her fears to rest was to make the journey and return her to her House. When she saw that her fears were baseless, she would realize that her night-thought had been no more than the troubled imaginings of an over-stimulated mind.

And so Cirin ignored her mind touch. It was the only true kindness he could offer.

Fortunately, they encountered no one on their walk back to the enclave. It amused him to see Tetralanna dart fearful glances at every corridor junction, as if someone might be waiting to leap out at her. Tetralanna's courage, unlike her arrogance, was only a thin veneer, and the environment of Tradepoint had quickly eroded it.

When they reached the enclave entrance, he keyed the door open and stepped into the antechamber. The two women followed, Tetralanna moving forward practically on his heels, her movements jerky with nerves. Despite Burlon's explanation about the bio-mist, she was clearly not yet comfortable with the process. Gredin, however, moved slowly, like one in a daze, and the doors nearly closed on her as she entered the antechamber.

With both sets of doors closed, the decontamination process filled the air around them with its fine, cool mist. He inhaled the familiar scent, and felt a faint dampness linger for a moment on his nose and lips before it evaporated. Tetralanna coughed several times, wringing her hands nervously. Gredin's breathing hitched as she tried to breathe deeply, and Cirin felt a renewed sense of pity for her.

The cycle finished and the interior doors opened, allowing the sounds of the enclave to reach them, and anticipation lifted Cirin's spirits. He bowed slightly to both of the women, crossing his palms. "I'm off to seek my Chosen. Gredin, stay alert for my call or, if you finish packing before you hear from me, make your way to the departure dais and await me there."

He left them then, eager to find Hayla. Her kisses would be a fine remedy for the taste this situation had left in his mouth.

Faced with her failure, Gredin felt a sick roiling in her stomach. Hot tears stung her eyes, and her nose had begun to run.

Tetralanna made a sound of disgust. "Cirin cannot possibly return soon enough to suit me. As the Power is my witness, Gredin, I have never seen anyone so undone. I am profoundly disappointed in your lack of discipline, and I plan to inform Unter that the House's funds have been very ill-spent on Frake te Santelle."

Gredin didn't waste her breath on an apology. No words were going to placate Tetralanna or change her decree that Gredin leave Tradepoint with Cirin. And it wasn't just Tetralanna who wanted her gone. Burlon agreed, and that had been enough to persuade Cirin.

Despair rose within her in a towering wave. What could she do? Burlon and Cirin were the organizers, and Tetralanna was the appointed Voice. Combined, the three of them were the recognized authority within the Vennan enclave.

Gredin knew that if she appealed to Ingarra and Beda to intercede on her behalf, they would try. But Tetralanna's Silencing made it impossible for her to explain by telling them of Venna's destruction, and their efforts were bound to fail without that vital information.

Tetralanna's voice interrupted her thoughts. "There. You see?" She pointed. "The departure dais is much closer to our chambers than the one we arrived on. It won't take you long to pack, so let us find a spot where you can wait for Cirin."

"He and I will be journeying to our deaths."

Tetralanna grimaced. "Stop being so dramatic, Gredin. Cirin is First Traveler of House K'lar. There is no one more competent to conduct you safely back to House Balamont."

"You are wrong."

"And you are a silly girl," Tetralanna snapped. "The sooner you disappear from my sight, the happier I will be."

...disappear from my sight...

She stumbled to a halt, struck by Tetralanna's words. Yes! Cirin believed that he could only return in time for tomorrow's Trisectoriana by leaving soon. If she could disappear, she could find somewhere to hide until time ran short and Cirin was forced to leave without her.

Gredin desperately wished that Cirin believed her warning so that he would remain safe, as well, but she had done all she could to persuade him not to go. And perhaps, without the burden of transporting her, he would discover she was right and still be able to return. She knew little of the River. And, as Tetralanna had pointed out, Cirin te K'lar *was* a First Traveler...

"Keep moving, girl. You have little enough time before your departure."

Gredin moved on, thinking feverishly. Could she find a place where they would not think to look for her? The departure dais was already clearly in sight, ahead of them. The crowd was thicker, too, as several dozen people worked busily. Gredin spotted a loom being assembled, and realized that it must be the area where the craft demonstrations would be held during the reception.

"Tetralanna!" a man called, waving his arm energetically in a bid for her attention. "We need your advice. Partha thinks these tables are too closely placed, but I believe we'll run out of space if we put them any farther apart. Your opinion would be much appreciated. Let me explain what-all is entailed…"

Still talking, he tried to maneuver around several knots of people who were engaged in a spirited discussion. Balked in his attempt to reach Tetralanna, the man hesitated for a moment, then moved sideways to bound up the steps of the untenanted dais. Venturing onto its unoccupied surface, he took three steps toward Tetralanna —

— and his presence triggered the dais's biodome. The floor vibrated, and the curved walls rose into place, with the man inside.

Tetralanna gasped, her hand rising to her throat. Other people reacted, some hurrying toward the dome, others retreating swiftly from it, in a crosscurrent of contrary movement. In moments, Gredin and Tetralanna were engulfed. People vied in their attempts to gain Tetralanna's attention, a babble of questions and concerns clashing in the air.

Gredin eased back, allowing one, two, four people to come between herself and the besieged First Speaker. Then, unheeded, she turned and slipped away through the milling crowd.

Life was good.

Fresh from mating with Hayla, and knowing that a journey upon the River was his next task and privilege, Cirin strode through the crowd in the reception hall with vigor, brimming with Balance. He felt a slight twinge of guilt over larking off to Venna and back while Burlon stayed behind, unaided, stuck with supervising the details and inevitable complications of the Trisectoriana. But it was only overnight. He would be back with ample time to recuperate before the ceremony.

His immediate plan was straightforward: scoop up Gredin, whisk her home to House Balamont, return to his own chambers in House K'lar for a meal and a rest, deliver Hayla's little present to her mother, and then return to Tradepoint.

There was just one snag. He was now a mere ten steps away from the departure dais… and Gredin was nowhere in sight.

Cirin supposed he ought to be annoyed. After all, he was primed and ready, and the girl was nowhere to be seen. But it was hard to feel too upset while his body was still humming with pleasure from Hayla's loving attentions. Of course, if he'd known Gredin was going to be late, he and Hayla could have lingered a bit more over their coupling... but hurrying had been fun, too, and neither he nor his Chosen had by any means gone unsatisfied.

Conscience nagged, however, because additional time spent here now meant additional delay in his return. Better to alert the girl that it was time to be on their way.

Focusing, he reached out to her private mind. =Gredin?=

But he received no response.

That was peculiar. Was Tetralanna's Silencing inhibiting the girl's ability to respond? Disconcerted, he reached out again, this time to Tetralanna te Balamont. =Voice?=

=I am the Voice,= came the smooth reply.

=And I am First Traveler,= he informed her, amused and annoyed by her smug air. =Where is your girl?=

=My...?=

=Your kinswoman. The translator. The girl you wish me to escort back to House Balamont. I am standing at the departure dais — and she is not. So, I ask again. Where is your girl?=

The undercurrent of self-satisfaction dissolved, replaced for a moment by flustered agitation, then a stern wash of Control. =She is not with me.=

=Nor with me,= he pointed out again, =which is a problem, unless you have changed your mind and wish me to leave her behind.=

=No! I thought she had gone to gather her belongings.=

=Well, Voice, I cannot transport that which I do not possess. You will just have to go on managing her yourself, here, if you cannot produce her.=

=No, please, a... a small delay. I will seek her out and have her with you soon.=

=*How* soon? I am ready to begin my journey.=

= Fetch a cool drink for yourself from the kitchens,= she urged. =By the time you have consumed it, I hope to have her with you.=

=Hope?= It was clear to him, by now, that the Voice had completely lost track of Gredin. And, although it afforded him a certain wry amusement to prod the humorless woman about the situation, he suddenly recalled that he had more serious news to convey. =I have been contacted by Director Wyve,= he informed Tetralanna. =When you finally locate your girl, tell her the Prett clinic confirms that the Hesch's foot is indeed broken, as she feared. As a result, House Balamont will be facing a substantial fine.= He couldn't resist adding, =I imagine Unter will be quite displeased.=

=Yes. Well. Kindly provide Unter with the details while you are there. And,= she added with asperity, =Gredin is most certainly not *my* girl.=

=She is your kinswoman. And Balamont is not my House, so communication with Unter about the Judgment is your responsibility, not mine. After all, as you have made abundantly clear, you *are* First Speaker of Balamont, and Voice of this delegation.=

Cold silence.

=I will be departing shortly,= he concluded. =If Gredin arrives before then, I will gladly convey her. If not, I will see you tomorrow at the Trisectoriana. For now, a fine day to you, Tetralanna.= And he disengaged the contact before she could protest further.

Slowly, methodically, he swept his gaze over the room, eyeing busy group after busy group. Nowhere among them did he see the errant translator.

He turned his attention next to his First Friend. =Burlon?=

=Cirin,= came the gratifyingly prompt reply. =Still here, are you?=

=About to leave. It sounds as if there was quite a tangle at the Traders' Market. Not that Wyve was generous with the details but...=

That drew a heavy sigh from Burlon. =The Beng shoved

their way into the Shodekeen maartza and frightened Gredin so badly that she Sent to get away from them. When she did, she stepped on a Hesch's foot.=

=I suppose you've already heard Wyve's update from the clinic?=

=Yes. Unter te Balamont won't be pleased. That's a hefty fine.=

The comment made Cirin grin. =That's what I just pointed out to the Voice. She wanted *me* to break the news to him. Imagine!=

=Let her attend to her own House's troubles,= Burlon responded. =Had she managed to calm herself, by the time the two of you spoke? Some impatient fellow tried to walk across the departure dais, here in the enclave. He set off the dome, of course, and Tetralanna panicked, as did half of the delegation — as if it wouldn't retract on its own shortly. You didn't hear about it?=

Cirin groaned. =No, I was with Hayla. I doubt we'd have noticed if Tradepoint itself had fallen from the skies.= He tried to marshal his thoughts. =So now, is there anything more I should know before I leave?=

=Not really. Is there any particular task you've shirked that I'll need to complete in your absence?= Burlon asked.

=Of course not. I have managed everything capably, as I always do. Just know that you may still have the translator girl underfoot. After the rehearsal, Tetralanna asked me to take Gredin home. Apparently that's something the two of you came up with?=

=In a sense. Tetralanna suggested it, and it seemed a fine enough plan.=

=Perhaps so, but I'm leaving soon, and Tetralanna doesn't know where the girl has gotten to, so I'll likely be going without her.=

=Well, I suppose it leaves us no worse off than we were before.=

=That depends. If the Voice can't find her by morning, the Silencing will wear off without an opportunity to reinstate it. That could certainly cause a difficulty.=

=So see to it that you return before it happens. Once Gredin sees that you've been home and back, she'll have to accept that her night-thought was just a piece of foolishness.= Burlon chuckled. =Bring her Chosen along. *That* should convince her.=

It was an amusing suggestion. =Not a bad plan. I'll see what I can do. Meanwhile, be well, Burlon. I'll see you tomorrow, before the Trisectoriana.=

=Indeed. Tomorrow. Fair Travels to you.=

With that attended to, Cirin considered whether to start on his way, since a scanning glance informed him that there was still no sign of the girl. If he were willing to wait a while longer, he supposed he could contact the historian and offer an account of how he had first chanced upon the Prett world and, from there, Tradepoint... But no. He could just as well do that in the morning, or even after the delegation had concluded its stay on Tradepoint and returned home. There seemed little point in standing around, waiting for Gredin to put in an appearance. If she was likely to cause difficulty for Burlon, it would be different. But the girl was Silenced, for now. She might even be able to draw some genuine pleasure from her last full day on Tradepoint, tomorrow, once he'd returned to set her mind at ease.

So decided, Cirin took one final, fond glance at the anthill of activity around him, then mounted the departure dais.

The dome descended and Cirin, embracing his gyfte, launched himself upon the River.

=Gredin?=

No response.

=Gredin?=

Walking toward the kitchen, Tetralanna found that she could not recall a day in her life that had been longer, or more frustrating, or more physically and mentally exhausting.

It was due, in large part, to this place. This *Tradepoint*. What sort of notion was that, to build a place entirely of metal and hang it high in the sky, away from the gardens and comfortable dwellings that made life so pleasant? What sort of people conceived of such a thing, let alone built it? And what sort of people willingly frequented such a place?

But the single greatest aggravation of the day was indisputably Gredin, who was somehow managing to create as much disruption by her unexplained absence as she had inflicted all morning through her equally annoying presence.

How *dare* the girl vanish?

=Gredin?=

Still no response. And this was at least the fiftieth attempt she had made to reach the girl's private mind, to no avail.

It was maddening.

When she reached the entrance to the kitchen, delicate aromas rose to greet her, summoning a wisp of appetite despite the tensions of the day.

Well, if the kitchen Tenders could carry out their tasks, so could she. Resolutely, Tetralanna prepared to carry on, then hesitated on the threshold, reaching out with her mind for one last attempt.

=Gredin!=

And again was met with silence.

Keegan's fingers were beginning to cramp.

Ignoring the pain, he smiled encouragingly at the woman who had just seated herself across from him. "Your name?"

"I am Nunellin te Vell. My gyfte is Making. I weave," she announced, smiling. She touched the shawl wrapping her shoulders, and the harsh lights of the dining hall caused the gold threads shot through the pale green fabric to glitter and shine with her movements. "I also have a minor gyfte for Music, but the music of my loom brings me the greatest satisfaction."

"It seems that you and the others of your House have been spreading the word amongst yourselves about my questions. My thanks for that."

The woman's grey-green eyes danced. "Oh, we of House Vell prize cooperation, Keegan te Fliss. We love nothing better than to help a task be done smoothly and well." She chuckled. "Besides, one would have to have been dozing not to notice that you've asked each of us the same questions for your history." She motioned at the paper upon which he had carefully written her responses. "You may add the fact that I am Unchosen. And now your work with House Vell is at an end."

Surprised, Keegan made the notation and laid his pen aside. "My thanks, Nunellin. Are you certain everyone from House Vell has spoken with me?"

"Quite certain," she assured him. "There are not so many of us here from Vell that we could fail to know each other by now." She grinned. "In truth, we are becoming somewhat tired of speaking only with each other at meals, and so we have agreed to divide into small groups tonight and seek the acquaintance of those from other Houses, and listen to their stories." Her merry gaze strayed to his writing tools. "Perhaps we of Vell have a bit of historian in us, as well."

"You and your House have certainly helped my task to go 'smoothly and well' today."

She laughed and rose from her bench. "Just so, Keegan te Fliss, just so. If there is anything more you require, you have only to ask, and we will be most happy to assist you further." She adjusted her shawl. "I would enjoy visiting with you more, but evening meal is not far off, and we of Vell need to review this plan for inviting ourselves to others' tables. I will hope to speak with you another time," she said and offered him her crossed palms.

"That would please me greatly." Standing, he gave her a slight bow and crossed his palms in return, then watched as Nunellin rejoined her group, which moved off in a cloud of chatter.

Keegan flexed the fingers of his right hand, spreading them wide, then closing them into a fist again and again. For his account of the thirty-seven members of House Vell, he had written in as small a script as he could manage, to conserve both paper and ink. Now, after a long afternoon of labor, he was feeling the effects of that decision.

Once his hand felt more normal, he packed up his supplies and began the long walk back to his sleeping chamber. Last night, he had made the error of taking his writing supplies along to a meal, only to discover that those with whom he ate were curious — too curious — about his gyfte and what he was recording. While he welcomed their interest, he had spent so much time answering questions and guarding his papers and other supplies from being touched that he had not finished eating until well after his dining companions had gone about their business.

Today's work was too precious to risk. He wanted everything safely stored away before he ventured out to seek companionship at evening meal.

He had walked only half the distance, skirting around various groups who stood chattering, and dodging others who crossed his path, when he encountered a group of six people carrying a heavy column of beautifully carved wood. It was clearly the work of an exceptionally talented Maker — one he would look forward to meeting as he continued to chronicle the other members of the delegation.

But that meant he would also need to speak to the blue creature again, or find some other source of paper, as well as purchasing ink and pens. And to do that, he would have to persuade Burlon to allow him to return to the Traders' Market, despite the tumultuous events of the morning.

He sighed heavily at the memory of Gredin weeping at the Judgment. He could only hope that Tetralanna was not adding to the young translator's burdens and distress...

As if the mere thought of her name had attracted her, Tetralanna te Balamont's imperious voice rang out behind him. "Keegan te Fliss! A moment, if you please!"

The words were more a command than a request, but he fastened a pleasant expression on his face before turning around to deal with Tetralanna for the second time that afternoon.

She bustled up to him, all angular energy, a few wisps

straying from the elaborate braiding of her hair, her pale blue eyes flashing. "Have you come across that accursed girl yet?"

Keegan took a step back. "Your pardon?"

Tetralanna's face was a portrait of annoyance. "Gredin. Have you seen her?" she demanded, then looked past him to scan the faces of the people moving around them.

"No, I haven't seen Gredin since the..." Well, perhaps it would be better not to mention the Judgment in the Director's office. "...since this morning," he amended. "Have you lost sight of her?"

"Of course I have, or I wouldn't be asking. She's nowhere about, which is as worrisome as it is vexing."

"Perhaps she's in her chambers, resting. Today has been difficult for her."

Tetralanna gave him a withering look. "Today has been difficult *because* of her. And I assure you, our rooms were the first place I looked, and I have rechecked them repeatedly since then." She shook her head. "Gredin has behaved so thoughtlessly that I am at a loss for how to deal with her."

It seemed that, given the opportunity, Tetralanna was prepared to continue her list of complaints indefinitely. To forestall her, Keegan said, "I regret not being able to provide more assistance, First Speaker," then searched his mind for anything more he could add that would neither offend nor encourage the agitated woman.

But Tetralanna turned away without a word of farewell and strode off, her head swiveling from side to side as she continued the search for her quarry.

Spirits low, Keegan watched her depart, then walked the rest of the way to his featureless metal door, anxious to reach a sanctuary from the atmosphere of strife that Tetralanna had left in her wake.

Entering, he keyed the lights on, reveling in the sudden quiet created by the closing of the door. Keegan placed his notebook and pen roll on the polished metal surface of the large table Burlon and Cirin had provided, and simply stood there, empty handed, shoulders slumped.

This room was now all the home he had. He was grateful for the small touches that softened it, such as the teal cushion on the bench, and his storage cabinet, which was painted pale yellow and decorated with a rainbow of blooming flowers... although, in a way, those graceful embellishments of color and craft only served to emphasize how much he had lost.

Drawing a shaky breath, he powered the tabletop luminth before returning to the room's entry door to switch off the blazing overhead lights.

The glow of the luminth was a welcome balm. Keegan hesitated, torn between easing his mind with a period of rest on his sleeping mat or easing his body in the bathing chamber provided by the Prett. With its lack of a tub, it was far from the comfort of the baths in House Fliss, but all Vennans loved the touch of water on their skin, and the cascade of water in the chamber was a novelty, like standing in the gardens at home beneath a warm, soaking rain.

He wished, not for the first time, that he had a Chosen. Someone to listen. Someone he could comfort and be comforted by, in turn. Someone to fill the empty spaces in this solitary life his gyfte had carved out for him.

Keegan squared his shoulders. Self-pity would not serve him well. He had built a good life around his gyfte; he would continue to do so and, in the process, make himself useful to Gredin and the rest of the delegation in the hard days to come. It would suffice. It would have to.

Eschewing the emptiness of his bed mat, Keegan decided on the baths, although the discrepancy between the Vennan expectation for such a chamber and what *this* chamber could provide made him shake his head. Perhaps he should just adopt the Prettian term for the small, functional room: *hygiene facili-*

ties. But the phrase seemed as awkward and strange as the room itself.

With a sigh, Keegan opened the door, triggering the bright light in the ceiling.

And gaped because there, huddled on the perforated floor of the bathing cubicle, fully dressed, was Gredin te Balamont.

The translucent door of the cubicle did little to hide the sight of her contorted body from him. Slender arms encircled her long legs, and her head rested on her upbent knees. It was a childlike pose, belied by her unfurled hlao. And spread before her on the shining metal flooring, incongruously, was a pattern formed from a dozen colored stones.

Stones! Where had stones come from, on this sterile, Prett-made station? They gleamed in the light, green and blue and cream and rose, earth colors, reminders of the natural world…

But his attention returned to the girl. Despite the sudden flood of light, Gredin remained motionless, seeming oblivious to his arrival. Was she ill? Injured? He triggered the door panel to slide aside. "Gredin?" he said quietly and reached in to touch her shoulder.

At his touch, she jerked away violently, pressing herself into the unyielding corner, and the movement of her soft-clad feet sent the stones skittering in all directions. "No!" she cried, and lunged forward, reaching for the scattered stones, gathering them up in quick, darting snatches as if she feared he might steal them away.

Startled, Keegan drew back. "Gredin, it's only me. Keegan. I won't hurt you."

Abruptly, she stopped moving, blinking at him blearily as recognition dawned. "Your pardon!" Her breath came in gasps. "I thought you were…" She hesitated, biting her lip.

"You thought I was Tetralanna."

A guilty nod of the head. Quickly, she counted over the stones in her hand, like a water hen tallying its chicks, then looked around wildly.

"There," Keegan said, pointing. "In the corner."

With a grateful nod, she leaned forward, extended her arm, and reclaimed the errant stone. Then, as he watched in curiosity, she funneled them all into a little cloth pouch, and slid that into her pocket. Only then did she lean back again, letting the wall support her.

"So you *are* hiding from Tetralanna?"

"Yes." Gredin rubbed her swollen eyes. "Has evening meal concluded?" she asked, on a note of cautious hope.

"No. Indeed, it has not yet begun."

She bit her lip. "Then please let me stay here a while longer, Keegan. I can't let Tetralanna find me. She intends to make me go back to Venna, and I cannot go. I will not go. I *dare* not because—" Her voice choked off abruptly.

"Because Venna is gone," he finished for her, matter-of-factly. Rising to his feet, he offered her a hand. "Come out of there, Gredin. Since you are staying, I can at least offer you somewhere more comfortable to sit."

"But Tetralanna is looking for me."

"If she comes to my door, it will take her but a few steps more to look in here."

She peered up at him, absorbing the tone of his words. "You aren't going to tell her."

It was a statement, not a question. He answered anyway. "No. I am not."

Gredin took his hand, rose stiffly, and let him lead her back into the main room.

Keegan settled her on the sole bench. Seating himself on his neatly made sleeping mat, he asked, "How long have you been here?"

Gredin flinched. "Since we returned from the rehearsal. I slipped away from Tetralanna after a man triggered the dome."

Keegan nodded. "I heard about that, while I was interviewing those of House Vell."

"House Vell? Why? Are they doing something special at the reception?"

"Yes and no. Quite a few are demonstrating crafts. Fairly few from their House Traveled here to Tradepoint, and so I asked Ellis te Vell if I might begin my lists with them." He nodded toward his notebook. "We now have a written record of each of their names, along with their major gyftes and whether or not they have their Chosen here with them."

"A written record..." Gredin stared at him. "You still believe me," she asked, "after everything that happened today?"

Keegan shrugged. "I am sorry for today's events at the Market and in the Director's office, but none of that affects what I believe about you." He captured her gaze again. "Gredin, you glowed. The Power spoke to you. Only a fool would ignore the Power's voice." He offered her a wan smile. "I may be only an historian, but I am not a fool."

Silence held between them for a time. Then Gredin said, "I owe you a great debt, Keegan te Fliss."

It was his turn to stare. "Why would you say such a thing? I have done nothing."

"You have believed me," she said. "You have allied yourself with me. And now you are sheltering me from those who do not and have not."

"As I said, I am not a fool. But you owe me nothing. You did nothing to force my choice, Gredin. You simply told the truth. There is no debt between us."

Gredin's chin lifted. "You are providing sanctuary, as we speak."

Keegan waved her tribute away, but his curiosity was stirred. "How did you decide on my chambers as your hiding place?"

"I knew of nowhere else to go," Gredin said simply. "I couldn't very well use my own chambers, since I share them with Tetralanna. And I couldn't use Beda and Ingarra's. They are my Guides, and so that would be among the first places anyone who knows me would think to look. I thought about seeking a place to hide at the Traders' Market, since it was certain that Tetralanna would never willingly venture there. But given my encounters with the Beng, and the harm I caused the Hesch, I was afraid they would report me to Prett security if they saw me, and Prett security would report me to Wyve, and Wyve would…"

"…report you to Tetralanna."

"Yes." She sighed again, sounding exhausted. Faint lavender shadows underscored her eyes. He supposed she'd had little peace of mind since receiving the Power's message, and the current day had been long and troubled.

"And so you thought of me?" he prompted.

"Well, no, actually. I hadn't yet decided on a hiding place, but then the dome was triggered, and Tetralanna was distracted… and your chamber was the only place I knew of that was close to the dais, other than my own rooms. I only intend to stay here until I can think of somewhere better. I don't wish to cause trouble for you."

"You are welcome to stay here for as long as you have need," Keegan assured her, and saw with regret that his offer brought a brim of tears to her eyes.

"I need to hide until Cirin leaves."

"Gredin…"

"I swear by the Power, I tried to convince him not to go."

"Gredin, listen…"

"I am so afraid for him." A single tear meandered down her cheek. "I know he is a First Traveler, but still… Should I try again to warn him? I don't know what I could say that I haven't already tried, but…"

"Hush. Listen to me. Cirin has already gone."

He expected her to be relieved. Instead, she bowed her head and began to sob.

Keegan wanted to curse. This young woman, little more than a green girl, had passed the Power's message to those in authority, and had received nothing in return but disbelief and impatience. And yet, even now, she had pity to spare for Cirin te K'lar.

He stood up. "Come and lie down."

"No, I should go. Tetralanna will be angry with you if she finds me here."

"There are worse fates than Tetralanna's anger, and you are in no fit state to withstand her wrath," Keegan said. "Lie down and rest. I will guard the door. And when the time for evening meal arrives, I will venture out and see what news I can gather."

With a tremulous sigh, Gredin allowed him to escort her to the bed mat, blotting her eyes with a trembling hand as she walked. Keegan waited until she had stretched out on the thickly quilted mat, then drew the covers up to her chin.

Gredin's lashes were already fluttering closed. "My deepest thanks, Keegan te Fliss."

"No need for thanks. After all that you and I have been through today, we are friends, wouldn't you say?"

"I freely acknowledge both our friendship and my debt to you."

He smiled, touched by her stubborn honesty. "Sleep well, Gredin. For now, at least, you are safe."

"Ingarra? Someone is seeking you."

Ingarra looked up from her needlework, somewhat dazed. She had been sewing since midday meal, her gaze and imagination fixed on the project that was growing in size and beauty beneath her hands. It was nearly complete, but she felt a little shaky, as she sometimes did when the work enveloped her, enthralling her spirit at the expense of her physical vessel. It took an effort of will to divert her attention from it now, but she made herself smile and say, "Thank you, Petron. Where am I needed?"

"Come with me," he invited. "I will show you the way."

And so she rose and set her work aside, draping the tucks and folds of the lovely garment so that it wouldn't wrinkle. Then she followed Petron through the twisty little maze of sleep alcoves, each separated from its neighbor by no more than a panel of cloth hung over one of the many ropes that criss-crossed Balamont's common space. "Such a bother not to be able to Send," she grumbled. "I am sorry to force such a tedious errand upon you."

"Don't trouble yourself about it," Petron said cheerfully. "I am only here at Tradepoint to accompany Dedelon, so I am glad to be of actual service to someone, in however minor a way." As they rounded another length of passageway, the metal door that separated House Balamont's space from the reception hall came into view. "There. The woman who wishes to speak with you is waiting, just beyond the door."

"My thanks," Ingarra said, and added, "You and Dedelon should seek us out, at evening meal. Beda and I would be pleased to have the chance to speak with you both."

"Indeed," he said, and turned away to retrace his steps.

Ingarra kept walking toward the big door, wondering who she would find beyond it. When a similar summons had reached her, earlier in the day, she had found herself in astonished conversation with Burlon te Bentain, and his errand had kept her busy, ever since. She wouldn't have been surprised if he was returning now to see how she was progressing with her work, but Petron said that the person awaiting her was a woman.

Still, it wasn't likely to be Gredin. Ingarra had been trying to reach her ever since Burlon's brief visit, with no success. Well, the rehearsal had been scheduled for some time after midday meal. She supposed it could have dragged on longer than anticipated. What did she know of such things? But the day was waning, and she was growing concerned.

The door loomed large, opening obediently at Ingarra's approach, and her spirits rose. She had feared that she might find Tetralanna waiting, thinking too well of herself to make her way through Balamont's crowded quarters. But no, the person standing there was Miri te Kendar, the kindly kitchen Tender who had dined with them last night. Beaming, Ingarra stepped out to greet her... then hesitated when she saw the look of agitation on Miri's face.

"What's gone amiss?" Ingarra asked, reaching out a hand to her. "How can I help?"

Miri's face crumpled further. "I am fine," she said. "But I fear the same cannot be said of Gredin."

A great stillness came over Ingarra, halting the forward progress of her feet, squeezing the air from her chest. "Is she hurt? Beda is a Healer. I can summon him—"

But Miri was shaking her head. "No, no, I didn't mean to frighten you like that. I don't think any bodily harm has come to her. But, oh, Ingarra, if you could have heard how that woman was talking about her…"

"What woman?" she asked. But she knew. Somehow, deep inside, she already knew. "You are speaking of Tetralanna?"

Miri bobbed her head in assent. "Yes. The Voice," she managed hoarsely. "I was working in the kitchens, preparing things for tomorrow night, and she — the Voice — came in to see how we were getting on. Rugen te Torr asked her when the next tour of the Traders' Market would be leaving, and she said there would be no more tours, and that no one was allowed to leave the enclave because… because Gredin had gotten into trouble with the Director of Tradepoint."

Ingarra pressed her hand to her chest. "How? What happened?"

"The Voice said that Gredin Sent."

"Well? What if she did? I know they've asked us not to, but would it be so terrible?"

"I don't know." Miri hugged herself. "The Voice made it *sound* terrible. She said that Gredin and several creatures were called before the Director."

"Creatures?"

Miri shrugged unhappily. "It's what she said. I suppose she meant traders from some other world. I gave her a message for Gredin, saying I was sorry for her trouble, and that I would set aside some of the Kendar pastries that she liked… but I haven't been able to put the matter out of my head, and so I came to find you. I hoped I might find Gredin with you or, if not, I at least wanted to be certain that you knew what was happening. I'm sorry to trouble you, but..."

"No, you did the right thing, and I am in your debt," Ingarra assured her. "Beda and I will find Gredin. And when we do, I'll be sure to let you know, so that you can end this day with a lighter spirit." She crossed her palms with sincerity. "My thanks to you, Miri. You have been a good friend to us, this day. But I will take my leave of you now. I must go to Beda, so that we can seek out our girl."

Despite having slept the remainder of the afternoon away, Gredin still felt profoundly weary. Keegan had gently awakened her before he left for evening meal, promising to bring back food and whatever news he could manage to obtain, and she appreciated his thoughtfulness. It would have been alarming to wake alone, with no way of knowing how far the day had progressed or how long he had been gone.

She was already quite sufficiently alarmed, for it was clear that she was still being sought. Tetralanna's mind touch demanded her attention again and again, troubling her sleep, forcing her to harden her will and resist the impulse to reply. Troubling in a different way, Ingarra and Beda had been seeking her, as well, but she was reluctant to involve them. There was nothing they could do to help. Better for them to be able to say, quite honestly, that they had no idea where she was, and had not been in contact with her.

Seeking comfort, she reached into her pocket and withdrew her pouch of stones, pouring them out onto her palm. But one of them bounced off another and careened away, striking the metal floor and rolling beneath the table with an audible clatter.

That never happened. Distressed, she put the others back into the pouch, set the pouch carefully aside, and crawled after the runaway.

She had watched it roll beneath the table, but now it was nowhere to be seen. It wasn't until she had fitted herself entirely under the table that she found it, tucked behind one of the table legs. When she reclaimed it, she saw that it was the same stone that had initially evaded her in the bathing chamber.

"Are you trying to hide from me?" she asked it, and examined it more closely. It was the stone she had found in the Balamont orchards, an odd one shaped like some creature's tooth, broad at the top and pointed at the bottom. "Or would you prefer to bite me?"

Its lacy bands of pattern were primarily beige and white and tan, forming intricate loops and swirls of subtle color. Still, one edge of the stone boasted intense reds and pretty pinks, as if the stone could not quite make up its mind whether it longed to be admired or wished to go unnoticed. "Don't go straying off again," she admonished, and crawled back over to Keegan's sleep mat.

But the stone almost slipped from her grasp again as she opened the mouth of the pouch.

Sobered, she closed her fingers gently over it, cradling it, and closed her eyes. "Don't you want to be safe with the others?" she asked. "Or are you like me?"

She hadn't meant to say that. She didn't know where the question had come from. However, now that it had been spoken aloud, it lingered. Why was she here, hidden away while everyone else was gathering for evening meal? She could stand up, right now, and walk out to join them. Ingarra and Beda would be pleased to see her. Miri would welcome her, as well. Gathering together was what Vennans *did*. Holding herself apart like this was unnatural. Perhaps Tetralanna and Burlon were right, after all. Perhaps Traveling the River had unsettled her.

Perhaps her night-thought had been nothing but a groundless notion that came to her in her sleep...

Gredin's fingers relaxed.

And the stone wriggled free.

This time it fell no farther than her lap, where it rested, gleaming in the light.

Defiant.

And she knew. Rather, she admitted to herself what she had already known. There would be no carefree meal in the reception hall for her, tonight. Her people were out there, the survivors, and their safety depended on her. And she could only keep them safe if *she* was safe.

That was why she had run away.

That was why, for now, she must *stay* away.

With solemn care, she picked up the stubborn stone and pressed it to her cheek. "I will do what I must," she promised. Then she slid the little tooth-stone into her pouch, put that into her pocket, and drew her jacket tightly around herself. The quarters she shared with Tetralanna had been a pleasant temperature, but Keegan's room felt uncomfortably cool. How did the Prett adjust a room's temperature? They probably relied on some mysterious sort of *griimoni*, whereas Venna Houses entrusted such matters to the attentive skills of their Weather-gyfted members...

That thought awoke a sharp new worry: what could those with gyfte of Weather do on Tradepoint? There was no sky here, no clouds, no sunlight, no rain. And what of people with a gyfte for Growing? Here, they would have no access to plants, or good, rich soil. One of Beda's major gyftes was Growing. How could he exercise it, on this metal world of Tradepoint?

Then she heard the near-silent whoosh of the room door opening, and fear raced through her like a poison.

It was Keegan, returning from evening meal.

"Good," he said. "You're still awake. No, don't get up. I've brought you something to eat." He advanced into the room, balancing a tray of small dishes, one of which had steam rising from it. "I wasn't sure what you might like, but you really should try to have something." He set the tray on the floor next to the bed mat, then sat cross-legged next to it.

Gredin surveyed the tray. Was she hungry? Her stomach felt uncertain, perhaps from nerves and grief. Something warm and nourishing might steady her.

The tray held an array of dishes. A bowl of creamy fish chowder, hot and inviting. Two small servings of sliced tinta, the hot-pink flesh of the fruit deceiving, since tinta was mild and sweet. A little basket of braided bread rolls, golden and fragrant. A tall glass of fruited water.

"I hope you haven't eaten, Keegen, for there is more here than I expect I can finish."

"Oh, I sampled a few bites, here and there, as I moved from table to table." He plucked a breadroll from the basket and broke off a small piece. "But I'll nibble while you eat, to keep you company. And I brought tinta for us both."

Gredin picked up the soup bowl and inhaled the steam rising from its surface…

"Did you enjoy the beach, nifflin?" Ingarra asked, spreading a cloth over the shaded table under the frond-trees. A moment later, the dishes and utensils that would comprise their midday meal appeared on the dark blue cloth.

Beda gave a hum of pleasure. "Fish chowder! Nice and thick, too, just the way I like it. We'll have to be sure to thank the Holding's kitchen Tenders before we leave."

Gredin could hardly sit still to eat. The warm breeze ruffled her curls, while waves advanced and retreated on the fine white sand, like fingers beckoning her to come back and search for more treasures. She dug into her pocket. "Look! I found a beautiful shell. I'm going to take it home and show it to Dreff…"

Gredin closed her eyes as the memory threatened to overwhelm her composure.

"Are you all right?" Keegan asked with concern.

"I'm fine," she assured him, resisting the grief that rose within her at the thought of Dreff, so beloved, now lost. With resolve, she began her meal.

The chowder was comforting, and she swallowed spoonful after spoonful, relishing both the taste and the warmth. To her surprise, it didn't take her long to finish the bowl, and she felt a bit better as she returned it to the tray. "Were you able to gather any news?" she asked.

"Indeed," Keegan replied, using a pair of finger-sticks to sample the tinta. "At the third table I visited, I met several companions of the man who accidentally triggered the departure dome. I professed ignorance and asked them to tell me all about it."

"Weren't they puzzled as to why you wanted to know?"

"Of course not. As the historian, I am already acknowledged

to be peculiar and interested in everything. Actually, the sixth table where I lingered was the most informative. A woman from House Shelahn was advising her group to avoid the Voice, if at all possible. She said she'd approached Tetralanna te Balamont earlier, offering to assist with preparations for the reception. But then— Well, here is how she recounted it." Keegan's gaze grew oddly distant, and his voice altered as he quoted, "'The Voice gave me a sharp look, and her mouth twisted up as if she'd bitten into an unripe citqua. She told me to attend to the business of my own House and she would attend to hers, whatever *that* meant. Before I could question her further, Burlon te Bentain came up and asked for a private word with her, and the two of them walked away and left me there, alone in the middle of the floor, while they spoke to each other in low voices, glaring at anyone who ventured near.'"

"The woman said all that? And you remembered it?" Gredin asked, astonished.

Keegan smiled. "My gyfte aids me in recalling conversations until I can find an opportunity to write them down."

Gredin thought about his account of Tetralanna in a temper. "I wonder what she and Burlon were talking about."

"I assure you, all at the table were wondering that, as well. I stayed silent during the idle gossip and speculation that followed, but I believe that Tetralanna and Burlon were discussing you, Gredin. I feel quite certain of it."

Her stomach lurched. "But why? Why should they care where I am, so long as I am out of sight and causing them no trouble?"

Keegan took another bite, his brows knitting as he pondered her question. Finally, he said, "Perhaps they fear you will speak of Venna's destruction."

Gredin shuddered. "There is no reason to fear that. Tetralanna's Silencing has been quite effective."

"But it will not last. She told us she would need to renew it, come morning. She cannot do that if she cannot find you, and so she is searching."

The notion was frightening to Gredin, as if she were a rista on a hillside, being hunted by a krag. "Perhaps so," she conceded unhappily.

The silence spun out again. Listlessly, Gredin speared a slice of her own serving of tinta, but she had scarcely placed it between her lips when another possible answer, a terrible answer, occurred to her. She chewed rapidly, nearly choking in her haste to swallow the juicy fruit. "There are other Travelers here, Keegan. Many other Travelers. What if Tetralanna and Burlon mean to have one of *them* take me back to Venna, when they find me?"

Keegan looked aghast. "Would Burlon risk using a Traveler less able than Cirin?"

"Why wouldn't he? Burlon doesn't believe what I've said about..." ...*Venna's destruction*, she tried to say, but the Silencing choked off her words. Frustrated, she pressed on. "The Travelers managed to bring the entire delegation and their baggage here to Tradepoint without any difficulty. Burlon will believe that conducting me back home is easily within any Traveler's gyfte." A dreadful sense of pressure began to grow again in her chest, making it difficult to breathe. "How can we prevent it?" Tears of fright sprang to her eyes. "What can I do?"

"To begin, you can stay here overnight," Keegan offered. "When I told Tetralanna that I knew nothing of your where-abouts, it was perfectly true. I'm sure that was apparent to her, so why should she begin to doubt me now? If you simply stay hidden here, you may well remain undiscovered."

"And then?"

"We can seek a more permanent solution in the morning, when we're both less fatigued. And Cirin is expected back tomorrow for the Trisectoriana. When he returns, he will confirm your tale… or, if he *doesn't* return, surely that will give them serious pause."

Fresh tears flooded Gredin's eyes, and she wiped them away with an impatient hand. She was so very tired of weeping. Would her body never run out of tears? "Thank you," she said, and pushed back the blanket that still covered her legs. "I will sleep in the bathing chamber, where you found me."

"That would be foolish, as well as uncomfortable. You can sleep next to me." His voice and gaze were calm, and a gentle smile curved his lips. "Though tall, you are slender. There will be plenty of room for you on the bed mat next to me — unless you are greedy for more than your half of the space. Or perhaps you kick?"

His teasing warmed her. And, truthfully, his chambers had become a sanctuary she was loath to leave. "I have been assured that I am a quiet sleeper," she said, not even attempting to speak Dreff's dear name. "You and I should both be able to take our rest."

"Then that is settled. Do you want anything more to eat?"

"My thanks, Keegan, but no." She smiled at him wanly, grateful for his steadying presence. But when the tray vanished in the next moment as Keegan Sent it back to the kitchens, Gredin felt a quick pang of remorse. "We shouldn't have wasted the extra rolls."

He looked surprised, then thoughtful. "You're right." He gave her a sober look. "I imagine I will soon long for what I just discarded."

Gredin flushed. "Each bite is precious now. And I was equally thoughtless about it."

"Then we will both strive to do better." He gestured toward the bath. "Why don't you ready yourself for bed? You still look to be in dire need of rest."

As Gredin rose from the bed mat, a wave of dizziness swept over her, and then receded.

Keegan peered at her, concern writ large on his face. "Are you alright?"

"I believe so." Her stomach moved uneasily. "I won't be long."

"Take your time."

Once inside the bathing chamber, Gredin found the room oppressively warm. She made hasty use of the now-familiar bench, then Converted her waste, and was shocked by how drained that small, familiar task left her. Leaning against the wall, she resolved to Freshen herself and her clothes despite her weariness. The day's troubles had bathed her in fear-sweat multiple times, and she had no intention of making Keegan regret his kind offer of sanctuary by coming to bed smelling like a Mamora.

But it took her a long time to summon the Focus and Control necessary to accomplish that basic self-care. Afterward, she pressed her face against the cool metal wall, each side by turn, to soothe the heated flush of her cheeks. Her legs were shaking, and she longed to lie down. As soon as she dared to leave the safety of the wall, she made her way back into the main room, moving gingerly.

Keegan, she saw, had been busy in her absence. The sleeping mat was neatly remade, its covers turned down in welcome. The luminth had been moved from the desk to a place at the head of the sleeping mat. And Keegan himself was seated at his table, writing. "Which side of the mat would you prefer?" he asked, straightening from his work.

She forced a smile, although the room was trying to dip and waver. "The closest."

He chuckled. "Then let's get you settled. Shall I help you take your jacket off?"

In the bathing chamber, heat had risen in her like a chimney. In the main room, however, she found herself shivering, chilled to the bone. Gredin stumbled to the near edge of the mat and sat down on it. "No. It's far too cold in here," she objected, clutching her jacket around herself.

"Cold?" Keegan repeated on a note of disbelief. He came to touch her cheek, then drew back in surprise. "I fear you may require a Healing. Let's get you flat in your bed, and I will call for Norian and Dint."

"No! You can't let them know that I'm here. They'll tell Burlon!"

"But you are unwell. We will ask them to keep the matter to themselves..."

"No. Please, Keegan, no. They would have no reason to risk Burlon's displeasure by keeping my location from him, and I can't risk being found. Just let me sleep. I'm sure I will be better in the morning."

"And if you aren't?" Keegan shook his head. "No, Gredin. You need to be Assessed, at the very least."

She opened her mouth to argue further... then hesitated as a new solution came to mind. "Don't speak to Norian or Dint. I will contact Beda."

"Your Guide?"

"Yes. He has a minor gyfte for Healing, and I can trust him to hide my location from Tetralanna and Burlon." She reached out to Beda's private mind before Keegan could offer an objection. =Beda? I have need of you!=

=Gredin! Praise the Power. Ingarra and I have been seeking you.=

=I know. I'm sorry.=

=Where are you? What do you need? Tell us where you are and we'll come to you.=

=No one else must know where I am. Tetralanna and Burlon te Bentain are seeking me, as well. I'll understand if you don't want the burden of keeping a secret from them.=

=Nonsense. We won't tell anyone. Let us come to you.=

She couldn't resist. And, in truth, she was feeling less well by the moment. =My thanks. I am in Keegan te Fliss's chambers.= It was difficult to concentrate, but Gredin closed her eyes and conveyed an image of the line of doors to him. "Keegan's room is at the end, on the left."

=Excellent. That's not far at all from where I've been working on Ingarra's display for the reception. We are coming.=

=Please take care. It is close to Tetralanna's door. She mustn't find me!=

=Peace, child. We will be watchful. Calm yourself, and we will soon be there.=

With Keegan's help, Gredin reclined on the sleeping mat, too exhausted to do more than murmur, "Ingarra and Beda are on their way. Beda will make everything right." She felt Keegan settle the covers over her and tried to protest, but fatigue was sucking the strength from her very bones.

"Rest," Keegan urged.

Too drained to resist, she let her eyelids sink down.

1933 OF 2000 ORBITS REMAINING

She had closed her eyes for a moment — surely it was only a moment — but she opened them to the sight of Beda and Ingarra standing over her. The relief of seeing them was so intense that her tears brimmed again.

Keegan cleared his throat. "Gredin is unwell. She says that you can Heal her. Is that so?"

"Give me a few minutes to speak with them first, please, Keegan," Gredin implored, before Beda could answer. "If he Heals me, I'll be asleep soon. A short delay will do no harm."

Ingarra sat down beside the sleeping mat, worry lines creasing her forehead. "You sound so weary!"

"It has been the most terrible day…"

Ingarra nodded. "Miri te Kendar sought me out to say you were in difficulty. And when we sat down to evening meal, we heard your name at every turn. Folks are in an uproar! What has been going on, child?"

"No, please," Gredin begged. "I can't speak about it all. Not yet. For now, I just want to see you, to know that you're here and that I'm not alone—" Her throat began to clog with fresh tears, and shivers chased each other up and down her arms.

"All right, my love," Ingarra said. "We won't speak of it now. There's no need for you to talk at all. Just listen, for I have news guaranteed to distract you from your troubles." Her eyes sparkled. "Burlon te Bentain came to see me, after midday meal, and he brought something with him." Her forehead pleated. "I don't understand why you're avoiding him. He seemed quite nice, despite being so busy with duties for the Trisectoriana. And you should see what he brought for you! Here, I'll Fetch it." She gestured, and suddenly her lap was overflowing with the gleaming red of galen berries, shading into a scarlet so deep-hued that it almost appeared black…

"The Shodekekeen fabric," Gredin whispered.

"Glorious stuff," Ingarra said, her tone reverent.

"But where did you get it?"

"I told you — Burlon te Bentain brought it," Ingarra said, and suddenly Gredin recalled how Burlon had approached her at midday meal, carrying a bundle wrapped in yellow paper, and asking where Ingarra might be found. "It's been an absolute wonder to work with," Ingarra continued.

Gredin's breathing quickened. "Work with?"

"Of course. I've been busy, all afternoon." She scrambled nimbly to her feet and, with a flick of her wrists, caused the fabric to billow out for Gredin's inspection. "What do you think? Is this not a dress worthy of the Trisectoriana?"

It was a marvel. Light danced over its folds, beguiling the eye to move from panel to seam to tuck, a visual delight so compelling that Gredin couldn't tear her gaze away. "Oh, Ingarra, it is an astonishment."

"Do you feel well enough to stand and try it on?" Ingarra asked.

Gredin shook her head, feeling a sharp pang of regret. "I can't wear it, Ingarra. They likely won't permit me to translate at the Trisectoriana, after all that's happened today. And even if I do attend, I couldn't wear something that beautiful. It would draw every eye. Tetralanna would be furious. I am only the translator."

Ingarra's smile took on a fierce edge. "Oh, I've no doubt she'd be displeased. But we can't have you insulting the Prett government by wearing less than your best. You'll go as the gyfted girl you are, and anyone who likes can look their fill. I've even fashioned the neckline to show Dreff's necklace to best advantage, and I've put in a little pocket for your pouch of stones. You'll do the House proud. And if Tetralanna has a problem with that, she can explain herself to Unter when we get home."

Gredin felt the strength draining out of her body. There would be no explanations to Unter. No House. No Venna. "Please, you don't understand. The dress is a work of amazing beauty, and I love you for the effort you've put into it, truly I do... but I can't wear it." She searched for some way to explain that wouldn't founder on the rocks of the Silencing. "To begin with, we cannot afford such a thing. I'm afraid to imagine how much that fabric must have cost Burlon, or why he made such a reckless trade."

"He says it cost him nothing."

Gredin shook her head. "That cannot be true. You know it cannot. Look at it! You've said it yourself — this fabric is glorious stuff."

"Glorious stuff which I've now cut and stitched," Ingarra pointed out, "so it isn't as if it could be traded back, even if the price *had* been dear. But it wasn't. Burlon te Bentain says this material was a present to you, from the Sho... Sho...."

"Shodekekeen." Memories of the Judgment in the Director's office rose in Gredin's mind, making her shudder. "But that's madness. I have brought nothing but trouble to the Shodekekeen, today. Damage was done to their fabrics and equipment because of me. I am the last person they would have reason to grace with such an extravagant present."

Ingarra shrugged. "Burlon told me the shopkeeper thought they were wrong to blame you for whatever happened today, so he gave us the material. And Burlon said he couldn't refuse it without insulting them, and that the merchant wanted you to have a dress made from it. Then — imagine! — he asked me whether I thought I could do anything with it, and I told *him* it would be a disgrace if I couldn't, since I've been sewing your clothes since you were a tiny babe." She stopped, a little breathless, and gave the gown another shake.

It was so beautiful that Gredin couldn't look away, but what could be be gained by enraging Tetralanna further? It pained Gredin to refuse the dress, when Ingarra had spent hours creating it just for her... but it seemed to be the only expedient choice.

As if the internal debate had stoked some inner fire, Gredin was suddenly too warm. The blankets were stifling, and her jacket was a torment. Panting with distress, she sat up, pushing the bedding away, wrestling with the jacket buttons—

"What's wrong?"

"I'm too hot! Don't you feel it? Aren't you burning?" she demanded in disbelief.

"Calm yourself," Keegan soothed, circling behind her. "I'll help you with your jacket."

Gredin felt him ease the material down from her shoulders and off.

Ingarra shrieked. "Your arm!" she exclaimed, pointing.

Gredin looked down... and stared. Three round wounds dotted her left forearm, small and evenly spaced, with angry red streaks radiating from each in stark contrast to the pale gold of her skin. The sight made her feel ill.

Ingarra knelt by her side. "That looks terrible. What happened to you?"

Beda moved Ingarra aside, then knelt and took Gredin's arm in a gentle grip. "I have never seen wounds like this. What caused this injury?"

"I don't know. I..." And then, suddenly, she *did* know. "The Hesch," she said, blinking against a rising sense of vertigo. "The Hesch grabbed my arm."

"Someone grabbed your arm?" Beda demanded, just as Ingarra asked, "What in the Power's name is a Hesch?"

"It was my fault," Gredin said to Beda, then told Ingarra, "The Hesch are another race of traders, here."

"And they're allowed to go about, injuring people?"

"No. I stumbled into him. I hurt him — I'm not sure how badly. It was my fault."

"Nevertheless, this should have been seen to," Beda chided gently.

"I didn't realize." Gredin fought back a new spate of tears. "My jacket covered it. I've been cold. I didn't think... It's been a difficult day. A complicated time. I was upset, and I thought that the way I felt was only..."

"Be at peace, nifflin," Beda said. "You felt unwell because you needed a Healing, and that is what you shall have."

Now that she had seen the injury, Gredin knew he was right. No Vennan coped well with a break in their skin's integrity. And this was no ordinary break. She had suffered punctures from the claws of an alien species, punctures that had been allowed to fester for the better part of a day. The very thought made her insides writhe, and her breath hitched in her throat.

"All will be well," Beda soothed. "No need to worry. You'll soon be restored."

All through Gredin's childhood, Beda's minor gyfte for Healing had eased her through various bumps and scrapes. But such accidents occurred far less often as she grew older. And never before had she needed a Healer's attentions twice in a single day. This morning, she'd felt guilty for troubling a Healer at all. Tonight, she had no choice.

"Close your eyes," Ingarra urged.

Gredin obeyed, and felt Beda's hands settle on her, one at her brow, the other at her wrist. A wave of gentle warmth surged into her, unknotting the lump of dread in her stomach, soothing her scratchy eyelids and swollen throat, easing the pain in her chest.

In a moment more, the room was lost to her as the sureness of Beda's Healing touch swept her awareness away.

Gredin drifted into awareness, savoring the warm cocoon of bedding. The soft cloud of her pillow invited her to snuggle deeper beneath the blankets, despite the dim glow of a luminth nearby. In the near dark, the room looked almost cozy.

And unfamiliar.

Gredin reached to push back the covers — and realized that someone slept next to her. For one sweet moment, she thought it was Dreff. Then awareness flooded in, swamping her hopes with the harsh truth of her situation.

Not Dreff.

Keegan.

A sob rose, and she pressed the back of a clenched fist to her lips in an attempt to stifle the sound. Keegan had been kind enough to hide her. Kind enough to believe her. Kind enough to save her life. Such a supportive friend deserved an unbroken night's sleep.

Fresh tears filled her eyes as a maelstrom of questions and emotions cascaded through her mind, squeezing her chest and making it difficult to breathe.

Why did this happen to Dreff and the others? I'll never see him or our home again. Oh, why didn't I refuse Unter's request?

Gredin's tears flowed faster, and she choked as she fought to stifle the sounds of her grief, determined not to wake Keegan.

I can't bear this. It's too terrible. The loss of Dreff, of Venna itself — I am broken. Surely the Power must see that it made a mistake by choosing me. How can I lead the survivors when the thought of what we've lost instantly reduces me to a sobbing heap?

I'm only Gredin, the girl who fails to live up to expectations, the girl who feels too deeply, the girl who can't fully realize her gyftes.

And yet how can I be ashamed of that? Every day of my life has brought me at least some measure of joy. The taste of life is a sweetness on my tongue, as if that were my truest gyfte, to feel life's joys so deeply. It was my consolation for my failings in more important things. Whatever else was true of me, I was happy.

But now that very ability to feel the full dimension of every experience is gutting me. I can't control my grief. I'm incapable of acting as the Power instructs me to act, and that is a failure worse than all the others combined.

Harrowed by that crushing realization, Gredin turned on her side and hugged her pillow. Grief and shame stained every tear until, exhausted, she toppled back into sleep.

After a time, however, the sense of darkness surrounding Gredin began to glow, lifting her back into awareness.

Gredin.

Dreff!

She flung herself toward the sense of his presence, and fresh tears claimed her — tears of love for him, of joy at his return, of anguish over the punishing day she had just endured, of longing for the shelter of his embrace...

Gredin, hear me.

But the tears had now been joined with sobs that rose from her very core, threatening to shake bone from bone as fear and grief consumed her.

Gredin.

She had a sense of being enfolded. Hushed. Calmed.

I'm sorry, she choked. *I want to do as you asked. I tried! But I can't. There's something wrong with me. I'm not strong enough.*

And I am sorry, too, Dreff told her. *Sorry to have asked so much — too much — of you. Sorry to have strained you past what you could bear.*

It's not your fault, Gredin assured him, bitterness coating her words. *I've always been this way. I am just grateful that you love me despite my failures.*

I have always loved you.

Acceptance, boundless and forgiving, filled her, lifting her spirits. A fierce desire to be worthy of that love prompted her next words. *Help me change. Please, Dreff. I need to be different.*

Silence. Then, *You don't know what you ask.*

I do, she insisted. *So many times, I've been a disappointment. So many times, I've fallen short, doing well but never well enough, never steadily enough to be counted on. That has to change. I have to change.*

If I altered you, a new Gredin would result.

I don't care, so long as it means I can do what needs to be done for those of us who have survived.

His voice gentled. *I hear you... but your old self would be gone forever. Are you sure this is a choice you wish to make?*

Gredin summoned her courage. *Today was impossible. I can't be like that again. I need to be calm and reliable. I need to be the one our people can trust. It's the only way forward. It's what I want. It's what we need. I won't change my mind.*

Silence, as her heart pounded.

Very well, he said at last. *I honor your choice.*

Nothing happened for a long moment. Then her breathing faltered, as if adjusted by some unseen hand, becoming slower... slower... slower...

Gredin shuddered, forced toward stillness, like a luminth being drained. It didn't hurt, but it was frightening to feel the life force within her waver and dim, guttering like a flame on the brink of flickering out.

It grew lower still. Smaller. Dimmer.

Then it gathered strength and steadied, much smaller now — a candle, where it had always been a torch.

It is as you asked. The old Gredin is no more.

You're certain?

Yes. You will be different. Calmer. Steadier. Able to cope with the loss of our world and the absence of so many loved ones from your life. Able to cope with the burdens that others will place upon you, and the responsibilities you will place upon yourself. Your days of following are at an end. It is time for you to lead.

Tetralanna would no doubt have something to say about that, Gredin reflected.

She may well, but events have passed Tetralanna by. Pity her, but you cannot afford to be influenced by her. She has nothing to teach you. This is no longer her time. She cannot be the leader our people need. It is up to you to make the hard choices that she cannot and will not. You must be the one to act, if our people are to be saved.

Still, Tetralanna was the appointed Voice. Tetralanna wasn't going to listen to her.

Tetralanna is no longer your concern. Focus on doing what you must do. The others will hear your words, and trust you, and follow you to safety.

The past day's debacle at the Traders' Market would make that harder.

This is a fresh start. A new Gredin. Beda Healed you. Now I have given you a new life.

Listening to that assured assertion, she fully accepted that this presence — for all its dear familiarity — was not Dreff. Or, rather, it was far more than Dreff. This was every face, every voice, every unique individual who was now gone. It was all the lost Chosens and children and parents. It was the sisters, the brothers, the kinsmen, the Heads of House, along with all the gyftes they had possessed, swept up into a whirlwind beyond imagining and... kept. Safeguarded. Cherished.

Returned to the Source.

That knowledge washed through her, scouring away the final remnants of the girl who had come to Tradepoint with such happy expectations about the life that lay ahead.

That path was gone. A new road was spreading before her now — a road she would be the first to walk.

I will be with you, Gredin. I am with you all. The way will be long and long, but the path is yours. Do not lose faith. This place is only your beginning.

A beginning?

Yes, but that is a worry for a later time. Tonight is for sleep.

Wait!

A wave of reassurance washed over her. *Sleep.*

But what—

A ripple of bodily ease. *Sleep.*

But—

A hint of amused affection. *Sleep, Gredin.*

And she slept.

[37]

THE RIVER

Traveling the River was pure joy for Cirin, the thing he'd been born to do. Nothing else was as deeply satisfying. Even finding his completion in Hayla's arms paled by comparison.

To return home was the sweetest journey of all. From his first short forays as a young man to the extended voyages that were now within his capability, Venna had sung to him, the one sure star in his firmament, the unfailing lodestone, the haven that called him back, however far he ventured. Where other destinations took concentration and cunning to reach, Venna drew him of its own accord, as if some unseen tether bound them together for all time.

And so it was the profoundest shock of Cirin's life when he closed the final distance and found... nothing. No haven. No harbor. No slightest ripple to indicate that Venna had ever existed alongside the boundless current that was the River.

Venna is no more.

Almost, the shock of it broke his Focus. Almost, the meaning of that absence caused his Control to desert him. But his gyfte was deep. Bound up in the River's embrace, the part of his mind that was not blind instinct or pure gyfte found a scrap of thought that clamored for his attention, and he clutched at it.

Palomar. If the impossible came to pass, he was supposed to go to Palomar. It was close. It was long-familiar. He could reach it. He could.

Gathering himself, he twisted and turned, like a fish fighting its way upstream, and found the bright path that would lead him to Palomar.

DAY THREE

THE TRISECTORIANA

Keegan woke to moonrise.

But this was Tradepoint. There should be no moon visible to him.

Unsettled, he opened his sleep-heavy eyelids... and saw that the silver light filling the room came from only inches away.

His bedmate, Gredin te Balamont, was glowing.

It was no subtle thing. He had to squint against the brightness, as if Gredin were a luminth intent on banishing the darkness of night.

I must notice every detail of how she looks, and ask Sill te Torr to harvest the memory, he thought, humbled at being — even indirectly — in the Power's presence. *I must record a description of this moment in my notebook for the histories.*

From instant to instant, he expected the glow to fade away, but he and Gredin seemed to be suspended in a bubble of time. As stealthily as he could manage, he rolled sideways off of the bed mat, onto the chill floor, nearly certain that the movement would wake her. But no, she slept on, her features serene. And so, at last, he dared to Fetch the notebook to himself and sit up, thumbing past his close-written pages about the members of House Vell.

In Gredin's silver radiance, the ink of his writing was clearly legible.

I can write by the light of her, he thought, shaken by the realization.

In time, however, even miracles grew less daunting. His breathing steadied and grew quieter. When Gredin and her glow remained unchanged, he opened his ink vial, set it carefully to one side, selected a pen from his roll, and wrote: *On our second night at Tradepoint, the Power came again to Gredin te Balamont as she slept.*

But there he stopped, lost in wonder and speculation. What further message was the Power delivering? Last night, it had announced the destruction of their world. Beyond that all-encompassing loss, what more was there to say? He couldn't begin to imagine... but that, no doubt, was why the Power was the Power, while he was a mere historian.

Still, because of his gyfte, there were things he knew that others had not troubled to learn, or had long forgotten. And one of those long-neglected accounts involved the Sixty-Six.

Where did we begin? As a youngling, that question had started him along a winding path from one kinsman to another, gathering stories from each, until eventually he found himself in the presence of Leel, who someone had referred to as House Fliss's Oldest.

"Ask your question, boy," Leel had instructed.

And Keegan, so young at the time that his hlao still firmly encircled his wrist, had asked the same question he had asked all of the others. "Where did we begin?"

"Clarify," said Leel.

No one else had requested that he do that. They had just brushed his question aside or referred him to someone from an earlier generation. Leel appeared to take him seriously, so

Keegan did his best to explain the purpose of his question. "I have a mother and a father. And they each have a mother and a father. And *they* each have a mother and a father, and so on. But where did we begin? Who was first? How could anyone be first? How could anyone not have a mother and father?"

Leel smiled, his expression warming. "You have selected a fine question, and you have finally asked it of the right kinsman, for I, Leel, have no mother and no father. I have a Chosen, Bessamel, who also has no mother or father. None of us did."

Each of Leel's words was like a crystal raindrop, falling with precision. And Keegan, because he was listening carefully, saw the question he needed to ask next. "Who is us?"

"Clarify," Leel invited, and his smile deepened.

"You said 'None of us did.' Of what 'us' do you speak?"

"I speak of the Sixty-Six."

It was not a term Keegan had ever heard spoken, nor had he seen it written down in the pages of the books he had begun to study. Feeling oddly breathless, he asked, "Who are the Sixty-Six, and why do they have no mother or father?"

Now there was a light in Leel's eyes, as if he were taking a deep delight in their conversation. Instead of answering, he asked a question of his own. "How many Houses are there on Venna?"

"Thirty-three," Keegan said, and felt a smile of pleased surprise stretch his own mouth as he saw the connection between Leel's question and his own. "Others of our House call you Oldest," he said to Leel. "Is that your Chosen's proper title, as well?"

"It is."

"And if I were old enough to venture to House Bentain or House Tetarrin, would I find a Chosen pair in each of those Houses who bore the title of Oldest?"

"You would indeed."

"And so there is a Chosen pair designated as Oldest within

each House. Thirty-three Houses. Thirty-three couples. The Sixty-Six."

"The Sixty-Six."

He gazed in wonder at Leel. "No mother and no father... Does that mean that you have always existed?"

Leel's laugh was gentle and amused. "No, it does not mean that we have always existed, youngling. We had a beginning, the others and I. A first day. But it was not like the day of your birth. I do not fully understand it, myself, but I will tell you what I recall. On a day of great beauty and promise, we — the Sixty-Six — awoke for the first time. We were then as we are now, fully mature. We were never infants, never children. We simply awoke in the presence of the Power. We did not know ourselves or each other, but the Power knew us, and named us, and joined us in pairs, and bestowed its gyftes upon us." His voice grew hushed. "And I will tell you one thing more. As the Power named each of us, we glowed."

"Glowed?"

"Our bodies gave forth the Power's own light." This time, his smile was wry and knowing. "Those whose gyfte it is to Travel the River say that they see the Power's light — that, as they Travel, they are surrounded by it, and that it upholds and sustains them. But we were not Traveling, that day, and the light did not come from around us, but shone out from within us. Our lives began on that day, and every Vennan who followed came from us."

It was a tale of wonder. When the time for midday meal arrived, he and Leel parted, with promises that they would meet again and speak more of that long-ago day of beginning. However, it had not proven so. One thing and another had intruded, distracting Keegan from his intent: other people, other tales, other opportunities. There had been no hurry about it; Leel would always be there, ready to resume the telling.

But now the world was gone, and Leel and the others of the

Sixty-Six were gone, and Keegan's written histories were gone — both those he had studied and those he had created. All that remained was his recollection of that single conversation he and Leel had shared.

Come morning, he would entrust that memory to Sill.

Looking down at the notebook on his lap, he realized that he could no longer read what was written there. The room was growing dim.

The glow was fading.

As he watched, Gredin's sleep grew restless. She turned onto her side, pushing the covers away, and Keegan saw that only her hands still glowed, as if the Power's light were escaping through her fingertips.

She made a soft little sound.

Keegan braced himself, ready to reassure her if a storm of frightened tears accompanied her awakening. With Beda's Healing to ease the way, he'd hoped that Gredin would have a night of unbroken repose, but that seemed unlikely, now that the Power had once again come to her.

Her eyes opened. One blink, two, and then she whispered, "Is it morning?"

"I'm not sure. I haven't heard anyone stirring."

She lifted one softly luminous hand. "Is this what woke you?"

He nodded.

"Well, it's fading now," she said, her tone matter-of-fact. "Come back to bed, if you think you can sleep again."

He shook his head. "I'm wide awake."

"Your pardon. I made a poor bedmate, after all."

"No, I would hate to have missed witnessing this." He wanted to ask what the Power had said to her, but he was reluctant to shatter her strange serenity. "Do you feel any better?"

"Yes. And I think I know a way to tell whether morning has arrived."

"How?"

"If a new day is upon us, Tetralanna's Silencing will have faded. Shall we find out?" She fixed him with a look and said, in a calm, clear voice, "Venna has been destroyed."

Keegan's breath faltered. He didn't know what pained him more, the repetition of that pronouncement of doom or the fact that Gredin could say it so dispassionately.

She offered him the saddest of smiles and added, with quiet determination, "I must speak with the Director. But first I'll need Ingarra's help."

Ingarra held her breath as she tiptoed past the little suite of rooms that Gredin and Tetralanna had been assigned to share, hoping its door would stay shut until she was safely inside Keegan's chambers. She had no desire to confront the woman while she was still fuming over the previous day, when Tetralanna boldly informed everyone she met of Gredin's woes. As if First Speaker had any right to discuss Balamont business with members of other Houses! As the delegation's Voice, she was supposed to solve problems, not create them.

For now, however, Ingarra was determined to make sure that Gredin was all right.

=Nifflin?= she ventured when she reached the door, her mind touch gentle in case Gredin was still feeling unwell.

The response came quickly, subdued but clear. =Ingarra. Please come in.=

The doors parted, revealing the sober face of Keegan te Fliss in the brighter light of the room. He motioned an invitation for her to enter, and Ingarra slipped inside.

Setting her laden tray on the metal table, Ingarra turned to the sleep mat, to judge how Gredin was faring after last night's storm of tears. She was relieved to see that the girl looked calm, if a little pale and heavy-lidded. It was a marked change from the flushed cheeks and agitated air of the previous evening. "I brought you some food, which Miri kindly provided. I was tempted to eat it myself on the walk here, it smelled so good. Would you like it down there or here at the table?"

Gredin sat up. "I'll eat down here, if you please. Come sit beside me. We'll leave the bench for Keegan."

It took Ingarra but a moment to Fetch the tray and place it on the bed mat. "Are you hungry? I hope I brought enough."

"There's plenty," Gredin assured her, selecting a roll and biting into it. "You and Keegan should help yourselves to anything you'd like."

Ingarra settled herself on the quilted mat, and selected a slice of cheese, smiling as Gredin consumed several bites of the roll in quick succession. "You seem to be in fair appetite, this morning."

"Mmm." Gredin swallowed. "I couldn't eat much, yesterday. This is very welcome."

Taking a bite of the cheese, Ingarra savored the mild flavor as it melted across her tongue. "I'm glad to see you in better spirits. This will be a big day."

"An important day," Gredin affirmed calmly. "Don't worry, Ingarra. I am fine now. No more tears, I promise. The time for weeping is behind me."

"I'm glad," Ingarra said, pleased and puzzled to find Gredin so composed. She hoped it would last. "Try the cheese and fruit," she suggested, and moved the square dish within easier reach for Gredin. "When does the Trisectoriana begin?"

"Shortly after midday meal." Gredin lifted a slice of the fruit and bit into it, catching an errant drop of juice with the tip of her tongue. "Thank you," she said with sudden intensity.

"It's only a placrim."

Gredin smiled. "Actually, I was thanking you for the gown

— although the placrim is delicious. But what you said last night was true. I need to look proper for the Trisectoriana, and the dress you've made from the Shodekekeen cloth will be perfect. I'm sorry I was difficult about it, last night."

"You were worried about Tetralanna, and you weren't feeling at all well," Ingarra said, wondering what had changed the girl's mind.

"I must seek out the Director as soon as possible. There are things he needs to know, before the ceremony."

"I see," Ingarra said, when she didn't really, but the activities surrounding the Trisectoriana were in Gredin's sphere of responsibility, while she and Beda were solely concerned with the activities of the reception. If Gredin needed to clarify some matter with the Director before the Trisectoriana began, that was her business.

"It will still be unfortunate if the dress upsets Tetralanna," Gredin continued, her voice steady, "but this meeting is more important than Tetralanna's reactions to what I wear. We'll need to present ourselves well when we face the Prett officials, and that will be harder for me to do if I'm not properly dressed." Her brows gathered. "I look too young," she said on a note of regret. "I wish I looked more reliable."

Ingarra stared, her attention snagged by something in Gredin's voice. It wasn't like the girl to fret over her appearance. "Shall I braid your hair and put it up? Would that help?"

Gredin brightened. "Yes, please. Could we do that now? I need to see the Director as soon as possible, and I need to look my best." She suddenly looked past Ingarra, her expression anxious. "Did you bring the dress?"

"Don't fret, nifflin. I left it in my chamber when I came out. Navigating those narrow halls is difficult enough without trying to carry something, as well." She grimaced and Fetched the gown. When it appeared beside her, she patted it and said, "I didn't want to trip and tumble through a panel onto someone who was sleeping. And I wanted to bring you some food, so I knew my hands would be full, handling the tray. It was simpler just to wait and Fetch the dress when you were ready for it."

Gredin took a last bite of her roll and pushed the bed covers aside. "I'm ready now, if you're done eating."

"As you like," Ingarra assured her. "Freshen your hands and I'll help you change. Do you need the bathing chamber first?" Her prompting re-awakened memories of Gredin's early girl-hood routines, and Ingarra smiled, cautiously relieved by how this day was beginning. Gredin already seemed much calmer. Soon, she would be back to her usual, buoyant self. "Just like old times, isn't it? Now, off with you."

Once the inner door had closed behind Gredin, Ingarra turned to Keegan, who was silently leaning against the wall, eschewing the use of the bench. "Is Gredin all right? She isn't just pretending to be brave for me, is she?"

"No," Keegan responded. "She's genuinely... different."

"Well, thank you for that."

"I deserve no thanks for the changes in her," he said, a distant look in his eyes.

"Then I thank the Power for the good that Beda's Healing gyfte has wrought in my girl."

Keegan's gaze seemed to sharpen, but he only nodded and said nothing more. The two of them waited in silence until Gredin re-entered the room.

Ingarra pulled the bench away from the table and motioned for Gredin to sit down. "Do you have something particular in mind for your hair?"

"No. You're bound to have a better notion of what will look good than I do. I just need to look... more reliable."

It was reminiscent of many mornings they had shared, and Ingarra felt the last knot of tension in her chest dissolve as she drew Keegan's brush over and over through Gredin's locks. Ingarra had always loved Gredin's hair, which was as full of life as the girl herself. The child-curls had nearly vanished, supplanted by a pretty tendency for her hair to wave. Soon, maturity would claim her completely, and even the waves would vanish, leaving her hair silky straight. But not quite yet.

Ingarra smoothed away the few night tangles that had formed, and divided Gredin's long locks into sections. Then, purposefully, she ordered the various sections into braids, large and small, thick and thin, twining and intertwining them in a complex pattern. "Beda and I are very proud of you," she said quietly as she worked.

Gredin stilled beneath her touch. "Proud? Why?"

"Why?" Ingarra repeated indignantly. "For any number of things. For working so hard, ever since you were small, to learn other languages and improve your gyfte. For being bold enough to come here to Tradepoint when your gyftes were noticed and your presence was requested." *For putting up with our sour-tongued First of Speech*, she wanted to add, but resisted the temptation. "For rallying this morning, after yesterday proved so difficult. You always make us proud, nifflin. Always."

For just a moment, Gredin tilted her head to rest it against Ingarra's palm. "I love you," she said, the words simple and sincere. Then she straightened on the bench.

When Ingarra had the final braid tucked into place, she and Keegan helped Gredin into the scarlet gown, careful not to disarrange her hair. Ingarra smiled her thanks for Keegan's assistance, then showed Gredin how the final panels draped and tied.

The finished effect exceeded even Ingarra's ambitions, and she felt a prickle of tears sting her nose as she gazed upon the picture that Gredin made. "Look at yourself," she invited, and opened her private mind to the girl.

Slowly, Gredin turned in place, then walked a few steps, first away, then back to stand before Ingarra. All the while, Ingarra watched her intently, projecting what she saw into the girl's mind — front, back, sides — more honest and complete than any mirror.

Gredin's cheeks grew pink. "This dress is a wonder," she said as she tucked her pouch of stones into the pocket. "Better than anything I could have imagined, and precisely what I need today. I am deeply in your debt, Ingarra."

"Never," Ingarra replied. "Making this dress was a pleasure, and making it for you was better still. If it pleases you, I am well content."

"Pleases me? It is perfection. In this dress, I can do all that is required of me."

"You look beautiful, Gredin," Keegan said solemnly, and bowed to her with crossed hands. "You wear the Power's touch well."

It seemed an odd thing to say, but Ingarra supposed historians knew all manner of strange expressions. "We could ask for no one better to represent us," Ingarra affirmed.

"I will strive to merit your faith in me." Gredin took Ingarra's hands between her own. "My thanks, Ingarra," she said with soft intensity. "My deepest, deepest thanks."

Ingarra smiled. "You know how it pleases me to please you. And I will tidy away your other outfit to our alcove, unless you think you will need it here again."

"Please do," Gredin said. "It would be a kindness." She turned to the historian. "Keegan, would you kindly check and make sure the way is clear? My need to speak to Wyve is urgent."

To Ingarra's relief, Keegan indicated that it was safe for Gredin to leave the chamber. The three of them walked silently to the reception area, which was still untenanted. "I wish you well, nifflin," she whispered, and watched as Gredin crossed to the bio-mist chamber with brisk, purposeful strides and entered it without a backward glance.

Ingarra drew Keegan into the reception area, farther from

Tetralanna's door. "In that dress," she said softly, "and with her hair all done up in braids, Gredin doesn't look like a young girl anymore." Then, unable to resist, she added, "And I hope Tetralanna chokes on her envy when she sees her."

With a twinkle in his eye, Keegan said, "If that should occur, I would very much like to witness it." He gestured toward the kitchens. "Do you suppose it is too early for us to beg a cup of besk for ourselves?"

"I am glad to hear it was a quiet shift," Wyve said to Figg, sitting down next to her behind the desk. "More to the point, I am relieved to hear that you had no further problems with the Hesch *or* the Vennans."

Figg offered him a tired smile. "The medical staff did what they could for Nitikikani of the Hesch, although that was little enough, beyond confirming that his foot was indeed broken..." She shrugged. "Perhaps some good may come of it, in time. I made it clear to him that we could have done far more if he and his people had cooperated with our past requests for medical data."

"The Hesch are a secretive lot."

"No worse than the Beng."

"No trouble from that enclave?"

"None." Figg frowned darkly. "I almost wish there had been. Silence from the Beng is rarely a good sign."

Wyve agreed, but unless and until the Beng contravened another station rule, he could do nothing. "Let us hope they cause no more trouble until after the Trisectoriana has been successfully completed."

A soft cascade of chimes filled the room, announcing an entry to the administrative area. Wyve shared a look with Figg. *What now?*

She shrugged again. "Today is bound to be unpredictable. Time enough for us both to rest tomorrow, when matters have returned to normal." She adopted a pleasant, expectant look. "So, who do you suppose has come calling, so soon after the start of your shift? The Hesch? The Beng? The Thalken?"

The mat under Wyve's feet vibrated, and he held up a hand to silence Figg.

"We will find out in a moment. They are here." He keyed the door to open, and copied Figg's receptive expression.

Then his heart sank, as Tetralanna te Balamont stepped inside the office. Was she here to demand an apology for their sharp words to her during yesterday's Judgment?

But even as he braced himself for the Vennan to begin vocalizing her displeasure, he realized two things, almost simultaneously: the woman had brought no one with her to provide translation… and he was wrong. It was not the Voice walking toward him with such poised confidence.

It was Gredin te Balamont.

She looked astonishingly different, dressed in an eye-catching scarlet gown, her elaborately braided hair making her seem even taller than before, while the office lights struck her flamestone necklace in a shower of colored sparks. Yesterday, she had been a pitiful sight, weeping and shivering as she stood before him. This morning, she walked with quiet assurance, head high, back straight.

She had undergone some profound change, and Wyve marveled, wondering how she had accomplished such a transformation. But it was doubtful she had come to discuss her new appearance, so he contented himself with saying, "Good day to you, Gredin te Balamont. How may Figg and I assist you?" And then he waited for her to speak, resting his hands comfortably on the desktop.

"Director. Assistant Director. My thanks to you for seeing me. I have information of grave importance to impart."

Indeed, she looked far too somber for Wyve's peace of mind. In an attempt to ease the tension, he asked lightly, "What? Has Cirin decided he prefers not to be honored?"

"Cirin is gone."

Not *Cirin isn't here*, which might simply imply that he was in the Vennan enclave while she was here, in the office. No. Gredin had said, *Cirin is gone.* A thousand questions and concerns awoke in Wyve's mind, but he settled for voicing a single word: "Explain."

His query did not appear to rattle her confidence. Instead, she murmured, "If I may?" and seated herself on the bench in front of them, calmly holding their gaze. "Cirin left Tradepoint yesterday, after the rehearsal. He said he would be back in time for the Trisectoriana, but he has not yet returned, and I have reason to doubt that he will."

She sounded utterly calm about it, far too calm to match the gravity of the situation. Wyve looked from Gredin to Figg, who was staring intently at Gredin, as if she could scarcely believe this was the same girl. He had always found the Vennan traders steady and unflappable. Did Gredin's youth and lack of experience account for her emotional liability?

Perplexed, he asked, more harshly than he'd intended, "Why would Cirin leave, when the Trisectoriana is happening today?"

"Because he was determined to prove me wrong."

"Wrong? About what?"

"I told him what I have now come to tell you — that Venna has been destroyed."

Wyve felt his jaw go slack. She had just used the word *tikbata* — a Prettian word that might properly be employed to describe the fate of a fragile vase hurled against a wall in anger.

Shattered beyond repair.

Obliterated.

Tikbata.

Wyve became aware that Figg was rubbing his arm, murmuring "Chee, chee, chee... chee, chee, chee..." as one might attempt to comfort a wailing child.

"How?" he asked Gredin in horror, turning his hands palms-up. "What happened?"

"I do not know," she replied. "I only know that Venna is gone."

"But how did you *learn* of this?" he asked, anguished on her delegation's behalf.

"The Power spoke to me in a night-thought."

Wyve blinked.

The Power?

In a dream?

A sick chill coursed through him, followed by a hot thread of indignation. Leaning back in his chair, Wyve demanded, "What foolishness is this?"

Gredin seemed unshaken by his withdrawal, showing no hint of tears at his sudden change of attitude. "It is not foolishness, Director. It is a truth."

"A dream," he countered.

"A night-thought from the Power."

"Yet Cirin disbelieves this dream?"

"Yes," she confirmed, and her mouth tightened. "I asked him not to go. I..." She shook her head. "I do not know the Prettian word. In Vennan, I would say I 'begged' him not to go."

"Distii," Figg said, her normally clear voice low and quiet. She cleared her throat. "The word you seek is distii."

Gredin nodded. "Begged. I begged Cirin not to go. I fear for him."

"Fear? Why?"

"Because he set out to Travel the River to a place that no longer exists. Because he has not yet returned. Are those not causes for fear?" she asked.

But she didn't sound frightened. Intense, yes, but not frightened. Where was the girl whose tears, just a day ago, had flowed so ceaselessly?

Wyve felt as if he had lost his inner balance, careening from his initial, heart-searing empathy over such a tragic disaster to angry skepticism at the unfounded nature of Gredin's claim. Now he was adrift between those two extremes, unsure what to believe. He didn't know this young Vennan. In the few days of their acquaintance, she had seemed wildly different at each encounter. And so Wyve turned again to his dependable counterpart, the one person he knew he could rely on. "Figg, what do you make of this claim? Do you believe her?"

"I do not have enough data, Director. But it appears to me that Gredin believes what she is saying."

This open discussion of their doubts did not seem to affect Gredin; she remained calm, her breathing steady and even, her hands folded quietly in her lap.

"Your skepticism places you in good company, Director, Assistant Director," Gredin said, breaking the silence. "Even the few Vennans I have told do not believe me... except for Keegan te Fliss."

"Keegan te Fliss?" Wyve echoed, startled afresh by the idea that the slender Vennan with the gentle smile, who had so eagerly observed Prettian writing, could believe such a horrific thing.

But it was Figg, as usual, who went to the heart of the matter. "Who, specifically, has heard this information and remains unconvinced by your story?"

"Burlon. Cirin. Tetralanna. Sill." Four names, clearly spoken.

"They and Keegan are the only ones you have told?"

"Yes."

"So few! Why haven't you informed your entire delegation of such essential news?"

Gredin's chin lifted. "Because Tetralanna used her gyfte to Silence me, to prevent me from speaking about the calamity to others."

Wyve felt as if he were wading into ever-deepening water. "I do not understand your use of this word, *silence*. What do you mean by it?"

"Tetralanna is First Speaker for our House. Her gyfte of Speech is substantial." Gredin's hands lifted from her lap, and she spread her fingers wide. "The gyfte of Speech is more than just the ability to speak to others in words that will be clearly heard and understood. The gyfte of Speech is like a... a... complicated braid." She interlaced her fingers. "One strand is clarity. Another is a facility for other languages. A third is the ability to speak of complicated matters in clear, simple terms. Yet another strand allows your voice to be heard over large spaces occupied by many people. And there are more." Her hands separated, and she settled them back in her lap, the move-ment causing the fabric of her dress to catch the light. "One of the less commonly used strands is the ability to Silence." She smiled without humor. "To be Silenced is to be ordered not to speak, and so you do not. Indeed, you cannot, if the Speaker's gyfte is powerful enough."

"At all?" Wyve asked, horrified.

"I am uncertain. My Mentor, Frake, knew of no such instance, but I suppose it might be possible, depending upon the strength of your gyfte. Still, Tetralanna did not attempt to leave me mute. She simply rendered me incapable of talking about anything related to Venna's destruction."

"You are talking of it now," Figg pointed out.

"A Silencing is a temporary thing. I came to you as soon as mine faded. Tetralanna's Silencing was entirely effective while it lasted, but it would need to be renewed daily in order to continue to curb my words. And I did not afford her an opportunity to renew it." A small, more genuine smile lifted the corners of her lips. "That is why I intruded upon you at such an early hour. I needed to leave the enclave before anyone was astir. Particularly Tetralanna."

Wyve felt as if he couldn't process Gredin te Balamont's information quickly enough. Questions and thoughts rose and fell in his mind. "How did you manage to convince the historian, if you could not speak?"

"Yesterday morning, I spoke the truth to all of those I just named, before I was Silenced. Keegan believed from the beginning. Sill stood apart, undecided. Burlon, Cirin and Tetralanna insisted that I was upsetting myself over nothing. They refused to believe the Power had spoken to me in my sleep. But it had, using my own Chosen's voice to inform me that our world was gone."

Her preternatural composure disturbed Wyve deeply. "How can you make that claim with such calm?" It all sounded too fantastic to be believed. Were Vennans prone to mental aberrations? Did this girl see visions and hear imaginary voices? Was she like the F'lala, who claimed that their every misdeed was something "the spirits" had ordered them to do?

But she said, "As you may recall, I *wasn't* calm, Director, not even when I encountered you later in the day. Far from it. I was consumed by grief and tears, utterly at the mercy of my emotions. It is why Tetralanna Silenced me, when Burlon suggested that my news should be kept from the rest of the delegation."

"Your extreme reaction did not convince Tetralanna te Balamont? She is the official speaker for your delegation. And she is of your house, is she not? Did that not make her sympathetic to you and more inclined to believe your words?"

"Tetralanna dismissed it as my tendency to be over-emotional. And she was frightened," Gredin said, "too frightened by my claim to allow herself even to imagine that I might be right. And I must with respect inform you that Tetralanna is no longer the official Speaker for the delegation. I am the official Speaker now, appointed by the Power."

Listening to that assertion, Wyve cautioned himself to take great care. "Appointed by the Power"? Religious beliefs of the races that frequented Tradepoint were specifically not the Prett's affair. And here he was, faced with a horrifying claim of destruction and a sweeping power grab, based on nothing more substantial than a young woman's claim to have had a nightmare. Wyve felt embarrassed and angry for having responded so viscerally to her initial shocking statement. Had that been its intent — to startle him into sympathy and cooperation?

"Chee, chee, chee..." Figg murmured again.

Wyve tried to slow his breathing. "So, it is only you and the little historian who believe?" he persisted, grasping for facts. "Does it cause you no concern at all that the more experienced members of your delegation resist belief in your tale?"

"I understood their resistance. But that may well change today, when I tell Tetralanna and the others about my second visitation from the Power."

Wyve felt Figg tense beside him.

"*Two* dreams?"

"Yes — the night of our arrival and last night. The Power has charged me with leading our people. I am not to heed Tetralanna any longer. The Power states that events have passed her by."

In her blond fragility, Gredin was an unlikely looking rebel, but appearance counted for very little on Tradepoint. Most distressing to Wyve was the contrast between Gredin's air of calm and the implied anarchy of her words. *The Power states* might be no more than a convenient euphemism, displacing direct responsibility for her actions. *I am not to heed Tetralanna* was a passive construction, again side-stepping accountability. And *Events have passed her by* — what was he to make of that statement, regarding the woman appointed as the Vennan delegation's Voice? It didn't matter that he found Tetralanna's manner objectionable. Burlon and Cirin had identified her as their delegation's official representative, and he was honorbound to respect that appointment until Cirin or Burlon informed him otherwise.

Assuming as neutral a manner as he could manage, Wyve said, "Your pardon, Gredin te Balamont, but you seem very little disturbed by this news that you bear."

To his surprise, she nodded. "Yes. The upset now is here, deep within." She pressed the palm of her hand to her chest. "Yesterday, it was—" Her hand extended, twisting, with her fingers aflutter. "—everywhere. I could not act. Could not think. Could not stop weeping. Could scarcely stand." A small grimace. "In that state, I could not serve as the Power needed me to serve, and so it returned to me, last night, and..."

In stubborn silence, Wyve waited for her to finish that sentence.

With a second little nod, she obliged him. "It... changed me. Adjusted me," she clarified. "Calmed me, to what you see now."

It was an eerie notion, one that strained Gredin's credibility. People were not engines. While a person could be temporarily calmed by medication, or might change their behavior over time through an on-going effort of self-will, that was very different from stating that some amorphous outside force had essentially recalibrated Gredin, as if she were a malfunctioning griimoni.

And yet the girl *was* markedly different, this morning. If it was neither drugs nor self-hypnosis, might it be the simple benefits of a night's sleep, or the effect of putting some distance between herself and yesterday's distressing encounter with the Beng and the Hesch at the Traders' Market?

Or had the change in her manner been accomplished by "the Power," as she claimed?

Wyve had never been comfortable with the Vennans' many assertions about the Power. Formalized religion was one thing. But a deity that intervened in people's lives and activities on a daily basis? A deity whose actions defied the tenets of science? How convenient that sounded. How extremely convenient.

Nevertheless, the most basic facts about the Vennans' presence on Tradepoint had defied scientific explanation from the very beginning. Had he not thought about them as the "eternal exception," just yesterday?

"I have angered you," Gredin observed. "How?"

Wyve searched for a response, disconcerted by her candor. "What you say is difficult for me to believe."

"It was difficult for me to believe, as well. But if you worry that I have misled you, it is not so. I have said nothing here that is not true, and I will answer any question you pose."

"Why so forthcoming?" Wyve challenged.

"Because our home is gone. Our people — all of those who stayed behind while we ventured here — are dead. We few who remain alive exist here now on your..." She shrugged helplessly. "Again, I do not know the word. One that means we need... shelter. Sanctuary. But also that we must rely on your good will."

This time, he supplied the word, first in Prettian, then in Vennan. "*Havonii.* Sufferance."

"Yes. That is the word for which I was searching," she

agreed. "We exist, now, on your sufferance, in dire need of refuge."

Beside him, Figg's fingers tapped methodically on the desk-top, and a written message took form on the clear glass in front of Wyve: *Of course we do not want it to be true. But what would such an enormous lie gain them?*

Her words were like a jolt of electricity, jarring Wyve from the dark spiral of his thoughts and doubts. The protective cocoon of his anger abruptly fell away, leaving a queasy ache in his middle. Figg had posed a salient question. Based on three hundred sectora of acquaintance, what could the Vennan delegation hope to gain by telling a massive untruth?

Slowly, he pushed back his chair and rose to his feet.

Gredin watched him, silent and unflinching.

Wyve walked around the desk, stopped directly in front of Gredin, crossed his palms to her in the Vennan fashion, and inclined his head. "Gredin te Balamont," he said in careful Vennan, "I ask your pardon. Your news..." To his own surprise, his voice wavered, and he struggled to regain his composure.

Gredin's smile was gentle and sad. In Prettian, she said, "I, too, longed with all my being not to believe. It is not news I ever thought that I would hear... or could bear. Only six of us know — and now you and Figg. The members of our delegation remain unaware of the Power's message." Her face took on a wistful look. "With your help, I wish to let them enjoy tonight's reception, if at all possible. They have worked hard, preparing for it, and they deserve the chance to celebrate the very things that unite us and make us most Vennan. But the news cannot be delayed past tomorrow morning. They expect to be taken home then — and there is no home." She looked at Figg, then back at Wyve. "Tomorrow morning, nearly a thousand Vennans will experience a grief that nearly crushed me, yesterday. By tomorrow evening, we must find a way to begin to feed them all, when we had assumed they would be dining from the bounty of their own Houses." She sat up even straighter. "I came here because I hoped to discuss our situation with you in some detail. If we can reach any sort of accommodation, we can then go on to use this meeting to prepare for the most immediate of my people's needs." She spread her hands. "But if, instead, you and the Assistant Director determine that the Vennan delegation must leave Tradepoint tomorrow as originally planned, I will excuse myself now so that I can meet with Burlon to discuss where else we might—"

Wyve held up a hand to silence her. "We would never treat any trading partner so harshly, in the face of such a disaster — not even the Beng."

"Graciously said, Director. But you are not currently housing a thousand Beng."

"For which," Figg said dryly, "we can all be grateful."

Caught by surprise, Wyve snorted, and Gredin smiled.

Then grim silence fell again.

"Understand," Wyve clarified, "there is no question of the Vennan delegation being required to depart from Tradepoint tomorrow. You have used only a small portion of your allotted rotations, as displayed on the countback monitor." *Only a small portion... although it feels as if a sectora has passed since your arrival.* "You may shelter with us until you know the truth of your world's fate, at the very least."

"I know it now," Gredin said, quietly but with utter conviction.

"I intend no disrespect," Wyve countered, "but we should seek objective confirmation. A planet does not easily cease to exist. If such a fate has befallen Venna, we may be able to detect evidence of it with our equipment."

"And if you do find such a sign?" Gredin asked.

"Pardon?"

"Will Venna be any less gone?"

As Wyve groped for a reply, Figg weighed in again. "If by

any chance you are mistaken, and Venna is unharmed, or has suffered damage but has survivors—"

"If that is so, Cirin will return to us, and I will rejoice. But I do not believe he will find that Venna still exists, and so I am mourning, for the Power was inescapably clear. Our home is gone. Our kinsmen, our Chosens, our children are lost to us."

Children. Wyve hadn't thought about the children.

His heart hurt.

Unable to contemplate such a devastating reality, he diverted his attention to a lesser problem. "Knowing now what sorrow you were bearing yesterday, I am sorry to have increased your unhappiness with my news about the Hesch."

Gredin's gaze sharpened. "What do you mean? I received no word from you yesterday, after the Judgment. I was... indisposed. Might I trouble you to repeat the message?"

"Of course. Our clinic confirmed that Nitikikani does, indeed, have broken bones."

Gredin's chest rose and fell as she sighed. "I was already quite certain of it, after hearing the way his foot cracked. But I thank you, Director, for the confirmation. Burlon was notified?"

"Yes."

She paused. "And the Beng, as well?"

He nodded. That had not been a pleasant task. But all parties had needed to be informed, just as the Hesch needed to know that the responsible parties were aware of the exact nature of his injury. Despite the windfall the injury would provide, Wyve suspected that Nitikikani wished the incident had never happened; the Hesch were notoriously protective of their privacy.

Gredin pinned him with a look. "And there is an additional difficulty to consider. Your government intends to make its presentation to Cirin later today, does it not?"

In the aftershock of her pronouncement, he had actually forgotten about the Trisectoriana. And that was dangerous, for while some might think him shallow for his concern over a formal presentation in the face of this far more devastating news, Wyve knew better. A thousand Vennans — the last thousand Vennans in existence, if Gredin's dream was to be believed — were now in need of refuge on Tradepoint. And permission for that sanctuary did not rest with him.

Wyve's position as Director of Tradepoint was an important one, but he was not its owner. His job required him to implement decisions made by the Prett government, specifically those made by the Vokastra. He would do everything he could to encourage those officials to support the continued presence of Vennan refugees on Tradepoint, but decisions regarding their treatment would ultimately be made on the planet below, including what would happen when they reached, and then exceeded, their forty-sect time allotment. Two thousand orbits — well, less than that, now — stood between the Vennans and a mandated departure from Tradepoint.

Nine hundred and thirty-seven Vennans. A few days ago, that number had seemed staggeringly large to him. In terms of the logistics of caring for them within the confines of the station, it still did. But when he reflected that it might well represent the total number of Vennans left alive in all of time and space, the number seemed small. Frighteningly small...

"Director? Does it not?"

How long had he just sat in silence, his thoughts spiraling ever deeper into the ramifications of this disaster? What had they been discussing?

Ah. The Trisectoriana.

"Yes." He took a furtive glance at the chronorb. Although time and its measurements meant little to the Vennans, punctuality was a firm expectation of the Vokastra, especially on occasions which were to be transmitted live to the planet-wide network. "The time appointed for the ceremony is still far enough off to allow us to formulate some plan. The first item on today's checklist for the Trisectoriana is a reminder to dispatch a security escort and transport pod to the Vennan enclave, shortly after your midday meal, to take the Vennan officials to the communciations chamber."

"What will their presence matter, if Cirin is absent?"

That question unsettled his breakfast. "Perhaps Cirin will yet return in time," he ventured.

"And if he does not?"

"Then I suppose..." he began, and found himself incapable of finishing that sentence.

Beside him, Figg straightened in her chair. "Gredin is correct. We need a contingency plan, in the event that Cirin does not return in time." She turned her attention to the girl. "This Trisectoriana has become a very public matter. The Vokastra has arranged to make an image of the ceremony widely visible, on our world. All who are interested have been encouraged to see and hear what happens. If the presentation has to be postponed, that will be a source of displeasure and public embarrassment for our government."

Having listened gravely, Gredin said, "Has Cirin met your government's representatives? If so, they must know that he is a reliable man. Perhaps they will understand, if we simply explain the difficulty."

Wyve shook his head in reluctant disagreement. "Three hundred sectora past, when Cirin first arrived on the Prett world, he did become acquainted with members of our government, but those original representatives have long since died. The current ones have not yet made his acquaintance, and I assure you that they would not be receptive to such an explanation. They have promised the people a broadcast, and so a broadcast is expected."

"In that case, we might do well to summon Burlon and ask for his thoughts on the matter," Gredin said. "He is Cirin's didana idia — his First Friend. He knows him better than anyone except Cirin's Chosen. Perhaps Burlon could speak at the Trisectoriana on Cirin's behalf, and they could broadcast that, instead. It would not be so very different than if Cirin were here. You would still have a Vennan speaking to your world from Tradepoint."

Wyve stared at her for a moment, wondering how to explain all of the reasons why that would not be an acceptable solution to the Vokastra... then found himself caught up in a new train of thought. "A fine suggestion," he said smoothly — so smoothly, in fact, that Figg shot a suspicious glance his way. Ignoring her, he nodded to Gredin. "By all means, let us ask Burlon to join us."

Morning meal had begun, with the members of the delegation fortifying themselves at the start of what promised to be a memorably hectic day.

Morning meal had begun... and Cirin wasn't yet back.

Burlon gave the hem of his tunic a nervous tug. The day had scarcely started. There was still plenty of time before the Trisectoriana. No need for concern. A dozen things could have delayed Cirin. Or perhaps he had already returned and was sleeping soundly in Hayla's arms, recovering from his journey...

But no. The members of House K'lar were seated not far from the arrival dais, Hayla prominent among them, and there was no sign of Cirin at her side.

Scabs. What if the Balamont girl *wasn't* crazy?

Burlon found that he had no appetite, although the aroma of fresh-baked pastries and bromin omelettes filled the air. Instead, he settled for Fetching a mug of hot besk, and went in search of the Balamont contingent.

Not that he wanted to talk to Tetralanna. Or the girl, for that matter. He didn't. But Balamont had brought more than a hundred people to Tradepoint; in a crowd that size, he ought to be able to avoid those two. What he wanted was to seek out a few of the Balamont Traders. They were people he knew, and he was confident they would be willing to answer his questions, if he could just spot them.

A familiar laugh caught his ear, and he swung to his left, scanning the Balamont tables for the source of it...

Ah, there he was.

Burlon walked over to the table where Riga te Balamont sat.

"Good day to you," he said. "May I join you briefly? I need a word."

The people seated nearby shifted obligingly, making room on the bench for Burlon to sit down beside Riga, who was watching him with wary surprise. In a cautious undertone that seemed calculated to avoid being overheard by their tablemates, Riga said, "I'm not doing it."

"Not doing what?"

Riga shushed him. "Not taking over for Ellis," he murmured, his lips barely moving. "It's not fair of you to blame Balamont."

Well, well, he thought, *the idle gossip has been flying*. "I'm not blaming anyone," Burlon assured him, reducing the volume of his voice. "And there won't be any tours of the Market today, so you needn't worry about being asked to take over for Ellis."

Much of the defensiveness left Riga's posture. "Oh? Your pardon. But Florrik te Calidane claimed you were putting together another group, and that you thought it only fair for Balamont to supply someone to head it, since —"

Burlon cut him off. "I haven't spoken to Florrik since we arrived. That man is far too fond of the breeze his tongue-flapping creates. When someone seems so very eager to tell you what I plan to do, I suggest you ask me directly, instead."

"Your pardon," Riga said again. "Well then, what *did* you come to discuss?"

"Gredin."

Riga recoiled.

"Not about what happened at the Market," Burlon assured him. He should have realized that Gredin would be a touchy topic for all of House Balamont, after yesterday's public loss of face and massive loss of profit. He'd probably been foolish to approach Riga here, where he was surrounded by kinsmen.

"What about her, then?" Riga asked, his earlier wariness back in evidence. "I've never met the girl. If you want to ask about her, you'd do better to speak with Nargo or Pleet. Or there's Sholif, over there. He knows her. Talk to him."

"Fine. My thanks. I will." Extricating himself from the bench, Burlon made his escape.

Sholif te Balamont, seated a few tables away, was just gaining his feet when Burlon approached him. "Sholif?" Burlon said in greeting.

"Burlon."

"Walk with me for a moment. There's something I'd like to discuss."

Sholif hesitated, and Burlon wondered whether Riga had just addressed the man's private mind, forewarning him. But Sholif nodded his assent, saying only, "I told Pleet I'd head to the Market with her when I finished morning meal. Would you like to join us?"

"That would work well. We can talk along the way," Burlon said, relieved. It would be much easier to engage the two Traders from Balamont in a conversation about Gredin if they were on their own, away from the distractions — and listening ears — of the rest of the delegation.

Pleet, a pleasant woman, accepted Burlon's presence with a smile, and the three of them crossed the crowded reception hall in companionable silence. When they reached the privacy of the decontamination chamber, it was Pleet who spoke first, as the bio-mist descended around them. "I'm just as glad we won't have groups of on-lookers wandering the Market, today. But I am sorry that things yesterday fell out as they did."

"Gredin injuring a Hesch," Sholif said, and shook his head. "Who could have imagined such a thing? She is the gentlest of girls."

Burlon decided he was unlikely to find a better entry point for his inquiries. "You know her?" he asked.

"Oh, yes," Sholif assured him. "Pleet and I have both known Gredin since she was a youngling. She wanted to learn Prettian, and who better than a Trader to teach her?"

"So you feel confident that there was no malice in what happened yesterday?"

"Panic, perhaps. But malice? Gredin? Never," Sholif said as the bio-mist dissipated.

"She has too kind a spirit ever to harm someone intentionally," Pleet agreed. "She's as bouncy as a rista kidlet, and I'll admit that she *can* sometimes be a bit clumsy when her attention strays. But any harm she did to that Hesch had to be accidental."

"Still," Burlon persisted, curious to know how far they would defend their young kinswoman, "Balamont is burdened with a brutal fine, as a result."

The outer doors opened, and they entered the public corridor and headed toward the Traders' Market at a comfortable pace.

"Only one-third of a brutal fine," Pleet pointed out.

Sholif glanced at Burlon and muttered, "Stub-toed Beng. Judging from your account, no such thing would have happened if it hadn't been for them. We'll explain it to Unter when we reach home tomorrow. The girl has been through enough."

"That doesn't seem to be the delegation's opinion of the matter," Burlon pointed out.

"Yes, well, what do they know? They only have idle gossip to go by," Sholif said. "They don't understand Tradepoint the way we do, and they didn't have you to explain it to them, the way we did yesterday."

"Maybe you should!" Pleet said to Burlon with sudden energy.

He eyed her uneasily. "Should what?"

"Explain it to the delegation, the way you explained it to the Traders. You could address them tonight, before the reception starts."

The thought of standing up to address nearly a thousand people, most of them unknown to him, made Burlon feel sick. Speaking to the Traders yesterday had been fine; he knew them, and it had been important for them to hear the outcome of the Judgment. But make some sort of speech to the entire delegation? No. He couldn't.

"It really only concerns House Balamont," he said, unwilling to admit how much the prospect of speaking out daunted him. "Or, if you feel strongly about it, address the community yourselves. You're of her House. It would be persuasive. But I think it's enough if you just speak privately to Unter. In little more than a day, these people will all return to their Houses, and most of them will never see Gredin again. Why belabor the matter when it will soon pass, on its own?"

Pleet offered something in reply but Burlon scarcely noticed, his attention suddenly claimed by a mind touch from Ellis te Vell. =Burlon? You're needed in the Director's Office, as quickly as you can get there.=

Again? he wondered in startled alarm, but he assured Ellis, =I'm on my way.=

So, Wyve needed to see him, did he? Well, he needed to see Wyve, as well, to alert him to the fact that Cirin had left Tradepoint and not yet returned.

Or perhaps not. Wyve would only fret. And Cirin would be back soon.

Surely, Cirin would be back soon.

Upon reaching the main intersection, Burlon crossed his palms to Sholif and Pleet. "Your pardon, but a matter has arisen that requires my attention — the first of several that will do so today, I suspect. I wish you fair trade."

And with that, turning left where they turned right, he set off down the corridor at a far more purposeful pace.

[43]

THE RIVER

Safe within the brightly flowing current of the River, Cirin allowed it to sweep him along the path to Palomar.

He knew the way, of course; every Traveler did. It was the first destination from Venna that the tutors taught, an easy destination once you selected the correct ribbon of Power to embark upon. Only the beginning was a challenge, requiring a neatly executed, twisting upward dive from the bright current that swept past Venna's door to the shining strand that would deliver you to the green, green world of Palomar. Once safely launched, the current became a gentle ride along broad, swooping bends that required minimal attention, affording ample opportunity for a new Traveler to recover their Focus and Control, conserving their energy after the excitement of a first launch.

He was hardly a new Traveler. Far from it. But the lack of challenge was greatly welcome since, once he was cradled in that warm, golden flow, it allowed him to examine his shocked and rattled thoughts — thoughts that kept circling back to one bitter, irrefutable fact: *Venna is no more... Venna is no more... Venna is no more...*

Though Gredin te Balamont had cautioned him, he, with the

reassuring presence of First Traveler's hlette on his arm, had given no credence to her warnings. But Venna was indeed gone, and a Traveler with a lesser gyfte might have lost Focus from the shock, unable to Control their journey, and been swept along until their body failed and they returned to the Source. That might be an easy ending, even a comforting one, in some ways, but he had no wish to try it.

...Venna is no more...

He shuddered, imagining what would have happened if, tomorrow, he had made that same discovery while burdened with a host of fellow Vennans and their cargo, including Hayla, his precious Chosen.

He needed to return to Tradepoint as quickly as possible and warn the others, so that no one else attempted such a return.

Grimly, he planned. Palomar would give him a safe haven to see to his vessel's needs. As soon he had eaten and taken a brief rest, he would launch back to Tradepoint.

On the journey to Venna, he had eagerly submerged himself in the Power's embrace, riding a path so familiar that he had Traveled it in mindless pleasure. Now, instead, he needed to stay alert and cautious, taking no risks. His sole purpose must be to return to Tradepoint as quickly as—

The River swept him toward an unexpected sight. Tight, looping coils of light arose, replacing what had always been a gentle curve in the River's flow — the gentle curve that marked the entry to Palomar.

And it was gone.

Cirin reached out with his gyfte, straining to keep himself from being swept into the unfamiliar passage ahead.

Palomar is no more.

His Control wavered, despair and grief clouding his mind, shaking his Focus. The tight, shining coils loomed closer. He had no idea what lay beyond them, except an ever-greater distance from Tradepoint.

No!

Pushing emotion aside, he hardened his will and summoned the strength to make yet another transition, all the while resisting the tug of the River's current.

But to where?

There were few choices on this part of the River. Palomar had always been the welcome oasis. The next safe world after it was a long Travel beyond Palomar, and this new configuration in the River might preclude it completely. And besides, he needed to Travel *toward* Tradepoint, not away.

That left only one possibility.

Zrach.

It was a cursed world, dangerous for the unwary, avoided by Vennans for long and long and long.

But it was the only option his battered mind presented.

With a major effort, Cirin dredged up the strength and clarity to make a twisting transition to the ribbon of light that would take him to Zrach.

May the Power protect me.

With that desperate plea echoing in his mind, he allowed himself to be carried forward on the new path, the only path of hope.

The dark world of Zrach was now his goal.

Outside of Wyve's office door, Burlon took the space of three breaths to center himself after his brisk walk down the corridor. He needed to set aside his worries about Cirin, and about the Balamont girl, and about the unsettled mood he had sensed within the delegation on what should have been a happy, industrious morning. Those were *his* problems, and he would deal with them all... but later. Right now, he was here because Wyve had summoned him. He needed to concentrate on addressing *Wyve*'s problems and concerns, whatever those might turn out to be.

Resolved to do precisely that, Burlon pressed his palm to the screen and entered, walking past the colored panels, heading straight for Wyve's door.

The two halves slid open silently at his approach, revealing Wyve and Figg seated behind their desk in their accustomed chairs. "Good day to you, my friends," Burlon said as he went in. "What can I do for you on this fine—"

Then he saw that someone else was already with them.

And who that someone was.

The easy phrases of greeting evaporated from his tongue,

and he heard himself say, more loudly than was appropriate in the Director's office, "Break a bone! Where have you *been*?"

Given Gredin's clash with the Hesch, that particular oath was all too apt, but Burlon was beyond caring. He felt as if his head might explode as he watched her rise and cross her palms to him. Her hair, braided by an expert hand, was fashioned into an intricate coronet that emphasized her already considerable height. And bruise him black and blue if she wasn't wearing a gown fashioned from the Shodekekeen fabric he had delivered to Ingarra te Balamont with his own hands, less than a day ago. The rich red bodice embraced her body like a Chosen's caress, while the skirt fell in graceful folds, the silhouette subtly elegant while the bold color stunned the eye.

She should have looked ridiculous, a youngling playing at the trappings of adulthood. Instead, slender and serene, Gredin projected an aura of quiet confidence. Her gaze was clear, her blue eyes free of the puffiness that had plagued her so persistently yesterday. "Good day to you, Burlon te Bentain. My thanks to you for joining us."

As if the meeting were happening at her behest, not Wyve's.

He looked to Wyve, ready to offer a hasty apology for Gredin's brashness in the Director's own domain. But Wyve and Figg appeared unruffled. "Sit," Wyve invited. "We have been waiting for you. There is much to discuss."

Something in the Director's tone struck Burlon oddly, causing him to wonder just how long Gredin te Balamont had already been there. Her presence made no sense to him. Why would Wyve have summoned her? Indeed, how could the Director have done so, even if he wanted to, when no one in the delegation had known where to find her?

Amend that, he cautioned himself as Gredin sat down again. *Clearly, someone has been acting as her ally. But who?*

Warily, Burlon moved along the curve of benches, picking one several seats away from Gredin, the better to keep an eye on her. Sitting down, he fixed his attention on Wyve, relegating the girl to a splash of scarlet in the corner of his vision. "What assistance may I offer?" he asked the Director, determined to return a proper balance to the meeting.

Wyve said nothing for a moment, then intoned, "We join our sorrow with yours."

Sorrow?

"It is a terrible loss," Figg said, her craggy face sober.

Burlon's insides clenched. What were they talking about?

And then their gazes moved from him to Gredin, and Burlon felt a horrified stab of comprehension.

She'd told them.

=Gredin!= he thundered at her with his mind. =What have you done?!=

But there was no least hint of response to his contact, as if she were not sitting in plain sight, two arm-lengths away. She kept her face turned toward Wyve and Figg, her expression tranquil.

Forced to it, he looked toward Wyve and Figg, as well. "What wild tale has she been telling you?" he demanded, unable to keep his voice quite steady.

"The same one that she told you, as we understand it," Figg answered, choosing Vennan for her reply. "That the Power came to her, in the night, and informed her that your world has been destroyed."

Destroyed.

The word could not be unsaid. Wyve and Figg had heard Gredin's claim, and Burlon was powerless to rescind their awareness of it. He turned again to Gredin. "So you took it upon yourself to share this notion of yours with the Director and Assistant Director, in spite of what we agreed?"

She faced him, appearing undaunted and unrepentant. "The rest of you agreed. I was not consulted. You and the others had all of yesterday to act on the knowledge I shared with you. You decided not to. Today, with my voice on the matter returned to me, I have selected a different path for us."

"It was not your place to make such a decision!"

"The Power has informed me that it is."

He wanted to storm from the room, or summon Tetralanna to Silence the girl once more. Yesterday morning, that process had sickened him. But now, when he saw the chaos Gredin was willing to create...

Figg cleared her throat.

A flush of mortification heated Burlon's face. Continuing this argument in front of Wyve and Figg was as unseemly as it was unwise. Whatever differences might exist, members of a Tradeteam *always* presented a unified front to outsiders.

But this was no Tradeteam. Gredin was neither a Traveler nor a Trader. And she was proving far too effective as a Speaker, now that she had pulled herself together. Cravenly, he wanted her reduced to yesterday's weeping creature. He wanted her incapable of talking about this claim that froze him with terror. He wanted Cirin standing safely beside him. He wanted all of these things, wanted them with a driving desperation, because if Gredin was right...

"Chee, chee, chee..." Gredin said in the Prett manner, her eyes wide with sympathy.

...if Gredin was actually *right*...

"Sit, before you fall," she said, and he realized that he was on his feet, dizzy with distress. When had he risen? *Yes, sit down, you great fool,* he told himself, and sank shakily down onto the bench again, aware that there was no longer any 'if.' Listening to her, being here in her presence, something within him had shifted, making it impossible to shelter any longer behind his protective shell of anger and outrage and disbelief. It wasn't a question of facts or proof. Such things were for the Prett. Instead, Burlon's very core, that intangible, infallible Trader's instinct that arose from his Power-granted gyfte, was telling him that Gredin was right.

He had to face up to it.

They were all going to have to face up to it.

He felt hollow.

Helpless.

Lost.

Figg came to him, offering a cup. "Drink, my friend, and compose yourself. We have need of your good wits."

He accepted the cup and took a swallow — then dissolved into a fit of coughing, for it was not water that Figg had brought to him, but fine Rodornon brandy. It sent a rush of heat all through him, and the familiar taste accomplished something more, reminding him forcefully that he had friends he could rely on. Wyve and Figg. The Rodorno. The Shodekekeen. The Wilra. The Mamora. They would all be supportive, once they were told.

Still, that mustn't happen yet, because races like the Hesch and the Beng would rejoice in the Vennans' misfortune, using the situation to their own best advantage in every trade they conducted. And trade might well be the only lifeline the Vennan delegation still possessed.

But that term was wrong. They were no longer a 'delegation.' They were now Venna, in its entirety.

Staggered by the thought, he took another, more judicious swallow of the brandy. *Kippi*, the Rodorno called it, and he had sipped many a cup of it in their company. Sometimes in celebration. Sometimes in silly drinking games. Sometimes in simple companionship.

Never before had he drunk it out of necessity.

A third sip emptied the cup and gave him the courage to meet Gredin's eye. "I crave your pardon," he told her, then couldn't resist adding, "unless, of course, you are wrong, in which case I will never let you hear the last of it. But if we were to make a wager on it, I no longer think I would be the winner of that bet." An odd shiver ran through him, chill and unsettling. "How is it that you sit there so calmly," he challenged, "when you spent yesterday choking on your tears?"

"The Power came to me again, last night, and Changed me," she said.

"What?"

She made a face. "I was of no use to the Power, distraught as I was, and so it returned and altered me. Someone needs to be able to think clearly, speak firmly, act with dispatch — and the Power determined, for reasons of its own, to remake me into that someone. Soon, every Vennan will be pierced by the news I must share with them. We will be forced to reflect on our lost kinsmen and the ending of our world. It will be a struggle for us to make sense of so much death, having encountered it so rarely in the past. If others among us can also remain calm and respond effectively, so much the better. But if they cannot, there will, at the least, be me."

One last time, Burlon tried to escape the blow that was descending on them all. "How can you speak with such certainty?" he asked. "Have you never before been convinced of a thing, only to find that you were mistaken?"

"Of course," Gredin agreed readily. "Often. But those were times when I had decided a thing for myself. This is different. I did not decide this. I did not want this. I could not have imagined this, and I did not sense its approach. The Power came to me and spoke, and that experience was like no other I have ever had, or ever will."

He longed to doubt her, but her words resonated within him.

"I make a pledge to you," she continued, "just as I have made this same pledge to Wyve and Figg — I will speak only the truth to you, and I ask for the truth alone, in return. This matter is too weighty for anything less. There is much I will need to learn from Wyve and Figg, and from you and the other Traders, and from those in our enclave who have had any hand in the running of their Houses. I am the youngest of us all, with the fewest life experiences upon which to draw. But I have my gyftes, and a willingness to serve, and a determination that this will not be the end of us."

"So now my Traders and I are to become your tutors?" he asked. It came out sounding like a wry attempt at a jest, when in truth what he felt was dismay at the notion.

"Of course," Gredin answered without hesitation. "And not only them. We must all become tutors of our strengths and specialties, insofar as others' gyftes enable them to learn. How else can we reduce the chance that some necessary skill will be lost to us for all time? There are few of us now, compared to what we were, and we will be faced with challenge after challenge in the days ahead. The old patterns will not suffice. Each of us must be willing to do more. We cannot be rigid. We must be willing to bend and change." A faint smile stole over her face. "That flexibility is a skill that Traders possess in abundance, is it not?"

But Burlon's thoughts seized upon a new and fundamental worry. "I can teach," he said, "and I can learn. So can we all, given time. But we do not *have* time. Past midday tomorrow, how are we to feed ourselves?"

Ever-practical Figg tapped at her tablet, then looked up from the data on her display screen. "Our records from the past twenty-five sectora show Venna exporting a variety of comestibles, but only importing a few edible luxury items."

Gredin blinked. "Comestibles? Those are what?"

"Food," Burlon replied. "True enough, Figg, which puts us in a fix. We're used to feeding ourselves, except for the occasional treat. Stuck here, we can't very well sustain our people on delicacies like lentz berries and amarantha wine."

"I love lentz berries," Gredin said, on a wistful note.

"Well, you'd get sick of them soon enough if they were all there was to eat, at every meal. They're not meant to serve as our main sustenance. We're going to need safe sources of vegetables, cheeses, grain…" He remembered the Judgment and made a sour face. "Grain. Well, *that* would certainly have been easier-arranged before yesterday's mess, wouldn't it?"

"Why?" Gredin asked. "What does yesterday have to do with grain?"

Naïve. Naïve and uninformed. Burlon sighed. "Only that much of the grain at Tradepoint comes from the homeworld of the Beng." He loosed a brief, mirthless laugh. "So it's either find a way to deal with them or we'll be stuck waiting for the next time it suits the Wilra to show up. Either way, it won't be good. Or cheap." He shook his head, fear gripping his insides. "We only have whatever random tradegoods the Houses currently have stowed here in their warehouses. Before long, those will be gone, as well. And then what?"

"We will find a way."

Her innocence and trust infuriated him. "Will we? By evening meal, tomorrow?" He rose from the bench and began to pace. "You're not in your House, where everything was provided for you. We are soon going to be in debt to every race that has anything we need, and to the Prett most of all, since they supply the roof over our heads, the floor beneath our feet, the very air we breathe. Once our own goods are gone, that debt will grow steeper with each passing day. Trade is life, here. Trade is pride. Trade is independence, and leverage, and self-respect. Soon, we will have nothing left to trade, and we will become nothing in this place. Nothing!"

Slowly, Gredin rose and confronted him, pressing her fingertips lightly to his lips. "We will not become nothing," she said, and her voice was suddenly different — not louder, but stronger. Clearer. "You are concerned, because you are an honorable man who pays his debts and takes his responsibilities seriously. But I tell you, Burlon, we will survive this dark time. We will create items of value for trade, even if we have nothing from which to craft them but air and light and the Power within us. For a time, yes, we will require aid, and we will accept it from those we trust, the Prett first and foremost. But we will not stand by with idle hands, taking what they offer and doing nothing for ourselves. We will not despair. We will serve our gyftes." She lowered her hand to her side. "We stand in the Power's grace, and it will *never* let us become nothing. Do you hear me, Burlon te Bentain? Never!"

Burlon stood for another moment, returning Gredin's gaze. His breaths were quick and sharp, as if he had just run a race, but her gyfte-laden voice steadied him. "Your words reach me," he confirmed, and sat down again, feeling the worst of the brittle tension in his body ebb away.

Gredin turned to face Wyve and Figg. "We are frightened." She said it as matter-of-factly as someone might say, *I'm hungry*, startling Burlon with her candor. "Excuse us. This will all become easier, once we can make solid plans. But keeping this secret from everyone in the enclave has worn us down. As horrible as the truth is — and it *is* horrible — it will still be a relief when we are able to name it and discuss it openly, as we are accustomed to doing." Her gaze returned to Burlon, and he felt the weight of it as she said, "You and the others were not wrong in your conclusion, yesterday, although your reasoning was amiss. You wished to Silence me because you thought I was wrong. I now wish to remain silent on this matter for a while longer, because I know that I am right. I believe that we should tell no one else in the delegation about Venna's fate, quite yet. Telling them now would be needlessly unkind. If the small group of us who know can simply remain strong, we can give everyone else one last busy day, one last happy evening, one last night of untroubled sleep."

Wyve shifted in his chair. "It is certainly your decision to make, and Figg and I will honor it. Additionally, holding the reception as planned, tonight, may serve as a positive chance for reunification within the trading community, in the wake of yesterday's Judgments. In the interim, however, it leaves us facing that difficulty we discussed."

Burlon realized, with a jolt, that the "we" Wyve had just employed included Gredin... and did not include him.

"What difficulty?" he asked.

"One, actually, that you are uniquely suited to help us solve," Wyve replied.

That was a relief. Or it should have been. But Wyve was looking at him with an oddly fixed gaze. "What difficulty can I ease?" Burlon asked.

"It involves today's Trisectoriana. And Cirin."

"We still have half a day before the event," Burlon insisted. "He may yet return in time for the ceremony. It was his clear intention to do so."

"And, if he does, we will rejoice," Wyve assured him. "But let us speak of what will happen if he is... delayed. The Vokastra sets great store by this event. Arrangements have been made for broadcast. Magnanimous tokens of recognition have been prepared. As an organizer, you know all of this."

"I do." Burlon swallowed, wishing he had another cup of *kippi* in hand. "I understand the importance of staying in good favor with the Vokastra — especially now."

"Especially now," Wyve echoed gravely.

"And so—" Scabs, he hated this. But he supposed it had to be done. "And so, if Cirin is not here for the Trisectoriana, I will step forward and thank the Vokastra on his behalf."

"No," Wyve said.

Had he misunderstood Wyve's point? Perhaps he could avoid addressing the Vokastra, after all. "Would you prefer that his Chosen do so? I am quite certain she would be willing."

"No," Wyve said again.

Sometimes, it was better just to stop guessing. "Tell me, then, what you require."

"We require Cirin."

Burlon's nerves twitched. It wasn't like Wyve to be obdurate or obtuse. "Yes. I have already told you that I agree. If at all possible, Cirin should be here to accept the Vokastra's tokens of recognition. But if he is not...?"

"Then you must."

"But you said—"

"For the length of the Trisectoriana broadcast," Wyve clarified, "you must *become* Cirin. You must wear his clothes, and accompany his Chosen, and answer to his name."

"I couldn't!"

"I believe that you could. It is not an easy thing for Prett who do not frequent Tradepoint to tell one Vennan from another."

Burlon felt panic rising in his throat like a tide. "Cirin and I look nothing alike!"

"Do you not? To other Vennans, perhaps. But consider it from the Prett perspective. You are both men. You are both tall. You are both fair. You both wear your hair in braids, and dress in the Vennan fashion. Compared to a Hesch, or a Polpethtira, or even a Mamora, you and Cirin are nearly indistinguishable. Moreover, the Vokastra will be seeing you through the medium of a hologram broadcast, with everyone else in your party treating you as Cirin. Be assured, Burlon, the Vokastra will see what they expect to see. I am confident of it."

"I am not!"

"Then present me with a better solution. But I do not think you can. And Gredin tells us that you are Cirin's particular friend. His..." He looked to Figg for assistance.

"*Didana idia*," she said, pronouncing the Vennan syllables with crisp precision.

"Yes. That. Or have I mistaken its meaning? 'First Friend,' Gredin termed it. This means the most highly esteemed? Or the friend of longest acquaintance? Or does it denote both?"

"No. It means your essential friend. Like a Chosen... but not." The words felt like stones on Burlon's tongue. *Don't you understand?* he wanted to shout at them. *You are speaking of my closest friend... and he may be dead. Even as we sit here, defining terms, he may be dead! And you want me to spend the afternoon pretending to be him, accepting honors in his place...*

But the Vokastra had the final say over what transpired on Tradepoint. And the welfare of the Vennan delegation was now — had to be — Burlon's greatest concern. Could he risk offending the Vokastra?

"Well then," Wyve said, "in your closest friend's honor, you will do this thing, yes? You will accept the token my government wishes to present to him, if he does not return in time?"

Burlon wished it did not feel so wrong. He tried again to explain. "I would still far rather accept it on his behalf, rather than pretend to be him."

"I understand that," Wyve said. "But the presentation, the entire ceremony, has been designed to honor him. If we say to our government that Cirin was here for the rehearsal but is not here to be honored now, that he left Tradepoint although he knew that the presentation was due to take place today..." Wyve sighed. "It would inevitably give offense — unless, of course, we share with them what Gredin has told us. Is that what you advise, Burlon? That we inform the Prett government of Venna's destruction?"

The suggestion horrified Burlon. "No. Not yet. Not until we have some plan for how to proceed. And certainly not before we've told our own people. Tomorrow, Wyve. Tomorrow will be soon enough. If Cirin isn't back by then, we'll have to tell your government then. But not yet. Not today."

"And in the meantime…?"

He was trapped. "In the meantime, scrape it, yes. You win. I'll be Cirin at the presentation, if that's what you need me to do." He grimaced. "But I don't like it."

That drew Gredin's attention. "You will need to like it," she cautioned, "or at least appear to like it, else what is the point? If we undertake this, it is because we wish the Prett government to be pleased with the Trisectoriana and with us. That will not happen if you look sad, or bored, or angry during the presentation. You know Cirin's mind and spirit. Act as he would act. In fact, I advise you to look as he would look."

"What do you mean by that?"

"Cirin knew he was going to be honored. Perhaps he brought special clothing for the occasion. Ask his Chosen. She will know. Indeed, have her braid your hair for the ceremony."

"And what about Tetralanna?" Burlon challenged. "She intends to be there, and *she* certainly won't mistake me for Cirin."

"You and I will just have to manage her between us, as best we can."

"You expect the Voice to have a problem with this plan?" Wyve asked.

"Yes," Gredin said. "She does not believe my news of Venna, which leaves us deeply divided. And my difficulties yesterday at the Traders' Market and the Judgment did little to endear me to her." She shook her head. "In all fairness, this has been a troubling time for Tetralanna. She came here to carry out a specific task, but events have now gone in a very different direction. Tetralanna stands for what we were. I stand for what we must become."

"Unfortunately, she is the one assigned to speak at the Trisectoriana," Wyve observed.

"But I," Gredin replied, the faintest twinkle briefly brightening her gaze, "am the one assigned to translate her words from Vennan into Prettian." She turned to Burlon. "Fair warning. You will need to school your expression at the Trisectoriana. Keegan and Sill and Hayla have no more grasp of Prettian than Tetralanna does, so their composure will be unchallenged. But you will recognize, all too well, those places where Tetralanna's speech and my translation differ."

Figg cocked her head. "Your pardon, but would it not be wiser simply to leave her behind at the enclave, if her presence is apt to prove disruptive? We do wish matters to progress without incident."

The thought had already crossed Burlon's mind, and he turned with interest to hear Gredin's reply.

"Wiser? Perhaps," she admitted. "But Tetralanna takes great pride in her role as First Speaker. I do not want to take this final occasion away from her, when countless days of sadness stretch ahead for us all. If at all possible, I will protect Tetralanna's dignity today, and afford her this last formal opportunity to act as Voice for the delegation." Gredin squared her slender shoulders. "Besides, the Vokastra expect her to be present, and you have already made it clear that they do not react well to surprises. Therefore, I think it best that we leave Tetralanna's role unchanged. But if she says things that are untrue, or that might upset your government and risk forfeiting their tolerance of our continued presence here, I will have to intervene. I cannot permit her to complicate our standing with the Vokastra, not when it could endanger the very survival of our people. Fortunately, her lack of Prettian greatly limits any impact she could have."

"Then that is how it shall be," Wyve affirmed. "And you, Burlon? We may count upon you to take Cirin's place, if he does not return in time?"

Troubled, but seeing no better alternative, Burlon nodded.

"Then that answers our main concerns about today's Trisectoriana. But there is a matter concerning tonight's celebration that I should clarify," Wyve said. "During Figg's shift, we received confirmation that the Hesch and the Beng still intend to send representatives to the reception, in spite of yesterday's incident."

It was not what Burlon wanted to hear. The last thing they needed, after yesterday's Judgment, was to open the enclave to those who wished them ill. "No doubt they hope to cause trouble. Tell them they can't come."

But Wyve shook his head. "Excluding them now would cause more problems than it solves. This was presented as an open reception. The number from each delegation has already been limited to three attendees from each race, with a one-to-one security ratio on all non-Vennan attendees, including the Hesch and the Beng. That should suffice."

"Should," Burlon repeated. "But I have my doubts. And I don't trust the Beng."

"None of the Beng directly involved in yesterday's incident will be permitted to attend. And Figg and I will both be there. In a reasonable universe, that ought to inhibit even the Beng."

"When were they ever reasonable?"

Wyve sighed. "Concentrate on strengthening your ties with the Beng, not tearing down the few positive connections that still exist. At a calmer moment, you will see the sense of that for yourself. The Beng are still smarting from yesterday's Judgment. Do nothing tonight to make a future relationship with them more difficult. Deal calmly with them. Offer them no harsh word. Trust Prett security to enforce station rules and safeguard the Vennan enclave while the Beng are among you."

"And what of the Hesch?"

"They are likewise limited to three attendees, and our security will attend them closely," Wyve assured him.

"I am sorry to have harmed Nitikikani," Gredin said, "and to have incurred such a debt. And I am sorry, too, for making our relations worse with the Beng."

"Yes," Wyve agreed, "the Beng dearly love a profit, so you have indeed seriously annoyed them, since two thirds of the on-going penalty the Hesch receive will be borne by the Beng, in the station ledgers. Still, you've likely endeared yourself to the Hesch, since they'll be reaping the profits long after Nitikikani's foot has finally healed."

"What do you mean? You speak as if Nitikikani's foot is still broken. Surely the Hesch Healers have interceded for him, by now."

Burlon looked to Wyve. "You see what I am dealing with," he said. "Our people know nothing but Vennan ways." He swung his attention to Gredin. "Other races do not have Healers — not as we mean the term. Their bodies must mend without intervention by the Power, when they can mend at all. Nitikikani must wait for his broken bones to mend themselves. It will take time."

"By this evening?"

"Well, there's little I know about the Hesch, but I imagine it will be far longer than that."

Gredin looked horrified.

"The situation is not so extreme as Burlon makes it sound," Figg objected. "There are a variety of treatments we can offer, depending on the race of the individual and the nature of their injury. We can lessen the pain and speed the mending. But the Hesch — like you Vennans — are protective of their privacy, and so we know fairly little about their physiology. If he were Shodekekeen, or Rodorno, or even F'lala, we could do more. As it is, Burlon is correct that the mending of Nitikikani's bones will take time. This isn't the case for you Vennans?"

"Of course not," Gredin said. "We have Healers. Injuries are not permitted to linger."

"Permitted?" Wyve said, and Burlon could see the gleam of

interest that sometimes entered Wyve's gaze when a new trait of a race who came to Tradepoint caught his attention.

But today was not the time to indulge Wyve in the pursuit of such an inquiry. The morning was wearing on, bringing the time for the Trisectoriana ever nearer.

Burlon stood up. "We should be going. I'll need time to speak with Hayla and make my preparations. Wyve, Figg, I suspect we've made a sufficient wreck of your morning schedule. Gredin and I will head back to the enclave now."

"Actually," Figg said, "I thought I might borrow Gredin." She smiled at the girl. "Am I correct that this is what you will be wearing for the Trisectoriana?" Figg asked her, indicating the Shodekekeen gown.

"Yes. What is it that you need from me?"

"Your company, nothing more. It sounds as if matters between you and Tetralanna have grown tense, and so I thought you might prefer to wait with me, instead of returning to your enclave. If so, I can bring you to the communications center at the proper time. Meanwhile, I thought we might venture down to the Traders' Market."

At that suggestion, Gredin brightened. "Could we visit the Shodekekeen maartza? I want to thank the merchant there for his kindness, and for donating the fabric for this dress."

Wyve blinked. "It was a present? Not a purchase?"

Burlon shook his head. "I tried to talk him out of it, but he insisted. It was a handsome present. A personal thank-you is certainly merited."

"Then I will arrange for a security escort," Wyve said.

Figg chuckled. "Hardly necessary. I walk these corridors with impunity, and anyone who accompanies me is perfectly safe."

Burlon felt a stab of concern, but he knew that she was right. As Assistant Director of Tradepoint, Figg had no need of a security escort. He mustn't let the news of Venna's loss taint his judgment about what was safe and what was not. And he could see the sense of keeping Gredin separate from Tetralanna, for the time being. Dealing with Hayla would be more than enough to occupy his morning, without adding a clash between the two Balamont Speakers to the mixture.

46

1904 OF 2000 ORBITS REMAINING

Tradepoint made Hayla te K'lar's skin itch.

Well, not literally. The enclave had been scrupulously clean when they arrived, and those with the gyfte of Tending had, among their other efforts, kept it that way despite the influx of so many people into so small a place.

But it was, essentially, a windowless box, cool and uncompromising. One member of her House had compared its bareness to a rock cave. In Hayla's view, however, that was unfair to the cave. Rock, at least, was a natural substance with inherent variations of color and texture, however subtle. The silver metal of Tradepoint had no variations. Isolated from the natural world, its impersonal precision gave off no sense of welcome at all.

And so, since practically the moment of their arrival, she had been using her gyfte in a variety of ways designed to counter that effect. Her current project entailed joining the ends of rectangles of lace-work to form little cradles, each of which could then hold a luminth. Someone claimed to have found a way to suspend them from the high ceiling overhead, and so she and several others were preparing the cradles, to create a pretty alternative to the garish glare of the overhead lights for tonight.

This evening's reception was intended to soothe people, putting them at their ease by wooing their senses. Of course, some of the 'people' attending would not be Vennan, and that was admittedly a challenge. Their taste in temperature, lighting, and scent might well differ, from race to race, and so their preferences could not all be simultaneously accommodated. But the races were not utterly unknown to her. She had heard many tales about these assorted folk, during her happy years as Cirin's Chosen.

You had best be getting your wandering self back here, she told him in her thoughts. *The morning is already half-spent, and I am beginning to fret...*

"Hayla? I need to borrow you."

Looking up from the lace-work, Hayla smiled, delighted to see Burlon's familiar face. The reception hall was packed with people, but the group from House K'lar was quite small. She found it disconcerting to be surrounded by so many people she didn't know. Tomorrow's homecoming would be a sweet relief.

Is Cirin back yet? The question balanced on her tongue, begging to be asked. But there was no point to it; when Cirin returned, she would be the first to know, not the last. "I am yours to borrow," she told Burlon instead. "What do you need?"

"It's complicated," he replied. "Let us seek a quiet place and I'll explain."

A quiet place? That seemed a feeble hope. Everyplace was noisy because everyplace was crowded. "I suppose you can come to our sleep alcove, if you like. At this hour of the day, few enough should be in that area."

She expected Burlon to offer some better suggestion, since he knew Tradepoint so well. But he nodded and said, "Excellent." For so early in the day, he already looked worn, perhaps the result of coordinating the last-minute details of such a massive undertaking as the Trisectoriana on his own, without Cirin's aid.

As she came around the table and reached Burlon's side, she detected an unexpected scent, and gave him a sidelong glance. "Kippi?"

He made a face. "It's been an unusual morning."

"It must be, if you're indulging in Rodornon brandy before midday meal," she teased.

Her words won only a wan smile from him, and so she stopped. Teasing was common between herself and Burlon, but it was never meant unkindly. If he was truly feeling the pressures of the day, she would do what she could to help, and keep her jests to herself.

She took him out through the antechamber, enduring the bio-mist, then down the public corridor to the enclave which held House K'lar's sleeping area. Another antechamber, another dose of bio-mist, and then they were into the enclave itself, where she led the way past the red-striped blanket that denoted K'lar's area, and through the narrow labyrinth to the little alcove that she and Cirin had been assigned.

When Burlon stepped into it, he made a soft sound of surprise.

"What?" she asked.

He waved his hand at the alcove, with its carpet and clothing stand, and the plump, multi-colored pillows that secured the rolled bed mat in place, out of the way. "You make this little pocket of space seem cozy, rather than cramped. Not easily done."

She smiled. "I doubt you sought me out in order to offer compliments on my gyfte, but I thank you anyway. Now tell me, how can I ease your day? What do you need?"

The sound of a conversation suddenly reached them from nearby, although blurred by the many intervening walls of cloth.

Burlon frowned. "It is a sensitive matter. I would prefer not to be overheard. May I…?" And she felt his touch at the edges of her private mind.

Mystified, she nodded. She knew that Burlon found mind speech a bit difficult to manage. Whatever he wanted to discuss must be sensitive indeed, if he was willing to make the effort of silent communication. =Of course, if you think it necessary. What is this about?=

=The Prett officials. The Sectoriana. Cirin.=

=What about him? He promised to be back in time, and he will be.=

=Perhaps, but Wyve is worried. He wants us to have an alternate plan, in case Cirin is late. He's being quite insistent about it. The Prett Vokastra have somehow enabled everyone on their homeworld to watch the ceremony, and it would be a great embarrassment to them if the Trisectoriana didn't happen — or even if it was delayed.=

She stared at him in bewilderment. =Why should it concern them so? The fault would be ours, not theirs.=

Burlon shrugged. =I don't understand it all, myself, but I have rarely seen Wyve so concerned. It isn't like him to fuss over nothing. I would like us to oblige him, if we can.=

=A kind thought, but what can we do? Either Cirin returns in time or he does not.=

=That isn't Wyve's view of the matter. He has come up with an idea.=

=Oh? The Director of Tradepoint is so powerful that he can produce my Chosen on command?=

=In a sense.=

=Don't be foolish. In what sense?=

Looking rueful, Burlon replied, =He wants me to attend the Trisectoriana and pretend to be Cirin.=

Hayla stared at him, laughter bubbling up within her. =You misunderstood him, perhaps.=

=No,= Burlon said, and stood there, looking grim.

=But you look nothing like him.=

=So I explained. And so Wyve already knows. But he says the Vokastra won't notice.=

That caused a little whine of muffled mirth to escape her. She stifled it quickly. =Not notice? Have the Prett no eyes?=

=They are little acquainted with Vennans, according to Wyve. He is confident that they will see what they expect to see, especially if...= He fell silent, shifting his weight from foot to foot.

=If?= she prompted, when he did not go on.

=My apologies to you, Hayla, but Wyve believes it would be best if I were to dress as Cirin intended to dress... and to have you at my side.=

Belatedly, she began to feel wary. =Dress 'as he intended to dress'... You mean wear the K'lar overvest, and the House sash?=

Looking miserable, Burlon nodded.

=And have me accompany you, and treat you as if you were my Chosen?=

Another nod.

=He is a bold man, this Director of yours.=

=A long-time friend to both Cirin and me.=

=And he expects *you* to be bold, as well, it would seem.=

Burlon sighed. =Yes.=

=And what of me? What am I to tell my House members, when they see Burlon te Bentain strolling through the enclave, adorned in K'lar finery?=

Another, deeper sigh. =You will tell them that it was all my scheme, not yours. But you can also tell them that it was a plan fashioned to permit the Prett government to pay tribute to your Chosen, as they intended, with no mention of House Bentain to cloud the matter. As First Friend, I will leave my name outside the door and stand there as a shell, with no intent but to enable the ceremony of the Trisectoriana to move forward in Cirin's honor.=

It was clear that Burlon was in earnest. However strange this intention sounded to her, *he* was taking it seriously, and had thought deeply upon it. And he was taking no pleasure from the proposal.

=When did the Director ask this favor of you?=

=Just now. I left his office and came directly to find you.=

=And what do you fear?= she asked.

=What do you mean?= he countered, looking shaken.

=What you are asking is bizarre. So tell me, what bad thing do you think will happen if we decline this 'plan' and tell the Prett they will simply have to honor my Chosen on some other day?=

A decisive shake of his head. =Your pardon, Hayla, but there is more to this than I am yet free to explain to you. For now, I can only say that it matters. It truly matters — for you, for me, for all of us.=

Well! Small wonder Burlon looked weary, if such a weighty and mysterious matter had descended on him unexpectedly.

He was asking her to take him on faith. To trust him. And, indeed, why should she not? The matter appeared to fall within his gyfte of Trade — *this* in exchange for *that* — even if she had no precise idea of what *this* and *that* entailed. And he was her Chosen's First Friend. He would never knowingly do her harm, or take advantage of her. Besides, the entire undertaking would vanish like a burst bubble as soon as Cirin returned, which was likely to occur at any moment.

=All right then,= she said. =Sit down.=

=Your pardon?=

=Sit down, so I can braid your hair.=

=My hair is fine as it is.=

Hayla paced to within a few inches of him and said aloud, softly but with fervor, "No. It's not. If we are doing this, we are doing it properly. Either sit down or leave."

47

1903 OF 2000 ORBITS REMAINING

Burlon looked shocked. She supposed she had never delivered any sort of ultimatum to him before. He had already long been Cirin's didana idia by the time she met him, and that had set the tone for all of their interactions. But this was different. She would have to explain her part in this action to her Head of House tomorrow, when they reached home. And that meant making sure that Burlon did nothing to embarrass House K'lar at the Trisectoriana today.

Burlon freed one of the big pillows and sank down onto it.

=Someday,= Hayla commented silently, amused by his capitulation, =some poor girl in House Bentain is going to recognize that you're her Chosen, and she is going to have a busy time, training you out of all your bad habits and peculiar notions.=

With that, she Fetched a comb and set about undoing the utilitarian plaits into which Burlon had gathered his hair for the day. It was nice hair, she reflected as she ran her comb through it. Good, obedient hair, darker in color and a little thicker than Cirin's…

He moved restlessly beneath her touch.

=Quit fidgeting,= she admonished.

Burlon heaved a sigh. =This really isn't necessary.=

Hayla gave his hair a little yank, then resumed her work. =Sit still and stop complaining. If Cirin were here, this is precisely what I would be doing for him.=

=Pulling out his hair in handfuls?=

=Braiding his hair so that his appearance would do both his House and the occasion the proper honor. I don't know what behavior House Bentain tolerates from you, but House K'lar expects better from its members.=

He subsided.

Hayla worked quietly for a time, her fingers deftly parting and combing and braiding. Finally, as if her silence unnerved him, Burlon asked, =You'll come with me to the Trisectoriana, won't you, if Cirin isn't back in time?=

=Of course I will. As if I'd let my Chosen receive such an honor and not be there to watch! It is painfully clear to me, Burlon te Bentain, that you are a man who has no least idea of how things are properly done.=

Glumly, Burlon remarked, =Cirin needs to get back here.=

=He will,= Hayla told him without hesitation, then amended that flat assertion. =Perhaps not in time for the ceremony, as you fear, but he will come back. There's no point in worrying. Cirin is First Traveler. No one is more adept at Traveling the River. You're just nervous about giving the speech.=

Burlon jerked beneath her touch. =Ow! Speech? I'm not giving a speech. Wyve will just hand me some token, after the Prett government officials have had their say.=

=Sit still,= she insisted again, and resumed her work on a small braid at his right temple. =No, I'm quite certain that Cirin said he'd been asked to give a speech. Weren't you paying attention at the rehearsal?=

=I wasn't at the rehearsal. I had a pair of trade negotiations, as well as an emergency consultation with the Traders about that Judgment with the Beng and the...= He hesitated. =Wyve may have mentioned something about a speech, the day before, when we first met with him, but it sounded as if all Cirin had to do was offer his thanks.=

=Hmm.= Hayla's fingers moved on to a new section of braiding, this time at Burlon's left temple. =That's not what Cirin said about it after the rehearsal, just before he left.=

Burlon made a skeptical sound. =As I understood matters, Cirin had better things than a speech on his mind when he came to you.=

=Of course he did.= Hayla smiled at the memory. =As if I would allow my Chosen to venture out upon the River in less than perfect Balance. But we found time for a bit of conversation, as well, in and amongst our pleasures. He told me about that poor girl he was taking home, the one who lost her senses. And he spoke to me about the speech.=

=I'm not giving a speech. And the girl didn't go with him.=

=You are obstinate, and you are wrong.=

=I am obstinate, but I am right about the girl, and I am not giving a speech.=

She frowned down at the final braid she was completing. =Oh, but you must. I suggest you begin to Focus on doing it properly. Otherwise, you will look foolish, which will make the Director look foolish, and Cirin will never let you hear the last of it.= She gave his head a pat. =There. You look almost presentable. I'll get the outfits.=

As she began to lay out the splendid finery she had brought out, Burlon looked more and more daunted. The K'lar overvest was a heavy garment, covered in elaborate embroidery. Every gyfted Needlecrafter ever born to the House had left her mark on it, in one place or another, creating some new bit of design or embellishing what was already there. There was a special shirt to be worn under it, with long, full sleeves formed from pleated panels of deep-green satin. And leggings. She hadn't forgotten the leggings. As a final touch, the pale green House sash bore an embroidered version of K'lar's crest, highlighted here and there with geddel crystals and beads of gold.

Objectively, Hayla supposed it was a faintly ridiculous outfit, old-fashioned and elaborate, but she loved it. The skilled hands of dozens of her House members had crafted and enriched it, over time, and the bold colors were a feast for the eye. It caused her a pang to think that it was about to be worn by someone not born to K'lar, for the first time ever... but she had come too far to rescind her permission now.

Burlon was staring at it in horror. =I'll drown in fabric,= he said. =I'll roast. I may not even be strong enough to walk along the corridor, weighted down with all of that.=

Hayla adopted a mock air of sympathy. =Oh, are the men of Bentain so very frail, then?= A mischievous smile broke through. =Cirin will be greatly amused to hear so.=

Burlon just groaned.

It was a surrender, of sorts. Losing no time, Hayla chivvied him out of his practical clothing and into House K'lar's ceremonial finery.

=I don't even feel like myself,= he complained once he had donned it all.

=Because you *aren't* yourself,= she reminded him as she changed her gown. =Lace me up. You are Cirin te K'lar, First Traveler, and you had best keep that in mind until this Trisectoriana is complete.=

He looked down at himself. =I suppose I should be grateful that these ludicrous sleeves cover the fact that I'm not wearing First Traveler's hlette.=

The comment startled her. If the hlette had been present, would Burlon actually have had the effrontery to slip it onto his arm? Would he have attempted to wear an object of power that belonged to someone else, simply to enhance this strange masquerade?

He surveyed her critically. =Such a solemn face,= he chided.

=Smile. This is a happy event, remember? You are about to see your Chosen honored.=

What he said was a dare, of sorts. She offered him a dare in return. =Certainly. And when it comes time for your speech, if you can think of nothing better to say, simply tell them all how much you adore your Chosen.=

She intended for him to laugh, but he held up a cautionary finger. =There is one thing I should warn you about — Tetralanna te Balamont.=

=The Voice? What about her?=

=She doesn't know that I'll be taking Cirin's place at the presentation.=

Hayla felt her eyes widen as she considered the ramifications of Burlon's words.

=We didn't see any point in upsetting her,= he went on, =not while there was still a good chance that Cirin would be back in time. And now… well, I'd rather not explain it to her, here at the enclave. She'll only fuss, and it isn't as if there's anything different we can do about it, under the circumstances.=

But Hayla had strong misgivings. =If she's apt to fuss, wouldn't it be better for her to fuss here and get over it?=

Reluctantly, Burlon shook his head. =Tetralanna doesn't easily 'get over' things. If she's going to make a fuss, it might be better to deal with it at the communications center. She'll be less apt to balk when she's faced with the Director and the moment is upon us. Besides, she speaks no Prettian, which will limit how much of an uproar she can create. Gredin te Balamont will be acting as translator, and she already knows that Cirin isn't back.=

=A difficult situation for Gredin,= Hayla observed. =Are you certain she's up to it? Cirin said she was deeply troubled.=

Burlon gave her a skeptical look. =I doubt that's how he put it.=

=All right,= Hayla conceded, =he said she was a sobbing,

runny-nosed mess. Whyever did she change her mind about going home with Cirin, if she was so unhappy?=

=House honor, perhaps,= Burlon said. =But I've seen her already, this morning, and she's quite calm now. There appears to be no reason to worry about Gredin. I've notified Sill te Torr and Keegan te Fliss, as well. Tetralanna will be the only Vennan in attendance who is unaware. Between the five of us, we should be able to contain her reaction.=

=Think you so? The woman is a Speaker.=

=Yes, but she will be a Speaker who cannot be understood. And if you make it clear to her that you approve of what I am doing...=

=Oh, *now* I see. You're counting upon *me* to calm her, are you?=

=Well, I will be busy being honored. Gredin will be busy acting as translator. That only leaves Sill and Keegan — who are there to observe and document the event, not to take part in it — and you.=

She narrowed her gaze at him. =Unkind, Burlon. You place me in a difficult position.=

=I know. And I am sorry. But you will help us, won't you?=

She did her best to assume a haughty look. =For my Chosen's sake,= she said, then softened the effect with a smile. =One way or another, we will all get through this presentation. And it will make a fine tale to amuse Cirin when he returns.=

But a strange sense of dread was building within her, a raw mix of worry over Cirin and a sense of wrongness at seeing Burlon dressed in House K'lar finery...

=If you are ready,= Burlon said, with an air of resignation, =we had best go and meet the others at the antechamber. The Prett transport pod is here to convey us.=

=Then let us be on our way,= she said.

But Burlon hesitated.

=Is there a difficulty?= Hayla asked.

Burlon gestured at his borrowed clothing. =When we step out into the reception hall, is someone from your House going to leap up and object to my wearing these things?=

Hayla smiled. =If they do, I promise to protect you. Just walk like a man of purpose. I doubt whether anyone will detain you. So, are we going or not?=

=We are going,= he replied in a tone that was unusually meek, for Burlon, and followed as she started to lead the way out.

But she balked at the panel of blue-patterned cloth that served them as a door, and used that final moment of privacy to turn and ask him, quite soberly, =What do you suppose it means, that the hour for this Trisectoriana has nearly come and Cirin has not returned?=

He paid her the respect of a sober look in return. =It could mean anything. K'lar and Balamont are on opposite sides of the world. Perhaps Unter was asleep and Cirin was reluctant to wake him, and so delayed for a time. Perhaps the River journey tired him more than he expected, and he needed more than a quick nap and a meal before he felt up to the return. Perhaps he will yet arrive before the ceremony begins, and he and I will be forced to huddle in the public corridor, trading clothes. All I know for certain is that he is not here now, and that we would not wish him to attempt anything unsafe, and so we are going to cope with his absence as best we can, from moment to moment.=

It was fairly stated. With renewed resolve, Hayla said, =Indeed. Let us go and do this thing, however it may play out.=

[48]
ZRACH

The entry to Zrach, deceptively accessible, gave no hint of the dangers that lay beyond.

Cirin had been to Zrach only twice, in all his travels, and he had never seen the sun shine there. Dense clouds, rain, and fog: those were the three faces of Zrach that he knew. And the temperature was never pleasant, veering between clammy chill and moist, oppressive heat. The only inhabitants he had previously encountered were tiny stinging insects that left painful welts on any skin they contacted, small reptiles that scuttled from mud to pool and back again with disconcerting speed, a variety of large, scavenging birds, and the occasional herd of ponderous creatures that thrust their way, uncaring, through whatever bushes and trees crossed their path. Under normal circumstances, Zrach was a place to avoid.

But these were not normal circumstances.

Weary and wretched, Cirin exited the River there and stumbled forward, arms flailing in an effort to regain his balance as muddy ground sucked eagerly at his feet. Cursing under his breath, he scanned his immediate surroundings warily in the dim light, and spotted a small hillock nearly covered in fleshy, broad-leafed bushes, off to his right.

Aware of the dangers that exposure could bring, he quickly Sent there, and was relieved to find that the ground, though coated in a thin film of moss, was firm and dry. Sinking to his knees, he cautiously parted the bushes, shuddering at the unnatural texture of the plump leaves, more like the slick smoothness of damp skin than plant, before peering into the shadowed cave they created at their center.

Empty.

Grateful, he crawled beneath the branches, letting the thick foliage spring back into place above him, obscuring him from sight. A moment later, he heard a distant, wailing howl, repeating several times before it abruptly ended. Cirin shuddered. Predator or prey? He had no way of knowing, and no desire to discover the answer, so long as it did not involve him.

Limiting himself to small, careful movements, he lay down in preparation for a much-needed sleep, but when he curled onto his side, a lump near his right hip reminded him of what he carried and had forgotten. Rolling onto his back, he withdrew the tidy pouch Hayla had pressed into his hands as he prepared to leave for Venna.

"Give these rostti to my mother. Tell her they were made among the stars." Smiling, she pressed a warm kiss to his mouth. *"And don't think of eating them yourself, you rascal, for I intend to ask her how she liked them, first thing upon our return."*

Cirin opened the pouch with shaking hands, revealing six small squares of sweetcake, densely studded with fruit and nuts — a present, now impossible to deliver, that was more than welcome as his depleted body clamored for sustenance.

He ate them in swift bites, then licked every crumb from the fine, white cloth that had enfolded them. Finished, he replaced both the cloth and the pouch in his trouser pocket, refreshed himself to cleanliness and, once again, curled on his side to court sleep. Raising a thin shield to keep insects and small creatures at bay, he pillowed his head on his arm.

Only then did he loosen the tight bindings on his emotions and allow himself to feel the pain and despair of the appalling truth he had witnessed.

...Venna is no more...

Tetralanna te Balamont disciplined herself not to pace as she waited near the doors to the antechamber that contained the hateful mist the Prett insisted they breathe every time they left the enclave or returned.

It should all have been so straightforward. Make the journey to Tradepoint. Meet with the Director. Oversee preparations for the reception. Speak at the Trisectoriana. Officiate at the reception. Return home.

Instead, with midday meal already an accomplished fact, she was the only member of their little group at the appointed place, ready for the arrival of the Prett security escort. There was no sign of Cirin te K'lar, the honoree. No sign of Sill te Torr or Keegan te Fliss, who were to commemorate the Trisectoriana. No sign of Burlon te Bentain, the supposed organizer of their delegation.

And no sign of Gredin, her appointed translator.

That was hardly surprising, although she had held out a faint hope that the wretched girl would show herself, given the importance of the impending ceremony. But it was increasingly a concern, since the Silencing she had performed on Gredin the previous morning had long since worn off.

Earlier in the day, Tetralanna had left her chambers for morning meal, expecting to discover that Gredin was spreading her wild tale within the delegation to anyone who would listen. Instead, the meal — and the morning — had proceeded without incident, with no sign of Gredin anywhere...

Despite her resolve, Tetralanna began to pace. The girl was unstable. What other explanation could there be? It was shameful!

Suddenly aware that her growing agitation had become visible, Tetralanna halted with her back to the room. She smoothed the silken folds of her skirt, letting the gesture mirror her mental effort to soothe her affronted feelings into some semblance of calm. She was the Voice, after all. *She* had no intention of bringing further embarrassment to House Balamont. If the journey to Tradepoint had disrupted Gredin's hlinga so severely, Tetralanna supposed that her absence from the Trisectoriana might actually be a good thing.

And it wouldn't matter, in the end, that the girl refused to respond when her private mind was addressed. Burlon had already agreed to act as translator at the Trisectoriana, at need, eliminating any disruption Gredin's absence might cause. It was only sensible, since he had no other role to play in the—

"Good. We're all here. Shall we go?"

Tetralanna looked around to find that a foursome of Vennans had gathered behind her: Sill te Torr, Keegan te Fliss, a rather elaborately dressed Burlon te Bentain, and an equally well-dressed woman who was unknown to her.

Tetralanna crossed her palms to the stranger. "Tetralanna te Balamont, First Speaker and Voice."

"And I am Hayla te K'lar, Chosen of Cirin."

"Oh! I am most pleased to meet you." Tetralanna craned her neck. "Where *is* your Chosen?"

"Perhaps he will meet us at the communication center," Hayla said, while Burlon moved past them to open the doors of the antechamber. Nonplussed by Hayla's strange response, Tetralanna was inside and breathing the mist before she truly realized what was happening. She tried to quell the panicky feeling that the cloud of mist brought on, coughing a little as the outer doors opened to reveal a pair of tall Prett security guards waiting in the corridor.

Burlon greeted them and turned to face the group. "The Director has summoned a pod for us. Very thoughtful of him. Go ahead and take a seat. I need a private word with the Voice."

The others exited and the doors closed, leaving her alone with Burlon in the metal box. She waited nervously, expecting the Prett mist to descend again. When it didn't, she said sharply to Burlon, "Well, what is it you wish to say? This is hardly a place where I wish to linger."

"Some changes have been made to the Trisectoriana. I wanted to make you aware."

"Changes? Now? But we've already had the rehearsal," Tetralanna remarked.

"It couldn't be avoided."

Tetralanna realized that Burlon looked grim. "Well?"

"Cirin has not returned."

"What? But he needs to be here! The ceremony—"

"Cirin has not returned," Burlon repeated, cutting across her protest. Then he added, "And so I will be taking his place."

Tetralanna got a grip on her rising panic. "But you are not the one who is being honored," she said sharply. "Burlon te Bentain did not discover Tradepoint. You cannot usurp an honor that rightfully belongs to House K'lar." She stared up at him scornfully. "The ceremony must wait for Cirin to return."

"That is not an option, according to the Director."

Impatience tugged at her Control. "Then how *does* he wish to deal with Cirin's absence?"

Burlon took a deep breath. "I am to be Cirin, for the duration of the Trisectoriana."

Did everyone at Tradepoint eventually go mad?

"But clearly you are not Cirin. Everyone *knows* you are not Cirin."

"Only those of us attending know. And Wyve and Figg, of course." He rubbed the back of his neck. "Wyve believes this is the only solution that will avoid offending the Prett governmental officials. To do otherwise, he says, would create an incident that makes yesterday's trouble at the Traders' Market appear trivial, by comparison."

Tetralanna grimaced. "This is all that wretched girl's fault."

Burlon shrugged, his heavy overvest glimmering in the harsh lights of the antechamber. "Nevertheless, I agreed with Wyve that it would be unwise to insult important officials of the Prett government. So, for this Trisectoriana, I will be Cirin."

"You should have included me in your discussion with the Director, Burlon. There is a major flaw in this plan of yours, the possibility of which you seem to have overlooked."

"And what might that be?"

"The fact that I am the Voice, and that I will not agree to such a deception!"

Burlon frowned. "Wyve assures me that those on the Prett homeworld will not see a difference. To them, he says, one Vennan looks much like any other."

Tetralanna drew herself up. "Indeed? How insulting."

"It's not intentional," Burlon said. "Can you tell one Beng from another? Or a Mamora?" He shrugged again. "And that is to our benefit today, since we do not wish Cirin's absence to cause offense."

"No. I am sorry, Burlon," she said, firmly, her sense of outrage growing, "but I cannot allow it. The truth will serve us best. It always does." She gave his fine clothing a dubious look.

"I will act on Cirin's behalf and accept the honors that the Prett wish to bestow."

Burlon stared at her for a long moment, no doubt giving her strong words due consideration. Then, with a reluctant nod, he said, "My thanks, First Speaker, but that will not be necessary. I am Cirin's First Friend. I will explain that he was unexpectedly called away, and I will accept the Prett's tokens in his name."

He reached for the control panel, but she grabbed his arm as a sudden thought reawakened the panic she had been feeling since Gredin's disappearance. It stirred uneasily now, low in her stomach. "I am still counting upon you to act as my translator, Burlon te Bentain."

Burlon gave her hand an absent-minded pat, and gently removed it from his sleeve. "Don't distress yourself, Tetralanna. When the need arises, translation will be taken care of. Time grows short. We need to go."

This time, she let him activate the controls. The door panels opened silently, and Burlon walked out, pointing to a row of gleaming benches on a slightly raised platform, where the others waited.

"It's a good thing Wyve dispatched a pod. Our trip to the communications center will be quickly accomplished."

She hadn't been expecting something new. On the first morning, they had walked to the Director's office. She would have preferred to walk again, rather than let Burlon settle her onto one of the hard benches next to Keegan and Sill. In front of her, Burlon took a seat next to Hayla, just behind the Prett, who were front-most of all.

A translucent barrier rose up on either side, curving to join in the middle, high over their heads. Then, smoothly, the platform moved forward.

It was unnerving. Without intending to, Tetralanna found herself gripping Keegan's arm.

He offered her a smile. "If we pass any Mamora today,

perhaps the barrier will prevent us from being troubled by their scent."

It was a comforting thought.

It was less comforting to think about their silent progress along the corridor. Burlon had called the platform a "pod," using the same word that Growers used to describe the seed sac of a plant in the House gardens. The analogy made her uneasy, as if that odd outer barrier might develop notions of its own about whether to release them from their confinement.

The barriers, however, also separated her from any creatures that might be walking in the corridor, as the historian had pointed out. And the relative safety of the pod did give her a chance to study those around her. Sill sat silent, quietly dressed in a soft, grey gown, First of Memory's hlette her only adornment. Her other seatmate's attire was equally modest. The historian's dark blue teslan and leggings were so plain that they bordered on dull, with only a narrow band of lighter blue leaves to decorate the hem of his teslan. Appropriate and proper, Tetralanna thought, for they were only observers today. By comparison, her own gown of rich gold brocade, embroidered with designs in silver thread around the neck and hem, was bright and eye-catching.

Her smile faded as she studied Burlon and Hayla, whose outfits mirrored one another. Hayla's rich gown matched Burlon's shirt in both color and style, the dark green satin falling in narrow, knife-sharp pleats from her bodice. Tetralanna wondered how Hayla felt about Cirin's absence. The woman certainly seemed calm enough. It was reassuring to think that Burlon, however wrong-headed he had been in attempting to contrive a solution to Cirin's absence, had been willing to listen to wiser counsel, and that he had continued to honor his agreement to say nothing of Gredin's foolish night-thought.

Burlon caught her staring. A moment later, she felt him contact her private mind.

=Yes?= she responded with exaggerated patience, hoping he wasn't going to attempt to change her mind about what needed to happen at the Trisectoriana.

=I forgot to tell you,= he said instead. =I found your girl.=

=You found Gredin? Where is she? I need to renew the Silencing!=

=Don't concern yourself,= he said. =She seemed much calmer. Ah, we have arrived. I will tell you more, after the ceremony.=

Looking around, Tetralanna realized they had reached the communication center much more quickly than she had expected. When the pod came to a halt, she was relieved to see that the barrier split obediently along its upper seam and retracted without incident.

Keegan steadied her as she stepped down from the platform, then offered the same assistance to Sill. Hayla and Burlon followed, and the Prett security guards ushered them into the communications center where the Trisectoriana presentation was to take place.

Several Prett stood nearby, fussing with their gleaming machines. Sill stepped to the side, apart from everyone, her expression remote and composed. Keegan seated himself on the rear bench. Hayla sat at the front, while Burlon remained standing. Then the doors of the room slid open again, and the Director appeared in the opening, conferring with security.

Hayla gestured an invitation for Tetralanna to take the seat beside her.

When Tetralanna hesitated, she felt a touch at her private mind and, opening herself to the contact, heard Hayla say, =Your gown is lovely. That shade of gold certainly becomes you. I think we are about to begin.=

It seemed churlish to refuse Hayla's invitation. Tetralanna took the designated seat, then turned to watch the entrance of the Director of Tradepoint. Another Prett followed him, head bent in intense conversation with a slender Vennan who commanded attention in a gown of eye-catching scarlet fabric.

Tetralanna gaped, the sheer effrontery of it stealing breath away.

Gredin had indeed been found.

"They are ready to begin," Figg said.

Waiting in the corridor outside of the communications center, Gredin considered the harried mind touch she had received from Burlon, scant minutes earlier: =*I did my best to reason with her, but Tetralanna is adamant that I not attend the Trisectoriana as Cirin.*=

Gredin had kept her reply short and firm: =*I will handle it.*=

But how she was going to handle it was still a question.

The doors to the communication center parted. As she and Figg walked in, an audible gasp caught Gredin's ear, and a single face claimed her attention: Tetralanna.

The older woman was glaring, her face reddened with emotion, every line of her body tense with outrage. Gredin saw her stiffen, as if bracing herself to rise from where she was seated. In another moment, Tetralanna would be on her feet, expressing her anger and indignation volubly to the assembled group. And that might prove disastrous, not only for the ceremony but for the fate of the Vennan survivors.

To prevent it, Gredin hurried toward her, smiling warmly.

Tetralanna blinked, as if confused by so eager a greeting.

Gredin came straight to her and swept up her hands, gripping them as she marshaled her gyfte and spoke, her voice pitched to Tetralanna's ears alone.

"Hear me, Tetralanna te Balamont. You are Silenced completely for the duration of this Trisectoriana, except when the time comes for you to deliver your official speech of thanks to the Prett Vokastra. Once the ceremony has officially ended, this Silencing will end. For now, however, you will sit still, creating no disruption, and wait to be summoned forward to give your speech, after which you will return to this seat and wait in silence for the conclusion of this Trisectoriana."

Gredin had no doubt that the Silencing she had just crafted would be effective. The Power welled up within her like a strong wind filling a sail, and her gyfte answered. Faced with the sudden threat, a selective Silencing had been the best way she could think of to prevent Tetralanna from endangering the Vennan delegation, while still permitting her to deliver her speech to the Vokastra. It wasn't ideal, but Gredin was reasonably certain that it would suffice.

Releasing Tetralanna's hands, she looked around, orienting herself.

Cirin, to her grief, was absent.

Tetralanna, flushed with temper, was not.

Sill sat calmly by, ready to create a Memory of the Trisectoriana.

Burlon, dressed in his borrowed K'lar finery, looked pale and nervous.

The woman beside Tetralanna was almost certainly Cirin's Chosen, Hayla, given the similarities between her elaborate outfit and Burlon's.

It took an additional glance for Gredin to spot Keegan, tucked away on the final row of benches, his head bowed industriously over his notebook. She realized, with a pang of conscience, that she didn't even know whether he had succeeded in procuring any of the yellow paper from the Shodekekeen, in the upheaval caused by her disappearance and the ensuing Judgment.

For the moment, however, she was needed elsewhere. At a signal from Figg, Gredin took her place near the front of the room and composed herself, ready to translate the Prett ceremony into Vennan so that Keegan, Sill, Hayla and Tetralanna would understand what was taking place.

Wyve spoke briefly to the workers, and the broad column of light she had witnessed at the rehearsal came to life. Within it, a semicircle of Prett officials stepped into view, wearing dark-brown robes, each robe bearing a different-colored border at its neckline.

The Director's clothing was no different from what Gredin had seen him wear on the two previous days, but she noticed that he had added a large pin — perhaps an official badge of office — centered on his chest. He nodded to the hologrammed presence of the Prett officials, then turned and crossed his palms to the assembled Vennans.

The Trisectoriana was about to begin.

"I, Wyve, Director of Tradepoint, welcome you all. Today's ceremony honors the peace that exists between the people of Prett and the people of Venna, and celebrates our mutually beneficial trade relationship." He paused, and looked to Gredin.

"The Director of Tradepoint greets us," Gredin translated into Vennan, "and acknowledges our relationship with the Prett as peaceful friends and trading partners."

Was it her imagination, or had there been a trace of unsteadiness in Wyve's voice as he said "the people of Venna"? She'd had a day and a half in which to absorb the horrifying news of Venna's loss — a day and a half, and the Power's calming intervention. For Wyve, that news was freshly received, and it was likely a struggle for him to sound calm and measured as he concealed that information from the officials of his world.

The first Prett in the semicircle stepped forward and spoke, in sonorous Prettian. "Our thanks to you, Director Wyve, for coordinating this event. I, Duv, current President of the Prett Vokastra and Chairman of the governing ministers of Prett, offer greetings to the visiting representatives from Venna."

"The senior Prett official, called Duv, welcomes us," Gredin supplied.

"We unite today," the brown-robed President continued, "in recognition of Vennan citizen Cirin te K'lar, and of the Vennans, our valued trade allies. Three hundred sectora have passed since Cirin te K'lar became the first of his people to make the journey from Venna to Tradepoint. Today's Trisectoriana is a public recognition of that accomplishment."

Gredin addressed the others. "He announces the Prett's intention to honor Cirin as the first Vennan to Travel the River to Tradepoint, three hundred Prett sectora past, and affirms us as valued trade partners." She saw Burlon's tension increase at the mention of Cirin's name.

Duv resumed. "For our presentation to Cirin te K'lar, I yield the floor to Arn, Senior Trade Commissioner, who is accompanied by Pord, the Melding Mediator."

Gredin wondered, *What is a Melding Mediator?* But this was not the time to ask. "Duv passes matters on to Arn of Trade," she translated, "and to Pord, whose role I will ask Wyve to clarify after the presentation."

Duv stepped back, and two new Prett came to the fore, the taller one dressed much as Wyve and Figg were, the shorter one in a brown robe bordered in green.

"Cirin te K'lar, step forward," the taller one intoned.

Gredin looked to Burlon, who walked to where Wyve was standing. Off to the side, she saw Tetralanna turn her head sharply, tracking his every move.

The short, brown-robed Prett said, "Cirin te K'lar, you exemplify your people's adventurous spirit. Vennans and Prett alike have benefited, these past three hundred sectora, from your presence on Tradepoint, and we confidently predict a productive future of trading for many sectora to come."

In Vennan, Gredin said, "Arn of Trade applauds Cirin's bold Travels, and speaks of prosperous future Trades."

"In recognition of your accomplishments," the speech continued, "we now award you with the following tokens. Director, if you will assist us…?"

Wyve turned to Figg, who handed him a small metal rectangle and a palm-sized box.

"This first present is for your personal use, here on Tradepoint," the Prett continued, and Wyve placed the rectangle on Burlon's palm. "It pleases us to present you with this credit token in the amount of three thousand station credits — ten credits for each sectora since your first arrival."

Looking astonished, Burlon nearly dropped the metal token, then tightened his fingers around it in a fisted grip. "You are too generous," he said in Prettian, his voice hoarse. "My thanks to you."

"The Prett present to Cirin is a token worth three thousand station credits," Gredin reported to the others. Was it her imagination, or did she see her words kindle an indignant fury in Tetralanna's eyes as the woman's gaze flicked from Gredin to Burlon and back again?

But Gredin had already selected her path, at Wyve's insistence, and she dared not deviate from it. The Trisectoriana was proceeding, and she needed to stop worrying about Tetralanna, or risk losing the thread of the presentation speech. "…honorary status here on Tradepoint," the Prett stated, "to be worn with pride as you move among us."

Wyve opened the small box, removed an object from it, and handed the empty box back to Figg. Then, approaching Burlon, he affixed something to Burlon's sash, above the K'lar crest, and stepped back.

Burlon turned slightly, and Gredin saw that the item was a pin — a miniature replica of the large one that Wyve was wearing.

Hastily, Gredin offered a translation. "Arn of Trade has given Cirin a small pin similar to the badge of office worn by the Director. The pin is ceremonial, a mark of respect in recognition of Cirin's long history here on Tradepoint."

"...appreciative if you would address the people of Prettig," the Melding Mediator said, speaking for the first time.

It was the cue for 'Cirin' to make his acceptance speech, but Burlon stood silent, color draining from his face, his eyes filled with panic as he looked to Gredin.

His distress startled her. Burlon never had trouble talking. He was a Trader, by gyfte. He could — and did — converse easily with everyone. But something — perhaps worry over Cirin's fate, or awareness of Tetralanna's livid disapproval, or a realization that the entire Prett world was watching — had shaken him badly.

She knew that there was no time for him to step aside and compose himself. The event needed to move forward. All eyes were on him. Already, Wyve was regarding Burlon with concern, and Gredin could sense the Vennans stirring uncertainly.

She shut them out of her awareness, Focusing solely on reaching Burlon's private mind.

=Burlon.=

=Gredin! I can't...=

She summoned her gyfte. =Burlon, listen to my words. Look at the Prett officials. Do it now. Smile at them, if you can. If not, at least offer them a nod.=

Stiffly, he turned to face the Prett again. Hesitated. Nodded.

=I will give you the words,= she assured him. =Do not worry. Do not try to think. Just repeat my words. Are you ready? =

Burlon nodded again.

=You humble me,= she prompted.

Nothing happened. Moments crept past.

=*Say* it,= she urged. =You humble me.=

"You humble me," Burlon said aloud in Prettian, and the unaccustomed roughness of his voice gave the words a surprising air of authenticity.

=I am a Traveler who has seen many worlds...=

He squared his shoulders. "I am a Traveler who has seen many worlds..."

=...but Tradepoint is unlike anything I have experienced.=

Obediently, Burlon repeated her words — not only the words, but the tone and inflection that breathed life and emotion into them. Gredin placed the phrases silently into his mind, and they issued from his lips with persuasive fluency.

=It is one thing to arrive upon a world...= A brief pause.

"It is one thing to arrive upon a world..."

=...and observe its people, and the society they have built.=

She had to be careful not to crowd too many words into his mind at once. He needed time to breathe, time to swallow...

"...and observe its people, and the society they have built," Burlon said.

=But Tradepoint is different from all of them.=

"But Tradepoint... Well, Tradepoint is different from them all."

It was difficult to gauge the response of the officials, who were only available to her as images. Instead, she kept Wyve at the edge of her vision, relying on his reactions.

=This is a place where many races can gather to deal with one another.=

The angle of Burlon's shoulders seemed less rigid than when they had begun. "This is a place where many races can gather to deal with one another."

Encouraged, Gredin concentrated on working toward a fitting conclusion.

=This fair and peaceful situation is only possible because of the guidance and oversight of the Prett.=

"This fair and peaceful situation is only possible because of the guidance and oversight we receive from the Prett," Burlon said.

Yes, Wyve seemed pleased by that.

=And so,= Gredin prompted, =while I am deeply grateful to you for honoring me today...=

"And so, while I am deeply grateful to you for honoring me today...."

=...I must, in fairness, also honor you, the officials of the Prett Vokastra.=

"...I must, in fairness, also honor *you*, the officials of the Prett Vokastra."

They were nearly done. It required only a final thought, to round it out.

=Your wisdom and dedication have created Tradepoint, a place that benefits all who venture here,= she began.

"Your wisdom and dedication have created Tradepoint," Burlon said, "a place that benefits all who venture here."

=And that is something of which you can be extremely proud, and for which we are all extremely grateful.=

"And that is something which should make you extremely proud, and for which we are all extremely grateful."

There. That should do.

Carefully, she lightened the touch of her contact with Burlon's mind and prompted, =Nod to them again, more deeply this time, then slowly turn away. Well done, Burlon. Well done.=

As he followed her instructions, she turned her own attention to the other Vennans. Quickly, she summarized Burlon's speech, partly for the sake of Sill's Memory of the event, and for the account of it that Keegan would write. But she also did it for the benefit of Tetralanna, who would be called upon in a few moments to offer her own remarks, and would therefore need to know what points had already been covered and what sentiments had been expressed.

Not that Tetralanna appeared appreciative. She might look calmly impassive to the Prett, but it was clear to Gredin that Tetralanna was still seething over what she and Burlon had just done.

Within the hologram, a new Prett stepped forward, with red edging on the neckline of his robe. He was by far the thinnest Prett that Gredin had seen, and his voice was less resonant when he began to speak, causing Gredin to wonder whether he was unwell.

"I am Gof, Senior Economics Commissioner," he began. "The Prett government wishes to convey its commemorative present to the Vennan government's representative at this time."

Gredin translated Gof's title and message, and stepped to the side. The moment had come. Would the Silencing permit Tetralanna to deliver her speech, as Gredin intended?

Tetralanna rose to her feet, smoothed the folds of her gown, surveyed the room, and made her way, slowly, slowly, to the appointed spot. When she reached it, she took a proud stance, cleared her throat... and spoke. "I am Tetralanna te Balamont, First Speaker and official Voice, appointed to speak today on behalf of the Vennan people."

Relieved, Gredin translated that information from Vennan into Prettian.

Gof lifted his chin and launched into what were clearly

prepared remarks, pausing after each sentence while Gredin translated his words for the benefit of Tetralanna, Sill, Keegan, and Hayla. Burlon, of course, had no need of her translation; he understood the Prettian words at least as well as she did.

"We, as representatives of the people of Prettig," Gof began, "extend our good wishes."

"The members of the Prett Vokastra greet us and wish us well," Gredin said.

"In the course of the past three hundred sectora, our world has come to know yours well, if indirectly, through the quality of the Vennan citizens who venture here."

Gof's words, politely complimentary, were spoken with little conviction, and Gredin found herself wondering whether he used the same speech for each race at Tradepoint when its anniversary date was honored. Nevertheless, she rendered the words with clarity. "In the course of our long trading history, the Prett feel that they have become familiar with us as a people."

"As our mutual trade has grown, our mutual trust has grown," Gof continued.

It was a simple sentence. Its ramifications, in the present situation, were less simple. Nevertheless, Gredin felt bound to translate it with accuracy. "Over time, both the trade and the trust between us have increased."

"Venna," Gof stated, "has proven itself to be a sound trading partner, honest and reliable in all things."

With a certain heaviness of spirit, Gredin made a slight adjustment as she said in Vennan, "The Prett official observes that he finds our Traders to be reliable individuals."

"Therefore, in honor of the upright character of the Vennan people, and our lengthy trading history with them, the officials of Prettig grant a one-sectora suspension of station fees and enclave payments for our friends from Venna, as an expression of our desire for many mutually prosperous sectora to come."

"Their present," she translated, "excuses us from station fees and enclave payments for the coming year. This is a reward for our long pattern of trade with the Prett, underscoring their wish for trade between us to continue for long and long."

It sounded well, but Gredin had left out the phrase "in honor of the upright character of the Vennan people."

Burlon would recognize the omission. Tetralanna and the others would not.

Coming to Tradepoint, Gredin had anticipated that her duties as translator would be straightforward and pleasurable. Right now, she was finding them to be neither.

Abruptly, Gof of the Prett nodded, signaling that his statement was complete.

It was Tetralanna's turn to speak. Gredin Focused her full attention on her, wishing she had more confidence in what was to follow.

"Senior Economics Commissioner Gof," Tetralanna began. "Arn of Trade. Prett President, Duv. Your generosity exceeds our worthiness. My gratitude to you, on behalf of the Vennan people, is deep and sincere."

Gredin conveyed those thanks in Prettian, hoping that Tetralanna would consider the matter of her remarks to be at an end.

But no. Drawing breath, Tetralanna said, "I had prepared a short address for today, in tribute to our friendship with the Prett, but it is clear to me that a weightier matter needs to be addressed."

=Don't translate that,= Burlon ordered silently, his thoughts urgent in Gredin's mind.

=I must say something,= she replied. =And it may yet be all right.=

She rendered Tetralanna's words with precision into Prettian, and the Vokastra eyed her with a sudden air of startled interest.

"Vennans have always prided themselves on being truthful," Tetralanna began.

=Careful,= Burlon cautioned.

Gredin hesitated, wanting to see what Tetralanna would say next.

But Tetralanna made it clear, with a glare, that she was in no mood to allow Gredin to wait. She stood silent, forcing Gredin to carry out her role and translate without further delay, or explain to the Prett why she did not.

Balanced upon a precarious point of decision, Gredin took Tetralanna's measure, and chose a third course of action. In her best Prettian, she said, "Hospitality is a door that must swing in two directions."

That drew a sharp glance from Figg, and a baffled one from Wyve.

Gredin looked back to Tetralanna. She might yet be wrong in her suspicion that the older woman intended to expose the matter of Cirin's absence. If so, there would be time to catch up with the gist of her speech...

Tetralanna's nostrils flared as she drew in a deep breath and continued. "But what you have heard today bears little resemblance to the truth."

=Bloody cuts,= was Burlon's pithy reaction.

Gredin remained calm. =Reassure the others,= she instructed him, knowing that they would understand Tetralanna's accusations all too clearly, but that they would find Gredin's 'translation' in Prettian as incomprehensible as Tetralanna did, unless Burlon let them know what she was really saying.

Assuming a sober expression, Gredin said to the assembled Prett, "And so tonight, at our reception, we will open our doors to welcome others and show them our ways."

"In particular," Tetralanna continued, as soon as Gredin stopped speaking, "the man who stood before you just now, claiming to be Cirin te K'lar and accepting your generous presents, is actually Burlon te Bentain."

Well. *That* was going to call for a bit more ingenuity.

Gredin composed herself. "Some who attend our reception tonight may be familiar with our Travelers, headed by Cirin te K'lar, while others are on friendly terms with our Traders, headed by Burlon te Bentain."

And still Tetralanna continued. "I will bring this to the attention of his House, when we return home tomorrow," she said. "Be certain that this day's actions will win him a serious rebuke. What explanation can be found to excuse Hayla te K'lar, Cirin's Chosen, who has sat by in silence through this deception, I cannot begin to imagine. I, on behalf of Venna, offer you our most sincere apologies."

=Caution Hayla to look solemn but not distressed,= Gredin alerted Burlon, and said to the Prett Vokastra, "Most of us who made this journey are neither Travelers nor Traders, but Tenders, and Makers, and Growers. And we are graced to include Hayla te K'lar, Cirin's Chosen, who thanks you for honoring him, as all of Venna thanks you for your hospitality, your generosity, and your creation of this unique place."

At that, she dared to glance quickly at Wyve, hoping that he would bring matters to a close before Tetralanna took some action that couldn't be explained away. But it was Figg who stepped forward and said briskly, "Our thanks to Tetralanna te Balamont." She made a gracious-looking gesture, indicating that it was time for Tetralanna to return to her seat.

Gredin held her breath.

With a curt nod, Tetralanna stalked back to her bench and sat down.

Figg smiled. "With your permission, President Duv, this concludes the speeches and presentations for today's Trisectoriana. Our Vennan guests have much to do in preparation for the evening's reception, which we deeply regret your inability to attend. Tradepoint Director Wyve and I will, of course, stand as your representatives. We will provide you with a full report of the event, tomorrow. Director, your closing statement?"

Gredin provided a hasty translation. "The Assistant Director acknowledges the Voice's words, and thanks the Prett officials for their time and attention, promising them an account of tonight's reception. She now invites the Tradepoint Director to make his concluding remarks."

Gamely, Wyve stepped forward, nodded to the Prett hologram and, in a nice touch, turned to nod to Tetralanna, as well, with a properly somber expression. Then, facing the hologram, he said, "President, members of the Vokastra, Melding Mediator Pord, thank you for taking time from your busy schedules for this presentation. The Vennans and we, the administrators of Tradepoint, are deeply honored, and we bid you a respectful good day."

Gredin translated. "The Director thanks the Vokastra for honoring us with their time. On his own behalf and ours, he respectfully bids them farewell."

The Prett President nodded graciously. And then, at a subtle signal from Figg, the image of the gathered officials winked out.

An uneasy silence fell over the room.

With the ending of the Trisectoriana ceremony, the Silencing ended, as well. Tetralanna paced forward instantly to where Wyve and Figg stood, crossed her palms to them, and said, "Director, Assistant Director, I apologize deeply on behalf of my delegation. Their behavior today was inexcusable." She flicked a glance at Gredin, and snapped, "Translate. Then we are leaving."

Keegan's glance was sympathetic, Burlon's indignant. Hayla and Sill were cautiously expressionless. But Gredin saw no point in contradicting Tetralanna openly. Looking to Wyve and Figg, she said in Prettian, "Director, Assistant Director, Tetralanna expresses her extreme displeasure at our conduct here, and offers her deepest apologies. I, on the other hand, congratulate you on surviving a uniquely challenging diplomatic ceremony. We will return to the Vennan enclave now, and we look forward to hosting you, this evening. Should you need me sooner, you have only to call for me."

"You and your people have our sympathy and our support," Wyve said. "We will join you tonight. For now, transport awaits to return the group to your enclave."

And he and Figg departed.

The pod ride back to the Vennan enclave was grim.

To begin with, the matter of seating became awkward. Tetralanna, stalking ahead of the group, claimed the center of the second bench, outrage written in every line of her stiff posture. Burlon bustled Hayla onto the third bench. Prett security settled on the first bench, each guard so large and muscular that the two of them filled it from side to side.

That left three seats available: one next to Hayla, one on Tetralanna's right, and one on Tetralanna's left.

For a tempting instant, Gredin eyed the spot next to Hayla. But Tetralanna was her House member and therefore was, in a way, her responsibility. And she was the one who had defended Tetralanna's right to exercise her role as designated Voice one last time, at the Trisectoriana.

How very differently matters had unfolded.

Leaving Keegan and Sill to settle the matter of the remaining two seats, Gredin gathered her scarlet skirts and sat down at Tetralanna's left.

With a huffy sigh, Tetralanna twitched her own skirts of gold brocade aside and, after giving Gredin a single burning glance, looked away.

A few moments later, with Sill seated on Tetralanna's other side, and Keegan behind them with Burlon and Hayla, the pod began its smooth journey. Since Tetralanna so clearly had no wish to communicate, Gredin felt free to gaze out at the intersecting corridors as they passed, allowing her thoughts to roam at will.

She was deeply grateful to Wyve and Figg — and to her Vennan companions — for helping her shield the Vokastra from any awareness of discord during the presentation, and for maintaining a properly sober demeanor when her translation strayed from Tetralanna's words. Without Tetralanna's inability to speak or comprehend the Prettian language, and, more importantly, without the Silencing Gredin had placed upon her, the Trisectoriana would have been a debacle.

But the Silencing was now at an end, and it was clear that Tetralanna's disapproval would soon be impossible to contain. They were returning to the enclave and its nine hundred and thirty-seven Vennans, all of whom would clearly understand any opinions that Tetralanna decided to express.

She had every right to do so. But the timing was regrettable.

One more night. Gredin was determined to let one more night pass before she revealed the devastating reality of Venna's destruction. Nothing could alter that terrible truth, but she could give her fellow Vennans one last evening to enjoy before circumstance stole their happiness away.

But doing so meant that she and Burlon would have to stand silent in the face of Tetralanna's fury, bearing the brunt of complaint expressed by the delegation's Voice. One more night would have to pass before Gredin could explain the reasons behind her actions at the Trisectoriana, and speak openly about the cause of Cirin's absence.

Fortunately, people's attention would be distracted, tonight.

The pod glided to a halt at the entrance to the enclave.

"You," Tetralanna snapped at Gredin, her lip curling in distaste. "Come straight to the room. Don't wander off and disappear again."

"Yes," Gredin agreed quietly, "you and I need to talk."

Tetralanna turned, followed Sill off the bench of the pod, and stalked away.

"Not good," Burlon muttered from the rear bench, plucking at the high neck of his overvest, as if eager to remove it.

Gredin stepped off of the transport pod and turned to face Burlon, Hayla, and Keegan. "I'll go and try to set matters right with Tetralanna."

"An ambitious goal," Keegan said, and offered her a sympathetic smile.

"Perhaps. But I'll do my best to calm her," Gredin assured them.

They entered the antechamber. The bio-mist treatment already seemed like a common occurrence, and Gredin breathed deeply, grateful that the Prett had created such a thing.

Tetralanna did not seem similarly inclined. She had isolated herself by taking several steps away from the group, but her unhappiness with the process was still apparent. She choked and coughed until the mist cleared, then broke from the chamber with quick strides as soon as the inner doors opened.

Entering the enclave, Gredin found the Vennan community teeming with activity as they prepared for that evening's reception. Magnificent aromas were already escaping from the kitchen to enhance the air, and she found herself inhaling occasional delicate floral scents, as well, as she walked as direct a path as she could manage through the throng. In one spot, a table loom had been assembled, with a demonstration area for carding and spinning arranged nearby. A variety of decorated dinnerware settings caught her eye, a little farther on, with paints and glazes standing ready next to plates and trays waiting to be adorned.

Somewhere else, she knew, Ingarra was one of several dozen craftspeople preparing examples of needlework and knitted items. And, through it all, an elusive wisp of melody made itself heard, as a sole harper practiced his part. The musicians, when they assembled, would supply a long evening of performances, some accompanying the dancing demonstrations, others as members of instrumental ensembles or as soloists in their own right.

As she walked along, people noticed her in her scarlet dress, and offered cautious nods of greeting. Contentment permeated the room, the byproduct of thousands of Vennans happily engaged in the pursuit of their gyftes. Spirits were high, eyes bright, mouths curving in ready smiles.

All too soon, she reached the door to the chambers she and Tetralanna shared. She paused for a moment, creating a centered core of stillness within herself. Then, Balanced, she opened the door and stepped inside.

Burlon had watched Hayla, all through the ride on the transport pod back to the Vennan enclave. He stayed close to her, not quite touching her but ready to support her at need, as they waited through the bio-mist in the antechamber. In the reception hall, which was now a hive of activity, she blundered into someone, and had to offer a choked apology. When it happened again a few steps later, Burlon could stand it no longer. "Come here," he said, gathered her to him, and Sent them both to the little sleeping alcove assigned to Hayla and Cirin.

The relief of being out of the noisy crowd weakened his knees. The look of frightened apprehension on Hayla's pale face weakened them even further.

"He didn't return," she whispered. "The Trisectoriana has come and gone, and Cirin missed it."

It was all coming unraveled. Now that the ceremony was over, and the Vokastra was no longer watching, Burlon couldn't bear to mislead her with little crumbs of truth. She deserved the entire loaf.

"Help me out of these clothes," he said. "Help me out of them, and then I will tell you everything."

She gripped his arm, her fingertips pressing hard against the pleats. "Where is Cirin? What can have happened to him?"

As he had done earlier, Burlon reached out to her private mind, and she admitted him instantly, dropping all barriers, letting him feel the raw panic that filled her.

=Truly, Hayla, I do not know where he is, or how he fares. But I know other things that you should hear, important matters that may account for his absence. I will tell them to you. I will tell them all to you. But first, please, help me to remove this outfit with the reverence it deserves. Let me go back to being what I am, Burlon te Bentain, Cirin's didana idia and your good friend. Then I will answer every question you have, and tell you all the things that you do not yet realize you need to ask.=

The promise quieted her, although he knew it could do nothing to ease her fears. In silence, deeply subdued, she aided him with the unfamiliar lacings and buttons, removing the crested sash, the embroidered overvest, the shirt with its long, pleated sleeves, and the sleek, fitted leggings.

It was an unspeakable relief to step back into his own comfortable trousers and tunic and jacket.

"Here," Hayla said aloud, her voice small and unsteady.

He turned to find that she had removed the ceremonial pin Wyve had fastened to the sash. She held it out to him.

"It isn't mine," Burlon said.

"Nor mine," she said. "Take it, for now. Keep it safe."

"If you like," he conceded. Accepting it from her, he tucked it into the deepest pocket of his trousers.

"And this," she said, and he saw that she had found the rectangular credit token, as well. Three thousand station credits, potentially enough to fill half a warehouse, depending on the bulk of the goods being purchased, and yet it fit tidily onto the palm of her hand.

Reluctantly, he added it to the pocket that held the pin.

=And now,= she said, reverting to the silence of mind touch,

=explain to me why my Chosen was not here to receive those presents.=

It was a bitter task, one he was unsure how to begin. =The answer is not short. May we sit? Would you like a cup of besk, before we begin?=

She tried to smile, but there was a wobble in it that touched his sympathies. =I suspect, from the look of you, that we might both be better served with a measure of Rodornon *kippi*.=

=That may be,= he conceded. =But it is a tale that deserves to be told sober.=

=Then sit with me,= she invited, and they each chose a pillow, and sat.

Burlon groped to find the proper thread for the unraveling of his tangled tale. =It began with Gredin te Balamont,= he said, =and a thing that happened… or did not.=

Hayla waited, looking at him askance.

=Some believe that Gredin te Balamont had a frightening night-thought, on our first night here.=

=And what do others believe?= Hayla asked.

Feeling sick, Burlon replied, =That the Power came and spoke a truth to her, as she slept.=

Hayla looked shocked, then amused, then concerned. =And if I were to ask one of those who believe, what truth did the Power speak to her?=

Oh, this was a grim thing to have to put into words, even within the privacy of his own mind. Reluctantly, Burlon said, =That Venna, in our absence, has been destroyed.=

Hayla cried out, then clapped both hands across her mouth. =Impossible!=

Burlon nodded. =So we told Gredin.=

=We?=

=Those to whom she confided her tale. Tetralanna. Sill te Torr. Keegan te Fliss. Myself. And Cirin.=

=Cirin! He heard her make this claim?=

=He did more than hear it. To reassure Gredin, he promised to make the journey to Venna and bring back a token to prove to her that all was well there.=

Hayla leaned back. =A token? No. He intended to take her home.=

=That plan came later. At first, he thought only to dash home, obtain some unmistakable keepsake from her House, and return. But Gredin entangled herself in the difficulty at the Traders' Market, and Tetralanna decided we would all be better served if Cirin simply removed the girl entirely from Tradepoint.=

=Then why didn't he?=

=She hid. She was afraid to go with him.=

Hayla looked indignant. =Afraid? He is K'lar's First Traveler. Nothing could be safer!=

=It was not Cirin's competence that she questioned. It was his destination.=

=Oh. Of course. Her night-thought.=

=Her night-thought… or the Power's message. She believes it absolutely. She begged Cirin not to go, with or without her, for fear of what might happen. But Cirin said there was no reason to worry. He believed that she was wrong — and that, even if she was right, there would simply be no exit from the River. He would Travel on to Palomar, rest himself there, and then return to us here.=

Hayla's face brightened. =But that would take longer. It would explain why he hasn't yet arrived.= Looking resolute, she added, =If that is so, then we have done the right thing. The Trisectoriana has been carried out, even if my Chosen had to miss it, and the Prett Vokastra are satisfied. It is not so very terrible a thing.= She cocked her head. =And yet you do not look relieved. Why? What am I failing to understand?=

He would have spared her, if he could. He would have kept the burden to himself. But she was asking, and he had promised to answer her questions. Gently, he asked, =What are we to do, tomorrow, if Cirin still has not returned? What are we to do when midday meal concludes, and everyone wishes to return home, if he is not back by then?=

Her shoulders slumped. =What are you saying?=

Burlon extended both of his hands and turned them palms-up, as if weighing two objects. "Either Gredin's night-thought was true or it was not. Either Cirin found Venna unharmed or he did not. If he found Venna unharmed, why is he not here with us now? And if he did not find Venna unharmed, what madness would it be for us to launch ourselves, tomorrow, upon that same journey?= He lifted his right hand slightly. =Perhaps all is well, and he has simply been delayed for some reason you and I have not considered. In that case, he will return to us as quickly as he can, will he not? Or, at the very least, would he not have some other K'lar Traveler come here, with a message for us?=

Hayla nodded. =He would.=

Burlon lifted his left hand. =But if all is *not* well... then we cannot leave this place until we know more. We cannot blindly follow Cirin's path, not knowing what has gone amiss. That is only sensible, is it not?=

=But...=

Burlon waited.

=But everyone will want to go home.=

=Yes. They will. But we cannot permit it. Not yet. Not as things currently stand. And perhaps not ever.=

Her breath caught. =Ever?=

Burlon lowered his hands. =Either Gredin had a groundless night-thought... or the Power reached out to convey a warning to us all.=

=And which do you believe?=

=Yesterday morning, I believed she was a young girl who had frightened herself over nothing. But today... Well, you saw her at the Trisectoriana. Yesterday, she was what Cirin described to you — a sobbing, runny-nosed mess. That's not how she is, today. I asked her why, and she told me that she had been of no use to the Power, the way she was, and so it returned last night and altered her so that she would be strong enough to face what lies ahead.= He shook his head. =Either she has parted company with her wits or she has, indeed, been altered. The young woman at the Trisectoriana who dealt with Tetralanna so calmly, translating all that went on, is not the weeping girl I saw yesterday. And that bodes very ill for our future, for it may mean that she was indeed visited by the Power, and that the message it delivered to her was a truth. Which means that we are now without a home.=

=And that I am now without…=

=No. Do not discount Cirin's cleverness yet, or his stubbornness. He may yet find a way back to us.=

Hayla drew a shuddering breath. =May the Power will it so.=

=May the Power will it so.=

Inside the rooms they shared, Gredin found Tetralanna waiting, arms folded across her chest. "Close the door."

"Certainly," Gredin replied, and cued the door to shut itself. The noise from beyond dwindled to nothing, leaving no sound but that of breathing as she and Tetralanna faced each other across the small table.

"I," Tetralanna said with quiet venom, "am ashamed of you."

Gredin nodded. "Yes, you've made that quite clear."

"Oh, I have not even *begun* to make it clear." Tetralanna drew herself up, seeming to grow taller and broader in the harsh overhead light. "Were you aware, before the Trisectoriana began, that Burlon te Bentain intended to pass himself off as Cirin te K'lar?"

"I was."

"And was that his idea or yours?"

"Neither. It was the Director's idea, but we agreed to it."

Tetralanna's lips pinched together in a thin, taut line. She shook her head. "You are a disgrace to our House. Worse yet, you are a disgrace to our gyfte." She pressed a hand to her forehead, then lowered it again. "I spoke the simplest, most basic fact when I told those Prett officials that we Vennans are honest people. I upheld the honor of our race, our House, and our gyfte when I unveiled Burlon's deception to them. Did you expect me to stand idly by and permit such a dishonest masquerade to proceed?"

"No. Burlon warned me of your views on the matter."

"Well, you were a fool to agree to such a lie in order to please the Director in the first place, and even more a fool to come there expecting me to support your lie with my silence."

"I viewed the matter differently."

"There *is* no different way to 'view' the matter," Tetralanna objected, her voice rising. "You are young and inexperienced, scarcely old enough to leave your House, and yet you took it upon yourself to disrupt our relationship with another race, one that is our respected trading partner, by telling them a falsehood on the very day they have publicly honored our friendship. I am in despair over how to account for your decision to do such a thing. What could possibly have compelled you?"

Gredin let the silence deepen for several moments, then asked, "Is that meant as a genuine question?"

Tetralanna's face flushed. "Of *course* it is a genuine question. What impertinence is this, that you would even ask me such a thing?"

"Until now, you haven't wanted to hear my explanation. Not really."

Tetralanna's glare grew glacial. "By all means," she said, each word a thrown stone. "Explain yourself."

"Very well. You ask what compelled me to promote an untruth that I knew you would immediately refute. I assume there are other things that you also wish to know, but that is your immediate question, yes?"

For a moment, Tetralanna looked confused — perhaps by the request for confirmation, perhaps by the calmness of Gredin's tone. Then her expression hardened. "Yes."

Gredin took a breath, organizing her thoughts. "Two things compelled me. You already know the first, since it has compelled my every action for the past two days."

"That 'night-thought' of yours," Tetralanna said with scorn.

Gredin simply nodded.

"And the second thing?"

"My belief, along with the Director's, that we would risk losing the goodwill of the Prett government if we caused them public embarrassment by revealing Cirin's absence."

"That makes no sense at all," Tetralanna said. "You subjected the Prett to an even worse embarrassment by passing off an impostor in Cirin's place, only to have me reveal Burlon's true identity to everyone."

"Actually, no," Gredin said, and a part of her marveled at how easy it was to stay relaxed in the face of Tetralanna's anger. "They suffered no embarrassment at all."

Tetralanna grew very still. "How can that be?"

"Because the confession you made to our hosts made no difference."

"No difference? I am First Speaker, the officially appointed Voice for this delegation. Why would my statement make no difference?"

"Because you do not speak Prettian," Gredin said.

"But my words were translated into…" Tetralanna began indignantly. Then her voice trailed off into silence.

Gredin waited.

"No," Tetralanna said, her voice little louder than a whisper. "No! You would not betray your gyfte in such a way."

"There is little I would not do to protect our people in this time of crisis. And, although I regret the circumstances, I do not see it as a betrayal of my gyfte. However, I understand why you might, since you refuse to believe in the truth of my words."

"What did you tell them? What did you claim that I said?"

"Nothing upsetting. I thanked them for their generosity. I

told them how pleased we were to be returning it, in some small measure, at our reception tonight. I thanked them on Hayla's behalf."

"Hayla! Why did she allow this travesty? Did you convince her to believe in this mad night-thought of yours, after the Silencing lapsed?"

"No. Hayla knows nothing about the Power's message. At least, I have not spoken of it to her. Burlon is the one who convinced her of his need to appear as Cirin. You must ask him what they have discussed. If he did not tell her, then she knows only that Cirin intended to Travel the River to Venna, and that he has not yet returned. Rather than disappoint House K'lar and upset the Prett, she agreed to help Burlon take his place at the Trisectoriana, since he is Cirin's First Friend. She is still expecting Cirin to return at any moment."

"Which he will," Tetralanna interjected, her chin rising obstinately.

"I long for both of you to be right, but I have little hope of it." As gently as she could, Gredin said, "Tetralanna, please, hear me. If I am wrong, we will discover it when Cirin returns, and no one will be more relieved than I to have it so. But can we not talk for a moment, here in privacy together, about the challenge facing us if I am proven right, and how best to help our people sustain that blow?"

"No."

Two days ago, such a terse rejection from Tetralanna would have intimidated Gredin into silence. A day ago, it would have caused her to dissolve in a flood of tears. Now, instead, she walked around to join Tetralanna on the other side of the little table and asked, "Why not?"

"Because I will not speak one more word or take one more action that encourages your belief in that ridiculous night-thought."

"I see," Gredin said calmly. "And yet a number of reasonable people don't find it ridiculous at all. Burlon te Bentain, for example, is a level-headed man, an experienced Traveler and Trader."

"Burlon doesn't believe you."

"He didn't, yesterday," Gredin conceded. "Today, he is... uncertain. Cirin has not returned and that worries him — that, coupled with the news that the Power has spoken to me twice."

"What do you mean, 'twice'?"

"The Power came to me again, last night."

Tetralanna slapped her.

In all her life, Gredin had never been struck in anger. It was not the Vennan way, in a race where physical integrity was so tightly linked to the ability to exercise one's gyftes. The blow was so unexpected, so outside acceptable behavior, the impact so physically and emotionally intense, that Gredin staggered back a step. But she stopped there, refusing to raise her hand to her stinging cheek and watering eye. Instead, in silence, she held Tetralanna's gaze.

The older woman turned away, shoulders hunched, arms wrapped about herself as if to prevent a further outburst of violence. "Wretched, deceitful girl," Tetralanna rasped, "to stand there calmly and tell such a lie."

"It is no lie," Gredin said. "Do you stand with your back to me because, by not looking, you can pretend to yourself that you did not just hit me?"

Tetralanna stiffened. Slowly, she turned around. Her face had grown pale, and tears shimmered in her eyes. "I did not intend to strike you."

"And yet you did."

"You should not have blasphemed."

"I spoke nothing but the truth."

That brought a renewed flush of color to Tetralanna's face. "So you believe."

"Yes. So I believe. Reflect on those words, Tetralanna. I am telling you the truth as I perceive it. It is the same truth I have been telling you for two days. Indeed, you were the first person to whom I confided it. The Power came to me, unlooked for, and entrusted this terrible truth to me. Ask yourself why, instead of supporting and comforting me, you have been so unwilling to grant even the possibility that what I say is true."

Tetralanna raised her hands in a gesture of pure frustration. "Use your good sense, Gredin. If the Power needed to convey a vital message, why would it choose you to receive it?"

A warning began to thrum, deep within Gredin's mind. Keeping her voice level, she said, "Who *should* the Power have spoken to?"

Tetralanna didn't reply, but the answer was there to be read in the glint of her eye, the proud lift of her chin, the way her fingertips stole up to stroke the gleaming hlette that identified her as First Speaker.

Frustration and pity stirred within Gredin, but they were muted grace notes, overshadowed by the startling realization that Tetralanna was jealous.

Gredin shook her head. "The Power does as it wills. I have no idea why it chose as it did. In truth, I wish it had passed me by. But none of that is by our choice. What we *can* do is plan how best to work together for the benefit of our people. We are the only two Speakers within the enclave. We will need to use our gyfte to reassure the others, tomorrow morning, when they are faced with the news of our fate."

Tetralanna recoiled, shaking her head in stubborn negation. "There is no 'our fate.' There is only your selfish insistence on enlarging your role far beyond its intended utility. That gown," she said, with a frown, "has the look of Mellian silk. Do you expect me to believe you brought such a gown from home?"

"No."

"Then where did it come from?"

"A Shodekekeen cloth merchant at the Traders' Market."

"And you think Unter will authorize the cost of such a purchase from House funds, simply because it caught your eye?"

"No. There was no cost." *Just as there is no House fund, and no Unter*, she could have added, but it seemed pointless and unkind.

"No cost?" Tetralanna scoffed. "What naive fantasy is that?"

"It is the truth. The Shodekekeen merchant made a present of this fabric to me, through Burlon, and Ingarra sewed the gown."

"Nonsense. Do you have any notion what a length of such fabric is worth? Why would a merchant part with such an item of value?"

"Ask Burlon to explain. Perhaps you will believe him."

"Don't think I won't — although his actions today with the Prett have done nothing to make him seem trustworthy. The Heads of House for Bentain and K'lar, as well as Balamont, will have a great deal to discuss, when we get home."

A wave of weary frustration dragged at Gredin, but she had to try. "Tetralanna, I will say this to you one more time. Our Heads of House are gone. Venna is gone. I very much fear that Cirin is gone, as well. We will not be going home in the morning, for the simple and terrible reason that our home no longer exists. If ever there has been a time when our gyftes are needed, tomorrow will be it. I am not your enemy, and never have been. I am your kinswoman, one who bears the same gyfte as yours."

"No." Tetralanna took a step closer and reached out. Her voice took on the intensity of their shared gyfte. "Gredin te Balamont, give me your hands."

Gredin felt the force of Tetralanna's gyfte clash with her own — and easily turned it aside. "No, Tetralanna. Your gyfte is not strong enough to compel me. The hand of the Power has changed me, and the fullness of my gyfte is now mine to employ. You cannot Silence me, not when the Power wishes me to speak and be heard."

Tetralanna stared at her, white-faced. "Take your belongings and get out," she demanded. "I packed your bag yesterday when I thought you intended to honor my decision to have you conveyed home." She laughed, the sound hard and desperate. "Imagine. I wanted to make things easy for you, and I didn't want Cirin to have to wait any longer than necessary. So there is no reason for you to linger now. I want nothing further to do with you, Gredin te Balamont. I rue the day you were born into our House."

The demand to vacate their shared rooms was unnecessary and demeaning, but Gredin saw nothing to be gained by insisting on her right to remain. For tonight, Ingarra and Beda would take her in, so that Keegan could reclaim his privacy. And tomorrow morning…

Tomorrow morning, everything would change.

[55]

ZRACH

It was thirst that roused him.

The instant Cirin awoke, a sense of great urgency gripped him, and he had to suppress the impulse to crawl immediately out from under the sheltering bushes. Instead, he forced himself to lie still and take stock of his surroundings. Zrach was an unforgiving world, one with dangerous consequences for those who acted in haste.

There was no way to determine how long he had slept. Dim light infused his leafy cave, little different from when he had first taken refuge there. A steady patter of rain on the thick, fleshy leaves above and around him obscured all other sounds, making it impossible to hear whether anything in the area was moving.

Cirin licked his dry lips, cursing Zrach. He was stiff, muscle-sore and thirsty. But tugging at leaves in the hope of catching a mouthful of rainwater was risky, and his other complaints could not be remedied unless he left his little sanctuary.

Swallowing a groan, he crawled to the edge of the over-hanging branches and carefully parted the stems until he could see the open area where he had arrived from the River. It looked much the same as it had, except that it was wetter, the muddy ground of his arrival now a shallow puddle of black water. The rocks had taken on a sickly purple sheen, and the acrid scent that rose from the moistened ground made him wrinkle his nose. It was likely just as well that he had resisted sipping at any rainwater. This was nothing like the fragrant rains were — no, had been — on Venna.

Patiently, he watched and listened, but noted nothing of significance. The clearing was quiet, with none of the noise of insects and little animals that had accompanied him to sleep. Nothing whirred or buzzed or rustled or moved. Perhaps the rain had compelled them all to seek drier shelter.

Thankful that nothing had invaded his resting place while he slept, Cirin eased out from beneath the bushes and stood up. His muscles protested, but it felt good to be on his feet, with departure imminent. He needed to bring his grim confirmation of Venna's destruction to Burlon without further delay, so that they could plan—

The pressure of the air around him rippled.

An immense black shadow took form over him, and something knocked him to the ground.

A line of fire bloomed along his back and arm. Stunned, Cirin rolled to his knees and scrambled to face his attacker, but he had only an instant before it was upon him again. Cruel talons raked his leg, scoring fresh wounds. Red eyes peered malevolently at him.

Cirin delivered a hard blow with the fist of his good arm to the scaled head, and the creature back-winged, hissing through its long, pointed beak, revealing rows of needle-sharp teeth.

Panting, Cirin shivered as a wave of vertigo washed through him.

The creature launched itself at him with a shrill cry. Cirin attempted to evade the attack, but the creature buffeted him with its wings, and the knife-like beak punctured his chest twice in quick succession, leaving white-hot agony in its wake.

Cirin screamed, arching beneath the torture. *I can't die here,* he thought in desparation. *Can't. Won't!*

Before the creature could finish him, he launched himself out of its cruel grasp and into the golden embrace of the River.

DAY THREE

THE RECEPTION

Gredin trudged across the crowded reception hall toward House Balamont's quarters within the enclave, baggage in hand, the hem of her scarlet gown swishing about her ankles.

"Gredin?"

She was trying to decide how best to explain her unexpected presence to Ingarra and Beda...

"Gredin te Balamont?"

The sound of her own name being spoken in the noisy hall finally penetrated her thoughts. Looking up, she was surprised to see Miri te Kendar hurrying toward her, carrying a large tray of fresh-baked sweetcakes. "Where are you taking your bag?" Miri asked. "You aren't leaving before the reception, are you?"

I'm not leaving at all, Gredin thought. *None of us are.* But she smiled in reassurance. "And miss all of this wonderful baking? Of course not."

Miri held out the tray to her. "Try one. See what you think of it." She beamed. "You wouldn't want us to serve less than our best."

"Indeed not. This deserves my full attention," Gredin said, and lowered her bag from her shoulder to the floor. Rows of crisp tindala, their ends dusted with spiced sugar, alternated with fragrant rostti, each golden-brown pastry bursting with fruits and nuts. "Tindala now, rostti later," she decreed, "if I'm fortunate enough to find that any are left."

"I'll set one aside for you," Miri promised.

Gredin bit off one end of the tindala and closed her eyes in honest pleasure as the flavors filled her mouth. Her second bite was the unsugared midportion, and her eyes flew open in surprise as she chewed it. "Kithris?" she asked.

Miri nodded. "Only the tiniest bit, but it makes its presence felt, even against the bolder spices. You do have an educated tongue. Perhaps your House should recruit you for its kitchens, if you ever tire of Speaking," she teased, and nudged Gredin's bag with the toe of her slipper. "You still haven't said where you're going."

Gredin popped the final bite into her mouth and chewed it with slow deliberation before answering. "To spend the night with my Guides. I've missed them, these past days."

"Well, I don't imagine you'll miss the Voice."

"Pardon?"

Miri's jaw took on a determined set. "It was unkind of her, yesterday, singling you out to Rugen like that."

Gredin blinked. "I know no Rugen. What was Tetralanna saying?"

Miri shifted uncomfortably. "She told Rugen te Torr that you had been called before the Director of Tradepoint... and that it was your fault that no more tours of the Traders' Market would be held."

"What else?" Gredin asked, then prompted gently, "It's all right, Miri. I would rather know than not. And I am already well aware that Tetralanna is angry with me. Just tell me what you heard."

Miri sighed. "She didn't say anything specific but she made it all sound dire. She said you were called before the

Director, and that several creatures were involved… and that you Sent."

Gredin almost laughed, to hear her misadventures boiled down in such a way. "None of that is untrue, although I can see where Tetralanna's account might confuse and distress you. The 'creatures' were traders from other worlds, some very nice, others not so pleasant. A group of the not-so-pleasant ones tried to take my necklace, and so I Sent to get away from them… but I wish I hadn't, because I stepped on an innocent trader's foot and injured it. And so, though I thank you for your sympathy, I did act against the rules, and the rest of the enclave *has* suffered for it."

"It doesn't matter," Miri said stubbornly. "The woman is from your own House. She should have stood up for you, there in the kitchens. It's clear that you're not a person who'd break a rule just to make trouble. But some folk dearly love having someone to blame, so please don't take it ill if any of them speak to you unkindly at the reception. And if you want a friendly face to talk to, even after we're home, I'd be glad to listen."

Miri's words were spoken in ignorance of the underlying disaster, but her kind sincerity touched Gredin to the core. "Thank you. I appreciate your concern, and I would truly like to become your friend. If there is anything I can do for you in the days ahead, please seek me out." It was as close as she dared come to revealing what a challenge awaited them all. She could only hope, when the time came, that Miri would remember her words. Leaning down, she grabbed the strap of her bag and shouldered it again. "And the tindala is absolutely delicious," she assured Miri, before moving on through the crowd.

A few questions asked along the way helped Gredin to find the area set aside for House Balamont, but it wasn't at all what she had expected. The Prett, she'd been told, had reserved four large storage facilities for the Vennans' use, which had then been subdivided to create housing for the individuals in attendance.

The only private accommodations were the rooms where she, Tetralanna and Keegan were lodged — rooms which, according to Burlon, were traditionally inhabited by visiting Tradeteams. The rest of the Vennans were staying in temporarily configured communal space.

She had known that. She had even thought she understood what was meant. But now, entering House Balamont's area, she was stunned by what she saw. The subdivision of space was no more than a maze of insubstantial 'walls' created by cloth panels draped over cords strung between one vertical support and the next. From where she stood at the entry to Balamont's assigned space, narrow walkways strayed off in several directions, a bewilderment of choices.

To attempt to search through it all for Beda and Ingarra would be a fool's task. Instead, Gredin set down her bag, composed herself, and sent her thoughts arrowing out to touch their private minds.

=Nifflin?= came Ingarra's reply. =Where are you? What do you need?=

Warmth blossomed in Gredin as she sensed Ingarra's ready goodwill. =I'm at the entrance to Balamont's quarters. In truth, I need a place to store my belongings and to spend the night. Tetralanna and I have parted ways.=

=I am glad to hear it,= came the firm reply. =She probably thought the dress should have been hers.=

That made Gredin smile. =It did cause a stir. But Tetralanna is upset by more than the dress. I know why, but it couldn't be helped. Truly it could not.=

=You'll be all the better for it. And Unter will understand, when you explain it to him. Don't let it fret you. Beda will be there in a moment to bring you to our alcove.=

Even as the thought reached her, Beda's familiar form come into view, down one of the cloth 'hallways.' "Gredin!" he said in cheerful greeting. "Come and be welcome. I'll take your bag.

Our space is not large, but we always have room enough for you."

She followed him through the twists and turns, threading her way past hanging panels and beneath loops of ropes. "I am sorry, Beda. I had no idea our people were crowded together this closely."

"Oh, it's not so terrible. Ingarra and I spend most of our time out in the reception hall. And today, of course, most everyone has been busy preparing for tonight's guests. I'll admit that it's strange, at night, to hear so many people murmuring to their Chosens as they settle down to sleep, and it takes a bit of practice to find your way in and out of here, since we must walk, but it will all make a grand tale to tell to those who didn't come. What would be the point of Traveling so far if it was just the same as home? I must admit, I am eager to see folk from other worlds, tonight. Do they look much different?"

Gredin thought about the blue-furred Shodekekeen. The tall, gaunt, bird-like Hesch. The towering bulk of the Prett. The small, sly Beng... "Very different," she assured Beda. "Very different indeed. I haven't seen a single one that could be mistaken for a Vennan."

"Wonderful," Beda enthused, and Gredin loved him all the more for his openness, quite the opposite of Tetralanna's uneasy recoil when faced with races other than her own. But would Beda's curiosity curdle into fear, once he knew that they were his new neighbors?

In many ways, Beda represented the best of Vennan traits: he was cheerful, industrious, steady, and optimistic. Gredin resolved to look on him as a marker in the days ahead. People like Tetralanna, habit-bound and cautious, would need a great deal of reassurance and support, once the news broke. But if Beda and those like him began to lose courage, Gredin would know that drastic measures were needed to prevent the Vennan survivors from drowning in despair.

"And here we are," Beda announced, sweeping aside a length of green cloth.

Beda and Ingarra's sleeping space, thus revealed, was even smaller than Gredin had feared. On Venna, each House included a multitude of wings built on a generous scale, with several stories of rooms, and innumerable nooks and crannies. Space abounded, and privacy was easily come by. But here…

"If I spread my sleeping mat, you will have to step over me to reach the walkway."

"I vow not to step on you," Beda said with mock solemnity. "For a single night, we will manage well enough."

A single night? A hundred nights. A thousand nights. A hundred thousand nights, for all she knew. No. This crowding was untenable, and it would make everything else seem worse, as well. She would have to speak to Wyve. They needed more space. Much more space. Urgently.

For tonight, however, it would have to do.

"Did you leave your sleeping mat behind?" Beda asked. "Shall I Fetch it for you? We cannot have you sleeping on the bare metal floor."

"That would be a kindness. You remember the room well enough?" But then memory sharpened, and she said, "Wait! Please don't. The mat that you recall from last night is Keegan's. You haven't seen my quarters. I will Fetch my own belongings." And she did, finding that the little task came easily to her; she Focused, and the mat and coverlet obligingly appeared on the floor at her feet, joined a moment later by her pillow and luminth.

Beda spread the mat and coverlet, smoothing the rumpled material. "There. Now you can crawl into bed and sleep, as soon as the reception is over."

"Ever thoughtful," she said. "You are the kindest man I know."

"Kinder than your Chosen?" he teased. "I should hope not."

Gredin felt a dull ache in her chest; she and Dreff would have no more opportunities to be kind to one another.

It was a thought that should have filled her with desperate anguish, but it seemed that the numbing calmness the Power had granted her was still holding sway. She was able to say, quite levelly, "The kindest man on Tradepoint, then."

"It is no effort to be kind to you," he assured her with a tender smile. "But I must go out soon to help Ingarra with the displays. Do you want to come along or shall I leave you here?"

"If you can spare a quick minute more, I will change my dress and come with you."

"Certainly," he said, and supplied a cheerful account of his recent activities while Gredin dug in her bag and pulled out the gown she had brought to wear for the reception — her sister Trethen's lavender gown, light as air, weighted only by its delicate shimmer of geddel crystals.

Trethen would never again have the chance to wear it. Gredin felt a sharp pang at the realization. Then, like a water hen bobbing on a wave, her resolve steadied. Trethen was gone, returned to the Source. Nothing could change that. But she would live on in Gredin's memory. And tonight, the Power willing, Gredin would dance in her honor.

She unfastened the various drapes and panels of the silken scarlet gown and stepped out of it. Slipping into the gossamer lavender, she reminded herself that this fabric, too, had come from Tradepoint. Some Trader had purchased it, perhaps from the Shodekekeen, back when she was just a little girl and Trethen had been embarking upon her first dance.

Where had those days and nights gone?

How had that life slipped from their grasp?

"You look a little tired," Beda said. "Has the day been difficult?"

She found a smile for him as she adjusted the cord on her flamestone pendant to accommodate the change in neckline.

Then she raised her fingers to her hlao, coaxing it to lengthen from its tidy circlet into a long and supple ribbon. Deftly, she wove it through her hair and tied it at her temple in Balamont's distinctive House knot. As a final step, she removed her little stones from their usual pouch and threaded them, one by one, into the narrow pocket that Ingarra had so sweetly sewn into the side seam of her skirt. In the course of her precocious childhood, it had become clear that Gredin was calmer and more Focused when she carried the stones with her. Eventually, Ingarra had resigned herself to the fact, and had begun including pockets in all of Gredin's outfits.

"This day has had its challenges," she admitted, "but I am prepared to put them behind me for tonight. We will dance, and eat delicacies, and I will introduce you to the Director of Trade-point, who is a Prett, very tall, very clever, with a huge, rumbling voice and a kind spirit. For now, however, let us go out together to find Ingarra and offer her whatever assistance she may need."

57

1896 OF 2000 ORBITS REMAINING

Cirin still wasn't back.

Blisters.

Burlon tried not to scowl as he moved to where he could keep an eye on the big doors to the antechamber. They were sliding open and shut frequently as more and more members of the Vennan delegation who were lodged along the corridor streamed into the reception hall, their bright, happy expressions undimmed by having undergone the bio-mist treatment. In hindsight, it had been a fortunate decision to house First Speaker in this main enclave. She had no need to leave for meals, unlike the residents of the other three enclaves assigned to them, and therefore no need to undergo the process she so disliked, multiple times in a day. If it had been otherwise, he was sure they would all have heard her complaints by now.

"Why so serious?" Jentana te Bentain asked, stepping into his path. Jentana was one of the older kinsmen from House Bentain to have made the journey to Tradepoint — which, if Gredin was right, might well mean that he was now the oldest living member of House Bentain. Given Cirin's continued absence, that was looking more and more like a real possibility, instead of some wild night-thought born of fear and strange surroundings.

It was far from a cheering thought.

"Just keeping an eye out for our guests' arrival," Burlon answered. "The sight of them is going to take a little getting used to, for most of our folks. The Prett and the others aren't like anything you're used to seeing."

Jentana chuckled. "We're not as frail as you Traders make us out to be. The timid ones mostly stayed home. People are looking forward to finally catching a few glimpses of someone from another race, tonight. Makes us seem foolish if we go home and have to say we came all the way to Tradepoint but only saw other Vennans. Everybody's excited. And it isn't as if we have to get any closer to them than we want to. This is a big room."

That it was, and tonight it seemed even bigger than usual, despite the crowd. The harsh, overly bright ceiling lights had been turned off entirely, and hundreds of luminth were floating overheaad in clever holders of lace, lighting the expanse and creating delicate patterns of light on the floor beneath. The overall effect softened the appearance of the reception hall, giving its lofty ceiling the look of a starry night sky.

"So, what does idle gossip have to say about our guests?" he asked Jentana, cautiously testing the waters of Vennan opinion toward Tradepoint's other inhabitants.

The older man grinned. "Apparently, some of them smell worse than rancid rista butter."

"True enough," Burlon had to concede. "That would be the Mamora. But there's no need to worry. Only one is coming, tonight, and I have Traders assigned to escort him and cleanse the air around him." It reminded him that he needed to notify all of the Travelers, before the night was out, to let them know that there would be an important meeting in the morning. They'd assume it was to organize the delegation's departure, and he'd let them believe that, for the time being. But the true purpose was to break the news that the delegation wasn't going anywhere. If the Travelers all agreed to stay put, it guaranteed that no one else could leave. Then, after morning meal, if Cirin still had not returned, he would have Gredin speak of what she believed had happened to their world…

"You're looking grim again," Jentana commented.

"I have a lot of details on my mind," he said, then deflected Jentana's concern by asking, "Any other worries about our guests?"

Jentana hesitated.

"Speak freely," Burlon said. "I'm truly curious about what you've heard."

"Well, I suspect someone was just teasing me."

"Don't be too certain. What did you hear?"

Jentana made a face. "That some of them look like… birds?"

Burlon nodded. "Tall, rather scary birds. Yes. The Hesch. If any Hesch come here tonight, and I've been told they might, my advice is to keep your distance. They are not particularly friendly. So, is that it? You've only heard talk of smelly ones and birds?"

"Tetralanna said…"

Burlon braced himself. "What wise words did First Speaker offer?"

"She said to watch out for the little ones."

That surprised a laugh out of him. "I suspect she meant the Beng, in which case I agree with her," he admitted grudgingly. "But Thalken are small, as well, and very different from the Beng. It's easy to tell them apart. Beng are loud, pushy, and untrustworthy. The Thalken are quiet and rather fragile, with fancy headgear." He shook his head. "Basically, short or tall, smelly or not, our guests are best admired from a distance. If you or anyone else is eager for a closer look at another race, I recommend approaching our hosts, the Director and Assistant Director of Tradepoint. They're Prett, which means they're tall and broad, with skin like tree bark. But they're good-natured, and they speak a few words of Vennan. And there will be Prett security guards present, in fair number, to make certain that all goes smoothly and all of our guests behave. It's perfectly safe for you to speak to any Prett you may encounter."

Jentana's eyes widened. "It wouldn't be safe to speak to the others?"

"It would be pointless. You don't speak their language, and they don't speak Vennan. Misunderstandings could occur. But it's really only a question of diplomacy, not of your personal safety. Everyone is coming to our reception to have a good time, and the Prett security will escort our guests and make sure no one gets confused or upset. Dealing with other races can be a tricky thing, but you're in no risk of physical harm tonight, and neither is anyone else. Please reassure anyone who seems nervous. Now, if you'll excuse me…"

"Certainly, certainly. This reception is quite an undertaking," Jentana said. "I'll go see how the pottery display is coming along."

As Burlon moved off, he spotted Tetralanna through the crowd, conversing earnestly with someone. Forewarned, he went the other way. If the only rumors emanating from Tetralanna te Balamont tonight were about the Beng, and not about his own dubious role at the Trisectoriana, he'd count himself lucky. She'd worked herself into quite a temper, and it still made Burlon's breathing quicken to think what might have happened if Tetralanna had known a few choice words of Prettian.

Fortunately, only he and Gredin and the Traders and Travelers had that advantage. If Tetralanna had calmed down enough to resist spreading her version of the event to everyone at the reception who would listen and was spending her time describing the Beng instead, Burlon suspected he owed Gredin a debt of gratitude for that.

Well done, youngling, Burlon thought, and felt a flare of

concern for the girl, despite her new, poised demeanor. Tomorrow morning, she would have to stand up in front of the entire delegation and tell them their possible fate. That would take more bravery than he was sure he could have mustered, in her place. He resolved to stand by her, as would Keegan in his own quiet way, until the truth could finally be determined.

But Tetralanna, the appointed Voice of the delegation, would doubtless speak out against both Gredin and her news, and that was going to be a problem. People would be devastated, not wanting to believe. And Gredin was unknown to most of them, and known to the rest as the young woman at the center of the Traders' Market incident, the one who had caused everyone else to be confined to the enclave for the duration of their stay on Tradepoint.

It wasn't an auspicious start.

Nevertheless, people would have to be told. And far better that Gredin do it, changed as she claimed to be by the Power's second visit, and with gyfte of Speech to aid her.

But even gyfte of Speech would be powerless to make the news of such a disaster easy to hear. How were they going to cope with an entire enclave crammed with frightened, worried people?

He wasn't a fanciful man, but he'd had a sour day so far. Cirin's absence crept into his thoughts every time he slowed down, causing his insides to feel as if they were slipping sideways. His spirits sank with the increasing certainty that Gredin was right, and that she *had* been right from the first morning.

An impending sense of loss, and a deep longing for the beautiful world that was their home, for House Bentain, for all the folk he knew there, and for Cirin, his First Friend, left Burlon struggling for composure whenever he relaxed the rigid Control he was exerting over his thoughts. And so he tried to stay busy.

He was particularly grateful that Gredin was no longer the weeping mess she had been yesterday. Today, with portents of doom roiling his gut, he'd have been tempted to join her in just such a display of emotion.

Burlon spared a thought for how the others were managing, particularly Keegan te Fliss. Gredin claimed that Keegan had believed her from the very first, unlike himself and Sill and Cirin and Tetralanna, but Burlon had yet to see any sign of grief on his face.

Come to think of it, Keegan hadn't said much at all since Gredin first spoke of her terrible news. Not at the Judgment. Not at the Trisectoriana. But Burlon thought, on reflection, that there had been a shadow in his gaze, one that made Burlon uneasy in retrospect. Give him somebody who complained loudly, any day. The quiet ones were the people you had to worry about. You never knew quite what they were thinking, or what they might do, and something in Keegan's manner made him think it might be wise to keep a kindly eye on the historian.

It was all too easy for the quiet ones to be ignored and neglected.

Burlon sighed. Stab it, what if they truly had no home? What if the Vokastra refused to let them remain on Tradepoint? They might be able to shelter for a time on Palomar, or Sprygale, or one of the other worlds where they went to Trade... but what sort of a life would that be, constantly moving from place to place for fear of outlasting their welcome?

He nearly groaned aloud. His beleaguered mind could find no peace.

He was good at making plans and coping with strange situations, and so were the other Travelers and Traders. In addition to convincing the Travelers to stay put, he'd need to meet with the Traders, as well, to discuss a number of pressing needs. If Cirin did not return by tomorrow's midday meal, they would need to undertake a thorough discussion of new trading strategies, based on the assumption that they were now stranded on Tradepoint. And he'd have to make an inventory of what remained in the warehouse spaces allotted to them — not just Bentain's portion, but all of it, from whatever House — including Houses that might no longer exist.

Sickened by the prospect, Burlon rubbed his jaw, thinking hard.

They should keep the news of Venna's fate to themselves while they figured out what necessary goods were in shortest supply. Once word got out at the Traders' Market, there were plenty who would take advantage of the situation. Better to trade for essentials while they still appeared strong...

But that would only work for a while. Sooner or later, folks were bound to notice that the Vennan delegation was still on Tradepoint. You couldn't hide nearly a thousand people forever. And as soon as their continued presence became apparent, folks would want to know why.

If the worst *had* happened, the Travelers and Traders would be the best ones to help him come up with viable solutions, once they got over their own initial devastation and gathered their scattered wits. They'd all just need a little time to catch their collective breath. He could count on the Prett to give them that much... couldn't he?

The Prett.

Scabs! The Prett were on their way!

Burlon realized he had been standing, frozen in place, for quite some time while others moved around him. That wouldn't do. He needed to stay alert. He needed to pay attention to everything at this reception, ready to handle any rough spots in the series of first interactions.

Keep things smooth with the Prett, on whose goodwill they might have to rely far more deeply than ever before.

Deal calmly with the Thalken and the Mamora, who would, with luck, pass the evening unaware that so many tensions existed just beneath the party's surface.

Warmly welcome the Shodekekeen, whose trader had

stepped forward to act as Gredin's unexpected ally at the Judgment.

Keep a wary eye on the Hesch, to whom House Balamont now owed a debt of ten point three one nine percent on every trading transaction they made for the next six sectora. A new and unwelcome thought struck him. Was that debt to be borne by House Balamont, as would normally have been the case, or by the entire delegation? Did the long-established rules of House-centric trading still apply, during a time when they were going to need every station credit they could muster just to pay for their own survival?

And, most of all, he needed to be prepared to take a hard line with the bleeding, scab-ridden, Power-forsaken Beng, who had now escalated beyond their former status as constant annoyance to the role of active enemy. The Beng, convinced that yester-day's Judgments had penalized them unfairly, would be brim-ming with spite — spite they wouldn't dare to vent on the Prett. Balked of that, the Beng would want to redirect their ill will. And the obvious and vulnerable target would be the Vennans — most specifically, Gredin.

A small parade of people walked past him, each carrying a laden tray of artfully arrayed food. The aromas were enticing, but the sight of such abundance sent a whisper of disquiet through him. Should he have counseled Gredin against allowing the preparations for this reception to go forward as planned, in light of the shortages they might soon be facing?

But no. Preparation of this feast was what the food Tenders had been brought to Tradepoint to do. Gredin couldn't have canceled or even reduced the reception plans without upsetting them, especially with no explanation given. And even if Gredin had decided to share the terrible news tonight, rather than wait until morning, nearly a thousand Vennans would still have needed to be fed, even if not quite so lavishly.

No, tomorrow's challenges would have to be dealt with

tomorrow, not tonight. And the guests for tonight made little difference. At most, the enclave might be hosting fifty individuals, if he included the Prett security guards in the count. Even allowing for the voracious greed of the Beng, that was a minimal outlay of food, compared to what it took to feed a thousand Vennans.

But he was going to resent every crumb that went down the throat of a Beng. Had Wyve taken leave of his senses, allowing them to come? What did it matter if excluding them caused hard feelings? The Beng were already in a froth over the Judgment. How much worse could it get? Slice it, he'd trade a whole enclave of Beng for one Rodorno...

A new sound startled Burlon from the darkness of his thoughts — a trill of music. Looking around, he saw that the assembled musicians were preparing to play in earnest. A cheerful dance tune made itself heard, and many of those not engaged in setting up tables or displays came to form impromptu lines and claim partners, waiting for the music to cue the opening steps.

The line closest to the entrance grew longer, extending toward him, and several people in it beckoned to him. "We're short a dancer. Join us," one entreated.

Burlon opened his mouth to refuse, then hesitated. It was a modest request, a small thing for them to ask of him. Their eyes were shining, their faces happy and hopeful...

"Certainly," he said. After all, the line wasn't far from the doors. When Wyve and Figg arrived, he could easily make his apologies and excuse himself.

For now, while he could, he would dance.

58

1895 OF 2000 ORBITS REMAINING

The pattern was a simple one, eight figures that his foursome would perform in time to the melody. Then he and his partner would turn up the line to greet a new couple and begin the figures again. He had learned the basic patterns as a child, as all younglings did, and had taken part in House dances with regularity since his hlao first unfurled.

But tonight was oddly different, and not only because of the unusual room in which they were dancing. The greatest and most startling difference was one he hadn't fully anticipated — the fact that he was mostly dancing with strangers.

House dances were just what their name implied — dances conducted within the privacy of the House, where every dancer present was a kinsman or kinswoman, some deeply familiar, some less so, some not yet known, but all related within the vast expanse of the city-state that formed the House.

Tonight, although the number of dancers was much smaller, he was hard put to spot a single individual that he knew. And if it seemed that way to him, despite his acquaintance with Travelers and Traders from other Houses, then most of these folks must feel even more isolated. It gave him a moment of panic to realize that these people might well be the sole inhabitants of his life now, the Vennans who would make up his entire world after tonight. Every stranger's face was a face he might need to learn. Every person was a person he might need to know. Right now, these people meant nothing to him, but that might have to change, starting tomorrow, if Cirin failed to reappear.

The pattern ended and repeated, ended and repeated, and Burlon went through the motions of the dance, his thoughts fixed on darker realities. There was no joy to be had from knowing in advance what these happy dancers would not learn until morning. If he had not shared morning meal with Sill yesterday, he would have been as unenlightened as they. And if he had remained unenlightened, he would not have taken it upon himself to summon Cirin to hear Gredin's strange tale. And Cirin would not have decided to venture home to Venna to quiet a silly girl's fears.

But if the girl had been devastated, not silly...

If her fears yet proved to be real...

Again, the pattern ended. Obedient to it, Burlon turned to make his progress up the line.

And stopped, staring down into violet eyes that stared back at him, wide with astonishment.

Violet eyes. A dainty button of a nose. A pink-lipped mouth the beauty of which made his own mouth go as dry as shredded ventic. Hardly any shape on her at all, which was funny, because he'd always been a man who admired a generous bosom, but it seemed obvious to him now that *this* was what a bosom was meant to be, just the sweetest little pair of handfuls, begging to be touched, and his ilian throbbing with the need to do just that, right here in the middle of the dance floor...

"Who *are* you?" he asked, and his voice came out all hoarse with longing as he drank in the sight of her face, the best face, the perfect face.

"Your Chosen," she answered, color flooding her cheeks. "Am I not?"

Of course! He was a dolt, too stunned to link one thought with the next. "Yes," he said. "Yes! And I am yours, now and forever, the Power be blessed. But what I meant was, what is your name?"

"Chenna. And you are...?"

"Burlon." He gave his head a quick shake, trying to clear it. "How is it that your face is unknown to me?"

"Perhaps because I am from the Holding. I Tend the hives."

But that made no sense at all. The Bentain Holding had no hives. "Chenna," he said, savoring her name, the taste of it sweet on his tongue. And then a wild thought struck him. An impossible thought, and yet... "Chenna, what is your House?"

She looked at him with loving concern, as if he were fever-addled. "Laith," she replied. "I am Chenna te Laith."

The next breath hurt as he dragged it in. "And I am Burlon te Bentain."

He realized that the music had stopped. He and Chenna stood alone, surrounded by a deepening ring of other dancers who stood still and watched them, some with excitement, some with distress, some with confusion.

Well, that was only fair. He was excited, himself. And confused. And, now that his brain had begun to work again, he was a little distressed, as well. Because...

"Chenna te *Laith*?" he asked.

Chenna nodded in solemn confirmation.

But Chosens came from within your House. Every child knew it to be so, and every adult lived out that truth. In all of time, back through the generations, there had never been an exception. You found your Chosen within your own House.

Yet there stood Chenna, his Chosen, unique and perfect; he knew it with every fiber of his being. Indeed, now that the first shock had passed, a giddy joy was bubbling up within him, making it hard to stand still, and harder still to think, when all he wanted was to be alone with her so that he could pledge his endless love to her as their bodies joined.

Voices were murmuring around the two of them: *A choosing. A choosing! How special, that it should happen here! Do you know them? Who are they? Do you know their House?*

Then a voice that was smooth to the ear but abrasive to his newly vulnerable sensibilities said, "A choosing? How very auspicious. Who is the fortunate couple?"

First Speaker.

At the sound of that unwelcome voice, Burlon reached out in search of Gredin's private mind. The instant she responded to his contact, Burlon told her hastily, =I'm near the entry doors. I need your assistance in dealing with Tetralanna.=

=I am coming,= Gredin assured him, without lingering to demand details.

The crowd of dancers was parting to make way for the Voice. Tetralanna arrived at the center of the ring of well-wishers, smiling benevolently. Then her smile faltered as she spotted Burlon. "Well," she said.

Burlon drew Chenna against him. "A fair evening to you, Tetralanna te Balamont. Indeed, the best of evenings," he stated, "for I have found my Chosen."

"Felicitations," Tetralanna said coolly. "I invite you to make her known to me."

"Certainly. This is Chenna." And then, because it was pointless to avoid the issue, and because he would not for a moment have his Chosen believe that he found fault with any aspect of her existence, he clarified, "Chenna te Laith."

Tetralanna's startled laugh was a surprisingly pretty sound, but it died away quickly, leaving Burlon caught in the cold disquiet of her gaze. "Say you so? You seem to be showing a lively disregard for House in all of your dealings today," she observed. "But this particular jest is a step too bold, even for you." Her voice took on a resonant authority. "Stand apart from her, Burlon te Bentain."

His arm, which had been holding Chenna snugly to his side, relaxed. His feet retreated, one step, then two, as he fought against the impact of Tetralanna's words. But he rallied his Focus quickly and stepped forward again to take Chenna's hand in his. "No. I will not stand apart. Chenna is my Chosen. And do not use your gyfte on me again. I am not some child blundering into danger who needs to be curbed."

"Are you not?" Tetralanna asked. Her voice was soft now, pitched so low that few beyond Burlon and Chenna would be able to hear it, but the disapproval in her stance was there for all to see. "What you claim is nonsense, Burlon — upsetting nonsense on what deserves to be an uncomplicated night of pleasure for our people. We have guests arriving shortly who will require your attention. I suggest you go and prepare to greet them. You can explore this strange notion of yours with your Head of House tomorrow, after we return home. Not now." Her gaze shifted to Chenna. On a kindlier note, she said. "And you, Chenna te Laith, deserve better than to be swept up in such a controversy. You are not the first of this delegation to be unsettled by the journey to Tradepoint. I do not assign blame to you, but I do counsel you to wait before you make any claim. Enjoy the dancing and tonight's reception, refresh yourself in sleep, and journey home tomorrow after midday meal. Once you are safely returned to Venna, you will feel far more clear-headed, and your Head of House will be available to advise you. In the meantime, I would enjoy seeing the display of House Laith's wares." She held out her hand to Chenna, and the resonance of gyfte returned to her voice as she said, "Come. Show me."

Burlon felt a flicker of panic as Chenna's hand began to slip from his grasp. "Chenna," he said with urgency, but he didn't tighten his hold on her. This wasn't about force. It was about love.

At the sound of his voice, Chenna turned to him, her expression warming. "Burlon!" she replied on a note of startled pleasure, as if he had just then appeared at her side.

"This," he said, gesturing, "is Tetralanna te Balamont, First Speaker, Voice for the delegation. Do you wish to go with her to see House Laith's display or would you prefer to stay here with me?"

Chenna began to speak, but Tetralanna overrode her. "If you are so concerned with identifying people, Burlon, perhaps you should explain to Chenna why you stood before the Prett officials today and claimed to be Cirin te K'lar."

It was a moment he had been dreading and had known was likely to arrive: a demand that he publicly explain the reason for his actions at the Trisectoriana. But he had hoped to avoid that need until tomorrow morning, when — if Cirin still had not returned — it could be explained in the context of Gredin's night-thoughts, and the desperate need to avoid causing public embarrassment for their hosts, the Prett.

And it had certainly never occurred to him that he might face such a demand in the presence of his newfound Chosen.

Burlon drew a breath, determined to find some response that would reassure Chenna that, despite Tetralanna's insinuations, he was an honest and honorable man. But before he could frame an opening remark, he heard someone else say firmly, "He did it because the Director of Tradepoint asked it of him."

Gredin.

She emerged from the ring of interested onlookers, her color a little high but her demeanor calm and commanding. "Why has the dancing stopped?" she asked, looking directly at Burlon for the answer, as if Tetralanna were nowhere about.

Taking courage, he said, "Because I have found my Chosen. Chenna te Laith."

He saw the double import of that statement register with

Gredin in a silent jolt of reaction, but all she said was, "Then I rejoice for you both."

"Rejoice?" Tetralanna protested. "Weren't you listening? They are of different Houses. It is obviously not a true choosing. If all you can do is encourage him in this wayward claim, then leave!" she cried, and flung out her arm toward Gredin in a gesture of imperious command.

As she did so, First Speaker's hlette flew from Tetralanna's arm in an eye-catching arc and landed neatly at Gredin's feet.

Burlon winced. The hlette wasn't just some pretty armband. It was an object of Power, and it was shocking to see it on the floor.

Gredin stooped and reached for it.

"Don't touch it!" Tetralanna demanded.

But Gredin's hand was already extended, and it seemed to Burlon that the hlette itself closed the final fraction of distance, completing the contact. He saw a ripple of reaction shiver its way through Gredin as she rose, the hlette resting on her upturned palm.

"Give that to me," Tetralanna demanded, her voice a growl. When Gredin didn't immediately comply, Tetralanna stalked over to confront her.

Burlon watched in horrified fascination.

"Give it back to me!" Tetralanna demanded again when she stood directly in front of Gredin.

Gredin extended her palm. "Take it," she invited.

Tetralanna snatched up the hlette and walked away.

"Wait," Gredin said sharply as the older woman reached the edge of the space that the crowd had cleared, and Burlon bit back a groan of frustration. If Tetralanna was willing to walk away, he was all in favor of that.

But Tetralanna stopped and looked back at Gredin, impatience etched on her features.

"Put it on again," Gredin said.

Tetralanna looked from the armband in her fist to Gredin. "What?"

"We would like to see you put the hlette on again."

Tetralanna hesitated, then slipped her hand through the opening and slid the intricate armband over her wrist and past her elbow to its customary position on her upper arm.

When it was in place, Gredin crossed her palms and inclined her head to Tetralanna in silent acknowledgment.

As courtesy demanded, Tetralanna began to do the same — and the hlette slid down her arm a second time and rolled to land once more at Gredin's feet.

A murmur of astonishment ran through the crowd like a wave.

Gredin bent and picked up the hlette for a second time.

Red-faced, whether from anger or mortification, Tetralanna pointed to a spot on the floor directly in front of herself. "Bring that to me. The hlette is mine!"

Instead, Gredin threaded her own hand through the band, slid it into position on her upper arm, and let go.

The hlette stayed where she had placed it, gleaming in the luminths' glow.

"It is *mine!*" Tetralanna insisted, her voice cracking on the final syllable.

"It would appear not," Gredin said. "But you may come and try to take it, if you are determined to do so."

There was little of smoothness or grace in Tetralanna's movements as she crossed the distance that separated her from Gredin. She moved warily, as if the floor were shifting beneath her feet. Her face seemed ravaged, and her arm looked conspicuously bare. She stopped in front of Gredin and thrust out her hand. "Give it to me!"

"No," Gredin said, her tone calm but firm. "It has come to me twice. I will not reject it again. But I will let you touch it. If it wishes to release me and go to you, it is free to do so."

Burlon could see the tremor in Tetralanna's hand as she pressed her fingers to the hlette, then attempted to slip her fingertips between it and Gredin's skin.

The band held firm, not budging as Tetralanna prodded and pushed and pried.

"Enough," Gredin said at last. She took a step to the side and looked past Tetralanna to the silent throng of observers. "First Speaker's hlette has passed," she informed them, her voice sounding effortless as it projected out to them. "I, Gredin te Balamont, am now First Speaker."

There was a stir at the sound of her name, perhaps the result of her misadventure at the Traders' Market, but silence quickly fell again.

"The passing of any hlette is a solemn act determined by the Power. Tetralanna te Balamont has borne First Speaker's hlette for long and long, and has served her gyfte ably, with its assistance." Gredin turned her head to look at Burlon, and he felt the affirming impact of her gaze. It was the only forewarning he received before she said, "But the passing of First Speaker's hlette is not the only change sent to us by the Power tonight. A choosing has been recognized — one unlike any that has gone before it, for it marks the joining of members from two different Houses."

Again, the crowd began to buzz.

Burlon felt a pang of gratitude and concern. Gredin, newly recognized as First Speaker, and handicapped by her extreme youth and the rumors about her role in the previous day's Traders' Market debacle and resultant Judgment, was risking her reputation by speaking out on his behalf. She had only his word to go by — his unprecedented claim that Chenna was his Chosen — and yet she was placing all her trust in him.

But how were they going to convince the others? There had never been a need for a choosing to be proven. The simple fact that both individuals sensed the bond was sufficient... or had been, until now. But Tetralanna had sown public seeds of doubt. And it was going to sound quite logical to people that he and Chenna should wait. After all, it was only for one night. Why not set the matter aside until tomorrow, and resolve the conundrum once they were home?

But if Burlon believed in Gredin's truths, that meant the old world and the old ways were gone, and their new life began here and now. Tomorrow, everyone in the enclave would be immersed in their loss. Was it selfish of him to want to share one night of joy with Chenna before that time of mourning began?

59

1894 OF 2000 ORBITS REMAINING

"Chenna te Laith and Burlon te Bentain," Gredin said, her youthful voice ringing out over the assemblage like a chime, "come and stand before me."

Burlon walked forward with Chenna.

"Most of us have witnessed choosing ceremonies conducted by our Head of House," Gredin said, "and many of us have been blessed to find our own Chosen and unite with them. We have no Heads of House with us tonight, but a choosing is the Power's will, and postponement of the Power's will is neither wise nor desirable. Therefore I ask you, Burlon and Chenna, whether you will permit me to act in place of your Heads of House, to show all who are assembled here that this is indeed a true union. Burlon?"

"Yes."

"Chenna?"

"Yes. Thank you, First Speaker."

Tetralanna gasped audibly at the use of her former title, but Gredin's smile remained a serene benediction. "Then it is my pleasure and honor to do so." She glanced over her shoulder.

"Sill te Torr? As First of Memory, will you come forward and witness this choosing?"

Sill obliged them, walking to a vantage point at the perimeter of the circle where she could see all three of them clearly.

Burlon knew what needed to come next, and he was struck by doubt — not of his devotion to Chenna, but of whether she would be willing to tolerate the intimacy that was about to occur. Normally, a choosing ceremony was handled by the Head of House, an authority figure known and trusted by the House's members, nearly as familiar to them as their own Guides. Burlon had known Gredin for only three days, and she was an utter stranger to his Chosen. But she was willing to act on their behalf, and in exchange she was asking for their trust.

"Are you ready to be joined?" Gredin asked.

Chenna looked at Burlon, her eyes wide and questioning.

He nodded to her in response, ever so slightly.

At that, Chenna smiled, the tension draining from her expression, leaving nothing behind but happy excitement, and Burlon felt his chest swell with love for her.

"I am ready," Chenna said, and Burlon added, "As am I."

"Then kneel and face each other," Gredin instructed, and they complied.

At the periphery of the circle, Tetralanna shook her head. "A travesty. It will fail," she said, her voice tight with anger. "I have tried to save you both from this public embarrassment. Just remember that."

But Gredin approached them, her face alight. "Chenna, Burlon, on the third day following your birth, your parents and Guides and Head of House called upon the Power, and a hlao was created for each of you. All your lives, those hlaos have upheld you, strengthening your hlinga and sharpening your Focus, attuned only to you. But those days are at an end. You have now discovered the person designated by the Power to be your Chosen, the person with whom you will become one, altered to your very core. Face each other now and join hands, just as your hlaos will join."

It was a command Burlon was eager to obey. Facing Chenna, he took her hands in his, and felt her tremble at his touch.

From the corner of his eye, he saw Gredin's hand nearing his face, and he flinched as he felt her fingers gently grasp the trailing end of his hlao. His breath caught in his throat, partly in apprehension at such a personal invasion, partly in anticipation of what he knew was to follow. Then Gredin brushed the end of his hlao against Chenna's.

And his soul caught fire.

When he recovered a sense of his surroundings, he and Chenna were clinging to each other. He drew back a cautious inch and saw that the filaments at the end of his hlao had interbraided themselves with Chenna's, as if they were a single ribbon.

"A proper choosing," Gredin said in affirmation, and a murmur of surprise and approval rose from the crowd. "You may separate your hlaos, now that the union has been witnessed."

Chenna touched her fingertips lightly to Burlon's hlao, while he did the same to hers. Under the influence of that mutual contact, the two hlaos separated, strand by reluctant strand, until at last the ends of each hlao hung free, separated but still yearning toward the other, as if sharing the stir of some private breeze.

"And so, in all kindness," Gredin said, "we should dismiss you now to savor your dydanin. But that poses a problem, crowded as we are in the enclave…"

"There is no difficulty," someone else said. "They can have my chamber."

Astonished, Burlon turned his head and saw Keegan te Fliss standing there, beaming.

"Thank you, Historian. The Power's blessing on you," Burlon said. "My Chosen and I are in your debt."

"I am only facilitating the Power's wishes," Keegan assured him. "My belongings are few. I'll remove them now, and you and Chenna may begin your dydanin."

"No!"

The voice, like a plunge into chill water, was Tetralanna's.

"What point is there in that?" she continued hastily. "A proper dydanin is twenty uninterrupted days and nights. We are all leaving in the morning. Let them wait and start their dydanin when they return — if indeed their Heads of House can be persuaded to sanction this strange union at all."

The woman was a menace. Determined not to be thwarted, Burlon addressed those who stood watching. "Ours is a true choosing, as First Speaker has just demonstrated. Surely even Tetralanna must concede that. Therefore, my Chosen and I accept Keegan te Fliss's generous offer of a chamber, and we will begin our dydanin tonight, in token of all that is yet to come. But I will emerge in the morning to confer with the other Travelers, and Chenna and I will resume our private time tomorrow night. In this instance, tradition can bend to necessity with no harm done to either." He kissed Chenna's cheek and whispered in her ear, "Do I have your trust in this, my love? For no lesser matter would I interrupt our private time."

She nodded. "You and I will be together evermore. Do as you must. It will make your return to me all the sweeter."

"Then we will go," he said.

"Wait." This time, it was Gredin who spoke, an expression of reluctant apology on her face. "Your pardon, Burlon, Chenna, but there is one matter more which we must resolve before your dydanin can begin."

"And what is that?" Burlon demanded, aggrieved.

Chenna placed a hand on his arm. "Tell us, First Speaker. We will listen."

Burlon subsided, soothed by Chenna's touch. Gredin had

acted as their ally in accomplishing this choosing. If she said there was still an issue to be faced, he would hear her out.

Gredin nodded her thanks. "Your choosing is true," she said. "Nevertheless, you are from two Houses — Bentain for you, Burlon, and Chenna from Laith. What of the children you will bear? They cannot be of two Houses."

Chenna's hand on his arm tightened. "Then what is to be done?" she asked.

Gredin's face seemed graven from stone. "One of you must leave your House," she said, "and align for all time with the House of your Chosen."

"Leave our House?" Chenna asked, her voice trembling. "How is that even possible? We are born to our House, each of us. Our kinsmen there created our hlaos. Our Guides raised us within the protection of our House's walls. House is who we are. House is everything!"

"Just so," Tetralanna affirmed, looking smug.

"And yet," Gredin said, "the Power has caused the two of you to choose beyond your House. Since each of us benefits from the security of our House, where are the two of you to live? What counsel would you offer to your children — to split their loyalties?" She spread her hands. "I am sorry, but I see no other solution. The two of you must choose a single House to claim, a single House in which you will reside, a single House to which you give your loyalty and support. This is a serious matter, deserving of respectful discussion. I advise you to speak with those of your House who are here, and with each other."

"And with your Heads of House, when you return home tomorrow," Tetralanna insisted, her voice strident. "You see now why this dydanin cannot — *must* not — begin tonight."

"I am so sorry," Gredin said. Burlon could see that she was, but it was equally clear that this was a point of impasse. On the matter of choosing a single House, Gredin was adamant.

But that, in turn, made matters simple, so simple that Burlon almost laughed, for the decision was already clear to him. He said, with utter conviction, "Then I align with my Chosen's House. From this moment forward, I am Burlon te Laith, and I will stand by my Chosen's side forever."

Chenna stared up at him, gratitude and concern in her gaze.

Tetralanna's face contorted, her expression less of anger than of shocked distress. "Think what you are saying," she cautioned. "Think what it will mean. This is no frivolous thing. Do as Gredin advised, since you are determined to listen to her, and take the necessary time—"

"I need no time," Burlon said. "Please understand, all of you, I have always been proud to belong to House Bentain. I esteem everyone there for what the House and its members have meant to me, and for the care they have taken in my nurture and instruction. But I am changed, and my loyalties have already departed from there. They lodge now with my Chosen, and so I will strive to make House Laith proud to claim me as one of its own. I step now from House into House, from contentment into joy." He turned to Gredin. "What more must I do? What else can I offer in pledge? Tell me, please, how to make everyone understand that Chenna is now my life."

There were tears shining in Gredin's eyes.

There were tears in his own, as well.

"We hear you, Burlon te Laith. You have done all that the Power could possibly require of you, except for the simplest thing of all — to live a happy life together, the two of you."

Burlon supposed that his decision would cause hard feelings. It was bound to. As a Trader and Traveler, he had long been a prestigious member of House Bentain, made visible to many by the nature of his gyftes, and he had added no small amount of profit to House Bentain's coffers. But those were business matters, matters of the head. This was his Chosen. And while Burlon would never have described himself as a sentimental fellow, he had spoken the honest truth just now when he said that

Chenna was his life. There was nothing he would not do to please and protect her.

In the morning, if Cirin did not return, and Gredin carried out her plan to reveal what she believed to be Venna's fate, Chenna would face the possibility that she had lost most of her kinsmen, and the Laith House itself, and its Holding, with the hives where she worked in service to her gyfte. He would act as her shield, softening the impact of the news, soothing her fears, reminding her of all that remained to them. And he would extend that comfort to the members of House Laith — his own new kinsmen.

But tonight was for Chenna.

Tonight was for joy.

"Keegan, I say again that my Chosen and I are in your debt for the generous loan of your chamber."

"I will walk there with the two of you," Keegan volunteered, "and bundle my belongings."

Hearing those words, Burlon realized how much he was about to miss. Turning to Gredin, he said with quiet urgency, "But the Hesch. And the Beng! If you need me—"

"No," she assured him. "Put it from your mind. Wyve and Figg will provide all of the assistance I require."

"But I was going to help you translate! I was going to keep an eye on the visitors, and contain the Mamora."

"Your fellow Traders and I will manage all of that quite well."

He looked at her — looked at her properly for the first time since her arrival to aid him against Tetralanna's interference. He looked past the gleam of First Speaker's hlette, the glow of her flamestone pendant, the sinuous beauty of the free-swinging ends of her knotted hlao, and the occluding aura of his own personal concerns, and felt another shock jolt through him. "By the Power's own gyftes," he exclaimed indignantly, "what are you wearing?"

She looked bewildered by the question. "My sister's dress. What concerns you?"

Burlon tried not to gape. "Are those all geddel crystals?" he demanded, incredulous.

Gredin gestured at the shining patterns on her gown. "Yes. Ingarra sewed them to look like ildarian vines, and then embroidered the blossoms. Isn't she clever? I think they're lovely."

"Change your dress," Burlon urged.

"What? No! I brought this gown particularly for tonight's reception. It's the only one I have."

"You have the Shodekekeen dress."

"I wore that for the Trisectoriana," she objected. "Burlon, you are making no sense. What's wrong with my gown?"

"Nothing. It's beautiful."

"Then why should I change out of it?"

There was so much that she and the other Vennans didn't know — about trade, about Tradepoint, about the Prett... Now was likely not the time to go into detail about any of it, but Gredin needed to know at least a little. "Because," Burlon told her, even more quietly but no less intensely, "you are wearing a sizable fortune's worth of geddel crystals on that gown, and geddel crystals are our principal trade item with the Prett. You might as well greet Wyve in a gown fashioned from station credits. And the other races know it, as well. You'll have the Beng trying to pluck them off like ripe berries from a bush."

She looked at him, incredulous. "They're just crystals. Ingarra sewed them on to make the dress look pretty."

"Well, I hope she sewed them on with a firm hand and stout thread," Burlon said, light-headed with anxiety. "If you should happen to shed a few of those on the floor, tonight, you'll have Beng and Prett alike diving under the tables after them, elbowing each other as they go — and possibly the Hesch along with them." He dropped his voice even further. "Seriously, Gredin, it isn't safe. It isn't wise. Take the dress off and hide it away before any of the guests get here."

"Is there a problem?" Tetralanna asked archly, approaching them. "Have you changed your mind already, Burlon te *Laith*?"

For a moment, he didn't understand; the argument with Gredin had driven the matter of House allegiance entirely out of his head. Then it flooded back to him, and he realized that Keegan was waiting for him. *Chenna* was waiting for him. And everyone else was watching and doing their best to overhear.

He put on his best untroubled Trader's smile and aimed it at Tetralanna. "Not at all. My mind is unchanged, my happiness complete, although I thank you for your concern. I was only resolving a few last details about the guests, before my Chosen and I leave the hall. But perhaps you are the perfect solution to my concerns, Tetralanna. Would you care to take my place at the entrance and bid a welcome to the Hesch and the Beng and the Mamora as they arrive?"

Tetralanna retreated a step, with a look of revulsion. "Most certainly not!"

"Ah well. Fortunate for us both, then, that I am able to leave such matters in the capable hands of First Speaker," he retorted, indicating Gredin with a little bow of his head. Then he turned away to escort Keegan and Chenna through the crowd of watchful eyes and avid ears, ignoring the undercurrent of murmured comments from the crowd, determined to devote his attention wholly to his Chosen.

Gredin would change her dress, or she would not. The Prett would bring a sufficiency of security agents, or they would not. The reception would go well, or it would not.

At worst, if he was needed, he would be only a short walk away. But Burlon fervently hoped it was a walk he would not be called upon to make.

60

"A reception. A *party*," Figg said, her tone glum. "Under the circumstances, this all feels eerily inappropriate."

"Ah, but those circumstances are known to very few," Wyve pointed out, walking at her side. He had suggested, against custom, that they travel the distance between their office and the Vennan enclave on foot tonight, and Figg had agreed, no doubt understanding that he wanted to glean a sense of the atmosphere in the halls of Tradepoint, after the strange dealings of the past two days.

So far, all seemed quiet.

A small contingent of security paced ahead of them. A much larger contingent followed behind, quietly alert. Assignments had already been handed down as to which of them would shadow the Hesch, which the Beng, which the Shodekekeen, which the Thalken, which the Polpethtira, and which unfortunate soul would stay with the lone Mamora. Sixteen guards for one-on-one escort duty of the foreign nationals. Two more for himself. Two for Figg. One for Tetralanna te Balamont, for form's sake. Two for Gredin te Balamont who, through no apparent fault of her own, seemed to excel at attracting trouble of all kinds. And ten extra agents, four of whom would guard the entrance while the rest circulated as he directed, once he saw how the reception was laid out.

In a reasonable universe, thirty-three Prett security should easily insure a peaceful evening. As things stood, however, the presence of thirty-three uniformed, highly trained guards was barely enough to steady his agitated nerves.

When they neared the entrance to the Vennan enclave, Wyve said, "Stay alert tonight, Figg. Don't hesitate to signal security if you see a potential problem developing. I would rather be over-reactive than risk falling behind the curve of events."

Figg offered him an artfully feigned smile. "Whatever do you mean, Director? We are simply here to celebrate the happy camaraderie that exists between Tradepoint's varied inhabitants."

He almost laughed aloud. Instead, he approached the entrance to the Vennan enclave, scanned his identification badge into the system, and pressed the keypad to request admittance. He could have opened the antechamber doors himself, but it would not have been polite. Instead, he waited patiently, giving the Vennans time to pass from their enclave into the antechamber and wait there while the bio-mist cycled.

Soon enough, the door panels parted.

Four Vennans — three men and a woman — stood revealed there. All four were traders whose features he recognized, all long-accustomed to Tradepoint and its ways. But their faces were all that was familiar. Gone were the serviceable pants and jackets the traders normally wore. Instead, all four wore gauzy tunics that ended at mid-thigh. Their arms were bare. Their legs were bare, as well, except for embroidered cloth slippers. The colors of the fabrics were an array of pastels, some embroidered, some not.

But the most striking difference was that the gleaming circlet of the hlao that habitually encircled each Vennan's brow had been replaced by a ribbon of gold, knotted elaborately at the left temple, its ends left to dangle free, long enough to graze the top of the shoulder.

All four traders crossed their palms, first to Wyve, then to Figg. "We welcome you," one said in polite Prettian. "Enter and be glad."

Another grinned and said, less formally, "Burlon certainly is."

It seemed that they wanted him to ask. "And why is Burlon glad?"

"He has found his Chosen," the female trader remarked, looking pleased.

Belatedly, Wyve realized that he knew her. This was Ellis te Vell, the assigned escort for the Vennan group's ill-fated visit to the Traders' Market. "Well! I will be certain to offer him my congratulations," Wyve assured her.

The fourth trader shook his head. "Not tonight you won't. He and his Chosen have already entered into their dydanin."

Wyve tilted his head in confusion. "*Dydanin*? That is not a word I recognize."

Smiles all around. "Their private time together," Ellis te Vell explained.

"Ah. I see. Tomorrow, then."

The smiles broadened. "Twenty sects. A dydanin lasts for twenty sects."

"You can congratulate him when he returns with the next trading mission," the tallest trader suggested. "For now, we will pass along your good wishes tomorrow morning, when he emerges."

"But did you not just say that a *dydanin* is twenty sects long?" Figg interjected. "Did I misunderstand? Or is he only shut away at night?"

"Dydanin is both night and day," the tall one clarified. "But we are Traveling home, tomorrow. He and his Chosen must come out for the departure, at least."

Ellis te Vell grinned. "Or perhaps Burlon will simply have the rest of us Travel home while he stays on here in the enclave with his Chosen, to enjoy their dydanin in peace," she suggested, and the others dissolved into laughter.

Wyve realized that they truly did not yet know about the destruction of their world. At whatever cost, Gredin and Burlon had maintained the secrecy.

"But we must not leave you stranded here in the entry, Director, Assistant Director," Ellis said as the good-natured laughter faded. "Please, come in. Join us."

And all four Vennans stepped aside to admit them.

Wyve found the habitual delay in the antechamber quite calming; he had long since trained himself to use each bio-mist exposure as a time to slow his breathing and clear his mind.

When the inner doors opened, he found the Vennan enclave so softly lit that it took his vision several moments to adjust.

"Many different sorts of clothing," Figg observed, and Wyve saw that she was right. Some of the men wore jackets and loose-fitting pants, while others were dressed in the same tunics as the traders who had invited them inside. A few of the women had also adopted jackets and pants, or tunics, but others wore brightly hued dresses, varying in length from mid-thigh to just above the ankle. Jewelry winked in the muted light on nearly everyone, most commonly necklaces and rings, and the same golden ribbon appeared on every head, knotted at the left temple in a variety of patterns.

"Their enclave, their customs," Wyve said in soft reply. Each race's enclave was theirs to run as they saw fit, barring actual physical endangerment of Tradepoint's infrastructure. And every race inevitably brought with them their own culture and taboos, their own attitudes toward matters of body modesty, personal space, and proper social behavior. It was what made him nervous about a night like tonight, where so many different races would meet in the relaxed freedom of an enclave.

The public corridors had regulated rules of conduct. The Traders' Market had regulated rules of conduct. The station offices had regulated rules of conduct. But the enclaves, technically, did not. And tonight's muted illumination and high population count within the Vennan enclave made supervision difficult. Thirty-three security agents? He found himself wishing for a hundred.

But that was foolish. The number of Vennans wasn't the issue, and the number of non-Vennan guests hadn't changed. It would all be fine. It would all be fine. It would all be…

"Chee, chee, chee…" Figg murmured, and patted his arm.

Startled, Wyve offered her a wry smile. "Am I so obvious?"

"Of course not, but I know you well. You fret."

The crowd in front of him parted, and he saw Gredin te Balamont walking toward him in a gown that instantly claimed his startled attention.

"Are those *geddel crystals*?" Figg demanded in a harsh whisper. "And look at what she's wearing on her arm tonight! Honestly, Wyve, who *is* this girl?"

He sympathized with Figg's question. Yesterday, Gredin te Balamont had seemed downtrodden and childlike, sobbing in shame and distress as she stood before him as the accused party in a Judgment.

This afternoon, at the Trisectoriana, stunning in her scarlet Shodekekeen gown, she had remained calm and in command even when events threatened to careen out of control around her.

Tonight — well, tonight, she had the impressive bearing of a government official. An elaborately knotted ribbon of gold glittered at temple and brow, its trailing ends grazing one bared shoulder. And, as Figg had been quick to spot, Gredin wore the intricate armband which, until now, had identified Tetralanna te Balamont as First Speaker and Voice of the Vennan delegation.

Wyve stopped where he was and crossed his palms to her in

the Vennan fashion. "Gredin te Balamont," he said, formally acknowledging her presence.

She reciprocated the gesture. "Director. Assistant Director. Our welcome." Her gaze touched briefly on the security guards behind them. "Indeed, our welcome to all within your group. Is it customary to acknowledge the security staff who accompany you tonight? May we offer them refreshments? A place to sit? Someone to accompany them?"

"Our thanks, but they are in service and require nothing but your tolerance of their presence. Two will attend you closely throughout the evening, with your kind permission."

"Unnecessary." Gredin gestured at the room. "We are within our own enclave."

"Yes, but there will be guests here soon who are not Vennan. I ask you to indulge me — especially given the value of your gown."

For some reason, that comment amused her. "Yes, Burlon mentioned that my gown might be a point of concern for you."

Before he could respond, Figg said, "A fine evening to you, Gredin te Balamont. Or, judging by what I see, should I now address you as First Speaker?"

"Yes," Gredin said.

Just that: *yes*. Wyve surmised, from her reticence, that there might be quite a tale involved. But Burlon, an ever-reliable source of interesting backstories, would apparently be absent from the entirety of the reception, to Wyve's increasing regret.

He spotted the former First Speaker coming steadily toward them, tension radiating from her as she walked.

In his position as Director, Wyve was often called upon to make quick decisions, based on fluctuating circumstances. He made one now. "Figg, transfer an additional agent to First Speaker's guard for the evening."

"Of course," Figg said, and Wyve was confident that the agent transferred would be Nur, who had originally been assigned to Tetralanna te Balamont. Shorn of her rank as First Speaker, she no longer merited individualized protection. And Gredin's importance and level of risk had, if possible, increased.

Figg turned slightly away and spoke into her wristcom.

Tetralanna te Balamont reached them and began immediately to speak, the Vennan words forceful and melodic as they flowed in a torrent from her lips.

Wyve understood much but not all of what she said, but Gredin still provided a translation. "She welcomes you and expresses her strong displeasure over the change in her status. It need not concern you. Would you care to see the exhibits and demonstrations?"

"I would greatly enjoy seeing the exhibits and demonstrations," Wyve assured her, and offered Tetralanna te Balamont only a shallow nod before turning to accompany Gredin deeper into the enclave. But they had only taken a few steps, with Tetralanna still hovering near Wyve's other side, when he felt a pulsation in his wristcom.

Then Figg said, "Beng."

Of course. Trust the Beng to show up early and linger late. "I had best greet them personally, if you'll excuse me," Wyve said to Gredin.

Her delicate brows lifted. "This is our enclave. I will go and greet the Beng."

"Then I will accompany you," Wyve said, and they reversed direction, leaving Figg to watch over matters.

Tetralanna te Balamont followed after them, looking aggrieved, but she balked and stayed behind when they entered the antechamber.

"She objects to the bio-mist," Gredin said calmly, and the doors closed, shutting Tetralanna from view.

When the mist cleared and the outer doors opened, Wyve saw that Security had stalled the Beng in the corridor, to their vocal displeasure. "We guest," one of them was protesting. "We invite. Director say we come."

"Better still," Wyve said as he emerged, "Director give special guard each Beng, keep Beng safe." There were, he saw, five of them standing there. "But Beng too many. Three only come inside. Beng agree. Three only. Which three register today my office?"

"We small," one Beng protested with a cheeky grin. "Three Shodekekeen same five Beng, yes?"

"No. Unregistered Beng return Beng enclave," Wyve insisted.

The Beng opened their mouths to argue… then hesitated, staring to Wyve's left.

Gredin had stepped up beside him, and her presence seemed to rattle the Beng. They muttered amongst themselves, and Wyve recognized just enough of their language to know that the words were not polite. In short order, however, two of the group separated themselves and scuttled back down the hallway, casting dark looks over their shoulders as they went.

"Red guard," Wyve said.

A security agent stepped forward.

"Number one Beng come stand here," Wyve requested. When the trio began to surge forward, he held up a single finger. "Number One Beng only. Here."

Grumbling, a single Beng presented itself.

Reaching down, Wyve affixed a glowing red disc to the front placket of the Beng's coveralls, and a matching disc to the back, between its shoulder blades.

"What this?" the Beng demanded. "What you put?"

"Small presents," Wyve told it. "Each worth one-quarter station credit. You wear tonight, redeem tomorrow, my office. Number Two Beng?"

The second Beng came forward with an air of reluctance, but stood passively while Wyve applied yellow discs, one on the front, one on the back of its coveralls.

"Number Three Beng. What you hold?"

The third Beng was carrying a cloth sack. At Wyve's question, it clutched the sack against its chest. "Present."

"Present?"

"Vennans give re-cep-tion. Beng bring present."

It was traditional, on Tradepoint. If one race played host on a given occasion, those who came as guests usually brought some token of appreciation. It wasn't required but it was always appreciated. In this instance, however, Wyve would have been better pleased if the Beng had bypassed the custom. "What bring?" he asked, trying to sound more curious than suspicious.

The Beng's face took on a stubborn expression. "Present for Vennans. Not show now."

But it was too big a risk, given the hard feelings the Judgment had engendered. "No show, no take inside. Show just to me."

"No. I show you, you maybe tell Vennans."

It was an impasse.

But Wyve was long used to dealing with the Beng. Faced with a stalemate, it was often best to let the Beng propose a solution, and then to negotiate if their suggestion was unacceptable. "How we settle?" he asked the Beng now. "You say."

The three Beng huddled together, debating the matter in tense whispers.

Finally, the third Beng stepped forward again, sack in hand. "I get Prett guard, like same they?" it asked, indicating its two companions.

The third Beng actually wanted a guard? That was fine by Wyve, but it didn't hurt to pretend a bit of reluctance. "You want same they?"

"Prett guard for me! Color buttons me! One-quarter station credit."

"Very well," Wyve conceded. He wasn't sure what the guard had to do with the present, but no Beng was going another step until they had identified the present to his satisfaction, so he motioned the third Beng forward. "Color buttons. Yes. Come."

This time, the discs were blue. When they were in place, Wyve said, "Blue discs, blue guard. Now tell how we settle."

The Beng tucked its chin to look down at the blue disc affixed to the front of its coverall. Then, appearing pleased, it looked up at Wyve. "I show blue guard. Blue guard tell you yes okay, no not okay. But not say what. Just okay, not okay. Blue guard stay me, not talk you until Vennan take present. Yes?"

It was an unusually long Tradetalk speech, for a Beng, and it seemed like an acceptable solution to Wyve. He reminded himself that the Beng were a space-faring race and therefore must be more intelligent than they seemed. If behaving foolishly and creating a stir caused other races to underestimate them, it was probably a tactic that suited the Beng's purposes.

The current plan placed a great deal of responsibility on the shoulders of the Prett security agent in question, but Wyve had chosen the three guards assigned to the Beng with care. It was an acceptable level of risk.

"Yes," he said to the Beng. Turning to the guard in question, Wyve said in Prettian, "Step across the corridor with him. Insist that he let you examine the bag and its contents thoroughly. Use your best judgment. So long as it doesn't seem dangerous, we'll let it through."

The process didn't take long. After a brief inspection, the guard nodded his approval. He looked unalarmed, perhaps even a bit amused.

Taking a firm grip on his curiosity, Wyve stepped back, clearing the way for them to enter the enclave. "Best Prett guards," Wyve assured the trio. "Keep Beng safe tonight. Beng behave, have good time."

All the while, Gredin had stood beside him, silently watching the Beng, listening to everything they said. Her expression was impassive, neither welcoming nor grim. Now, as the three Beng and their assigned Prett guards approached the entrance to the antechamber, she crossed her palms, nodded to each of them, and said in Tradetalk, "Come inside. Be happy."

The Beng, less gracious, edged past her with exaggerated

care, rolling their eyes as if she posed them some physical threat. Then Red Disc pointed at her gown, and all three of them exploded in an incomprehensible chatter of Beng, likely commenting on the fortune in geddel crystals that adorned it.

Once the Beng and their guards were inside and the door had closed, Wyve said to her, "Those discs I fastened to them blink, which will make them easy to spot, even in dim conditions. The discs also house a signal that will show us precisely where they are."

That won a grudging smile from Gredin. "We do admire Prett ingenuity. Let us hope it will not be needed." Then she looked past him and smiled. "Ah. Our next guests."

Wyve turned to look, and saw the blue-furred Shodekekeen approaching. Upon arrival, all three rose onto their hindmost legs, which made them taller than Wyve and Gredin.

"Welcome," Gredin said in Tradetalk, brightening. "It is good you come!"

The foremost Shodekekeen touched its chest and said, "Shamkalak Urmo Memelo. I see you, our maartza." To Wyve's relief, it made no mention of seeing Gredin at the hearing. Instead, it nodded its head toward her. "You say Shamka."

"Shamka," Gredin repeated in acknowledged, and gestured at herself. "Gredin te Balamont. You say Gredin."

"Grrdin," the Shodekekeen said, elongating the 'r' sound, perhaps in deference to the shaping of its muzzle. Then it disquieted Wyve be tracing a line of geddel crystals on Gredin's gown with a careful claw. "Fine work," it stated. "Who sew gown?

"Her name Ingarra."

"Gara. Shodekekeen fabric, this! Color not good you," Shamka said. "I show better, next time come."

Gredin blinked, appearing nonplussed by Shamka's comment, but she said nothing.

One of the other Shodekekeen mewled and growled in that

peculiar blend of sounds that comprised their language, and Shamka translated, "Mamora come. We go in now."

But the nearest Prett security said, "Bag?" The third Shodekekeen turned, and the guard opened the pack it wore, briefly inspected the contents, and closed it again. "Thank. All good."

Gredin waved them toward the entrance. "Go in. Music. Food. Drink. Welcome."

Shamka rotated his front paws so that the pads were exposed, and crossed them, in imitation of the Vennan gesture. "Grrdin. Thank."

As the three Shodekekeen moved into the antechamber, the first taint of Mamoran scent reached Wyve, making his nostrils twitch.

Usually, the Mamora walked the corridors of Tradepoint in groups, moving with a unified precision that looked almost military. Tonight's solitary Mamora arrived, kitted out in the traditional yellow shirt and black trousers, and Wyve's eyes began to water. Whatever trick the Vennans had come up with for countering the smell, he wished they would put it to use.

A moment later, his wish became reality. The Mamora simply stopped stinking — or so it seemed to Wyve. And it was Gredin herself who offered to escort the Mamora inside, saying lightly to Wyve, "Will you remain here to greet the final arrivals, Director?" Then she returned her attention to the Mamora. "Come. We find Vennan Traders to walk, talk with you." A Prett security guard joined them, and the three vanished into the antechamber.

"The Polpethtira are coming," one of the Prett security guards announced, nodding to their right. And there, rounding the nearest corner, came a cluster of lean Polpethtira, their purple skin gleaming under the corridor lights.

Their interest in the reception was a mystery to Wyve, for the Vennans and the Polpethtira had never been trading partners.

The Polpethtira specialized in solar devices and resonance amplifiers, along with an array of gel-tech accessories, none of which were of interest to the Vennans. And the Polpethtira's purchases on Tradepoint focused on high-end griimoni, which again made the Vennans irrelevant to them as trading partners.

Nevertheless, here they were.

The three who approached were all female, their entire bodies were covered with designs depicted in white that gleamed against the dense purple of their skin. Two were empty-handed, while the third carried a large fabric sack.

"Welcome. Good you come," Wyve said in greeting.

The first two exchanged a flurry of hand signs, then looked to the bearer of the sack. She took a small step forward and said, "Director. Greet you."

The foremost security guard said politely, "I look your bag?"

The Polpethtira opened the sack.

After a token glance, the guard said, "Yes. Thank," and gestured toward the doors. The Polpethtiran party and their trio of guards passed into the antechamber.

"Director, there may be trouble developing," one of the remaining guards said.

Wyve looked down the corridor.

The Thalken approached with tiny, mincing steps, their towering headgear swaying as they walked. Clad in an array of pastels, they resembled a flock of butterflies. They were only half the height of a Vennan, shorter even than the Beng. The Thalken, physically fragile, rarely emerged from their ship without hiring Prett security to escort them to and from the Traders' Market in transport pods.

Wyve wondered how well they would cope with the crowd inside the Vennan reception hall... then realized that the guard's warning was correct: the Hesch had just come into view behind the Thalken, traversing the same corridor.

Both Hesch and Thalken were prideful races, and the

Thalken — perhaps due to their tiny stature — were prone to lodging complaints, taking every perceived transgression against them as an intentional threat. Their defensive attitude was wearisome and wore Wyve's patience down. Sometimes, he was tempted to ignore their complaints. Other times, he was equally tempted to issue a rebuke to the accused party just to appease the Thalken and get them out of his office.

Instead, he frequently deflected the Thalken to Figg's attention, then felt guilty for having done so. Figg deserved better from him...

The long-legged Hesch were rapidly closing the distance separating them from the Thalken. What was more, the Hesch were walking three abreast, tightly bunched, as unified in their progress as the Mamora usually were. At the present rate, they would soon overtake the Thalken, either forcing them aside or treading on their heels.

The Hesch began to clack their beaks, creating a staccato uproar.

Startled, the Thalken looked back over their shoulders, then faced resolutely forward again, their pace unchanged.

The distance between the two groups shrank rapidly.

"Move!" the center Hesch shouted in Tradetalk. "Move!" And his companions continued to clack their beaks.

As things stood, this wasn't going to end well.

Wyve signaled to a pair of security agents, then stepped into the center of the corridor. "Thalken stop," he bellowed. "Hesch stop, too. I, Director, come talk you there."

The Thalken stopped immediately.

The Hesch came forward three more steps, stopping only when they towered over the Thalken, still clacking their long beaks in irritation, although more softly.

"Hesch make much fast," one of the Thalken accused as Wyve reached them, its voice high and thready. "Make order us. Make push if Director not say stop."

Wyve held up his hand. "No push. No harm. You give quiet." He looked over their tops of their headwraps to the Hesch, noting that the middle Hesch's long, skeletal arms rested along the shoulders of its two companions. It was an odd posture, and Wyve had the sudden sense that he was being invited to jump to hasty conclusions and take actions he might regret. Instead, he looked more closely at the middle Hesch's face, trying to see past the surface similarities of beak, bald pate, and shining eyes.

Ah.

He inclined his head slightly. "Nitikikani, yes?"

A quick bob of affirmation from the dark head.

"Surprised see you here," Wyve continued. "Hesch small wait." He redirected his attention to the Thalken. "Hesch have hurt foot. Need sit. Let Hesch pass. Long legs, they go fast. Thalken move with me, wait moment only, then we go in together, honored guest."

They opened their mouths to protest.

Of course they did; they were Thalken. But Wyve was having none of it. Counting on his considerable size advantage, he simply herded the three Thalken aside.

It took no physical contact. Thalken always shied away from contact with another race. Wyve spread his arms and gestured expansively, they moved in hasty avoidance, and the deed was done. And the Hesch, at least, didn't linger to gloat. They strode past without another word, although the one closest to the Thalken did give its bill one final clack.

He'd once asked Figg how she stayed so calm in the face of such petty provocations. Smiling, she'd remarked that she found it helpful to think of most other races on Tradepoint as over-indulged children who had never been taught how to behave properly in public.

The memory put a slight smile on Wyve's face, which seemed to disconcert the Thalken. "Much thanks," he said to them. "Hesch hurt. Thalken much kind to help. Come. I walk you now, make you welcome, bring you meet important Vennan."

Flattery and the offer of special attention forestalled whatever further complaint they might have been prepared to make, as he had hoped it might. But Wyve found himself longing for the quiet of his office and the comfort of his bed, which was not a good sign since the evening was only now about to begin.

When Gredin first reentered the reception room with the Mamora, Tetralanna had been lurking at the edge of the crowd near the antechamber, but the sight of a Mamora had sent her scuttling away. Now Tetralanna was back, having added a brocade shawl to her sleeveless gown, perhaps to mask the absence of First Speaker's hlette on her upper arm. Her expression was pinched, and she seemed to radiate anger and frustration — or fear.

Although aware of her presence, Gredin could think of no cure for Tetralanna's dilemma. The older woman longed to stand at the center of events but dared not approach, repelled as she was by the presence of the other races attending the evening's reception. It would have been an unsolvable conundrum, even if First Speaker's hlette had still been hers to wear.

Some of the Vennans in attendance seemed to share Tetralanna's apprehension, clearly startled by the assorted shapes and sizes of their guests. What had sounded exciting and exotic in the abstract was proving more daunting for them when seen close at hand.

Gredin was grateful that she had already encountered all but one of the races in attendance, and she drew further comfort from the presence of Wyve and Figg. It was up to her to set a calm example, and to help the evening move beyond the tension of these preliminary moments. As soon as a little time passed without an alarming incident, the atmosphere would ease. People wanted to be happy, tonight. They had put great effort into their preparations for the evening. In truth, the Vennans all wanted this reception to be a success. But she realized that the tension in the room was not solely from Vennan reaction to unusual visitors. Of the other races present, none but the Prett seemed entirely at ease with one another.

The single Mamora looked the most relaxed, although it stood apart, of necessity, surrounded by the four Vennan Traders whose task it was to keep it company while they continually cleansed the air around it.

The three Shodekekeen took up an impressive amount of space as they sat on the floor together, the expanse of their blue fur looking rather like an irregular blue pond. Gredin believed them to be the friendliest of the guests, but she hoped the Shodekekeen would find no reason to extend their large, curving claws until everyone was more relaxed.

The Polpethtira stood in a tight arc, their strangely decorated bodies motionless except for their hands and long, multi-jointed fingers, which gestured and fluttered constantly. Was it nerves, or were they communicating with one another?

The Hesch looked frightening, standing at their full, formidable height. Their eyes glittered in the light from the luminths, and their long bills clicked and clacked as the outer two supported Nitikikani, a Hesch she would recognize anywhere after the terrible ordeal of the Judgment. The two unfamiliar Hesch moved their hairless heads in quick jerks, alternately eyeing the crowd and her gown. Tonight, the strips of cloth bound around their bony forms were all black, not the variegated black and green she had previously seen Hesch wear.

Nitikikani stared solely at her, not even seeming to blink.

The Beng were in their usual green coveralls, shifting restlessly from foot to foot as if standing still was impossible for them. Wyve's security discs blinked in synchrony on their chests, one red, one yellow, one blue, and the looks they cast at Gredin were openly hostile.

And then there were the Thalken. She wished she had Burlon beside her to relate his thoughts about them. Smaller even than the Beng, and far slighter of build, the Thalken were as hairless as the Polpethtira, but with pale skin that looked almost translucent, like the white of a partially cooked egg. Beneath their elaborate headgear, large, deep-set eyes dominated their faces, while their noses and mouths seemed little more than slits. Elegantly dressed, they stood with composure, but Gredin did not warm to them. She would reserve judgment, but something about their manner unsettled her.

Finally, Figg gave her the nod she had been waiting for, indicating that all of the Prett security agents were in place and that the outer doors of the Vennan enclave had been secured.

Cirin, to her sadness, was gone. Burlon was absent, having already embarked with Chenna upon their dydanin. And Tetralanna no longer had any formal role to play. As a result, Gredin would act as both Speaker and translator. But she was not alone. Sill stood ready to form a Memory of what was to follow, with Keegan beside her. And Wyve had taken up a position on Gredin's other side. The evening was as official as they could make it.

Looking at the half circle of guests who sat and stood before her, she said in Tradetalk, "All Vennans say welcome all you. We start."

A murmur of acknowledgment from the Shodekekeen was the only response.

She continued, "Eat our food. Hear our music. Watch Vennans Make things. But first Director announce present each you bring. We thank for honor."

Beside her, Wyve announced in Tradetalk, "Mamora come, give present."

There was a little stir from the other guests, but Gredin's careful inhalation detected no faintest scent of the Mamora as he came toward her, flanked by the Vennan Traders who were his escort. Arriving directly in front of her, he reached into a pouch affixed to the waistband of his black trousers and drew out a small, prettily carved wooden box. Balancing it on the palm of his hand, he extended it to Gredin and said, in Tradetalk, "Vennan fair traders, fine goods. Glad many sectora deal Vennans here Tradepoint. Present three nuts kithris. Enjoy."

Gredin accepted the box, crossed her palms, and bowed her head to the Mamora. "Much thank! All enjoy much," she assured him. "Vennans thank. Vennans remember."

Then she announced to the delegation, in Vennan, "Our guest from the Mamora has generously presented us with three entire nuts of kithris for our enjoyment."

A spontaneous murmur of appreciation rose from the assembled Vennans, and the Mamora looked both surprised and gratified as he and his accompanying quartet of Vennan Traders returned to their original position.

A movement at Gredin's elbow caught her attention. She turned and found Beda beside her, offering a tray on which she could place the little box of kithris nuts, freeing her hands for the next presentation. She smiled her thanks, grateful to have him near.

Wyve, in Tradetalk, said, "Hesch come, give present."

Gredin felt a prickle of unease trace down her arms as the trio of Hesch came forward. It troubled her to see that Nitikikani still required support to stand, and she crossed her palms to him solemnly as the three Hesch halted in front of her. Two seemed transfixed by the sight of her gown, and she remembered Burlon's caution about the geddel crystals. But Nitikikani looked higher, cocking his head to one side and then the other, his bright gaze flicking from her shining hlao to the gleaming hlette that encircled her arm, and from there to the rainbow fire of the flamestone at her throat.

The silence dragged on, and Gredin wondered if he expected her to speak first. Then he lifted his beak sharply, once and again, and said, "Amarantha wine. Vennan traders like. Hesch give." The Hesch on his right came forward with a large, rough-woven sack from which he produced a stone jug carved in the shape of a squatting creature with its tongue outthrust.

The Vennan Traders accompanying the Mamora chuckled, nodding their approval.

The Hesch who held the jug said softly, for Gredin's ears only, "Nitikikani say give now. Celebrate you leave tomorrow, be gone." Then he warned, "Heavy, this," as he handed it to her.

"Heavy" was an understatement. Even forewarned, Gredin nearly dropped the jug. But she firmed her hold on it and said, "Hesch kind. Good present. We much thank."

The Hesch bobbed its head and stepped back into place beside Nitikikani, who continued to stare at her with an air of fixed concentration.

Gredin raised her voice, addressing the delegation. "Our guests from the Hesch enclave bring us a container of amarantha wine, which our Traders indicate is very fine indeed."

That won a new round of enthusiastic cheers from the Traders, with an undertone of amusement that she didn't understand. Perhaps amarantha wine was particularly potent. If she sampled it, she would do so with care.

As she placed the jug on Beda's tray, she warned, "Take care, Beda. It's very heavy."

His knuckles whitened, and his eyes widened as the full weight of the jug descended. Moving quickly, he crossed to the table, no doubt eager to relieve himself of the burden.

Wyve said, in Tradetalk, "Thalken come, give present."

A Thalken nodded. Beneath its fantastical headgear of pale green, it was dressed in muted shades of peach, with lacy trim in the same shade of green. It came forward slowly, each step precise, and extended a tightly rolled scroll to Gredin. "To look, at end of day. To make mind quiet," it said in a wisp of a voice, its eyes lambent in the glow of the luminths. As Gredin accepted the scroll, it added, "Open now."

A silken ribbon secured the present. Gredin untied it and extended the scroll by slow degrees, revealing a delicately painted scene: a clouded sky, a lake, an ancient, many-branched tree, a trio of birds.

The beauty of the depiction impressed Gredin. She could almost feel the breeze and hear the gentle lapping of water against the shore. The artist had used a minimum of brush strokes, with only the subtlest traces of color, and yet the scene came alive.

"Much, much fine," she told the Thalken, regretting the limitations of Tradetalk. "Make eye glad. Find place where all Vennan eye enjoy. All Vennan thank Thalken."

The Thalken gazed up at her for a moment, and the shape of its mouth altered slightly. A smile? Gredin couldn't tell, but she hoped that the Thalken understood her delight in their gift.

"The Thalken have given us an exquisite scroll painting," she told the room. "We will arrange for it to be displayed tonight so that everyone can admire its artistry." She turned and, as she had done with the other presents, placed it on Beda's waiting tray. At the same time, she contacted Keegan's private mind, commenting silently, =You'll wish to examine this more closely. The brushwork and the quality of the paper are remarkable.=

Wyve looked to her, as if gauging her readiness. When she nodded, he said, "Shodekekeen come, give present."

It was Shamka himself who rolled onto all six feet, then rose onto his hind legs, his sudden bulky height eliciting a whisper of apprehension from the Vennan crowd.

Gredin said firmly, in Vennan, "Do not be alarmed. I am pleased to present my friend, Shamka." Then, in Tradetalk, she said, "Shamka, much welcome."

Shamka opened the pack worn by one of the other Shodeke-keen, and extracted a large, paper-wrapped package which he tucked beneath one furry arm before crossing his paws and bowing his head to Gredin.

She returned the gesture.

Shamka held out the package. "For Grrdin. Better color. Show friend Gara, yes?"

Gredin smiled. "Yes," she affirmed. "I show Gara."

"Open now," Shamka urged.

The paper bundle was tied with glossy teal ribbons, which Gredin unknotted and placed on Beda's tray. Carefully peeling back the outer paper, she gazed down at its contents: fold upon fold of teal fabric, bearing hair-fine traceries of bronze at irregular intervals.

"Much better you this," Shamka said.

"Beautiful," she concurred.

"More present under."

Gredin looked up at him, surprised. "More?"

"Under," he prompted. "We interrupt, other day. Bring now."

Carefully, Gredin turned back an edge of the folded fabric and smiled at what she found there. "I see. Many thank!" Placing the fabric next to the ribbons, she turned to catch Keegan's attention. "See what Shamka has brought for you," she said, and handed Keegan a thick stack of the mottled yellow paper that had first led them to Shamka's maartza.

Keegan took the paper with evident delight. "Bahnt!" he said, and bowed his thanks to Shamka.

Shamka returned the bow, dropped down onto all six legs, and rejoined his fellows.

Collecting herself, Gredin said to her fellow Vennans, "The Shodekekeen have brought a length of fine fabric for us, as well as a generous sample of their paper for use by our historian, Keegan te Fliss. We thank them for their thoughtfulness."

Wyve called the Polpethtira forward next. "Polpethtira come, give present."

After the delight of conversing with Shamka, it was easy to turn a welcoming face to the Polpethtira. Gredin bowed to the trio, crossing her palms. "Welcome. Glad see you come."

Fingers flew, then stilled, and the purple individual on the left stepped forward, a large sack in hand. "We bring present. You say Polpethtira make beauty." It stroked a design that curled from eye to chin, its dark purple gaze intense. "Give new idea for trade. We thank," it said, and handed Gredin the sack.

Curious, Gredin opened it, and exclaimed aloud in pleasure. "Wonderful!" She withdrew a set of baskets, three in number, nested one inside another. The baskets were brightly colored, woven in intricate, raised designs. They were eye-catching, and she found that running her fingertips lightly over the texture of the designs created a pleasurable friction. "Much thank!"

The Polpethtira tugged on its earlobe and strode back to the other two, fingers fluttering, as they reformed their arc-shaped stance.

Gredin told the Vennan delegation, with genuine pleasure, "The Polpethtira have given us a set of woven baskets made by their artisans. Please be sure to examine them closely, for they are wonderfully made, pleasing to the touch as well as the eye. We are delighted by the Polpethtira's present."

The delegation murmured as she placed the baskets on Beda's ever-ready tray.

That left only the Beng. She suppressed a shiver of distaste, and gave Wyve full marks for allowing no reluctance to enter his tone as he said, "Beng come, give present."

One of the interchangeable Beng bustled forward, carrying the big sack Wyve's guard had searched. Holding it up, the Beng said plaintively, "Beng see presents other traders bring. Much nice. Beng plan nice present. Now Beng have big Judgment debt pay Hesch, much unfair."

Figg cleared her throat.

The Beng scowled and boldly muttered, "Beng no see Hesch. Beng no touch Hesch. Judgment say Beng pay Hesch. Unfair!"

Wyve took a step forward. "Beng want leave now?" he asked, his voice rumbling ominously, and the Prett security guards stiffened.

The Beng hunched its shoulders and glared, first at Wyve, then at the guards, and finally at Gredin herself. "No. Beng no leave. Beng bring present. Beng do nice thing. *Beng* not unfair."

"Suggest Beng stop talk, give present," Wyve said. "Now."

The Beng stepped toward Gredin, and it took an effort of will for her not to back away from that malevolent little figure. Flint-eyed, it looked up at her with rebellious animosity in its gaze, but its voice, when it spoke, took on a false air of sweetness. "Beng plan present for Vennans. Now, Beng no afford that present. Is okay. Beng find other present, do best Beng can." It thrust the sack toward her. "Here."

If Gredin hadn't seen Prett security examine the bag and its contents, she might not have dared to take possession of it. But she schooled her face to impassivity, accepted the sack from the Beng's hands, hefted it for a moment, then parted the folds of coarse fabric.

A pungent, earthy smell rose to up to meet her.

Not permitting herself to wrinkle her nose, Gredin cleansed the air within the bag, much as the four Traders were doing with the Mamora's scent, and leaned closer to look inside.

The Beng appeared surprised, and perhaps a little disappointed, by her failure to recoil.

In the bag's dim interior, Gredin saw half a dozen lumpy shapes, each roughly the size of her fist, some with pale sprouts emerging from them. Emboldened, she reached in and grasped one, pulling it out into the light.

Brown and misshapen, it appeared to be a sort of tuber, possibly edible, or perhaps the eventual source of some flowering plant.

A soft ripple of uncertain laughter ran through those in the front ranks of the crowd.

"I thank," Gredin said levelly to the Beng. "What call this present?"

"Flagle," he said, scowling at the crowd's laughter, and added defensively, "Good eat."

"Good eat," Gredin repeated, straight-faced. "We thank."

She placed the little tuber gently back into the bag and placed the bag on the tray Beda held, doing so with all the ceremony she had exhibited with the other presents. Then, in Vennan, she said firmly, "Politeness to our guests, please. No laughter. The Beng have given us a bag of tubers which they call 'flagle.' I have no idea how to prepare them or what they taste like, but the Beng claim that flagle are good to eat, and so I have thanked them for the gift."

Silence fell, and the Beng retreated, darting between its two compatriots.

Gredin looked to Wyve, who nodded.

"Now the present giving is at an end," she announced to the delegation, "and our reception will begin. Kitchen Tenders, please offer food and drink to all in attendance. Musicians, play on. Dancers, begin your performance when you wish. For those Houses which have prepared demonstrations of crafts and trade-goods, deal kindly with the curiosity of our guests. Our Travelers and Traders will make themselves available to offer translation if the visitors have questions about what they see. Above all, enjoy this evening. You have all worked hard, and you deserve a pleasant time. Prett security accompanies all of our guests, so there is no need to be uneasy around them simply because they are different."

She offered an encouraging smile to the assembly. "Let the reception begin!"

As the Vennan members of the crowd began to stir, Gredin turned her attention back to the visitors and said, in Tradetalk, "Enjoy Vennan reception, you. We greet, show things we make, show how we dance, give music your ears. Give food, drink we make. Vennans say welcome."

Wyve held up a hand and added, also in Tradetalk, "Station rules. You wish eat food, swallow drink? You choose. You risk."

Gredin found that a sobering warning, but none of the visitors looked alarmed.

The musicians began, the soft strains of their melody providing a welcome backdrop. The buzz of conversation ebbed and flowed as Vennans moved to their assigned places, setting out trays of food, preparing to dance, or preparing to demonstrate their appointed craft or skill.

The visitors hesitated, some eyeing each other openly, others more covertly watching Wyve, Figg, and the security agents. But the tension eased somewhat as the Vennans dispersed, leaving more open space available.

Gredin spoke again for the benefit of their guests, making

expansive gestures. "Tables for food, drink, there. We try make safe, eat same you, drink same you. Enjoy."

The Beng scuttled in that direction, with their Prett security in hot pursuit.

Approaching the Shodekekeen, Gredin smiled at Shamka. "Cloth that way. Many different kind. Watch make, watch sew. Meet Gara, maybe."

"Gara," he echoed brightly, and lumbered off, while his two companions moved, instead, toward the food tables, their bulk causing a visible eddy in the crowd as they passed through.

Taking a few steps toward the Hesch, Gredin said, "Bench for Nitikikani? If yes, you tell. We bring food, drink, place small table here."

Nitikikani made no reply, but one of the other Hesch bobbed its head in what she thought might be a nod. Turning, she said to Beda, "Could you ask someone to see to that? A bench for the injured Hesch, and a tray of assorted food and drink for the three of them? I'm sorry to ask it of you, but—"

"You have your hands full," Beda said, smiling. "Go on. We'll arrange it."

Relieved, she left the Hesch and moved to offer a bow to the Thalken. "Gredin te Balamont, I," she said by way of introduction. "Thalken welcome in Vennan enclave. Do what pleases. Go where like. Talk me if you have need. Over there, Crafters create bowl, vase, plate. This way, paint same. In corner, create…" She realized that she lacked the word for 'jewelry.' Raising her hand, she touched the flamestone pendant she wore around her neck. "…to wear." She gestured toward the rings that adorned several thin fingers on the nearest Thalken's hand. "Like that, also."

"Like that?" a Thalken asked, pointing at First Speaker's hlette on Gredin's upper arm.

"No," she disavowed. "Is… different. Not create."

"Like so?" the third Thalken inquired, reaching toward the trailing end of Gredin's hlao.

Gredin straightened hurriedly. "No. Is like this," she said, pointing from her hlao to First Speaker's hlette. "Not create. Different."

The Thalken looked disappointed. After a quick conference amongst themselves, however, they nodded dismissively to her and drifted toward the corner of Craftspeople she had indicated.

And Keegan, she noted, followed after them.

The gazes of the Polpethtira seemed riveted on the musicians. Gredin had no idea whether it was the music, the performance, or the instruments themselves which captured their attention. "You like? We create music. Go. See. Hear. Vennans dance soon."

All three Polpethitira tugged on their earlobes, then glided off, winding easily through the milling bodies, their security guards following with less finesse.

That left the Mamora. But Gredin found, when she turned to approach him, that he already looked quite content. One of the Traders was handing a glass to him, and Figg had joined the little group, chatting animatedly. Ellis beckoned for another Trader to come and take her place at the Mamora's side, then walked to where Gredin stood.

"An evening well begun," Ellis observed.

"An evening scarcely begun," Gredin countered. "But I am relieved to have weathered the giving of presents without a major difficulty."

Ellis shook her head. "Those Beng. I despair of them. A bag of flagle!"

"They wished to make a point."

"Their eternal point seems to be that no one is as shamefully ill-used as they are."

"Do you suppose they believe it?" Gredin asked. "Or is it all bluster?"

Ellis shook her head. "With the Beng, who knows?" But then

her expression brightened. "Such a surprise tonight for Burlon! I am happy for him, although the timing is awkward. Do you really think he and Chenna will come out, tomorrow morning, or do you suppose we'll have to leave them here to make their own way home?"

"I believe they will come out," Gredin said firmly. "In fact, no plans should be made in the morning until Burlon has come out to join us. Will you pass that word on to the Traders and Travelers?"

"I will... but folk will be anxious to start the journey home after midday meal is finished."

"Anxious or not," Gredin replied, wishing she could be more forthright, "no one should leave Tradepoint until Burlon has had a chance to speak." She nodded toward the Mamora. "All goes well with our guest? Would he care for something to eat?"

"Oh, he assures us that he is quite content simply being part of the group, for once," Ellis replied. "And, truth to tell, I'm not quite sure what to feed a Mamora."

"Wyve would know, would he not?"

Ellis blinked. "The Director, you mean? It seems you've come to know him well, in just these few days."

"Because I do not use his title? I mean him no disrespect. He requested that I call him by his name, so I complied. Do you and the other Traders find it too familiar of me?"

"Not 'too familiar,'" Ellis said with a sigh. "Just a bit bewildering. Pardon me for saying so, Gredin, but you were called into his office yesterday to have Judgment pronounced against you. You were in tears. And now..." Ellis waved her hand. "Well, now the two of you seem to be on the friendliest of terms. What are we to think?"

"That he is a kind and forgiving man, I suppose. He understands that, although harm was done, I did not intend it. He has handed down his Judgment, and now he is ready to move beyond it, for the sake of our festivity. What sort of reception would it be, if the Director glowered at me throughout the evening?"

Ellis sighed again, this time more heavily. "Yes, but you had best hope that your Head of House will be equally understanding, tomorrow, when he learns of the Judgment and the fine." She offered a wan smile. "I will speak with him about it on your behalf, if you wish me to."

It was a generous offer — pointless, under the circumstances, but generous. "Thank you," Gredin said. "I will think about it. Tonight, though, is for pleasure. Fetch something for yourself to eat and drink, Ellis. You have earned it."

"You should do the same," Ellis urged. "Come and see what the kitchens have prepared."

Gredin glanced again at the Mamora. "I shouldn't stray far."

Ellis laughed. "All seems well enough. If a difficulty should arise, I am certain you will be among the first to know."

The food tables, when they reached them, were astonishing in their variety and beauty. Puddings and pastries, breads and vegetable dishes, fruits and confections — they were arrayed in groups, the portions small to encourage sampling of many different flavors.

Under the censorious eyes of their Prett guards, the Beng had camped out at tableside, where they were gorging themselves on berry tarts, with smears of red and purple juice staining the skin around their mouths.

As Gredin approached, one guard cast an anxious glance her way, but she smiled and shook her head. Let the Beng eat what they would. There was a display of the same tarts at the other end of the table, as well, for anyone else who might want one. And it was better for everyone's peace of mind to know precisely where the Beng were, and what they were doing.

Miri te Kendar bustled up. In one hand, she carried a small

plate that held two tiny pastries and a single rostti. In her other hand, she bore a glass of deep-red galenberry cordial. Handing both to Gredin, she said happily, "Here. Take these. People are in good appetite tonight," and hurried off again.

Gredin stared after her, pleased to see that the little pastries bore the Kendar crest. She knew what she would find inside: minced benroot and tongue peppers. Resting the slender glass on her plate, she popped a pastry into her mouth, chewed and swallowed it, and sighed with pleasure. "How kind of her, to bring this to me when she is so busy," Gredin said, and realized that the rostti was the one that Miri had promised to set aside for her. A woman of her word.

"Eat," Ellis encouraged. "Drink. And do it now, before someone comes along to interrupt." Then she gazed past Gredin, and her eyes widened. "Too late. Turn and greet the Director," she prompted, and slipped away into the throng.

Forewarned, Gredin welcomed Wyve, who held a mounded plate of fresh-baked items.

"The food," he said in greeting, "is beyond excellent."

Gredin smiled. "Our food Tenders are a gyfted group, representing many different Houses," she said, and lifted the cordial glass to her lips.

It was then that it happened: one of the Shodekekeen approached the table, and the Beng with the yellow disc, seeing it, let out an ear-piercing shriek and bolted away, dodging past his guard and careening hard into Gredin. The rostti and the remaining pastry flew into the air, and the little glass of galenberry cordial spilled down the front of her gown, leaving a bright stain of red on the lavender fabric.

Yellow Disc fled through the crowd, with his assigned guard hurrying to follow.

Blue Disc snickered.

Wyve and the Shodekekeen both moaned, their eyes wide with distress.

"No matter," Gredin said. Separating the cordial from the material it had soaked, she tidied it back into the glass.

Wyve gaped — which, in turn, surprised Gredin. Cleansing and Tidying were skills that all Vennans possessed, abilities they developed in childhood and honed to perfection as they grew older. The liquid of the cordial was one thing; the fabric of her gown was quite another. Separating them was primarily a matter of Focus and Control, the fundamental skills that lay at the center of every gyfte.

Behind her, the musicians struck a chord and repeated it twice more — the signal that the dancers were ready. Gredin drew breath and announced, with gyfte-enhanced clarity, "Your attention, please, everyone. The dancing demonstration is about to begin."

The hum of conversation in the reception hall subsided, and she shifted into Tradetalk.

"We create music now. Show dance all Vennans know. You watch."

Overhead, luminths dimmed, except for those directly over the dance platform. Food and drink were still available, and the craft demonstrations would continue unabated, but most of the Vennans directed their attention to the dancers, and the visitors soon did the same. A single harp note sounded and repeated, quickening rhythmically. The dancers stirred, crossing palms to their neighbors. Flutes spun a high, thin melody, and the dance began.

Watching, Gredin felt an ache in her throat for all those who, like Trethen, had stayed behind on Venna and would never dance again.

Beside her, Wyve's gaze was fixed on the shifting couples. Nearby, Gredin glimpsed the slender Thalken threading through the crowd to get closer to the platform where the dancers bowed and whirled. The other observers stood still, caught up in the ethereal atmosphere woven by the performance, as if holding their collective breath.

Then, off to the side, a shimmer brightened the air.

And someone gasped.

And someone screamed.

1891 OF 2000 ORBITS REMAINING

Time fractured as Gredin struggled to understand what she was seeing.

The bio-dome had sprung to life, covering the arrival dais, and a man stood within it, swaying, his clothing stained with broad, wet splashes of galenberry cordial.

Gredin blinked.

Not cordial.

Blood.

A trickle spilled from the man's mouth. "Venna is destroyed!" he rasped, his words muffled by the barrier. "Palomar is destroyed!"

Cirin had returned.

He staggered forward. Colliding with the transparent barrier, he pressed both hands against the dome. His knees buckled, and he slid down, his splayed fingers leaving streaks of crimson.

Reeling with horror, Gredin shook free of her paralysis and ran toward the steps, but Sill darted unexpectedly into her path, and they collided. The impact sent Gredin sprawling headlong.

"Cirin!" Hayla, Cirin's Chosen, Sent herself within the dome and crouched beside him protectively. "Who did this to you?"

she quavered, her voice high-pitched with shock, and then, not waiting for an answer, shouted, "A Healer! He needs a Healer!"

The dome retracted, its cycle complete. Robbed of its support, Cirin toppled sideways into Hayla's arms. "Zrach," he whispered, gasping for breath as his head lolled against her. Then his gaze found Gredin, where she still lay sprawled upon the steps. "Your night-thought was true, Speaker," he said, his voice little more than a husk. He reached one hand toward her, and she saw that his shirt was torn. Through the rips in his shredded sleeve, First Traveler's hlette gleamed visibly around his upper arm. His trousers were torn, as well, and the flesh of one leg was scored so deeply that the white bone lay revealed.

Caymen te Indirin, Assessor for First Healer, raced up the steps to kneel beside Cirin, wrapping her long fingers around his wrist, seeking the lifebeat that resided there. As soon as she found it and began her Assessment, Cirin's pain-wracked expression eased, though the blood still bubbled between his parted lips. Hayla looked to the Assessor, her face alight with hope.

But Cayman shook her head in slow negation, tears glimmering in her eyes.

Cirin's hlao was a sleek, narrow circlet around his head; all Travelers wore their hlaos thus when they embarked upon the River. Reaching down, Hayla pressed the tips of her fingers to it, and the ends of Cirin's hlao instantly shook free in recognition of her touch. A moment later, one trailing end of her own hlao brushed against an end of Cirin's and clung there, the filaments entwining.

Bending low, Hayla kissed her Chosen's brow, then his cheek, and finally, for an instant, his bloody, panting lips.

Cirin whispered something to her, and then began to shimmer, as if a luminth had been lit within him. The light was soft, at first. Then it intensified, growing brighter and brighter until Gredin was forced to squint against the force of its glow. The stains of blood on his clothing grew radiant, as well. Even the smear of his blood on Hayla's lips began to shine, and Cirin's hlao became a ribbon of cool white flame.

The radiance that was the essence of Cirin te K'lar flared, so intense for an instant that it painted its afterimage in Gredin's eyes. Then it was gone, extinguished except for a shower of tiny golden sparks that settled softly over Hayla and winked out, one by one by one.

Gredin blinked, then stared.

Cirin's body was gone. His clothing lay crumpled on the dais, torn but unstained, and the remnants of his empty shirt had fallen aside to reveal the hlette he had worn for long and long as First Traveler. But Cirin's life had ended. His body was gone, as was his hlao. They had evanesced, returning to the Source.

Hayla began to weep, and Sill embraced her.

Wyve's huge hands closed gently around Gredin's upper arms, lifting her to her feet.

Those closest to the dais began to react, some drawing back, some crowding closer, all aghast, while those in the rest of the vast room stirred restlessly, murmuring questions in confused agitation.

Gredin turned within Wyve's grasp, looking up with urgency into his astonished gaze. Pitching her voice low against the increasing uproar around them, she said, "Director, have your security people remove all of the foreign guests. Immediately."

"But what *was* that?"

"The Power." With each new breath she drew, Gredin felt more certain of her course. "We have just witnessed the end of Cirin te K'lar."

"The end? He disappeared. Are you saying that he's *dead*?"

Power grant her patience. "Yes. Please, Wvye—"

"But... can Cirin be correct? Venna is destroyed? *And* Palomar?"

"Yes! Wyve, please, *go*, and take the others with you." When he still hesitated, she said, "I will come to your office in the morning. We can discuss everything then. But now I need everyone who is not Vennan gone from this place. I must speak to my people."

He seemed to wake, for the first time, to the growing chaos around them. "Yes. Yes, of course." He crooked his elbow and raised his wrist to his lips. "Escort out. Immediate escort out," he said, and added grimly, "Tell them there has been a death."

Gredin knew that rumor and speculation were already flying through the room, some spoken aloud, some passing silently from mind to mind, none of it well-informed, all of it alarming. She looked for some sign that Wyve's order was being carried out, but it was hard for her to see over the crowd. "Tomorrow morning. Early." she promised Wyve again, and left him.

As she mounted the lower steps of the arrival dais, hoping for a less obstructed view, she heard a series of piercing screeches from the direction of the food tables. Turning that way, she saw a Prett guard leave the area, moving toward the enclave doors. Over his shoulder, still protesting loudly, was a Beng with a berry tart clutched in each fist.

Elsewhere in the crowd, she saw the dark, hairless skulls of Hesch, and the red-brown head of Mamora. She spared a thought for the three tiny Thalken, glad that they had a contingent of Prett guards to keep them from being stepped on, in the crush. She spotted Figg, and there, nearly to the doors, stood Wyve. Prett security streamed past him, crowding into the antechamber, each of them likely escorting a foreign visitor.

An agonized wail rose and fell and rose again, people drawing back from the desperate sound. From her raised vantage point, Gredin looked, and saw that the dreadful lamentation was coming from Tetralanna, who writhed in the supportive hold of several members of House Balamont. They were trying to steady her on her feet, but she kept collapsing into their arms as she keened and cried.

Gredin took a step toward her, to offer what comfort she

could... then stopped. She was the last person from whom Tetralanna would accept comfort. And so she stayed where she stood, looking again toward the doors to gauge Wyve's progress, anxious for the outsiders to depart.

But the choice haunted her. In the space of a few short days, a vast chasm had opened between herself and Tetralanna, created by everything from Tetralanna's fear of the other races on Trade-point to her refusal to believe in Gredin's visitations from the Power. And the estrangement had crystalized in an inescapably public way when First Speaker's hlette leapt from Tetralanna's arm and refused to return.

Even now, in the midst of chaos, the presence of First Speaker's hlette on her arm made her feel steady, her Control unwavering. Was Tetralanna suffering equally from its absence, at this most difficult time? Should Gredin go to her, after all?

The harsh overhead lights flickered on for an instant and off again, startling everyone.

Gredin spotted Wyve at the control panel; he lifted his hand in recognition, then pointed at the doors, which she took as a signal that the removal of the foreign guests was complete. Then Wyve, too, walked to the antechamber. With a last look over his shoulder, he entered it.

And the big doors closed behind him.

Looking out at the sea of shocked Vennan faces, Gredin realized that the moment she had dreaded had come, even sooner than she had planned.

She waited as Sill te Torr escorted Hayla from the dais, noting the growing swell of anxious voices as the two women passed her on the steps. Tears ran silently down Hayla's white face, and her gaze was vacant. She seemed unaware of Sill's murmurs of comfort or the arm Sill had wrapped around her in an attempt to steady her descent. A weeping woman met them, once they were on the floor — someone from House K'lar, she guessed — and drew Hayla away along the narrow pathway the crowd made for them.

So then. Gredin squared her shoulders and climbed to the top step, getting as high above the crowd as she could without triggering the dome. Her personal hopes and concerns would have to wait. Right now, it was time to address her fellow survivors.

With a flick of Power, she brightened the luminth above her, setting the crystals on her gown ablaze, and drew deeply on her gyfte.

"Hear me, people of Venna. Attend my words."

Heads lifted, and faces turned toward her as one, captured by the compelling command in her voice.

"Some of you were close enough, just now, to see Cirin te K'lar arrive in our midst, to hear the terrible news that he imparted, and to watch as his life ended and he evanesced, returning to the Source. But most were too far away to clearly see or hear what occurred. Therefore, I speak now to all of you, that we might know the truth together."

She took a deep breath, and the geddel crystals flickered like flame. "Cirin spoke a terrible truth — that Venna, our home, is gone. Our world was destroyed in an instant. Our kinsmen, our Houses, all of our dear ones who did not journey with us to Tradepoint have returned to the Source."

A discordant melody of grief and protest broke from the mouths of the crowd and began to build, but Gredin pressed on, lacing her words with her gyfte to assure they would be heard.

"Here on Tradepoint, the Power has spoken to me twice as I slept, first on the night of our arrival, and again last night."

She saw stunned confusion mix with grief on the faces closest to her.

"On that first night, when the Power told me of Venna's destruction, it chose to speak to me in the voice of my Chosen, Dreff te Balamont. Even then, I struggled against believing that horrible truth, as you are struggling now. I was deeply saddened and gravely shocked. Any of you who saw me yesterday will recall my obvious distress. I was grieving, as you now grieve. My tears were as thick and hot as yours."

Wet eyes and faces glistened as her haunted audience listened intently.

"But the Power is with us. We have not been abandoned."

A voice from the back shouted, "Say you so? Then how could this happen? Where was the Power's sheltering hand when it was needed most?"

Gredin touched the hlette on her arm, steadying under its

calming warmth as it responded to her touch. "I have no sure answer for such questions. I can only assure you that the Power is with us still. Did we not all witness Burlon and Chenna's choosing, earlier tonight? Did their hlaos — our personal connection to the Power — not respond as the hlaos of all past Chosens have responded?" Her voice rang out clearly. "The Power did not destroy our world. The Power is as it has always been. And it is with us still, in this very moment."

Gredin offered them a sad smile. "I have no idea why the Power has Chosen me to lead us in this difficult time, but it singled me out and spoke to me, and I will do my best to safe-guard and preserve us, as it requested that I do. We few in this room are all that is left of Venna. We must take care of one another, comfort and rely on one another. We know, thanks to the assurances the Power gave to me, that this is not our end. We will find a path forward."

Another voice, torn between grief and hope, asked, "How can we be sure that what you say is true? Perhaps those were only night-thoughts!"

"They were not, but I have no better word to describe them. They were like nothing I have ever experienced. But if you doubt my words that Venna is gone, and that our loved ones have returned to the Source, Sill te Torr will be able to offer you proof. She was present at Cirin's side, tonight, when he Traveled back to us at such great cost to confirm the truth of what the Power told me. If Sill is willing, I would have you all share those vital Memories. That way, all will have the same knowledge, and there will be no room for doubt about the truth of our situation."

A sea of faces stared up at her, mirrors of their ravaged thoughts and emotions. She saw despair. Numbness. Grief. Anger. Denial.

Faced with all of that, Gredin said, "Once Sill has shared the Memory of this event, we will need to grieve together as a people. Let no one be neglected or forgotten as we mourn. And rise tomorrow in the awareness that each of you is precious, regardless of House. We can spare no one in our struggle to recover from this tragedy."

A woman standing in the front row, near Gredin, cried hoarsely, "But where will we go? Our home is gone!"

"Thanks to the Prett, we have safe shelter here on Tradepoint for the time being. Beyond that, tomorrow is soon enough to discuss our situation and begin making plans for our future. Tonight, let us offer our lost kinsmen our tears and sorrow. Let us clothe our grief in our remembrance of loved ones and loved places." She turned to Sill. "Will you show them what you witnessed here tonight?"

Sill nodded and mounted the steps to her side.

Gredin turned back to face the delegation. Her people. Her family, in the truest sense. "After Sill has shared this Memory with us, I urge you to gather together by House and return to the quarters allotted to you. Be gentle with one another in your grief." Her voice wavered, and she touched the hlette again, drawing on its strength. "For reasons beyond our comprehension, we have been spared the devastation that swallowed our world. In time, we will prosper again. Do not let despair build a permanent home within you. None of us is alone, nor are we gyfteless. And we are not without hope or the blessings of the Power. Let us remember all of these things as Sill shares with us, and afterward, when we head to our beds. I will hold you close in my thoughts, this night," she assured them. "But now is the time for all of us to sit down and open our minds to Sill's gyfte as we accept the Memory she is prepared to share." With that, Gredin stepped aside, making way for the First of Memory. "If you are ready, please begin, Sill te Torr, with my gratitude," she said, and sat down on the lowest step.

Gredin braced herself, although she hoped that the Memory of Cirin's death would be less intense for her than for the others in the room, since she had been nearby to witness it for herself.

But then, without warning, she became Sill, frightened and choking with pity as Cirin te K'lar gasped *Venna is destroyed... Palomar is destroyed...* and crumpled to his knees. Next, in answer to Hayla's frantic questions, she heard him whisper, *Zrach.* And, last of all, she watched as Cirin looked directly at Gredin te Balamont and said, his voice barely audible, *Your night-thought was true, Speaker.* The kiss from his Chosen, as their hlaos entwined. Some whispered final words, too faint for any ears but Hayla's to discern. And then, blindingly beautiful, his evanescence, as the torn and bloody body and its hlao were transfigured into the Power's pure light before vanishing altogether, leaving nothing behind in Hayla's embrace but empty clothing and First Traveler's hlette.

Abruptly, the Memory ended, and Gredin was herself again, shaken by the impact of all that she had just experienced.

If she was shaken, the others in the room were utterly shocked, driven into frightened, sobered silence. Climbing unsteadily to her feet, Gredin became aware that hundreds of people were staring at her, stunned by having lived through the Memory. Many looked at her with a trace of fear, as if she had become irrevocably 'other' as a result of having been touched by the Power. But they no longer challenged her. Hearing Cirin's words as he died had bludgeoned them out of their attempts at denial.

Gredin moved onto the upper step again, Fetched First Traveler's hlette to her hand from where it had fallen when Cirin evanesced, and Sent his clothing and boots to her small sleeping chamber for safekeeping. In time, she would return them to Hayla, but not tonight, when they could only remind her of Cirin's loss.

She touched Sill's shoulder in apology and gratitude, then looked out over the pale, distraught sea of faces. "This has been an evening of unwanted revelations for us all. Mourn your dead. Weep for the pain their loss causes you. But remember that all of them, like Cirin, have returned safely to the Source. Tomorrow, we will begin to plan how best to carry on with our lives in their absence. For tonight, we need to sleep — or, if sleep evades us, at least to rest. Go now, all of you. Seek your kinsmen. Seek your beds. In the morning, upholding one another, we will turn our faces forward and confront the new day."

Slowly, in pairs and clusters and occasional larger groups, people rose and coalesced, most walking toward the antechamber, others toward the areas within this enclave that had been designated for their Houses. The sounds of weeping began again, and few individuals were altogether steady on their feet, but Gredin's final exhortation seemed to have penetrated at least the outer shell of their grief, freeing them from the frozen tableau that had engulfed them all during Sill's sharing of Cirin's demise.

"And you need your rest, as well," Gredin said to Sill, whose face showed the strain of the dire Memory she had just conveyed. "You have done our people a great service tonight, though I know it was neither easy nor pleasant. You will be much in demand, these coming days, as people seek to preserve precious memories of those they have lost. Please be sensible about your need for rest and replenishment as you respond to their requests."

Sill's Chosen, Marin, had come to the foot of the dais. Gently, he gathered her into the curve of his arm and walked with her toward the doors, with a sober parting nod.

[66]

Holding First Traveler's hlette, which had graced Cirin's arm for so long, Gredin stayed where she was, watching until the last stragglers had vanished. She hoped that, somehow, they would manage to escape the realization of their loss long enough to tumble into sleep.

She had no such expectation for herself, not anytime soon. Although her limbs ached with weariness, she was filled with a trembling tension, the residue from having called so strongly on her gyfte. She felt as if she still stood within the force of the Power's flow, and the sensation was one she was helpless to dispel. She would have to wait for it to dissipate gradually, releasing her back into the calmer realm of workaday normality. Then she might find sleep. She supposed she needed those things any Vennan needed after they had drawn deeply on their gyfte in a sustained fashion. Rest. Sleep. Food.

But sleep seemed a distant goal. Even rest was beyond her, in her current jangled state. Perhaps she could eat a few bites, once a little time had passed, but not yet. Right now, she needed something to do. She needed a task. Something simple but necessary. Some way to put the energy singing through her body to good use.

She looked around... and realized that she was not quite alone, after all. Four people sat on the edge of the dancer's platform, watching her in silence.

Ingarra and Beda.

Miri te Kendar.

And, notebook in hand, Keegan te Fliss.

"Greetings," she said to them.

It was a stupid thing to say, but she was feeling rather stupid, as if she had just spent most of the words in her head and had few left to offer.

Only Ingarra managed an answering smile through her tears. All four people looked haggard as they rose from their perch and walked toward her.

As glad as she was to see them, it was a sad and solemn reunion, with the specter of the night's tragic news hovering over them. "I wanted to tell you," Gredin said as Beda reached out to pull her into a hug that both gave solace and sought it. "The few who knew pledged themselves to silence while they awaited Cirin's return, and Tetralanna Silenced me. They thought Cirin would be back, this morning, but he didn't come, and..." She shook her head. "Even today, when the Silencing had worn off, I didn't speak. I hoped to give the group one last, happy night." Her voice trailed into silence, and she shook her head again, in sadness and regret.

"And what of you?" Keegan asked, his voice gentle. "Are you all right?"

Gredin nodded. "Relieved, in a way, to finally have it known. But regretful, as well, since everyone must now bear the grief. And you? How have you fared? Our visit to the Traders' Market seems so long ago..." She looked to the others. "Keegan was one of the few who learned of my night-thought, that first morning — and he was the only one who believed it. I will always be grateful for that." Her gaze strayed to Miri. "And you — you have been working in the kitchens all day. You must be so tired."

Miri's eyes were red-rimmed, her shoulders slumped. "Weariness can be cured with a decent night's sleep. It is the least of my woes. But the loss of my Chosen and my children..." Her chin wobbled. "I don't know how to carry that load. I was going home, tomorrow morning!" She looked down and shook her head. "It is just as well that you had Sill te Torr share that Memory with us. Even now, having experienced Cirin te K'lar's passing, I can barely keep myself from asking you whether you are certain. It seems so impossible. How can they not be there? How can our home be gone?"

Gredin nodded. "It is why Cirin went — not to prove me right, but to prove me wrong. To him, I was just a child frightened by a night-thought." She could see his face, so confident and brave. Then that memory was supplanted by her all-too-clear recall of his face as she had seen it tonight, riven by pain as he protected them all by delivering the vital message of Venna's loss, despite the lifeblood spilling from his lips...

Gredin willed her breathing to steady, aware that the pain she felt at the thought of Cirin's death would have driven her to the floor, sobbing, if not for the blunting of emotion the Power had wrought in her.

"We're all tired," she said instead. "Let us retire for the night, in the hope of facing tomorrow's challenges with the courage they deserve." She turned to lead the way... and was confronted by the huge tables that still stood arrayed, loaded down with tray after tray of food.

She staggered back a pace, daunted by the sight. "Oh dear."

"And there's that much again and more, in the kitchen," Miri informed her. "Such a waste."

"No," Gredin cautioned, distressed by the thought. "No, none of it should be wasted. Not a bite. Not a scrap. Oh, Miri, we have nearly a thousand of our people to feed, tomorrow, and the next day, and every day thereafter. I trust that none of us will starve — the Prett will help us be sure of that much. But these things—" She waved her hand at the laden tables. "—these are Vennan delicacies. The last of their kind. Once these are gone, and we exhaust whatever ingredients may yet remain in the kitchen stores, there will be no more of these flavors. We'll be eating food from other worlds, grown by others, harvested by others, brought here to Tradepoint by others. But if we can salvage all of this, then at least for the next few days we can dine on food from home." She managed a mirthless laugh. "Indeed, it looks as if we will be dining on party fare at every meal."

"Or not." A steely look of determination came over Miri's face, warring with the lines of grief and fatigue. "Might it not be better, given all you say, if we packed these things away and stored them? That way, from time to time, everyone could have a few bites of Vennan fare as a special treat, when spirits are low, instead of eating all of them now until we're thoroughly sick of them. Unless I miss my guess, few folks will have much appetite, these next few days. They'll scarcely know what they're putting in their mouths, and they'll care even less."

Gredin looked at her in confusion. "Store this food? Can that even be done? Won't everything simply go stale or begin to rot, depending on what it's made of?"

"No, not if we deal with things properly. We can pack up most of the extra and store it cold, or freeze it entirely, keeping out just what we think we may need for tomorrow. The Prett showed the Traders, and the Traders showed us. They say freezing is easy, floating in the sky as we are, and that there's no shortage of room for such things."

"Well then," Ingarra said, speaking for the first time since the terrible news, "the sooner we begin, the sooner we can go to our beds." She turned to Miri. "Where do we start?"

"Come with me," Miri said, and took them all toward the

brightly lit kitchen. "We'll rescue what's already been heated and see where matters stand."

For a goodly while after that, time passed in a blur for Gredin. After setting First Traveler's hlette on a safe shelf, out of harm's way, she worked as a team with Keegan, grateful for the chance not to think as they followed Miri's directions, Fetching trays from the tables and transferring food into huge, square, metal containers that Miri said had been provided by the Prett when they equipped the kitchen.

At last, all of the food had been dealt with. Miri looked around the kitchen blankly, as if stranded by the end of the task.

"Show us where House Kendar resides," Beda said to her gently. "Ingarra and I will walk you there." He looked over Miri's head at Gredin. "And don't forget, nifflin, that you are staying with us."

It was a sharp reminder of her clash with Tetralanna. Gredin nodded, grateful that she had already secured a friendlier place to spend this difficult night. "Indeed," she acknowledged. "I will see you there shortly."

The trio walked away, leaving only Keegan behind with her. He was standing at one of the gleaming metal counters, writing something in his notebook.

"Will that not wait for morning?" she asked, in the gentlest of teasing. "I doubt you could forget the details of this night if you tried to do so."

Without looking up, he said, "I'm busy. Go to bed."

Something, perhaps his oddly peremptory choice of words, perhaps a trace of hoarseness in his tone, snagged her attention. Whatever it was, it sank a hook into Gredin's gut, a sense that something more was badly awry. "No," she said, retrieving First Traveler's hlette from the shelf, "I would rather wait and walk with you. Where is House Fliss residing?"

"At the moment?" he asked — a peculiar question. And then he closed his book and closed his eyes.

"Yes. At the moment."

He gestured vaguely. "Here."

"I don't understand," Gredin said. But she was increasingly afraid that she might.

Keegan took a breath, and another, and finally said, "I am House Fliss." He turned to her, his gaze bleak. "I am the only member of my House who came to Tradepoint, and so I am its only survivor." He swallowed, and said again, with stark simplicity, "I am House Fliss."

Every Vennan on Tradepoint had lost multitudes of their House members.

Only Keegan te Fliss had lost them all.

He'd believed her night-thought, and so he had known of his utter isolation for the past two days, saying nothing, lending assistance where he could, carrying out his task as historian. He had even given away his room so that Burlon and Chenna could savor their dydanin.

Gredin had not thought she could feel any worse than she had for the past two days.

But she could. She did.

"Come," she said. "We will Fetch your belongings from wherever you have tucked them. You will bide with us in House Balamont for as long as you wish. At the very least, it is where you will sleep, tonight."

Keegan hesitated.

"Tonight," said Gredin, "none of us should be alone."

With a sigh as deep as the void that had swallowed their world, Keegan yielded.

And they went forth together.

Gredin collapsed into her bed, hoping for a sleep deep enough to block the sounds of others' grief that rose from all around her.

All day, events had battered her like storm waves breaking over the rocks at the shore, threatening to overwhelm her. But her newfound calm, like those shore rocks, had stood firm, and she had kept her footing, doing her best to move forward with steady authority. Now it was time to set down her burden and sleep.

But as she settled herself to attempt it, she saw that she had begun to glow.

Gredin, you have done well.

The Power's message blossomed vibrantly in her mind, with only faint echoes of her Chosen's beloved tones. The praise was sweet, but the painful realization was inescapable: Dreff was lost to her. She would never hear his voice again, except in memory.

He is gone but not lost, First Speaker. The hlette on her upper arm warmed briefly, a soothing touch. *The life you antici-pated is no more. Your Chosen, along with so many others, has returned to the Source. But your memories of his love remain and are yours to cherish forever.*

In their brief, beautiful time together, she and Dreff had talked and planned and hoped…

Yes. But your future now lies in a new direction.

True. And she was not alone in her pain. Loss and grief pierced every Vennan survivor.

Those survivors are now yours to Guide and protect. Never let them despair or believe they have been forgotten or forsaken.

Gredin sighed. How could words, even words spoken with the authority of First Speaker, mend their collective grief?

With time, and tears, and remembrance.

Time? Time was as much a burden as a blessing. In the morning, they would all wake to the shocking remembrance of Cirin's news and Cirin's death, and the images of a dark tragedy that had forced the celebration to so abrupt an end. They would look to her for answers — answers she didn't have.

Be at peace, Gredin. Have faith.

Her smothering sense of guilt and sorrow and worry began to ease, swept away on a comforting wave of warmth.

You have already begun to walk the proper path. Do not doubt yourself, and do not let others shake your resolve. They will wish to cling to the known, but new thoughts, new ways, new goals will be needed for this new future.

Gredin felt acceptance seep into her, warming her from the inside, like a hot cup of besk on a brisk morning. Yes, they were bound to need new goals. Venna was gone. The survivors on Tradepoint would need to adapt and embrace new attitudes in order to survive. That would be a challenge for people so steeped in tradition, but the Power would speak to her at need, correcting their direction, guiding their steps.

No. Not so. My words to you end tonight.

Panic tried to blossom in her chest.

You have everything you need to accomplish your task.

Task? Gredin felt the sting of tears. Already, there were a dozen tasks she needed to undertake. A hundred. A thousand!

Our people must help themselves and help each other. Your most essential task is to dispatch the Travelers.

Dispatch...? No! No, her goal was to gather everyone in and keep them close, where they were safe. Every life was precious — far too precious to be risked. Surely Cirin's death had taught them that bitter lesson.

Dispatch the Travelers.

Her mind wailed the question: Why?

Dispatch the Travelers to begin the search for your new home. All that you do, all that you Speak, all that you decide must in some way be in aid of this. Our people cannot stay on Tradepoint forever, separated from sea and sky and the good green earth. Dispatch the Travelers so that, in turn, they can find New Venna.

The Power's reassuring touch steadied her.

They can find New Venna.

It was a plan, a pledge, a bulwark against the storm of uncertainty that tomorrow morning — and every morning thereafter — would bring.

Find New Venna.

"New Venna," she murmured into her pillow.

And slept.

CPSIA information can be obtained
at www.ICGtesting.com
Printed in the USA
LVHW050049271020
669864LV00014B/110

9 781949 890648